The DEVIL'S TIDE

Matt Tomerlin

For two fiercely lasses... my mom and my sister.

PROLOGUE

The water gently lapped at *Ranger's* hull as her sharp bow slid through the calm night sea, like a knife silently cutting glass. The waxing moon shimmered in the delicate ripples that spread from the ship's wake. Sails fluttered softly, plump with the mild yet persistent wind that urged the ship forward. A pirate snorted in his sleep, his hammock swaying as he rolled onto his side.

"This won't last," Bastion said, gesturing at the brilliant starry sky. A storm had been chasing them since departing Nassau, a dense cloud growing heavy and black on the aft horizon. No matter how fast they pushed the ship, the cloud slowly gained on them, like a stalking predator that had all the time in the world. The wind was constant, and *Ranger* was a fast sloop, but the storm could overtake them in a few easy steps if it so desired.

"Nothing lasts," Bart replied, plucking the last sliver of meat from a chicken bone. His belly was full to bursting, but he knew better than to waste good meat in the early stages of a journey. The crew would be living off of hardtack and rum before long, and chickens would plague their dreams. Bart savored the final juicy bite and tossed the bone to the sea, watching as it tumbled downward and made a little splash in the dark water.

Not much of a meal for the sharks, he thought.

He rested his arms on the rail beside Bastion, letting the cool breeze sweep over his face.

"How long before Governor Rogers comes for us?" Bastion asked in his thick islander accent. His dark skin would have rendered his features indiscernible in the night if not for the moonlight.

Bart had specifically chosen a best friend who enhanced his mental and physical appearance in every way he could possibly conceive. Bart was a head taller and more powerfully built. Bastion was five years older than Bart, who was twenty-five, but Bart thought him no wiser than a teenager. There were few aboard *Ranger* who Bart considered his intellectual equal.

"I don't know," Bart said with a lengthy sigh. He didn't care to think about what was behind them, only what was ahead. He had run away from his overly strict parents in New York when he was eight and had never looked back. He spent much of his youth moving from family to family, conning each with various fictions that detailed a tragic heritage, though in truth he had suffered no tragedy. He spent a year or two with each family before growing tired of them, gathering up any valuables he could conceal, and moving on to the next.

Eventually he ended up working on a merchant ship, where he became skilled at mending sails. He remembered little about his mother, but he was certain she had been a gifted seamstress. That gift must have trickled down.

Bart had been recruited into piracy when the trade ship he served aboard was set upon by Benjamin Hornigold and his protégé, Edward Teach.

"Rogers isn't after us," Bart continued. "He's after our dear captain. You and me, we're ghosts. Once we get that treasure, we'll disappear."

"What if there be no treasure?"

Bart shrugged. "Then we'll disappear as poor men, same as always, and move to the next venture until we can disappear as rich men." Bastion was always dwelling on what might go wrong. As far as Bart was concerned, there was an easy way out of any situation, if one only bothered to look for the escape route.

"Captain Benjamin cannot disappear so easily as us," said Bastion.

"He's a fool," Bart growled. Hornigold, a former pirate turned pirate hunter, had been Governor Woodes Rogers' right-hand man, and he had thrown it all away thanks to a mysterious woman's promise of a buried fortune. Under cover of night, Hornigold held a covert meeting with his crew in Nassau harbor, informing them that he planned to abandon his duties and seek out this treasure. Hornigold would bring the woman with them as a guide; a kind of human treasure map. She was a pretty thing who called herself Kate, with untamed hair that might have been colored in blood.

Bart and the majority of the crew, most of whom had been former pirates, were more than happy to oblige. They weren't making enough under the employ of Woodes Rogers. If Rogers apprehended them, they could feign ignorance and say they had simply followed Hornigold's orders and hadn't realized that he had acted without the governor's permission.

"Once pirate, always pirate," Bastion said. Probably something he had heard one of the men say. Like a parrot, Bastion often latched onto phrases he had overheard, even when he didn't fully understand their meaning.

"Problems arise when a pirate makes a name for himself," Bart replied, digging a strand of meat out of his teeth with a fingernail. "A man can't disappear when everyone knows his face." He nudged Bastion with an elbow. "You and me, we're nobodies. You know why history doesn't tell of successful pirates?"

Bastion thought about that for a moment, frowning. When he came to a conclusion, he looked like he might throw up. "Because successful pirates do not exist?"

"No, you fool," Bart spat. "Because the successful pirates are nobodies, like you and me. They're smart enough *not* to make names for themselves. They keep to the shadows and keep their mouths shut. Men like Hornigold want the fame *and* the fortune. You can't have both. The smart ones, we'll never know their names, and that's the way they like it."

"Maybe them not smart," Bastion suggested with a shrug. "Maybe them just lucky."

Bart ground his teeth. "Luck's got nothing to do with it. A real man makes his own luck."

"No," Bastion said, shaking his head ardently. "You cannot make luck. My father told me this."

Bart pushed himself angrily off the bulwark. "Well then your father was a bloody idiot! You really don't know anything, do you?"

When Bastion regarded him with a raised eyebrow, Bart flung his hand contemptuously through the air. "You've gone and sullied my jovial mood," he said. "I must recover it from the bottom of a bottle."

Bart left Bastion standing there staring dumbly after him. His anger slowly waned as he zigzagged through several sleeping crewmen sprawled about the deck and made his way below.

He found a dozen men in a corner of the hold, where they were huddled about a few candles, passing around a large jug of rum. He squeezed between Andrew Harrow and Fat Farley, who were seated on a long crate. Harrow slapped Bart on the back and handed him the jug, which had a third of rum left in it. Bart eagerly tipped the jug and took a huge swig.

"Slow down, Barty," Farley chuckled.

Bart righted the jug and handed it back, wiping his mouth. A bubble of air climbed his throat, and a massive belch popped from his lips. "I needed that," he said.

"Have another," Francois Laurent, one of *Ranger's* gunners, said with a grin. "We're fully stocked."

"For now," Bart said. "A few more nights like this will make short work of it." But that didn't stop him from taking another swig, and another, and another. Soon the bottle was empty, and Francois stumbled across the hold to fetch another. As Bart groggily watched him disappear into the dark, he saw something. A ways off, at the edge of the candlelight's reach, he could see a bare foot dangling from a crate. He scaled the leg to a vague, slender figure sitting in the dark. Even in the shadows, her hair shone red. Her hand rested on a bottle of her own, which was half drained. Black linen breeches hugged her hips, fastened tightly around her thin waist by a black belt. She wore a man's white shirt with ruffled sleeves, loosely laced at the neck to reveal her cleavage. Her hair shadowed her eyes, but her mouth was visible. She was smirking.

"She's been there all night," Farley whispered in Bart's ear. "She just watches us. Gives me the creeps, she does."

"Why isn't she shacked up in the captain's cabin?" Bart wondered. It seemed to take minutes to form a sentence, and he heard himself slurring the words. The rum was doing its job.

"I reckon the captain is asking hisself that same question,"

Harrow replied. The rest of the men chuckled . . . but not too loudly. They glanced apprehensively at her, as though they didn't want to offend. Bart winced in revulsion. What kind of pirate was intimidated by a woman?

Francois returned with a new bottle, filled to the brim. He sat down, popped the cork, and stole the first gulp. He offered the bottle to Farley, but Bart snatched it first. He took a swig and then dropped the bottle in Farley's lap.

He aimed a finger at the woman in the dark. "Has anyone had a go with her yet?" He said it loud enough for her to hear.

Everyone suddenly shifted in their seats, looking anxiously at each other. The woman didn't react. Her fingers lightly drummed her bottle of rum in dawdling succession.

"Don't think so," Farley answered under his breath.

"Captain wants her unspoiled," Harrow whispered.

"Unspoiled?" Bart said, curling his lip. "He said that? That's a downright aggravating choice of words!"

"Not so loud," Farley urged, holding a hand out flat and lowering it in a hushing motion.

"And why not?" Bart snapped.

Farley's mouth fell open, but he had no answer.

"That's what I thought."

Harrow's hand grasped Bart's shoulder. "Bart, I think that's enough."

Bart stood. His fellow crewmen pulled away as he stumbled between them, knocking over one of the candles with his heel. It rolled against a crate, flame sizzling out as the wax spilled over the wick. "Have you forgotten who we are? We're pirates! There is no 'enough' for the likes of us!"

Farley and Harrow exchanged a woeful look. Francois sniffed and looked down at the deck.

"She's the reason we're here," a young blonde crewman Bart didn't recognize said timidly.

"And that affords her the right to strut about our deck un-spoiled?" He sneered the last word.

"Bastion!" Francois suddenly cried, extending a hand. "I think it's time your friend found his hammock."

Bart turned. Bastion had entered quietly behind him and was standing between two crates. "I come only for rum," Bastion protested with his palms up. "I do not solve disputes."

"Damn straight," Bart said. "That's Reed's trade, and he's not here." Quartermaster Reed generally put an end to quarrels before they had a chance to begin.

Bart faced the woman. The hold swirled as he turned, and he thrust out a foot before he fell. "The very least she can do," he said, pointing at her, "is let a few of us betwixt her thighs."

At that, the woman gathered her rum and slid off the crate. She departed without looking back, hips languidly swaying. Wayward orange streaks in her hair ensnared the diminished candlelight after her figure had faded.

Bart turned to the group, spreading his arms. His right hand raked against a crate, grinding splinters into his knuckles. He clenched his teeth, but refused to openly acknowledge the pain. "She departs before I can finish," he said.

"You had more to say?" Francois quipped with a little smile.

Bastion took the seat between Farley and Harrow, where Bart had been seated. He took a sip of rum, stared at the bottle for a moment, and then fixed Bart with a very serious look. "This not a good idea. Captain Benjamin won't suffer dis . . . dis . . . what's the word?"

"Disobedience," Francois answered.

"Yes, that one."

"Last I looked, we're pirates again," Bart hissed. "What's a little disobedience among scoundrels?"

"Bart," Farley said, pointing, "your hand is bleeding."

"Shuttup," said Bart.

Bastion shook his head sternly, his large eyes unblinking. "Captain Benjamin worked with Blackbeard. Him learn a thing or two about dealing with disobedience."

Bart gave an exaggerated shiver. "See how I tremble!"

"Bart," Farley said, "your hand looks ill, mate."

Aggravatingly, Bastion was still shaking his head. "Captain Benjamin won't be happy if you kill the only person knows where the treasure is hiding."

"He's got a point there, mate," Farley said, grabbing the bottle of rum.

"I don't mean to kill her," Bart replied uncertainly, blinking at the blurry blob that had just spoken, until his vision focused. "Maybe I'll just teach her a lesson."

Harrow tittered. "From the look of her, I'll wager she's learned many lessons."

"None so hard as mine," Bart said, and he swiftly pivoted on his heels and made for the exit before bravado could flee him.

"No stopping him now," he heard Francois say.

"I'm not about to try," Farley muttered.

Bart shouldered through many crates, which seemed to be sliding in on him. The walkway seemed far more constricted than when he had first entered. A chicken scurried about his feet, flapping its wings and squawking. He kicked the bird with all his might, propelling it into a crate. The chicken landed flat, one wing flapping spastically. "Might want to cook this one now," he called back at the others. "I tendered it up for you."

"Stairs are the other way, Bart," Harrow called.

"Don't need stairs," Bart guffawed.

He found a ladder leading to the deck and started climbing, scraping his nose on a rung. He cursed, shaking the dizziness from his head. Halfway up, he peered over his shoulder. The crewmen stared after him from their distant patch of light.

Farley waved, his face bright red as though he was ready to burst out laughing. Bart spat at them and continued climbing.

His hand slipped on the next rung, leaving a smear of blood. A massive splinter was jutting from his knuckle, blood seeping between his fingers. He tore the splinter free with his teeth, feeling no pain, and wiped his hand on his pants.

He slapped both arms on the deck and wrenched himself upward. He stood, invigorated by the cool air. He scanned the deck, his vision blurring in and out of focus. Pirates were scattered everywhere, sleeping soundly. He looked to the bow but didn't see anyone. Had she run to her captain at last, fearing the inevitable?

He looked to the captain's cabin, set in a stairway carved in the deck. The door was shut. Bart started toward it. They were pirates again, after all, and the captain's quarters on a pirate ship were not exclusive to the captain. Bart would barge in and take what was rightfully his, and there was nothing Hornigold could do about it.

A slender shadow stirred on the quarterdeck directly above the cabin. Her hair was unmistakable. Bart sprinted up the steps to the deck. No pirates were sleeping here tonight. It was just him and her. She smirked suggestively and slowly moved to the aft bulwark. She set the bottle of rum at her feet and faced him. She was framed by the black storm clouds in the distance, ever vigilant on the horizon. "What took you so long?" she said.

"I knew you wanted me to follow you," Bart slurred.

"Picked up on that, did you? And here I thought myself too subtle."

Bart moved closer, wobbling on unsteady legs. He had overdone it with the rum, but that never seemed to damage his libido.

"The others wouldn't have picked up on it," he said.

"You're smarter than them," she replied knowingly. She placed her elbows on the rail behind her, stretching her shirt across her chest, nipples pressing against the fabric. Bart's heart thumped in his chest as he advanced.

"You were right," she said. Her voice was wincingly raspy, almost masculine, as if she had screamed too many times.

"About what?" Bart asked. He needed clarification; he was right about a great many things.

"About ghosts."

"What about ghosts?" he said, trying to sound casual. The ocean was moving slowly away from the ship, the sails billowing with all the haste of a snail struggling through molasses. If Bart didn't get to his business soon, he would pass out.

"When ghosts disappear, no one notices," she said, running her tongue across her upper lip.

He frowned, gradually recalling his earlier conversation with Bastion. "You were listening in?"

She laughed. It was a harsh sound, like pebbles grinding. "I was passing by and overheard."

"You have good ears."

"I only have the one, you see." She trailed a finger across her temple, drawing back her hair to reveal a garbled mess where her right ear had been. Bart flinched. What had happened to this woman? "Don't look so appalled," she chuckled. "It's only an ear. I have a spare."

He swallowed his revulsion, pushing the unsettling image from his mind. She was still very attractive, two ears or one. It was fortunate that her hair concealed the mutilation. He supposed he could get past it.

She curled a finger, summoning him closer. "You'd better hurry," she said, eyes descending to his crotch, "before the spirit absconds."

He moved fast, crushing her against the bulwark. His hands

fumbled at her waist, sliding down and around to cup her ass. She gasped as he squeezed her. Her wet lips grazed his cheek, breath hot on his face. Fingernails dug into his ribs. He smashed his chest against hers, her nipples piercing his pecs. Her hair smelled like salt and sand. He licked her neck and struggled to untuck her shirt from her pants. She seized his arms and shifted her weight, turning him around so that he was between her and the bulwark. Her foot kicked the bottle of rum as she moved, and it clinked noisily as it rolled onto its side.

"Oh dear!" she exclaimed, giggling lightly. "It's spilling. Can't have that." She held up a finger, halting him, and bent down to forage for the bottle. She stumbled, and her fingers tapped the neck of the bottle. It rolled behind his leg. "Raise your foot," she said. He did as instructed, and she reached under him.

"Hurry up, down there," he urged impatiently.

Her gaze lifted suddenly, the glint of predatory eyes glaring at him through the red tresses of hair that had spilled over her face.

"What are you . . . ?" he started, scowling. Everything was moving so slowly.

She pushed upward, her shoulder catching the underside of his foot. Her left hand shot into his stomach, knocking the wind out of him, and when she withdrew it, something flashed silver and red. She summoned all of her power to shove him up and over the rail.

The deck tumbled out of view, his legs flailed in the air, and every notch of his spine grated against the rail as he slid off. The world spun end over end, sea and ship swirling in a dizzying blur. And then he saw her looking down on him, hair burning crimson in the moonlight, face eclipsed in darkness.

Bart's back slapped the water.

He struggled to stay afloat as the ship sailed away from him at startling velocity, much faster than it had seemed to be moving when he was aboard. He opened his mouth to scream and sucked water into his lungs. He hacked violently, ejecting something dark and red into the water, where it expanded in a black cloud around him. He continued to cough, salt water biting at his esophagus. He thrashed his arms, slapping at the rolling waves, and pain shot through his torso like a bolt of lightning. His legs started to sink, as if gripped by invisible hands. The water lifted above his nose, and he thrust himself upward, but the pain in his stomach was paralyzing him. The muscles in his arms were quickly growing numb and stiff.

The ship moved quietly into the horizon, and the woman remained a shadow at the stern. The last thing Bart heard was a crack of distant thunder from the storm somewhere behind him.

1

NATHAN

Flies circled the churned mess of Henry's ravaged kneecap, buzzing incessantly in a near perfect sphere. He swatted fiercely at them, his remaining eye gleaming with defiance. A sickly-sweet aroma wafted from the ghastly wound.

He doesn't know he's dying, Nathan realized with a wry smirk.

"What're you smiling about?" Henry barked.

"We hang on the morrow," Nathan chuckled, "and still you swat at flies."

"They'll have me soon enough," Henry nodded. "But not tonight."

The late afternoon sun cast a ray of light through the small square window, projecting two bars across Nathan's legs. He found it amusing that someone had bothered placing bars in the window at all. Not even a ten year old girl could squeeze through that opening.

Large flecks of dust trailed through the sunlight, in no hurry to greet the cold stone floor of the cramped cell. Straw was scattered about, and a brown river of feces streamed from the rusty pail Henry had carelessly kicked over in his sleep. The black sewage was littered with the corpses of greedy flies that had realized their mistake too late.

Occasionally, a fresh breeze would sweep in through the window, combating the mingling stenches of feces and Henry's festering wound. Nathan could taste salt on the wind, carried in from the harbor nearby. Two days ago, after he had been thrown in here, he would stand on his toes to peek out the window and catch glimpse of the impossibly blue water, white sails, and flocks of birds gliding above. Now, he didn't want to look at everything he had lost. He was certain that no one was coming to his rescue, and he would hang alongside his pitiful cellmate in the morning.

He would never again see his beloved Annabelle, the beautiful strumpet he had spent a month with before so foolishly returning to sea. She was the first woman he had ever been with, and she would in all likelihood be the last. When fate brought him back to Nassau, Annabelle was gone. According to gossip, she had left for Tortuga with her pimp, Charles Martel, after she had been viciously raped and disfigured. Nathan also heard that she'd fallen in with Blackbeard, but he didn't believe that for a second. He tried desperately not to think about her copper skin, her full breasts and hips, her thick black hair, and, above all, her big brown eyes and luscious lips.

He scratched the stump just beneath his elbow, where his left arm had once been, lost at sea thanks to a collapsing yard-arm. In dreams the arm remained, and he had no knowledge of its absence until he woke. In dreams he wasn't trapped in a tiny cell. In dreams he scaled the ratlines of *Harbinger*, the ship he had served aboard under the command of Captain Jonathan

Griffith. He climbed and climbed until he finally reached the top, where he was greeted by cool winds and curious seagulls. The deep blue sea stretched in an endless radius, with no sign of land in sight. The sky was a perfect cerulean, unblemished by clouds.

And then a fly or a foul scent or someone shouting orders in the harbor would rudely stir him from his oblivious slumber, and he would find himself back in the darkened cell, minus a limb and smelling of shit and death.

The larger cells had been filled to the brim with pirates when Nathan and Henry were first brought in. Nathan recognized several of them as fellow crewmates from *Harbinger*, which now rested in blackened pieces at the bottom of the sea. Nathan and Henry were put in a "spare cell," as the guards called it, which was considerably smaller than the others, and minus a bed or even a bench. It felt extremely isolated, and it was the only cell partitioned by solid walls instead of bars.

Henry had made friends with the next inmate over, even though they were separated from view. Nathan couldn't be sure what the man in the next cell looked like, as his sight hadn't yet adjusted to the dim dungeon block when he was first dragged past. He sounded older, with a coarse voice that broke on words with too many syllables, sending him into wheezing fits. He called himself Jethro, and claimed to have served alongside the infamous pirate Charles Vane, who had set fire to a ship in the harbor when Governor Woodes Rogers first arrived to establish order. Jethro maintained that Vane was on his way to rescue him. "Vane's men are highly placed, they are," he claimed. "Some o' them work right under the governor's nose, they do, and he hasn't the foggiest notion. They wait for Vane's order, and when he gives it, the governor's in for a surprise. I can only imagine what they'll do to that pretty wife o' his."

Nathan wrote the old man off as crazy, but Henry seemed utterly convinced that Jethro was his key to freedom. "He knows an awful lot of detail," Henry said whenever Nathan balked openly at Jethro's wild claims.

"You can laugh all you want," Jethro said nonchalantly. "But ask yourself why they bring me wine, and bring you soiled water."

"No one brings you wine!" Nathan scoffed.

"I'd show you," Jethro replied, "if not for the wall betwixt us."

"Convenient," Nathan said. Jethro would probably swear his rescuers were right around the corner even as the noose was fitted around his neck.

A heavyset guard named Ferrell approached, raking his keys across the bars, as he liked to do every few hours. Sometimes he would wait until they were sleeping before he did it. When Ferrell reached the spare cell, Nathan fixed him with a hard glare. He was met with obnoxious laughter. Ferrell enjoyed provoking a reaction from men who would soon be too dead to challenge him.

"I wonder," Nathan grated, "would your keys ring so loudly if we were not scheduled for execution?"

Ferrell's eyes went fierce at that, his sweaty cheeks blooming red, and he clutched his musket threateningly. "I wonder," he furiously intoned, "would you speak so boldly if you weren't destined for the gallows?"

Nathan stood and clutched one of the bars. "If I weren't destined for the gallows, I would return for you."

Ferrell slammed the barrel of his gun against the bars, and Nathan recoiled just before his fingers could be smashed. "You've got one more night to dream of revenge," Ferrell said, grinning through his teeth. "Shame you'll have to wake up." He lumbered off, giggling to himself.

Nathan sat back down, his cheeks burning furiously. How had it come to this?

"Katherine Lindsay," Henry rumbled as he flicked a fly from the black mess of his gaping knee. He had uttered her name at least once every waking hour over the past two days, as though he would forget it if he didn't recite it regularly. But how could anyone forget her? "She's killed us all."

He's right, Nathan reminded himself. She had left him to die here. She could have saved him so easily. There was a reward for her safe return to London, and Nathan had hoped to claim it under the guise of an innocent sailor who had been kidnapped alongside Lindsay by *Harbinger's* pirates. In truth, Nathan was far from innocent, but he had hoped the friendship he *thought* he shared with Lindsay would compel her to corroborate the lie.

Katherine Lindsay had apparently vanished into the wilds of Nassau or booked passage on a ship to God only knew where, leaving Nathan to rot in a cell. Her mane of red hair burned in his mind like a sunspot seared in the retina. He could scarcely recall her face, which was overshadowed by that shroud of hair. There had been a time when he felt so sorry for her, held against her will by Captain Griffith, who probably thought he had found a wife. Griffith murdered her husband without hesitation and took her without bothering to consult his crew.

Katherine had seemed so lost, so ready to give in, and for a time Nathan thought Griffith might have won her over, as insane as that notion seemed now. And then something changed. Nathan had no idea when or why it happened, but survival suddenly became a priority for Katherine, at the expense of every man aboard *Harbinger*, including Nathan. Griffith let his guard down, and Katherine took his life as quickly as Griffith had taken her husband's. Nathan wondered what went through Griffith's mind in that final moment, other than the shot from his pistol. Did the justice of the deed occur to him, or did he see nothing more than a betrayal?

"That bitch shot me leg," Henry whimpered for probably the hundredth time.

"Yes, Henry," Nathan sighed. "You mentioned that once or twice."

"I done nothing to her," Henry went on, firmly shaking his head. "I done nothing!"

"That's not exactly true," Nathan said. If there was one thing Nathan had learned, it was that not a single pirate held himself accountable for his own actions. The disreputable paths they had chosen were irrelevant to whatever indecencies they were suffering presently.

"They'll probably take it off," Henry groaned. The flies were growing more courageous now, deftly avoiding the frantic sweeps of Henry's hand and landing on dark flakes of dried blood. "One-eyed, one-legged Henry," he went on, shaking his head.

"Don't think you'll need to worry about that much longer."

"So says you," Henry sourly fired back, aiming a finger at Nathan's missing arm. "Yours healed up nicely."

Nathan massaged the stump at his elbow, fingers rolling over the bone just beneath the skin. "Not really," he shrugged. "It didn't grow back."

He felt older than he imagined any twenty-one year old should. He had lost much of his appetite along with his arm, and his skin felt taut over his bones. His ribs ached with every breath, and his eyelids were constantly threatening to close. His sandy blonde hair was starting to fall out in tufts. There was, of course, no bed in the cell, and his ass was sore from sitting on the hard stone for so long. Shifting his position no longer assuaged the pain. He had grown accustomed to discomfort. "Life is pain," his father told him years ago, after Nathan had been thrown from a horse and had scraped up the elbow of the arm that was now shortened. "So long as you're in pain, you aren't dead."

Henry hissed through his teeth, jerking his leg sharply. "Oh God," he moaned. His forehead was drenched in sweat. "Will this never end?"

"Very soon," Nathan reminded him.

A distant door creaked open, and a column of white light spread down the hallway. "Whossat?" Henry said, leaning forward with a crazed look in his eye. "WHOSSAT??"

Nathan set his head against the closely-notched bars, trying to see who was coming. *The fat guard on his way to taunt me with the keys again?* Maybe Nathan could break the guard's arm, unlock the cell, and make a run for it. What other chance would he get?

Three long shadows split the column of light on the floor, stretching in size as the footsteps grew louder. The shadow in the middle was tall and large, and his pace was less stiff than the flanking shadows.

Nathan pulled his head away from the bars and propped himself against the wall with one leg flat and the other raised, his one arm dangling casually over a knee. He wasn't about to let them see him sweat.

"This one here," came a gruff voice.

"I remember."

The three men stopped before the bars. The two on the right and left were guards, and the middle was Woodes Rogers, Governor of the Bahamas. Nathan had met Rogers once before, after Nathan approached one of the soldiers in town and demanded to be taken before the governor. He was promptly thrown in this cell, and Rogers came to him a short time later.

Rogers was a tall man with a great round belly held aloft by a sloping belt, the huge buckle facing downward. He wore a deep blue coat with polished brass buttons. His head was covered by a full white wig, the curls of which rested on his shoulders. He had a broad nose and bushy eyebrows that were just as black as his impenetrable eyes. His chin was inconsequential, descending into the frill of a white collar. His left cheek was engraved with a round scar bordered by a thick ring of rubbery skin that was split in several places, like a crater on the moon. His upper jaw on that side was slightly caved in, forging an uneven face. His skin was surprisingly tan and leathery, as if he had spent much of his life outdoors.

"I watch the hangings whenever I can," Rogers said without delay, peering directly into Nathan's eyes. "Not because I enjoy them. Nay. In fact, I loathe death. I feel a man who hands out judgment must witness the consequences firsthand."

Nathan rolled his hand, opening his palm to the ceiling. "You came here to tell us that?"

"Pay him no mind, Nathan," Henry spat, shaking his head. "Thinks he's better than us because he talks fancier. He's just a pirate for the King."

Rogers seemed unaware that Henry existed, despite the stench of Henry's wound. "I do not respect those who would condemn a man to death without the decency to watch them die."

Nathan fronted a casual smirk, though he felt a nervous twinge in his cheek. "That sentiment will comfort me as the rope constricts about my neck."

"You're not a typical pirate," Rogers noted. "Your speech is long and clear, and you are evidently bred of fairer stock."

Henry grunted loudly at that, but he failed to divert Rogers' attention.

"Not all sailors are simpletons," Nathan said.

Rogers leaned against the bars, furrowing his considerable

brow. "Is that what you call yourself? A sailor?"

"Governor," Nathan sighed, "my time is running short. What do you want?"

Rogers wasted no more time, pushing himself off the bars. He broke into a pace, walking back and forth outside the cell while the guards remained dutifully still. "You claimed to have sailed with Katherine Lindsay, a woman whose name continues to plague my desk. Her husband's family is nothing if not diligent. And it seems I may have let her slip through my fingers."

"That's too bad," Nathan said, suppressing a curse. "If only someone had warned you."

"I am a busy man, and I sent Benjamin Hornigold in my place. That was a miscalculation. Now, Hornigold has fled my employ, last seen in the company of a redheaded woman, before he sailed his ship and crew out of my harbor to . . . well I think you know where."

"I don't follow."

"I think you do." Rogers adjusted the buckle that his belly rested upon. "In fact, *following* is exactly what I expect you to do. Benjamin Hornigold was a former pirate. Also of fairer stock. He surrendered himself to me under the condition that he hunt down the criminals he once crewed alongside. I came to regard him as a friend. A fellow adventurer. We traded many tales in a short span. I suppose, over the years, politics have made me a sterner man." Rogers' gaze faltered only for a moment, a shadow passing over his face. He almost looked sad. "It seems Benjamin's ambitions got the better of him. The only reason he would have fled is if that woman promised him something I could not."

Nathan snickered. "A fuzzy nook between her legs to rest his face?"

Henry choked out a laugh.

Rogers bristled. "Now you pretend to be a less cultivated man than I know you are. No doubt such vulgarity was a necessity to keep your place amongst scoundrels, but it will gain you nothing in my presence."

Nathan embellished a sigh. "And what could I possibly gain from you?"

"I suspect you're a man of at least two faces," Rogers said, studying him. "It takes a rare sort of intelligence to blend so effectually with one's environment."

Nathan shrugged. "If I was so smart, I wouldn't be in here." His teeth gnawed at the inside of his cheek. *I certainly wouldn't have trusted Katherine Lindsay to do the right thing.*

"He's got you there, Gov," Henry added.

"There's no greater crime than wasted talent," Rogers said.

"So hang me," Nathan chuckled. He was starting to enjoy this. If he was going to die, he might as well have some fun first.

Woodes Rogers gripped his belt buckle and shifted his girth. "Though my resolve in suppressing piracy is encouraged by your lack of respect, I fear I must decline."

Nathan's arm slid off his knee and his hand slapped the cold stone ground. He curled his fingers, dragging his nails along the irregular surface. "You want me to tell you where they went?"

"No. I want you to *show* me where they went."

Henry's back straightened. His lone eye widened. "My name's Henry," Henry declared, his voice pitched strangely high.

Rogers blinked in annoyance, reluctantly shifting his line of sight. "Pardon?"

"My name's Henry," Henry repeated. "We was introduced once before." Henry had been there when Rogers first granted Nathan a meeting.

Rogers' eyelids fluttered with irritation. "Strange. I must have forgotten you."

"I know where she took your man." Henry looked totally ridiculous, absently leaning over his rotting leg with a desperate look in his lone eye. "I know where she took him, and I can take you there."

Rogers smirked. "Do not mistake me. One of you will hang tomorrow. Judging by the smell of that grotesque wound, you're dead either way. I'll do you a kindness in shortening your torture."

"This?" Henry said, tittering down at his leg. "I've had worse." He aimed a thumb at his eye. "Rotted clean out of me skull, it did. I can handle a ruddy leg."

Rogers motioned to the guard on his left. "Open the cell."

"Sir," the guard acknowledged at once and fumbled with his ring of keys.

"Bless you," Henry said, slapping both palms together and resting his forehead on his thumbs.

The guard opened the door, which screeched on its rusty hinges, and stepped in. "Just the boy," Rogers instructed. The guard nodded and lifted Nathan by his armpits.

"Wait!" Henry pleaded. "Wait!" He seized the guard's leg. The guard jerked away and gave Henry's wound a nudge with his heel. Henry shrieked, clutching his knee. Nathan was dragged out of the cell as Henry wailed behind him. "Tell them they need me, Nathan! You won't find the island without me! And even if you do, you don't know where he buried all them chests! I do!"

The guard put Nathan before Woodes Rogers. Nathan struggled to keep his balance, his legs wobbling underneath him. The guard steadied him.

Nathan saw Ferrell a few cells down the block, watching anxiously. When Nathan made eye contact, Ferrell's eyes flickered away, and he went about his duties.

The other prisoners were leaning against the bars of their cells trying to see what was happening, jittering to one another.

Nathan could see Jethro now. The man was lounging in his bunk, his back against the wall, not a care in the world. He wasn't as old as Nathan had guessed. Maybe forty. His close-cropped hair and mustache were peppered grey. A deep scar was carved in his forehead, from his scalp to his right eyebrow. He was surprisingly well dressed, with a clean white shirt, ruffled at the neck, and maroon breeches. A black cap with a red ribbon sat in his lap. An empty goblet stood on the floor, and Jethro tapped it repeatedly with the tip of his boot.

"Tell me, Rogers," Jethro wheezed, "How many ships did you plunder in your expedition around the world, with that treacherous scallywag Dampier for a navigator? How much gold and silk did you return to England before you determined piracy an ill affair?"

Rogers was unfazed. "I am not addressing you, sir. My business is with the young man."

"If not for business with former pirates," Jethro said, "you'd have no business at all."

"Persist in this fashion," Rogers countered flatly with a sideways glance, "and I shall be unable to ignore the wine that magicks itself into your cell."

Jethro inclined his head politely. He didn't say another word.

Rogers returned his attention to Nathan. "I care naught for lost treasure that probably doesn't exist."

"It *does* exist!" Henry bellowed. "I know where Griff buried it!"

"My only concern is in ending piracy," Rogers continued, ignoring Henry. "Benjamin Hornigold was a trusted ally, and now he's spit in my face and returned to the ranks of piracy. I must retrieve him and make an example of him. Mr. Adams, you will be transferred to a ship called *Crusader*, where you will report to Captain Dillahunt. You will lead him to Hornigold's destination. That is the extent of your role. Nothing more will be required of you, and afterward you will be free to do whatever you like, with the exception of engaging in further piratical activities. There may even be a position available on Dillahunt's ship, should you desire."

"I understand," Nathan said. A swell of relief was steadily rising in his breast. His fortune had shifted as swiftly as the wind, but he knew better than to let the moment overwhelm him. The wind was fickle.

One detail was nagging at him. "What of Lindsay?"

Rogers paused. Apparently he hadn't considered that. "Her family will want her returned safely, but her recent actions do not bode well her mortality. Lindsay has deprived me of my best man. If anything were to happen to her, I can't say my slumber would be diminished."

"Noted," Nathan said. He wasn't sure what he would do if he encountered Katherine again, but it was good to know that his freedom was not contingent on her survival.

"This little shit doesn't know where the island is!" Henry screamed, sweat trickling down his forehead.

Rogers clutched Nathan's collar and drew him closer. "If you require this man, tell me now."

The words came easily. "He's no use to anybody."

Rogers nodded. "Then he will hang with the others." He patted Nathan's shoulder, just above the missing arm, and smiled for the first time. His gnarled jaw did not allow the smile much leeway on the left side. "And before you depart, you will witness the executions."

2

CALLOWAY

"I must confess disappointment," Jacqueline Calloway said, strutting around her room in nothing more than a feathered tricorn hat. "I expected them to strangle for minutes on end. The snapping of their necks was shocking, but it was over too fast. I see no real punishment in a brisk death, do you?"

"You're lucky you got to see anything at all," Guy Dillahunt replied, watching her from the bed.

"So are you," she shot back, turning away from the window to face him. The morning light projected her slender silhouette across the room. The establishment had no name, as yet. It was fairly new, and so far Calloway was the only tenant occupying one of the four rooms on the second floor above the tavern. She wondered how long this place could stay in business with only her to support it, since pirates were now steering clear of Nassau.

Dillahunt was sitting against the crude headboard, one hand

behind his head, the other fingering a polished black pistol with silver sloops set into each side of the grip. Calloway had noted that the gun was never far from his person, which was probably smart for a man of his vocation. Dillahunt was a famed privateer who had lingered in Nassau over the past month to aid his friend, Governor Woodes Rogers, in ridding the Caribbean of piracy.

The covers were drawn to his lean waist. His stomach was etched in muscle, ascending into a broad chest. He had bulky shoulders and biceps the size of Calloway's thighs. Blonde strands permeated his thick brown hair. Calloway guessed him to be in his mid-thirties. Upon close scrutiny, Dillahunt was not particularly handsome, with a narrow mouth, puffy cheeks, and eyes displaced too far apart. His nose was round and flat, as though he had been punched one too many times, and there was a perpetual crease between his eyebrows. Still, Calloway found him irresistibly attractive. In her opinion, a man did not need a perfect face. Character and strength were far greater virtues, and Dillahunt possessed an abundance of both.

"I've been afraid to ask," he said, setting his gun on the cockeyed bedside table. "How old are you? Or, should I say, how *young* are you?"

"I am fifteen as of two days ago," Calloway said, grinning proudly.

Dillahunt considered that, chewing on his bottom lip. "You are considerably talented for a fifteen year old."

"I've been at it since I was twelve," she admitted. Her mother, a beautiful French prostitute named Elise, had raised her in a small brothel at Port Bayou St. Jean in Louisiana. Calloway's father had been an impossibly handsome raven-haired explorer who her mother had spent no more than a single night with, or so she had claimed.

"Your accent sounds vaguely French," Dillahunt said. "Yet

your surname is English, is it not?"

"I don't know anything about names, 'surs' or otherwise," Calloway said. "My mother probably took it off one of her many suitors. We had so many last names, you see."

"Your mother? A stunning woman, I'm sure."

"Prettier than me."

"I doubt that," Dillahunt said, beckoning her back to the bed with a hooked finger.

She stayed where she was, enjoying the soft breeze on her naked back as it swept through the open window. "She was more womanly." She trailed a finger over a disappointingly small breast. "I could pass for a boy."

"So you've said," he drawled, rolling his eyes. She had been not-so-subtly hinting at joining his crew since meeting him yesterday. "Never met a boy with skin so smooth as yours."

"I'm as tall as you, Captain," she chuckled. She was nearly six feet tall, with long legs and strong broad shoulders. Her mother said Calloway had gained her stature from her father. Jacqueline's piercing sapphire irises, fair complexion, and the faint smattering of freckles about her nose, however, had been gifts from her mother.

Dillahunt gnawed at a fingernail. "I knew a strumpet taller than Edward Teach," he said between bites.

Calloway recoiled at the name. "Do not speak that name to me," she barked. She had good reason to despise Teach, but she wasn't about to share that with someone she had just met. For all she knew, Dillahunt was one of Teach's spies.

"You have a quarrel with Blackbeard?" Dillahunt said, the crease lengthening in his brow.

"No," she lied. "I've just heard unspeakable things about the man."

"Exaggerations mostly," Dillahunt replied. "But not all. He is exceedingly dangerous."

"I told you not to talk about him."

"Fine," he said, raising his hands innocently. "My point was I knew a very tall strumpet. Of course, her hips were wider than yours. Too wide for my tastes. I'd hate to see the plump bastards she popped out of those things."

Calloway ran her fingers through her straight black hair, which reached all the way to her waist. "If my hair was shorter and I wore boy's clothing, you wouldn't know the difference. There is very little that separates a boy's face from a woman's."

"I can't say I've ever been aroused by a boy," Dillahunt replied, spitting out a curl of fingernail.

"Maybe you have and didn't know it."

"That would be most alarming," he muttered to himself, as if experiencing a revelation. "Where would you stick the bloody thing, anyway? Jesus! I'd not blame a man for taking a cutlass to himself and flinging his cock to the sea, should such urges arise. The choice between a cock that excites for men and no cock at all . . . well that's not really a choice, is it?"

"I can't say," Calloway shrugged. "I don't have one."

"Precisely the reason you are absent clothing in my presence."

"It seems to me," she said, tapping her chin with her index finger, "that the only real difference between men and women is what's found betwixt our legs."

Dillahunt screwed up his face. "This conversation has taken a turn for the unpleasant." He retrieved his gun and suddenly became preoccupied with polishing the already spotless silver sloops.

"Well, that and tits," she went on, lowering her head to gander at her own bust, "which I don't have a whole lot of." She checked them often, for fear they might vanish if she didn't. She had hoped they would increase with age, but they had stubbornly refused.

"I'd like my hat back," Dillahunt muttered childishly.

Calloway turned away and set her palms on the windowsill, inhaling the morning air. Port Nassau was a bustle of activity below, as it always was after a hanging. Nothing brought out the liveliness in a town like an execution. The villagers were conversing with one another in the markets, navy sentries were stealing gossip while patrolling the docks with their long muskets, and several children were playing with turtles on the bright white sands of the beach.

The port was much cleaner now than when Calloway had first arrived a year prior. Many structures had been reinforced and repainted, and the town was beginning to distinguish itself from the lush jungle surrounding its borders. The streets had been cleared of tropical vegetation, which had found little resistance from the pirates when it threatened to overwhelm the town. Governor Rogers was rebuilding the fort on the hill that overlooked the bay. It was an ominous structure that served as a warning to all pirates who would dare return to the port that had once served as their primary base of operations. He had erected a new palisade around the fort, strengthening its defenses.

Not a year prior the harbor was filled to the brim with so many pirate ships that it was difficult to see the water between them, but now it was lightly sprinkled with the clean white sails of merchant vessels and a few official navy sloops. Shiny new mounted guns skirted the harbor. A hulking man of war loomed in the distance, near Hog Island. It was flanked by two heavily gunned navy sloops.

Fashion was gradually blending. It was difficult to tell one woman from the next, as they all seemed to be wearing the same style of dress. England had come to Nassau and had smothered much of its color along with its pirate populace.

Calloway looked past the white beach to the translucent

shallow waters that shimmered vibrantly in the early light. "They can take the town," she murmured distantly, "but they cannot take the water."

"What's that?" Dillahunt called from behind her. "Is that poetry?"

She faced him, propping her ass on the sill and folding her arms beneath her breasts. "You're taking me with you."

Dillahunt tossed the covers away and shuffled out of the bed. He stepped into his trousers and lifted them to his waist, fastening them. "I don't even know you," he said. "You wanted to see the hanging, so I used my influence to get you to the front, despite a full crowd. I wanted a night's pleasure. We were both obliged. Now you want to stowaway on my ship. What's in it for me?"

"A night's pleasure *every* night," she replied mischievously.

"You've scarred me," he whined, rubbing the back of his head. "If I'm ever to rise again, I'll require a blow to the skull that renders this morning's conversation forgotten."

She leapt off the window and moved towards him. He stared, transfixed by the movement of her hips. She cupped his crotch, which immediately hardened in her firm grip. "This tells me otherwise."

"Seems it has a mind of its own," he said, swallowing. "And a shorter memory."

"Why are you getting dressed? I wasn't through with you."

He pulled away, retrieving his shirt. "My ship impatiently awaits. We depart within the hour. As we speak, the crew scurries about the deck like rats, inclined to anarchy when starved of leadership."

"How do they feed themselves in your absence?" she drawled sarcastically.

"That is a good quest—" He paused, scowling. "Oh. You're making fun of me."

"I'm coming with you," she insisted, placing a hand on her hip.

"Some of my crew are former pirates," he said, slipping a bright red shirt over his head and buttoning it. "They do not tolerate females at sea, and neither do I. It's bad luck. Just ask Jonathan Griffith, if you can find his corpse somewhere at the bottom of the harbor."

"Which is why I will not board your ship as a girl," she said, reaching up and gathering her hair into a ponytail behind her head. "I'll cut it off. I'll dress as a common sailor. No one will know the difference. Except you. At night. When I steal into your quarters."

"Someone will notice that," Dillahunt said, curtness rising in his tone. He dropped to his knees and reached under the bed to retrieve his long black coat. "Sailors have nothing but time on their hands, and they spend that time studying every-one around them. Little details that bore you and me become exciting gossips worthy of reenactment over a campfire. A captain sleeping with a cabin boy, while not exactly suitable for reenactment, would prove particularly exciting gossip. And possible cause for mutiny. Not to mention what could happen to you if your true gender were discovered."

"I'll be careful."

He slipped on the coat and straightened the sleeves. He paused, fixating on her head. "This can no longer be ignored. You are wearing my hat."

"You can't have it." She flicked the white feather dangling over the brim.

"It's my finest hat."

"Buy another. The market's open."

"Jacqueline," he sighed.

"Jaq," she corrected, raising a finger.

He set his hands on her shoulders and massaged them with

his thumbs. "Jacqueline, this next voyage is dangerous business. I must track a former associate of the governor. A very smart man by the name of Benjamin Hornigold." He stared at her portentously. When she didn't respond, he added, "I may be violently murdered for my trouble."

"I thought Hornigold was hunting pirates now."

"Indeed he was," Dillahunt said. "But now he's gone on the account with that Lindsay woman."

"Who?" Calloway replied, playing dumb. She knew exactly who Katherine Lindsay was—everybody on the island did— but she also knew that men liked to inform women of things they thought women didn't already know.

"Some bitch from London who spent too long with pirates. That idiot Jonathan Griffith kidnapped her, and she apparently repaid him by setting his ship ablaze in the harbor."

"Hmm, I might like her."

"She's all mixed up in the head, as women tend to be after enduring fearful circumstances. Rogers believes her to be leading Hornigold to a supposed bounty that Griffith may or may not have stashed before his untimely demise. Promises of gold seem to follow this woman wherever she goes, but so far as I can tell, no one's been paid."

"No time to lose, then!" Calloway declared. She rounded the bed and gathered her plain brown breeches and tan shirt. She felt Dillahunt's eyes on her back. She was almost fully dressed by the time he spoke.

"Why are you doing this?" he asked.

She turned as she laced up her shirt. "I'm tired of this place," she answered, not looking at him.

"I don't believe you," said Dillahunt. "There's something else."

She finished with the laces. "That will have to do for now, captain. Now if you don't mind, I have need of your sword, and I don't mean the one betwixt your legs."

Dillahunt picked up his rapier. The thin blade was razor sharp, and the hilt was ornamented with gold accents and several red rubies. He moved around her. "I'll do it," he said, removing the hat from her head and placing it on his own.

"Afraid I'd cut myself?"

"Afraid you'd cut *me*," he replied. He gathered her long hair, pinching it at the base of her skull. "Are you sure about this?"

"Just do it."

He set the blade flat against her neck and sheared upward. She shuddered as the long black locks fell away, settling on the floor. When the deed was done, dark swirls surrounded her feet. She brushed strands from her shoulders and chest. He circled her, eyeing his work. She ran her fingers through her hair, shocked at how little resistance she encountered. "How do I look?" she asked as she ruffled her hair.

Dillahunt grimaced. "Like a boy."

He left the room without another word, pausing only to sheathe his sword and adjust the feather of his hat. She would know where to find him, because he had taken her on a boastful tour of his ship last night.

Calloway left the room a few minutes later, heading down the narrow spiral staircase to the bottom floor. She waved at the fat, jolly barkeep as she passed him polishing some mugs behind the bar. The tavern was empty, and it probably wouldn't get much busier later in the day without any pirates to fill it.

Calloway stepped into the fresh morning air and wandered down into the market. She nodded to the various merchants, but no one recognized her without her long hair. The women gave her strange looks. Calloway hoped they were trying to determine her gender.

She purchased a wide-brimmed brown hat from one of the vendors. It was very plain, so it wouldn't draw any attention to her. It fit snugly over her head and shaded her features. She would have to be careful about crewmen getting too close and noticing her thin eyebrows, pretty eyes, and petite nose.

She passed Sassy Sally's tavern, and her nostrils caught an enticing whiff of turtle soup, but she didn't think she would have enough time to sit down and enjoy a meal. Sassy Sally's chef was notorious for taking his time, and he probably wasn't awake yet at this hour.

She came to the docks and hesitated, staring at the ships as they bobbed gently in the water. A young man missing his left arm below the elbow was carted past her by two guards, his head held high. He was handsome, but the puffy circles under his eyes made him appear older than his years. He looked like he had been freshly bathed, clothed, and shaved. His sandy hair was slicked back, though a wayward lock fell over his brow. "I can walk on my own, thank you," the young man said to the flanking guards. They did not relinquish their grip as they marched him down the pier. Calloway wondered briefly who he was. Every person in Nassau had a story. His might be more interesting than most, but she doubted she would ever know.

She still had a little time before Dillahunt departed, so she continued onward to the beach. The sun was already reflecting brightly off the white sand, causing her to squint. The rays projected a netted pattern upon the rippled sand beneath the water. A turtle was wavering in the current with no apparent destination in mind.

Laughter skittered along the beach. A batch of grinning young boys sprinted toward her, and she made no attempt to get out of their way. Lean muscles worked beneath their dark skin. They spared her with brief glances as they ran around her.

She was nothing more than an obstacle in the path to some imaginary adventure. They continued up the beach until their distant laughter was overpowered by a crashing wave.

Calloway welcomed the approaching tide, stepping forward as it rolled over the sand. It washed over her bare feet, dousing her legs. She closed her eyes and smiled. The water was warm and inviting, and she resisted the urge to keep walking until the seafloor dropped away. She wanted to swim into the horizon and keep swimming until she reached the ends of the world.

"I birthed a fish," her mother had told her after their first week in Nassau. Jacqueline had spent an entire day swimming. She had never known waters as warm as the Caribbean.

"Perhaps my father was a merman," was Jacqueline's reply.

"I assure you," her mother laughed, "he was a man." She then grew distant as she thought about him, and they didn't talk again until the next day.

There was a time when Calloway wanted nothing more than to find her father and run away with him. There was a time when she hated her mother intensely, for reasons she could not explain. But her mother was gone, and Calloway missed her terribly. It wasn't important who her father was. She never knew the man, but she knew her mother, and that was all that mattered. Her mother had not abandoned her. Unfortunately, she hadn't realized any of this until it was too late.

She opened her eyes as the water retreated, sand hollowing beneath her feet. Dillahunt's ship, *Crusader*, was the first thing she saw. It was a brigantine, recently commissioned. Everything about it looked new, with clean white sails, polished decks, and guns that sparkled in the sun. A beautiful mermaid decorated the bow, both arms spread above her head, grasping the bowsprit suggestively. The mermaid's large breasts hung freely beneath tangles of wooden hair. Her face was elegant, with curved cheeks, full lips, a small chin, and impossibly large eyes with tiny pupils. Her human body transitioned at the waist into the scales of a long fin that stretched down the bow. Her tail dipped into the water.

A man stood at the bow, arms folded as he watched the crew busying themselves about the deck. Calloway knew from the feathered hat that it was Dillahunt.

"He sure paints a pretty picture, doesn't he?" she mused aloud. That was something her mother would say about men like Dillahunt. Her mother had commanded a lofty fee, so she rarely took a poor man to bed. Calloway had remained equally stingy, which earned her the hatred of other whores but filled her pockets. She had branched out from the local whorehouse, The Strapped Bodice, after her mother died, choosing her clients rather than letting them choose her.

She had chanced upon Guy Dillahunt in the market, as he was buying that feathered hat. Calloway was looking forward to sharing the captain's bed as often as possible. He seemed far more experienced than most of the younger men she had slept with. He had worked to pleasure her, which made her eager to please him in turn.

She considered turning to take in Nassau one last time. She had no idea when she would see this place again. The town had changed so much in so little time. It would be unrecognizable by the time she returned.

Her thoughts were interrupted by a sudden commotion on *Crusader's* deck. Several of the crew rushed to the starboard rail, peering over the edge. The one-armed young man she saw earlier was being escorted up a long ramp onto the ship, but one of his guards had slipped and tumbled into the water. The young man made some sort of jest Calloway couldn't hear, and the crew broke into uproarious laughter. The guard cursed at all of them as he struggled in the water.

Calloway smiled and started for the docks. Perhaps she would learn this one-armed man's story after all.

As she made her way up the pier toward her new home, she forgot to give Nassau a final consideration.

3

KATE

"Do you make your bed every morning, captain?" Kate asked, subduing a chuckle. The large bed was freshly made, with several decorative pillows propped up against the headboard, which was engraved with an impressive ship cresting rolling waves. The coverlet was a deep maroon with gold patterns that smoldered in the candlelight.

"Only when I have company," Benjamin Hornigold replied between nibbles of chicken. He studied the contents of his plate instead of meeting her gaze. He was a very prissy eater, tearing bits of meat off the bone with a fork and chewing rapidly like a rabbit. He washed it down with a sip of red wine from a polished silver goblet.

Kate had long since finished her meal and was enjoying a third goblet of wine. Her fingers were greasy. Bones littered her plate. She sat with one arm hanging over the back of her chair, legs crossed, watching Hornigold barely make a dent in his half of the chicken.

"Only when you have company?" she asked nonchalantly. "Even men?"

"I'm rarely afforded the opportunity to entertain women in my cabin," Hornigold said. "I keep tidy quarters, and I find my cleanliness influences the men to do the same with my ship."

"*Their* ship," Kate corrected. "You are pirates again. This ship does not belong to just one man anymore."

"Aye," he conceded with a scowl, setting down his fork. Apparently he had lost his appetite. "I suppose it doesn't."

Kate had not once seen Hornigold smile since they departed Nassau as fugitives. She didn't know him very well, so it was possible that he was just a stern man, but she thought it more likely that he was regretting his hasty decision. Hornigold's history as a pirate ran deep, and the promise of treasure had awoken something in him that he could not deny.

Kate was willing to bet Hornigold would have lived out the rest of his life as a pirate hunter had she not come along to alter his course. Perhaps Hornigold was realizing that as well.

"Do you expect me to sleep in it?" she asked.

"Pardon?"

"Your bed. Do you expect me to sleep in it?"

To his credit, he didn't feign ignorance. "It would ease my mind."

"Oh," she laughed mockingly. "Are you worried for me?"

"Do you prefer sleeping out there with the men?"

"They don't bother me."

"With your looks, I find that hard to believe."

"I remain unspoiled," she replied with a smile.

Hornigold tweaked at his moustache with thumb and forefinger. "I would think it difficult to sleep when you might be stirred at any moment by a man crawling aloft, weighting you down. You might scream, but sounds are easily quashed below decks. The deed would be done before anyone could come to your aid, assuming anyone apart from me would bother to save you."

"Maybe they fear I would do more than scream," she said, narrowing her eyes.

"There is very little these men fear," Hornigold replied.

"I spent a year in Captain Griffith's bed, and look what happened to him. Are you certain you want me in yours?" She was not ignorant to his errant gawking. More than once she caught him stealing glimpses of her breasts beneath her loose shirt, which she never laced all the way because she enjoyed the sun on her chest. His eyes lifted whenever he realized she was looking at him.

When he agreed to let her lead him to Griffith's buried treasure, he had probably assumed she was part of the deal. She knew she should have fancied him, but the attraction refused to muster. He had a distinguished manner that commanded respect. He was tall and handsome, with a trim mustache that was finely pointed on each end. He typically wore a long maroon coat and a black hat, but tonight he was absent both. Tonight he wore a black shirt, ruffled at the neck and wrists, with dark brown breeches and polished leather boots. His thick black hair was slicked back, collected in a ponytail.

Kate felt a bit absurd in his presence. She was suddenly very conscious of her messy red hair, her shirt that was too large, and her dirty bare feet. A year ago she wouldn't have been caught dead looking like this, but she had grown fond of casual clothing. The skinny pale girl from London was no more. She had grown lean muscles, and her skin had been darkened by the perpetual Caribbean sun. She no longer ate like a bird. She heartily finished every meal, and her breasts and hips had filled out.

"Why should I fear you?" Hornigold said. "Unlike Jonathan

Griffith, I have not brought you here against your will."

"Nor I you," she countered.

He scowled at that. "I go where I please."

"That's a relief. I was concerned that you blamed me for abandoning your new station."

He chortled without smiling. "You flatter yourself. I am responsible for my own actions. No one else."

"That epiphany has yet to occur to most pirates."

Hornigold's right eyelid flickered at the word. "In truth," he said, waving his hand carelessly, "I have more important things to worry about than you in my bed."

Men are as quick to lie as women, Kate mused. *They just aren't as good at it.*

"Like what?" she replied, deciding to play along.

"Like the crewman that has mysteriously gone missing, with naught but a few drops of blood to mark his passing."

"I heard something about that." She swallowed too much wine and winced as it went down bitterly. "I would think the mystery easily solved."

"Pray tell," Hornigold said, raising an eyebrow.

She shrugged. "Well, I've developed a taste for rum on this journey, and I can safely say the waters of the Caribbean can seem positively inviting under its influence."

"If rum influenced men to leap to a watery grave," said Hornigold, "none would remain to crew the ship."

She reached across the table to retrieve the wine bottle, which was nearly empty. She poured the last few drops into her goblet. "Murdered?" she suggested offhandedly, recalling Bart's dumbfounded expression as he toppled over the rail and plummeted into the black water. The dirk she had used to stab him had been easy to dispose of, but the blood on her shirt was problematic. She couldn't exactly take it off, throw it over the side, and return topless to her bunk in the hold, with dozens of pirates ogling her. Bart had left a red smear in the fabric at the stomach. She tried scrubbing it with rum, but it wouldn't come out. So she returned to her bunk with the bottle of rum clutched over her stomach. She quickly changed shirts and, the next day, tossed the blood-saturated evidence over the side when no one was looking.

In the days since Bart's disappearance, few of the crew made eye contact with her. They knew he had gone after her that night, and now he was gone. None of them could prove a thing, of course, but they all suspected her. If Bart hadn't been notoriously hotheaded, they might have held a grudge.

Hornigold went to his cabinet to retrieve another bottle. He kept a large supply of wine in his cabin. "Bartholomew was talented with the sails," he said as he searched for a specific vintage. "And he was equally talented at making enemies amongst his peers. It's possible someone tossed him over the side in a fit of anger."

"How dreadful," Kate muttered.

Hornigold returned with a new bottle, popped the cork, and filled both goblets. He leered sideways at her as he poured. "The crew is uncharacteristically mum on the issue."

"Maybe you'll never know," Kate teased, picking up her glass.

For a long moment he looked at her. She stared coolly back at him. "Something on your mind?" she asked when she grew weary of the game.

"Why did you not return to your husband's family?"

She blinked. She hadn't expected that question. Over the past week she had pushed all thoughts of Thomas and his family out of her mind. She had last seen Thomas in a dream, in which she promptly fled from him. After killing the man who had murdered her husband, she saw no reason to dwell on the past. "What exactly would I be returning to?"

"Safety. Security."

Those words, which emerged so easily from his lips, were alien to her. "I thought I had those things once. Until my husband was killed, and I was taken."

"So why squander a chance at freedom?"

Laughter bubbled out of her. "This is freedom, right here! The two of us, seated across from one another, neither with power over the other. Those other words . . . safety? Security? Those are illusions that may be stripped of us at any moment."

"Was your freedom not stripped from you by Jonathan Griffith?"

"No!" she said, slamming her palm on the table. A bit of wine dribbled over the rim of Hornigold's glass, which he hadn't touched since refilling. "Griffith could not take what I didn't yet possess."

"So you've discovered freedom in the Caribbean, amongst pirates, and now you want to be one yourself, is that it?"

"Call me whatever you like," she said on a sigh.

"You'll never be a pirate, Katherine."

"Kate," she barked with a glower.

"Ah yes. Kate. I'm sorry."

"No you're not."

"Well," he continued, "you'll never be a pirate, Kate. Those men will never accept you as one of them. They come to sea to escape your kind."

"My *kind*?"

"Women, if I must be precise."

She grinned. "We are a scary lot, aren't we?"

"Life is simpler without you," Hornigold said. "Women complicate matters beyond necessity. If I present you a red flower, you will complain it's too bright a color. If I buy you an orange flower, you will say, in retrospect, the red wasn't so bad. If I bring the red back, you might accept it, but secretly you won't be happy with it, because the truth is no color is good enough for you."

She gawked at him. "Is this anecdote based in fact?"

His jaw tightened. "That's not the point. The point is women are unhappy with normalcy."

"Pardon," she said, again having to suppress a laugh, "what is normal? Murdering and pillaging? Is that the lone alternative to giving women flowers?"

"The sea is the only place you are *not*," he informed her with a condescendingly slow drawl, as though she wouldn't understand him if he spoke too quickly.

"And here is a woman, infiltrating your glorious sea."

"That's how they feel," he said, tipping his glass. "It is a subconscious thing, mind you, which they would never express even if they came to the miraculous comprehension of it overnight."

"I don't blame them. It's an embarrassing sentiment."

An awkward silence followed.

Hornigold shifted uneasily in his chair, pretending to take an interest in the opposite bulkhead. Kate hadn't decided what she thought of Benjamin Hornigold yet, but he was far more interested in her than he wanted her to believe. After narrowly escaping a perilous relationship with one pirate captain, she wasn't eager to leap into another. As far as she was concerned, this was a business arrangement and nothing more. When she had finished her wine, she thanked him for dinner, bid him goodnight, and allowed him to stare at her ass as she took her leave.

A harsh wind greeted her on the main deck, threatening to tip her over. The full moon was partially obscured by a cloud that was moving fast. The deck wobbled more than usual, and at first she wondered if she'd had too much wine. She stumbled to the port rail, setting a hand on one of the cannons to keep from falling over. The ship rocked this way and that, cresting huge rolling waves. The cannon trembled beneath her hand, breeching tackle stretched taut. She looked aft and saw a black mass trailing the ship, threatening to engulf the stern. Lightning flashed somewhere within the clouds.

"It's like to be a rough night," said Billie Dowling, one of the few pirates not afraid to speak to her. Billie was the younger brother of *Ranger's* master carpenter, Avery Dowling. She didn't care much for Avery, who her first day aboard had unnecessarily threatened dismemberment if she touched any of his tools. Billie, on the other hand, seemed genuine enough. He couldn't have been more than twenty, but his teeth were already mottled brown, and the whites of his eyes had gone yellow. The dark skin on his shoulders and arms was blistered and peeling. "The storm is catching up at last. Best get below, as that cannon won't offer much shelter."

"Thank you, Billie," she said, meaning it. "No rest for you?"

"I fear I'd wake at the bottom of the ocean."

Kate wished Billie luck and descended into the hold. She rolled into her hammock, and it swayed dizzyingly. Her head was swimming with wine. The creaking of the hull filled her ears. Several crewmen that she couldn't see in the dark were snoring loudly in their bunks. A few of them were awake in a corner, playing a game of dice. She heard Fat Farley laughing boisterously at a joke. Did that man never sleep?

Heavy lids quickly closed over her eyes.

When she came to, the hold was immersed. Crates were floating around, knocking into each other. Her back was resting in the water, which was level with her hammock. She jerked upward in shock, smashed her head against a deck beam, and tumbled into the water. Her body twirled, and she thrashed her arms and legs. The water was black. She swam up, or so she thought, until her head hit the deck. She spun around, placing her feet flat on the deck, and projected herself upward. Her head emerged from the water, and she gasped hoarsely. She looked around, crates bobbing in and out of view, until she found the main hatch. Water was cascading down the stairway, lit from the opening above. Was it daylight already? Had she slept that long?

She swam for the exit, making her way through the maze of floating crates.

A slender shadow split the light.

Kate clutched one of the larger crates.

A foot appeared on the first step, and then another. Slender legs came into view, and then fully curved hips that arced into a thin waist, and then small breasts with black nipples. She was completely naked, her wet skin faintly tinted in green. She was tall and lean, like a well forged cutlass. She continued her descent, stepping into the water without hesitation.

Kate blinked the sting of salt out of her eyes, struggling to focus on the woman's face. She saw black hair, as short as a man's, elegant lips that were neatly pursed, a thin nose, and sharply arched eyebrows. Her eyes were closed. She continued her methodical descent, following the steps into the water until her head vanished beneath the surface.

Kate scanned the water, but it was impenetrable. She was about to swim in the opposite direction when two blue orbs materialized, impossibly bright, illuminating everything beneath the surface in otherworldly cerulean hues. The naked woman was crouched three feet from Kate's legs. The orbs were her eyes, blank and passionless, and they were transfixed on Kate.

She woke with a start, twisting in her hammock. She sat up, looking around. The hold was not quite flooded, but water was streaming down the steps from the main entrance. Large puddles had collected all around.

She heard men shouting at each other above, footsteps thudding rapidly along the deck. Someone loosed a high-pitched shriek, or maybe it was the wind gusting through the hold. A crash resounded, bowing the planking just above her head. *Ranger* shuddered violently, and Kate was nearly thrown from her hammock. Water seeped through a crevice between planks, pattering her chest. And then the water darkened. She looked down.

Her shirt was drenched in blood.

4

HORNIGOLD

"Get to safety, you fool!" Benjamin Hornigold bellowed. "That man is already dead!"

The idiotic surgeon either hadn't heard Hornigold or was deliberately ignoring him as he scrambled through a wave that cascaded over the deck. He was stubbornly trying to get to a deckhand who was pinned beneath a fallen yardarm. If the pool of blood that was spreading steadily from the deckhand's compressed torso was any indication, he was beyond saving.

Hornigold drew his pistol and aimed it skyward. In all his years of captaining, he had learned that nothing commanded attention like a gunshot. He pulled the trigger, but the hammer clacked without firing. The powder was soaked through. He angrily threw the pistol at the surgeon, but he missed his mark by a few feet.

Hornigold could only watch in horror as the surgeon's feet were swept out from under him. The current carried him across the deck, legs and arms flailing. For an instant, his eyes, insane with terror, met Hornigold's. And then the surgeon was dashed against one of the starboard cannons, his head splitting like a watermelon on the cascabel knob. His limp corpse slipped through the gunport and tumbled over the side of the ship, lost to the roiling sea.

The surgeon was a recent addition to the crew. Hornigold couldn't even recall the man's name. Copernicus Ryan, the boatswain, had recommended the surgeon a month ago, but Hornigold had been too busy to get to know him. *How many more will die,* he wondered, *without that idiot around to provide proper medical attention?*

Bastion, who had been securing the foresail, leapt from his perch and scrambled toward the cannon where the surgeon had vanished. "Back to your post, sailor!" Quartermaster Reed bellowed from the bow, his arm wrapped around a swivel gun for support. Bastion skidded to a halt just short of the cannon, staring dumbly at Reed. He was starting to turn back when a massive wave raised *Ranger's* bow high into the air. Bastion was lifted off his feet as the ship crested the wave and slid steeply down the backside. Bastion touched down, his ass taking the brunt of the damage. He rolled over, moaning as water splashed over him.

The long bowsprit plunged into the black water, shuddering on impact. The jib topsail snapped free, taking a three foot splinter of the bowsprit with it, and whipped back toward the deck. Two deckhands were quick enough to duck, but a third man never knew what hit him. The sail catapulted him over the side as it swept past. *Another man without a name lost to the sea,* thought Hornigold.

The topsail arced on its tether, the long splinter of bowsprit still attached. Reed released the swivel gun he had been clinging to and tried to leap out of the way as the sharp piece of wood shot toward him like a spear. But he was too late. He was sliced nearly in half, from crotch to shoulder, and then dragged across the bow and smashed against the railing.

What remained was barely distinguishable as human, let alone any semblance of the man Hornigold had once called friend. Entrails spilled from a gaping torso, slipping through exposed ribs. The legs were splayed in opposite directions, one foot missing, the other twisted at an impossible angle. The head was pulverized, face raked clean off, skull smashed in. An eyeball dangled from an open socket.

Hornigold fell to his hands and knees and retched. *Ranger* collided with another wave, but the sound was distant and inconsequential. As Hornigold's vomit was washed away, he barely recognized the man he saw mirrored in the water. The ripples hyperbolized his scowl. A stream of blood swirled into view, darkening his face. The rain was heavy on his back, weighting him down. His joints ached. His elbows quivered. He wasn't sure if the water was rising or if he was sinking.

I'm so sick of all of this.

Woodes Rogers had promised him security, and Hornigold had considered himself fortunate to be spared the gallows. He had thanked Rogers profusely, befriended him, and eagerly rushed out to sea to hunt his former friends. They saw it as a betrayal. They called him a coward. And he knew they would murder him given the chance. Now he was a pirate again, and his circumstances were no less precarious. Except his enemy was neither a pirate nor a noose. His enemy was the sea. It didn't matter whether he served the crown or ambition, he would be claimed by the sea either way. He knew that now.

We're not meant to be out here, he realized for the first time in his life. *So far from land, on tiny floats of wood. Every time we venture out, our odds of success decrease, until the odds abandon us altogether. The dangers are too great, and those that survive are made evil by the horrors they see. And who can blame them for that? Certainly not I. What pardon did Woodes Rogers truly offer in sending me back into this hell? I am bound to it no matter what I choose.*

And then, with that sudden realization, it all stopped.

Complete silence.

Patches of blue materialized in the water. Hornigold looked skyward.

The clouds were breaking.

The storm had claimed four men in less than five minutes, and just like that it was over.

Hornigold balled his hands into fists and pushed himself to his feet. He wiped a hand across his wet mustache, sniffing as he took in the devastation. The sails were in tatters, and the topsail jib was dangling over the side.

Hornigold helped Bastion to his feet, setting him against the cannon that the surgeon had collided with. The blood had mostly been washed away, but a few bits of brain dribbled down the cascabel. "Are you alright?" Hornigold asked him.

"I think so, captain," Bastion rasped between a fit of coughs. "Reed?"

Hornigold shook his head.

"Him deserve better," Bastion said with a woeful shake of his head.

"It was a fast death," Hornigold said, sniffing hard. Salt went down his throat, and he struggled not to cough.

"Him deserve no death at all."

"The sea has no regard for what we deserve," Hornigold replied. Reed had told him that a long time ago, after a very young deckhand had been crushed while careening the ship. The deckhand had been scrubbing the keel when a tidal wave washed over the beach, pitching the ship in the sand.

Hornigold figured he should be used to death by now.

"Someone must clean that up," Bastion said, staring at the bow.

Hornigold refused to look that way again. Someone else would have to worry about that mess. He patted Bastion on the shoulder. "Don't stand until you've recovered your breath, and maybe not even then. You've earned your share today. The foresail would look even worse if not for your diligence."

"Thank you, captain."

Hornigold left Bastion's side and started aft. Fat Farley and Francois Laurent were securing a cannon that had come loose. They glared at him as he passed. He noted no reverence in their manner, only blame. They started whispering to each other. He had convinced them to come along, promising riches beyond their wildest dreams. They would never need to work again, not for Woodes Rogers and not for themselves. They could disappear and live out the rest of their lives, as all pirates dreamed. *How many have actually succeeded?* Hornigold knew the percentage wasn't favorable, but he had promised his men they would be the exception to the rule. Had Jonathan Griffith promised his crew the same? Those men were all dead now, and Hornigold sought to claim what had been theirs.

With thirty-eight men, *Ranger* had little more than a token crew, but that was the most he could muster on short notice, and it meant more shares for everyone. He would have sailed with less if he could have, but he needed all the help he could get. He had convinced himself that the ends would justify the means. He knew he might lose a few. He knew he might lose *everyone*, including himself, but this was his last and only chance. He hadn't realized how much he hated what Woodes Rogers had turned him into until Kate Lindsay offered a way out.

In sync with his thoughts, she climbed from the hold. Her red hair appeared first, the very same color as the blood that swirled beneath Hornigold's feet. She was drenched from head to toe, translucent shirt clinging to her breasts, stained with blood.

She chooses a fine moment to emerge from safety, thought Hornigold.

"What happened?" she asked, looking mildly concerned.

"Are you wounded?" he asked, indicating her shirt.

"It's not mine. What happened?"

"What do you *think* happened?" he muttered gratingly. "The bloody storm overtook us. My quartermaster is dead."

Lindsay flinched when she looked at the bow. "Was that him?"

"Yes," he replied, not looking. He needed no reminder of the ghastly image.

"I'm sorry."

He chuckled cynically. "For what? Do you take hold of the weather and guide it as easily as a man's ambitions?"

Lindsay stared at him blankly. He couldn't be sure if she was purposely unreadable, or if there was nothing to read. He decided he didn't care. He carelessly brushed her shoulder as he passed by her.

The next two hours felt like days, though the sun hardly moved in the sky. The storm was small on the horizon and rapidly fading. It was suddenly very hot, and the damp wood started to stink. Before Hornigold's clothes could dry, he began to sweat profusely from the humidity.

He put several men to work on the bow, first to clean up the ruin that was Reed, and then to repair whatever damage they could. He set his best sailmakers to work on a new jib topsail, though it would be hard to secure with a diminished bowsprit. Most of the others attended to the flooded hold, bucketing water over the sides. A crate of rum had toppled, every bottle within shattering on impact, and the intense smell saturated the hold. "I'm drunk off the stench," Billie Dowling said, and everybody laughed.

Laughter comes so easily. How have they grown accustomed to tragedy when I have not? He wanted to scream at them, tell them that this was no laughing matter and to stay focused on their tasks, but they were a democracy again, as Lindsay had been so quick to remind him, and he had no say over their conduct.

He retreated to his quarters. Most of the wine bottles had rolled out of his cupboard, broken shards twinkling in the variegated light that issued through the stained glass window. The wine collected in a large puddle about the shards, like a red ocean encompassing glass islands.

Hornigold fell into a chair and set a hand on the table, atop a map of the Caribbean that he had been studying earlier. His eyes fell on the bright red X where Lindsay claimed they would find the uncharted island that concealed Jonathan Griffith's vast fortune. Hornigold drew a dagger from his boot and dug it into the X. The tip hit an inch short of the center. He wrenched the dagger loose and slammed it down again, and again it came up short of the mark. He angrily hurled the dagger across the cabin, where it slapped the ornate headboard of his bed and tumbled down, slipping behind the mattress.

His frustration swiftly gave to exhaustion, and he slumped in the chair, closing his eyes. He knew it wasn't proper for a captain to rest while his crew was dealing with disaster, but he needed just a moment to recover his strength. *That isn't too much to ask, is it? Just a moment?*

It couldn't have been more than a few seconds before he fell asleep. He dreamed of an island, lush and beautiful, with impossibly white beaches, crystal waters, and green trees bearing fat fruit. The island was small but dense with tropical vegetation. A parrot colored like a rainbow flew overhead, looking down at him as it sailed toward the island. "This way," it called. "This way. This way. This way." The bird's voice faded as it disappeared into the jungle.

The breeze was cool on his face but not cold. The sun was warm on his back but not hot. He felt renewed as energy coursed through him from the legs up. *Where am I? Am I on a ship? No, I must be in the water.*

He looked down and, sure enough, found himself submerged to his waist in shallow water. He could see straight through to the white sand. Colorful seashells were scattered all around, big and small. A red crab scurried away from his foot, taking shelter in one of the larger shells. He bent down and plucked the shell out of the water. He turned it over, but there was nothing inside. He looked down at the water again. The crab materialized in the hollow from which Hornigold had removed the shell. It scuttled away, staring at him with bulbous eyes that rested on long stalks. *I've been deceived by a crab.*

The island looked inviting. A man could live his entire life off of fruit and crab. A waterfall with a little lake at the bottom would be nice too. He was certain there had to be a waterfall somewhere in that jungle.

He took a step forward . . . and halted when something grey darted through the water before him. He scanned the water, but he couldn't see where the grey thing had gone. And then something flashed silver in his peripheral vision, rising above the water to the right of him and then sinking before he could look at it. Another silver flash, this time from his left. He spun in place, things shuffling in the water all around. He looked down. Dozens of grey streaks were circling his legs.

A fin broke the surface.

A yawning mouth with two sets of razor sharp teeth lunged at his face. He recoiled in horror . . .

. . . And woke to a loud rap on his door. "Come in," he

mumbled.

Another knock.

"Come in, I said!

The door opened, and Dumaka, very tall and very black, stuck his head in. "Captain?"

"Yes, Dumaka, what is it?" he asked, wiping sweat from his brow.

Hornigold had recruited Dumaka from a slave ship two years past. Dumaka learned English in under a month, and he spoke it better than most of the crew. After complaints of leakage in the barrels, Dumaka made some barrels of his own, and Hornigold instantly promoted him to cooper. The last cooper, a middle-aged man named Jeremiah, did not take kindly to a black man stealing his job, and drew his pistol on Dumaka later that day. The shot missed Dumaka but hit another man in the forehead, killing him instantly. Jeremiah was marooned on the next island they came to, with nothing more than his unreliable pistol for company.

"Ship off the starboard bow," Dumaka said.

The words didn't register at first. "Merchant ship, navy, or pirate?" Hornigold managed.

"Merchant," Dumaka said. "They've hailed us. Want to know if we need help."

Hornigold frowned. "They must think us reputable sailors."

"An unfortunate mistake," Dumaka quipped with a grin.

Hornigold followed Dumaka out on deck. A two-masted merchant ship, slightly larger than *Ranger*, had pulled close and was running parallel. Her crew was lining the rail, exchanging friendly words with Hornigold's men, who were acting the part of honest sailors. The captain, a distinguished looking man with white hair, dressed all in blue, stood at the forecastle with a profound look on his face, as though contemplating the meaning of the universe.

Copernicus Ryan moved close to Hornigold and whispered, "These simpletons don't seem to know the hazards of the Caribbean. The Lord sends a gift." Copernicus produced a crude wooden cross from within his shirt and kissed it.

Hornigold seized the boatswain by the arm and drew him near. "We ask before we take, and we harm no one."

Copernicus pulled away, raising an eyebrow. "Who are you to deny the Lord's gift?"

"If that ship is a gift of the almighty, then he steals from honest merchants in the offering."

"We need their sails," said a raspy but unmistakably female voice. Hornigold turned. Kate Lindsay was smiling at him.

"They willingly offer help!" Hornigold said, a little too loud.

"Then they are fools," Lindsay replied. "I'm amazed they've made it this far."

"Maybe them not fools," Bastion said as he approached, rubbing his back. His face was racked with anguish.

"Maybe a trap." Dumaka suggested.

"We clearly outgun them," Hornigold said with a dismissive snort. *Ranger* was probably the most heavily gunned sloop in the Caribbean, and the merchant vessel was sporting under a dozen cannons and swivel guns combined. "I'll not deprive them of their sails and leave them stranded out here to ease our temporary misfortune."

"Every second we waste," Lindsay said, "allows Woodes Rogers to advance. Do you honestly think he hasn't already dispatched his best man to hunt you down?"

"I am his best man," Hornigold said, trying to maintain his calm.

"You *were* his best man," Lindsay corrected.

"Who are you to deny what the Lord offers?" Copernicus whispered eagerly in Hornigold's ear. Hornigold caught a whiff of the boatswain's foul breath, which stunk of rotten teeth saturated in rum.

"The Lord is very generous today," Lindsay said, winking at Copernicus.

"Aye," Copernicus replied, nodding firmly at her.

Another comrade easily forged. This woman was tricky. Hornigold's fingers found his mustache, tugging at it furiously.

"We mustn't deny His offering," Copernicus insisted.

Hornigold shoved the boatswain away. He straightened his shirt. "We are not savages. Our sails are mendable."

"Lost time is not so easily mended," Lindsay insisted.

Hornigold glared at her. "I'll decide how time is best spent, thank you, Mrs. Lindsay."

She advanced on him, raising her voice so all around could hear. "Give them our sails and the tools to mend them, if your conscience worries at you so. Take theirs. Our time is far more precious, is it not?" A lock of red hair fell in front of her face, and she flicked it away with a fast hand.

"That's true, captain," Copernicus agreed.

"She's right, captain," Dumaka agreed.

"Reed would say the same," Copernicus added, "if he were here."

"Reed's not here!" Hornigold shot back fiercely, a bit of spittle pattering Copernicus's cheek. "Reed's in pieces! Puzzle him back together and you would see me dumbstruck enough to accept counsel from a dead man!"

"We can't do that, captain," chimed in Billie Dowling. "We put the pieces over the side."

Lindsay lowered her head, hair shielding her face. Her shoulders trembled slightly, and Hornigold realized she was chuckling. "What is funny about any of this?" he demanded.

"Many things," she squealed.

"Suspicion is mounting," Copernicus reminded them as he

gestured at the opposite ship.

Lindsay slowly raised her head, recovering herself. "They won't wait much longer, captain."

Hornigold glanced over his shoulder. The captain of the merchant ship was staring at him from the quarterdeck. His men had stopped talking. They were starting to sense something was wrong.

More of Hornigold's crew were drawing near, eyeing him expectantly. "Our true prize is to be found on Griffith's Isle," he told them. "We do not need to inconvenience others in the taking."

The crew mumbled to one another. They didn't like that.

"I'm confused," came that annoyingly raspy female voice. Lindsay stretched a beseeching arm to the crew. "Are you not pirates? Is inconveniencing others not what you do, when you're not murdering them?"

Everyone fell silent and looked at her.

"This is unwise," Hornigold insisted.

"Have you truly forgotten who you are?" She moved past Hornigold. He grabbed her shoulder, but she shook free. One of the men giggled at that, nudging a friend.

"Are you not pirates?" she repeated.

The crew exchanged uncertain looks. Some of them were starting to smile.

"Are you not pirates?!"

"I am!" someone in the back called.

"So am I," agreed another.

"Me too."

"I don't like labels, but I suppose I is."

"A vulgar term," Francois Laurent said with mock revulsion. Then he grinned. "But aye, I am."

The sporadic voices swiftly merged into a collective roar. The sailors on the merchant ship were pulling away from the railing, horror settling in. Their captain stared uncertainly from his perch. A very young first mate was jabbering nervously in his ear, but the captain was too petrified to listen.

"Look into their eyes!" Lindsay said, and everyone followed her gesture. "Look at the fear you inspire!"

The pirates stomped their feet, and the report cracked as it echoed off the sails. Many of them drew cutlasses and pistols and raised them to the sky. Hornigold couldn't believe what he was seeing. He reached for his gun, but his hands slapped at an empty belt, and then he remembered that he had thrown the gun at the surgeon during the storm.

"See how they tremble before you!" Lindsay said, her voice transcending the ruckus.

"This is madness!" Hornigold started forward, but he was halted in place. Copernicus had a firm grip on his shoulders. "Unhand me right now, Ryan," Hornigold ordered in as deadly a tone as he could muster.

Ryan blinked, remembering himself, and released him.

"Claim your prize!" Lindsay bellowed.

Andrew Harrow fired his pistol, and the pirates loosed a deafening howl and surged forward. The deck quaked beneath them. The crewmen on the merchant vessel stumbled over themselves to get away. Grappling hooks flew, catching in the ratlines. Ramps were spread across the two ships. Gunners raced to the cannons, though Hornigold knew that not a single cannon would be fired this day. Fear was the greater weapon.

Ryan was good enough to favor Hornigold with a contrite bow of his head before hurrying after his peers.

Kate Lindsay watched confidently as the pirates swept over the merchant ship like a plague of locusts. Her hair tossed in the breeze, but she didn't blink when the strands pervaded her vision. She had taken control of the crew with a few easy words.

"You do realize that they may kill someone on that ship?" Hornigold growled.

"I know that better than anyone," was her even reply. "When you accorded to this bargain, did you not think there would be consequences?"

He stepped into her line of sight. "Under normal circumstances this would be considered an act of mutiny."

She moved around him. "'Normal' circumstances? As you pointed out, captain, women are not fond of normalcy."

He glared at her, but her gaze refused to shift his way, not even when her lips curved into a smirk that was surely meant for him.

5

ANNABELLE

"Help me with these, would you, love?" said Edward Teach.

Annabelle stepped into the soft candlelight, hoping he would notice how nice her breasts looked in the silk robe she had discovered while rummaging through booty in the hold. Her nipples were perfectly outlined beneath the thin material.

Teach handed her four hemp cords. She took a seat atop the desk before him, dipping the makeshift fuses in a solution of saltpeter and lime water. She worked the first fuse into Teach's thick beard. "You'll set yourself alight one day," she scorned.

"They'll have to amend my name to Firebeard," he said with a guttural laugh.

"Is that not the sort of fiery end you dream of?"

"Already you know me better than I know myself."

"Oh, I don't think anyone truly knows you, Edward."

"You look ravishing tonight," he said. His beard twitched, and the creases in his sun-scavenged cheeks told her there was a smile cloaked beneath that black thicket. His piercing blue eyes scaled her body up and down, halting momentarily to fixate on her breasts. Perhaps tonight would finally be the night.

"I didn't think you'd noticed," she said as she started on the second fuse.

"I always notice."

Annabelle merely nodded. It had been two months since her ship had been intercepted by *Queen Anne's Revenge*, and in all that time Edward Teach had done nothing more than sleep beside her in bed, fully clothed. She had tried every trick in her considerable array, but nothing worked. She was starting to wonder why Teach had taken her. When he first brought her aboard, she was still suffering nightmares from a brutal rape at the hands of a loathsome pirate named Edward Livingston. When Teach brought her into his cabin, she was frightened out of her wits that he would do the same, night after night. She had heard horrible stories about the things he had done to whores, but he had done nothing of the sort to her. He didn't so much as touch her until she made the first move a month later, after her fear had been replaced by extreme boredom. Now she would give anything for him to tear her clothes off and ravish her. She was a strumpet, and she feared her talents were going to waste. She wasn't sure how much more of this she could take.

"What devious notions crowd that mind of yours?" he said. His bushy eyebrows were pinched together as he studied her, the many creases of his brow bunching tightly.

"Many at once," she answered with a smile.

"I prefer to tackle each in the order it came." He looked to the stern window. The curtains were parted, and it was pitch black beyond the faintly lit rail of the stern gallery.

She finished the second fuse and went to work on the third, tying as fast as she could. "I'm sorry. My fingers are clumsy today."

"Don't fret," Teach said. "The longer they're made to wait, the more nervous they be when I emerge."

"Are you going to kill them?"

"Aye."

"All of them?"

"Enough to leave a mark on those I don't."

"That's good," she said, finishing the third fuse. "It's been too long since the last. I overheard John Garretty saying you'd gone soft."

"Garretty?" he said, looking puzzled.

"The cook's boy."

"Oh, aye. He said that, did he?"

"Mmhmmm."

He seemed unconcerned. "Two months deprived of murder and they think me Benjamin Hornigold."

"I suppose you'll make up for it tonight," she reassured him.

Annabelle could scarcely forget Teach's last murder. He had killed Charles Martel, her employer. She held no love for Martel, who was vicious with all his whores, and he had been particularly angry with her for getting raped and bruised up, as if she'd had any say in the matter. She told Martel to take up his grievance with Edward Livingston, and Martel gave her a fresh bruise for her smart mouth. When the pirates abandoned Nassau due to the impending arrival of Woodes Rogers, Martel decided to spirit the best of his whores to Tortuga. He never made it that far. Teach killed Martel first, making an example of him, severing his head from his neck. Annabelle would never forget the sound Teach's massive cutlass made as it tore through skin and muscle in a sawing motion. "The spine be the most stubborn part," Teach had said, gritting his teeth as he worked through the bone. When Martel's limp body finally dropped away, Teach held the blank-faced head aloft for all to see. He found no quarrel with the rest of the crew after that.

Teach's crew took everything in the hold and enjoyed the company of the whores. When Teach looked on Annabelle, he allowed no other man to touch her, and he promptly escorted her to his quarters. Even in her post-Edward Livingston state, with a deep scar running down her right cheek, she knew she was far more beautiful than her sister whores. Her breasts and hips were perfectly curved, her skin was toned copper by both day and by candlelight, and a mane of thick black hair ran the length of her back. Countless men had stared into her large brown eyes and told her she was the most beautiful woman they had ever seen, and she would not humbly deny it.

Teach said the same, nearly every night, though he had done little more than talk. She had stolen a kiss, but his lips proved less deft with kissing than they were with words. *Has he kept me here for conversation and nothing more?*

She supposed it could have been much worse. She reminded herself that most women would have been violated by the entire crew until they were nothing more than a semen-crusted corpse.

She finished the final fuse and set her hands in her lap, watching him stare out the window, as he often did at night. "What are you always looking at?" she wondered.

"The night."

"There's nothing to see out there."

"Everywhere I look, there be something to see. The world brims with obstacles begging for notice. Out there my gaze finds no quarrel. Strike the fuses, would you?"

She set a slow match in the candle until it took flame. She gingerly lit each fuse, taking care not to light his beard on fire. The cabin quickly filled with smoke, and Annabelle plugged her nose.

Teach stood in the haze. "My coat," he instructed. She took

his long black leather coat off its hook and dressed him. She set a black tricorn hat over his dark locks, fitting it in place. The smoke rolled up over the brim. He looked every bit a devilish wraith, blue eyes gleaming beyond the haze.

"Come out with me," Blackbeard said.

She lowered her head. "I should get dressed."

He pinched her chin. "Nay. I want them to see you like this. I want them to see what I return to after my business be resolved."

"As you wish," she said. She opened the neck of her robe to reveal her cleavage. "Is that better?"

If he heard the question, he made no attempt to acknowledge it. "Follow me as far as the quarterdeck, but stray no further."

She nodded dutifully. He turned at once and threw open the door, his pace quick and deliberate. She followed him out, trying not to cough as the smoke from his beard trailed into her face. She stopped at the end of the quarterdeck and watched him descend the stairs.

Much of the crew was gathered on the cut-down forecastle, with three prisoners lined up in front of the capstan. A small merchant ship flying Dutch colors bobbed in the water off the port of *Queen Anne's Revenge*. Blackbeard's men were presently ransacking the ship while its crew looked on in horror. A few of the merchant ship's crew had been killed, their corpses left to bloody the deck. One poor soul was facedown in a puddle of his own blood with a cutlass sticking out of his back.

Queen Anne's Revenge loomed over her prey like a giant hawk that had claimed a small bird. She was a three-hundred ton frigate, originally named *Concord*. She had been a gift from Benjamin Hornigold, who captured her near the island of Martinique. Teach had served in the Royal Navy, and he confided to Annabelle his undying respect for Queen Anne. He said her death had left him heartbroken, and he thought it especially tragic that not one of her seventeen pregnancies had resulted in a surviving child. He renamed *Concord* out of sympathy. Benjamin Hornigold was quick to point out the irony when Blackbeard set *Queen Anne's Revenge* upon every British vessel he encountered. That was the beginning of the end of their alliance.

Blackbeard's men stepped out of the way as he approached the prisoners. He stopped, allowing the smoke to roll over his face. He was very tall and very darkly dressed, and all men around him looked small and colorful by comparison. He turned to take in his surroundings, his fierce eyes meeting Annabelle's for an instant. The fuses in his beard were roused by a sudden wind, and his features kindled with hellish hues for a brief moment, before the smoke obscured him again. He fixated on the three prisoners, and they trembled visibly before him.

The man in the center was the Dutch vessel's captain. He was middle-aged, with long blonde hair and a short beard of the same color. It seemed to take every bit of courage he had to match Blackbeard's gaze. A teenaged girl in a spotless white dress stood at his right, with doe eyes and golden blonde curls. To the captain's left was a man who couldn't have been more than twenty. He was the spitting image of the captain, with a decade and a half removed.

"What course, men?" Blackbeard asked his crew, spreading his arms. No one offered an answer, because they knew him well enough to know he wasn't actually looking for one. "Do we leave this skullduggerous fool to an island with naught but a pistol for comfort?"

"Nay!" they shouted in unison.

"Nay, indeed!" Blackbeard agreed. "That be too kindly a penance for the likes of him. Neither do I see an island on yonder horizon. It would seem fate makes the decision for us."

"Please, sir," the captain said, lips quivering.

"Please, sir?" Blackbeard said, his tone laced with sarcasm. "If you hadn't run, I'd be encouraged to oblige your plea, and you'd already be on your way . . . minus your cargo, of course. Unfortunately, you ran, and I be encouraged to make an example of you. Did you truly think a ship such as mine outmanueverable? Have you not heard the name *Queen Anne's Revenge*?"

"I did not know this was *Queen Anne's Revenge*," the captain stammered.

"Then you do not know the waters upon which you sail. Have you not heard the name Blackbeard? Did you not know who the Caribbean belongs to? Be that why you have not yet toppled to your knees in my presence?"

The captain fell to his knees, pulling the young man and young woman down with him. "Do whatever you want to me," he said, "just don't hurt my daughter, please."

The girl in the white dress whimpered softly, tears glistening on her pale white cheeks. She had the complexion of a porcelain doll and looked just as easy to break.

"Nay," said Blackbeard, wagging a finger. "She's no longer your concern. Men, take her below!"

Four pirates scooped up the captain's daughter and dragged her kicking and shrieking into the darkened hollow beneath the quarterdeck. "No!" the captain exclaimed. He tried to stand, but two more pirates held him in place. "What are they going to do to her?" he demanded, tears welling.

Annabelle couldn't see Blackbeard's face, but she knew he was smiling. "Those men are going to ravage your daughter until she speaks naught but nonsense or speaks no more, be that clear enough? They have gone too long without womanly company. And after they've done with her, I'm going to set you and what's left of your daughter back on your ship, and you're going to sail straight to Nassau and relay to Woodes Rogers exactly what happens to ships what put *Queen Anne's Revenge* to their rudder."

"You release her right now!" cried the young man at the captain's side.

Blackbeard drew back slightly. "Be this your son?"

"Yes," the captain said. "He's only twenty, sir."

Blackbeard loosed a guttural laugh. Smoke lifted from his beard, tendrils swirling in the wind. "You think that not old enough to die?"

"I most certainly do not."

"You most certainly do not think it *not* old enough to die?"

The captain's eyes went wide as terror mounted. "No, no, wait, no. I think it . . . I think it *not* old enough to die. What you said, sir."

"Well, now I be thoroughly perplexed."

"There's nothing perplexing about it," the captain insisted, anger overwhelming him. "Twenty is most certainly not old enough to die."

"What age be proper?"

"I don't know," the captain blustered. "Not *his* age, that's certain."

Blackbeard looked to his crew and scratched the back of his neck. "This man would have us believe twenty an unkillable number. Refresh my memory, gentlemen. Have we not seen men of twenty or less killed?"

"Aye," they said.

"Are you certain? The captain says nay."

"That's not what I said," the captain protested.

"Then a man of twenty *is* killable?" Blackbeard asked, embellishing a confused tone.

The captain's head dropped. "I cannot win this game."

Blackbeard looked to the son. "Your father quits easily. If I didn't know better, I'd think he wishes you dead. What do you think? Don't I know better, or do I?"

The son thought about that for a moment, eyes darting back and forth until he came to a conclusion. "You don't?"

"Then your father *does* wish me to kill you."

"Wait!" exclaimed the son. "You *do* know better!"

"Well that be a dismal conclusion, in light of the sentence preceding it."

"This is absurd, sir!" the captain protested.

"I agree," Blackbeard said. "Neither of you can muster an intelligible sentence even when your lives hinge upon it."

"Goddammit, Teach!!!" bellowed the captain, his face blooming red with rage.

Blackbeard's crew started to laugh.

"I'll do the only damning this night," Blackbeard promised. "Starting with your son. Boatswain, fetch my sword."

The lanky boatswain, whose name Annabelle had never bothered to learn, shuffled off on a bum leg, sporting a sinister grin. He returned with a massive curved sword and laid it flat across his captain's palms. Blackbeard gestured, and two pirates dragged the son before him.

The captain squirmed beneath his captors. "Teach, I beg you!"

Blackbeard moved behind the boy, giving Annabelle a clear view of what happened next. He set the massive sword across the boy's neck, standing behind him with one hand on the hilt and the other gripping the tip. He jerked back hard, drawing the blade deep into the boy's throat, and a waterfall of blood gushed down the thick steel. The boy's eyes rolled back in his head and his jaw fell open. He made a gurgling sound before slumping against the sword.

"Hmm," said Teach, frowning at the fresh corpse. "Appears

the boy yielded no fervor for life. I pray your daughter be putting up more of a fight, though the lack of screams troubles me."

"Oh, God, why?" the captain moaned.

"Absent parties rarely offer riposte," Teach said, bending over to wipe the blade on the dead boy's shirt. He faced the captain again. "If there truly be a god, I exist by his design. He allows me free reign over this ocean. It be God what placed me in your path. Think on that."

Blackbeard handed his sword back to the boatswain and quickly ascended to the quarterdeck without another glance at the devastated captain. He nodded curtly at Annabelle as he passed, and she obediently fell into step. She knew the entire crew was watching. Unlike most pirate crews, they had no minds of their own. They were the men no one else wanted. They had no ambitions beyond thievery and murder. Life meant nothing to them. Tomorrow did not exist, only today. They would live and die at sea, because land had no tolerance for them.

Annabelle felt a weight lift from her as Blackbeard closed the cabin door. She knew they would have savaged her by now if not for his protection, just as they were savaging the captain's daughter this very instant. She wished to thank him for that in the best way she knew how, but he had not permitted it.

Tonight would be the night.

Seeing him murder Charles Martel had awoken something in her, and tonight had given her another taste of his power. The ferocity in his eyes as he took a life was like nothing she had ever seen. Men shrunk before him.

Teach took off his hat and coat and began tugging at the fuses in his beard, which were all but extinguished. She shrugged out of her robe, enjoying the way the silk felt against her skin as it slid off. She stood naked before him, the candles accentuating her mahogany skin, dancing shadows exaggerating every curve of her body.

He regarded her incredulously. "Not tonight, love," he sighed. "Murder steals my strength."

6

NATHAN

She might have fooled the others, but she hadn't fooled him. One sidelong glance from under the brim of her comically wide, low fitting hat and Nathan knew this boy was not a boy. She had wisely avoided mixing with the rest of the crew, never drawing attention. Not everyone on a ship was a bundle of personality, and it was easy to fade into the background if one so desired. Many were content to settle into a quiet corner, reading or drinking, with no one taking issue. The boisterous jokers more than made up for the reclusive types.

She was standing between two cannons on the main deck, arms resting on the port rail, watching dolphins as they leapt out of the water in graceful arcs near the bow of the ship. Their silver skin glittered in the sun. They had followed the ship tirelessly for nearly an hour now. Nathan had been thrilled the first time he saw dolphins, but they soon became too common a sight to rally his interest.

The sun beat down from a bright blue sky, and Nathan wondered how the girl's bare feet could stand the heat of the deck. The wind matted her frumpy clothes against her body, revealing the curves of her hips and ass for an instant. She shifted into a more boyish pose, sniffing and crossing her arms. Her short and jagged black hair fluttered beneath the hat. Her height and broad shoulders aided the ruse.

"I never got your name," Nathan said.

"That's because you never asked," she replied in a gruff voice.

Nathan set his hand on the rail beside her, noticing the faint patch of freckles under her eyes for the first time.

"I'm no good for company," she said, sustaining the false masculinity in her voice.

"That will be a welcome departure," Nathan quipped. "I've had nothing but good company since stepping onboard this ship." Nathan had been treated as something of a celebrity after his uproarious entrance. Most of Dillahunt's crew were former pirates, and Nathan's previous captain was held in high regard among them. Any man who had nearly been executed for serving under Jonathan Griffith was a friend of theirs.

A small minority of the crew were not so kind, however. They muttered choice slights whenever he passed, "traitor" chief among them. They did not welcome a pirate who was assisting the governor in hunting down other pirates. The irony of their own involvement apparently escaped them. Or maybe Nathan was the personification of their guilt. He was getting used to being a scapegoat.

The most worrisome was a man known only as Red Devil, who was said to be half a native from America. His skin was indeed tinged red, and his broad jaw was completely without bristle. His hair was long, thick, and black. Nic Lawsome, the cook, had told Nathan that Red's father was a noble-born

Englishman who had kidnapped and raped a native woman who strayed too close to his property. He sheltered her until she gave birth, and he murdered her shortly after. Why anyone would do such a thing, Lawsome couldn't say, but there was something in Red's merciless eyes that made the tale believable, as though he knew he had been born of an evil act.

Other than a few dissenters, Nathan felt mostly at home on *Crusader*. The ship was similar in design to his old ship, though it was kept in far prettier condition. The many cannons were spotlessly polished, the sails were bright and new, and the decks had been freshly tarred.

"I have an idea," the boy who was not a boy suggested. "You tell me my name and I'll tell you yours."

"Not a fair game," Nathan frowned. "You probably already know my name."

She shook her head, careful not to look at him. "I have no idea who you are."

"I see," he said. He found that hard to believe, given that they wouldn't be here without him as a guide, but he couldn't think of a way to dispute it without coming off as egotistical.

After a long silence, she said, "You're not going to leave, are you?"

"Thought I'd enjoy the view."

She groaned. "That's what I thought."

A dolphin leapt precariously close to the ship, its fin scraping the hull, and then arced back into the water. The girl let out a little gasp, then remembered herself. "Don't worry," Nathan said. "Never seen one hit by a ship. They're too smart for that."

She curved a lopsided smile his way. She was obviously the flirtatious sort, and she was having a hard time subduing her nature.

"Sarah?" he asked offhandedly.

"What?"

"Your name. You seem like a 'Sarah' to me."

Her expression turned ugly. "Is that some sort of joke?"

"No more than that hat," he said, flicking the brim with his middle finger.

She jerked away, glaring at him. He offered a smile, and her expression gradually softened as she realized there was no point denying it. "Have you told anyone?" she demanded, trading her manly tone for her true voice, which was refreshingly feminine.

He placed a hand over his heart. "Not a soul."

She looked around in distress, then seized his collar and drew him near for a conspiratorial whisper. "Do you think anyone else figured it out?"

"No. I'm dying of boredom. Captain Dillahunt doesn't want me working any part of his precious ship, so I've nothing better to do but notice details I normally wouldn't give a second thought."

"He doesn't trust you," she said, releasing his collar. "I'm starting to see why."

"Why?"

She regarded him with an upturned eyebrow. "You're too smart for a pirate."

"A low hurdle, easily vaulted," he chortled. "It seems their ranks are easily infiltrated by smart men and pretty women."

She blushed. "A charmer, I see. No wonder he doesn't trust you."

"Are you his?" It would be a lot easier for her to sneak aboard if she had been aided by Dillahunt.

The redness in her cheeks brightened, but this time it was not due to his charm. "I belong to no one, thank you very much."

"You know what I mean."

She looked to the sea, eyelids fluttering rapidly. "Yes. I am his."

"I thought so." He pulled away slightly, instinctively. He didn't want to invite a captain's jealousy. "I saw you steal into his cabin the other night. You didn't leave."

Her lips curved into a naughty smile. She seemed relieved to be able to express herself with someone other than Dillahunt. She stuck out her hand. "Jacqueline Calloway. Not Sarah."

"Nathan," he replied, shaking her hand with a full grip as he would a man's. "Pleased to meet you, Jacqueline."

"Jaq," she corrected. "Or Calloway, if you like."

He winked knowingly. "Of course."

"And does anyone belong to you, Nathan?"

"She also belongs to no one," he replied matter-of-factly, though he could only *hope* that was true. He tried not to think about the rumors regarding Annabelle and Blackbeard. He'd spent too much time dwelling on that in his cell in Nassau.

"I see," she said, intrigued.

"I'll probably never see her again." He vacantly rubbed the stump where his left arm had been.

"Her fault or yours?"

"Must there be fault?"

She let out a tart laugh befitting an older woman. "Where people are concerned there is always fault. I may be young, but I know that much already."

Nathan ground his fingernails into his stump, wincing. "The fault is mine. I could have stayed, but the sea was too tempting."

She smiled. "When I look at it, I forget everything else."

"A part of me knew she wouldn't be there when I returned."

"Oh, Nathan," Calloway said with a reassuring smile, "who's to say you won't see her again?"

He returned the smile, but the muscles of his face felt dense and stubborn. "The world is too large, and too much time has passed. It's likely she's forgotten who I am. She is a strumpet, after all."

She wrinkled her nose, freckles gathering close. "A whore cannot love?"

It took a moment before comprehension struck him, and when it did, the girl before him was illuminated. "Of course she can," he stammered. "Apologies."

She giggled. "Don't worry, it's very hard to offend a whore. We develop thick skins even at my age."

"Twelve?" he suggested with an impish smirk.

"Very funny, but a few years short."

"You're only fifteen?" he said, mouth hanging open. His jest wasn't as far off the mark as he had intended. She nodded, setting her arms on the rail again. He joined her. A couple of dolphins were still leaping out of the water, but most were just swimming now, keeping pace with the ship.

"How old was your woman?" Calloway asked.

He started to answer, and then he realized with a shock that he had no idea. "You know, I'm not sure we ever discussed it."

She angled scornful eyes his way. "You don't know how old your one true love is, Nathan?"

"It never came up," he replied defensively, warmth filling his cheeks. "We had other things on our minds."

"Like as much frolicking as there are hours in the day?"

"Exactly," he said, nudging her with his stump without thinking. As usual, he had forgotten. To her credit, she didn't flinch.

"I think you've mistaken lust for love," she stated flatly.

He gaped at her audacity, unable to form a retort.

"I've seen it many times," she went on. "If I had a piece of eight for every pirate that thought himself in love with me, I'd be rich before I reached adulthood. They all say the same thing, especially the young ones having their first go. They've coin to spend and they set eyes on the prettiest whore they can find—"

"That would be you?"

"—and not surprisingly they fall in love. And yes, I was quite pretty before I cut my hair. I fancy my hips and my legs and my arse, and I think I have a fetching stomach that curves inward rather than outward like most women." She was droning on now, lost in herself. "My breasts are dreadfully small, though. I can't do much about those."

Nathan swallowed, glancing downward. "Hard to gauge beneath a dowdy shirt."

"Well, I do have breasts, of course. Small, but noticeable enough in shapelier garments. The shirt serves its purpose, except where meddlesome pirates with nothing but time on their hands are concerned." She smiled shrewdly at him.

"That last bit was about me, wasn't it?"

She nodded solemnly. "Afraid so."

He had trouble not staring at her. She was so young, with her entire life ahead of her. "You know," he said cautiously, "the sea is a very dangerous place."

"Oh dear," she said, feigning fear.

"You jest, but this is a dangerous mission."

She sighed. "You think he hasn't told me that time and time again?"

"People may die."

Her eyes flashed with genuine excitement. "Really? Do you think so?"

He frowned. "Well, yes."

She gripped his sleeve. "Have you seen a man killed by a sword?"

He raised an eyebrow, leaning away from her. "Many times."

"Is it true that blood gushes all over the place when the blade is pulled out?" She was grinning now.

"Well, it depends on the—"

She glanced past Nathan, and her eyes widened. "Shuttup! He's coming."

Nathan looked over his shoulder and saw Guy Dillahunt approaching, scanning the ship for anything out of place. His hand rested atop the hilt of his shiny rapier, poised to draw it at any moment. His gaze settled briefly on Calloway as he approached.

"Captain Dillahunt," Nathan greeted with a nod.

Dillahunt seized Nathan by the good arm and turned him starboard, pointing to a cannon across the ship. "Do you see that cannon?"

"Aye, captain, it's difficult to miss."

He heard Calloway stifle a giggle.

"Does it look properly lined to you?"

"It looks a cannon like any other, captain."

Dillahunt looked at him expectantly. "Is it not misaligned in relation to the others?"

Nathan took another look. All the cannons seemed perfectly lined. "It appears straight to me."

"Very well," Dillahunt said, releasing him. He straightened Nathan's sleeve where his grip had ruffled it. "I've made a mess of your shirt."

"It's fine."

Dillahunt shifted his chin to the horizon. "We should be within sight of Griffith's island in three days, if it truly exists."

"It exists," Nathan assured him.

"No offense intended. Pirates are inclined to devious plots, and you are a pirate, last I looked."

"I'm a guide," Nathan reminded him. "Nothing more."

"You'd claim yourself a furry little ferret if it helped you elude the gallows. I've had dealings with pirates all my life. In fact, I can't seem to crew a ship without them. If you want the truth, I'm not certain any man here has earned my trust, apart from my loyal first mate. Governor Rogers believes he can make honest sailors of pirates. I told Rogers the line between privateer and pirate is a thin one, drawn in sand, too easily swept away by a strong tide. He wrote off my words as 'overly dramatic' at the time, yet now he sends me to catch Benjamin Hornigold. You can't blame me for keeping my . . . guard . . . up . . . "

Dillahunt's gaze trailed away with his sentence. "Are you absolutely certain that cannon is not out of place?"

Nathan did not look again. "It may be a notch off."

Relief washed over Dillahunt's face. "I suspected as much."

"Should I adjust it, captain?"

"No. I just wanted to make sure I wasn't the only one who saw it. Carry on." Dillahunt took his leave, glancing fretfully at the cannon in question as he walked toward his cabin.

"Queer man," Nathan muttered.

Calloway sighed. "He woke up out of sorts this morning. I suppose I must attend to him, if you take my meaning." She favored Nathan with a little smile before adjusting her hat and starting after Dillahunt. She cleared her throat and stiffened her poise, and she was all boy again. As always, none of the other men seemed to know she existed.

Nathan returned his attention to the sea. Only one dolphin remained, leaping out of the water with that perpetual grin they all had, oblivious to its absent kin. Nathan couldn't spot any other dolphins in the water, no matter how far he looked. He prayed this one wouldn't be permanently separated from the group, forever indemnifying a moment of glee.

7

KATE

The ship was an indistinct blur beneath the surface, resting in a relatively shallow grave just off the eastern beach. Kate peered over the edge as Dumaka and Andrew Harrow rowed the little boat around a charred mainmast, which was the only part of the ship that remained above water. If not for the mast, they might have mistaken the sunken ship for the carcass of some great whale that had come here to die.

"Cunningham's ship?" Hornigold asked Kate.

"Yes," she replied gravely. "*Abettor.*"

"I met the man only once," he said. "I liked him instantly. He was a true pirate, but he abstained from murder."

"The same can't be said of Griffith," Kate replied. "When Cunningham figured out who I was, Griffith killed him."

"And everyone aboard?"

She nodded. "Collateral." *All for me.*

The island was greener than Kate remembered, with a dense

jungle circumventing a treacherously steep grey summit that must have been volcanic. The peak was surrounded by haze. It had only been a few hours since dawn, and a morning fog was rolling down the mountainside, collecting in the many nooks and outcroppings. The jungle wrapped around the base of the mountain in a thick ring, sloping down to the beach. The trees were tall and dense, with only a few openings large enough for a person to stroll through. Dread crept into the pit of Kate's stomach as she stared into the largest opening just beyond the eastern beach. Jack Cunningham had gone in there willingly, and he never came out.

Just then, something skittered in that dark hollow. Kate tightened her grip on the rail of the boat, fingernails digging into the wood. She glimpsed a splash of color, a flutter of crimson. Her heart thumped in her chest and hairs prickled along the back of her neck. She seized Hornigold's wrist. "Do you see that?"

"See what?"

Another flash of red. Blood? What was happening in there? "There!" she hissed, pointing.

Hornigold squinted. He opened his mouth to speak . . . and then froze. "What in the bloody hell is that?"

More flashes of red. Something was rustling within. And then a terrible shriek. It sounded like—

A parrot burst from the opening, wings brushing against leaves as it escaped some unseen predator in a panic. It squawked frantically, ascending above the tree line, and then turning back toward the mountain. It disappeared into one of the crevices far above.

Kate released Hornigold's arm. He massaged his wrist where her fingernails had left pink gouges. "Sorry," she said.

"It's fine," he replied, clearing his throat.

It was not long before the boat's keel slid onto the white

beach. Dumaka, Harrow, and Hornigold leapt out quickly, feet splashing in the water. Hornigold offered Kate his hand. She was reluctant to get off, despite the sun already beating down on her back from its low position on the eastern horizon. It was going to be a hot day, and the shade would be a welcome respite, but that would mean taking shelter near the jungle. There were a few trees scattered randomly about, but their shadows wavered in the breeze, and they were not closely packed enough to offer much of a canopy.

Hornigold stared at her, his hand hanging in the air, palm facing up. "Something wrong?"

"No," Kate replied. She took his hand and swung her legs over the rail, sinking her bare feet into the soft sand. A little wave splashed the back of her legs, and she wobbled slightly. Hornigold's grip tightened. Kate felt his other hand on the small of her back, steadying her. She jerked away. "I can walk, thank you."

Frustration flashed in his face, but he blinked it away. He looked to Dumaka, who he had appointed quartermaster shortly after the death of Reed, without the consent of the crew. "We'll set up camp here and send several two-to-three man groups into the jungle. According to Mrs. Lindsay, there are thirteen chests. She doesn't know the exact location of each chest, but this island is only so large. A thorough search and keen eyes will yield our fortune, gentlemen. It will probably take us a week or more, but we are well rationed and Governor Rogers has no idea where we've gone."

Kate swallowed. *That might not be true.*

She thought of Nathan Adams, the young pirate who had called her a friend, yet wasted little time in attempting to turn her in for the reward her husband's family had offered. Nathan was surely dead by now, but there was a slim chance Rogers had thought to interrogate him about Kate after she had corrupted his precious Benjamin Hornigold. Even if Rogers was as smart as everyone claimed, she doubted Nathan knew how to get back to this island, because Griffith had kept the charts in his cabin.

She smirked at the silly thought, pushing it aside.

Dumaka took the boat back to *Ranger*, which was moored in the distance. Another boat passed him on its way to the beach, carrying more crew. The two boats ferried back and forth until half of the crew had been transported to the island.

Kate strolled along the beach, warily skirting the jungle. She found a long green iguana and chased after it until it retreated into the trees, well out of her reach. Birds and bugs formed a symphonic ambience from within the jungle. She squinted, trying to discern details between two trees, but it was black as pitch in there. She took a few steps back, not wanting to put her rear to the trees for fear that something would leap out when she wasn't looking and drag her into the darkness, never to be seen again.

When she turned, she was shocked at how far she'd walked. Her footsteps trailed off in a long bend. Hornigold and the others were far down the beach. If she'd walked any further, they would have been out of view entirely, beyond the curved perimeter of the trees. She started back, veering into the water so she could soak her hot heels.

By the time she got back, the pirates were already setting up camp. The sun was in the middle of the sky, searing the crown of her head. She bent down and splashed water into her hair. Bastion approached, reaching into his pocket and withdrawing a black piece of cloth. "You need it more than me," he said, offering it to her. "For the head."

"You sure?" she said, squinting up at him.

"It will look better on you," he said.

A charmer, she thought. *Naturally he'll want something in return. They always do.* But that didn't stop her from taking the bandana. She fastened it over the top of her head, tying a knot in the back, with her hair spilling out the sides. She made certain her mutilated ear remained concealed. "I must look quite the pirate," she quipped.

Bastion shrugged. "I don't know what a pirate look like." He awkwardly pivoted on his heels and shuffled off before she could ask him what he meant. Bastion was very shy, but Kate suspected there was much more going on beneath the surface. He would quite often sit and stare pensively at his peers, studying their every gesture. Kate tried to talk to him a few times, but the conversation always ended abruptly, as Bastion would suddenly seem to remember his duties and hurry off. She suspected he wasn't comfortable around women.

The pirates finished making camp by midafternoon. Kate helped Avery and Billie Dowling unpack several tents and hammocks. She exchanged a few words with Billie, while Avery silently scowled. She knew Avery didn't care for her and cared even less for her fraternizing with his younger brother. Billie was not the smartest lad in the Caribbean, and Avery was understandably protective of him. Kate respected Avery's position, but Billie was far too friendly to ignore.

When there was nothing more to do, Kate found a nice perch on a long rock formation that jutted over the tide. She leaned back and put her arms behind her head, bending one knee while stretching the other leg across the rock. A cool breeze caressed her body as the sun drew nearer the horizon. The sapphire sky gradually gave to purple hues.

Kate caught a few pirates stealing glances at her, but she didn't care. She fell asleep once or twice with no dreams to disturb her, just the gentle swish of the tide on either side of the long rock formation. Whenever she was awake, she would tilt her head and watch the pirates from time to time.

Bastion and his newest friend, Keith, were gathering thorny green fruits from the trees. Keith was a lanky, badly sunburned young man with stringy red hair and a maze of freckles. He tried to bite into one of the fruits, but winced at the thorns. Bastion was far more experienced, slicing through a fruit with his cutlass and offering one half to Keith.

Copernicus Ryan and Fat Farley were building a firepit with poles to support a skewer. A fat hog was tied up near them, rooting gleefully in the sand, oblivious to its impending doom. The hog was one of three which, according to Farley, they were saving for special occasions. Kate felt sorry for the beast, but her growling stomach was at odds with the sentiment.

Francois Laurent, Gabriel Elegy, and Jeremy Clemens went exploring, disappearing into the jungle. Laurent and Clemens took muskets while Harrow and Elegy carried shovels, in case they stumbled upon one of the thirteen chests.

A hundred or so paces from Kate, Hornigold was sitting by himself in the sand, staring at *Ranger*. One arm rested atop a raised knee, while his other hand was twirling his mustache. His expression betrayed no emotion, good or bad.

Laurent, Elegy, and Clemens returned shortly after the sun had retreated beyond the horizon and stars lightly speckled the sky. Laurent reported to Hornigold, but Kate couldn't hear them over the waves. Hornigold merely nodded, not taking his eyes off *Ranger*. Laurent lingered for a moment, as if he wanted to say something more, and then took his leave.

The hog squealed as Farley wrestled it into submission, securing his arm around its neck. Ryan slit the animal's throat, spilling its blood in the sand. The hog instantly collapsed beneath Farley's massive girth. They stuck a skewer through it, from mouth to rear, and hefted it over the firepit. Ryan's knees nearly buckled, his face turning bright red. Bastion rushed over to help him lift. Farley prepared the fire. The flames kindled swiftly, bathing the beach in orange ambience. It was not long before the intoxicating aroma of roasting hog filled Kate's nostrils, and her mouth watered as she watched the juices pop and sizzle, streaming down the darkening meat.

Francois Laurent took a seat near the fire and started playing an achingly beautiful tune on a polished violin. More pirates drew near the fire. Harrow handed out a few bottles of rum. It was not long before they were all singing drunkenly, making up whatever lyrics they thought went along with that tune. Laurent increased the tune's fervor to accommodate their boisterous singing.

Farley cut off the first slab of meat, tasted it, nodded, and then stepped back as the pirates descended on the hog like vultures. Kate waited patiently, despite her rumbling stomach, and when they were all seated and happily gorging themselves, she leapt off her perch and approached the firepit. Farley offered her his cutlass, which she took with a grateful incline of her head. She cut off a huge chunk of meat from the hog's hindquarters, the blade slicing through the meat as if it were butter. She handed the cutlass back to Farley and plopped herself in the sand beside Bastion and Keith, who were seated near the water. She spared them with a brief smile before eagerly sinking her teeth into the meat. The skin was crunchy and the meat tender, savory juices dribbling down her chin. She ate until she thought she might burst, and then she kept eating.

Bastion handed her what was left of a bottle of rum and half of one of those thorny green fruits. Kate threw back her head, draining the bottle in a few gulps. She savored every bite of the fruit, which was white on the inside and sweet on her tongue. She fell into the sand. Her head settled into the tangles of her hair, thick curls grazing her cheeks. Her lips were wet with meat juices and rum, and the fruit left a pleasant aftertaste. She had never felt so thoroughly satiated in all her life.

A large wave crashed over the beach, rolling so close that Bastion and Keith sprang to their feet in alarm. Kate shuddered when the water touched her heels, but she did not move. The two men looked at her, then each other, and then laughed and sat back down.

Countless stars seemed to swirl above her, with the waning moon holding steady. She raised her index finger and trailed patterns between the stars, fashioning a constellation that resembled a ship.

"What did you mean earlier?" she asked Bastion. "When you said you didn't know what a pirate looks like? And please don't run off before you tell me."

It was a long time before Bastion answered. "I see too many pirates," he said finally. "They look the same as everybody else. The governor say pirates all bad men, but I see good men that are pirates, and I see bad men that are not pirates. Captain Benjamin . . . him was a pirate. Then the governor give him a piece of paper saying him a good man. A piece of paper can change a man? Now him a pirate again. Him a bad man now? Captain Benjamin rescue Dumaka from slaver ship. Them slavers was bad men. Them do bad things to other men, things I wish to never see.

"Captain Benjamin not a bad man, him just want better things. Him not like Edward Teach. Teach do terrible things him have no reason to do. Captain Benjamin not like that. But the governor say them both pirates, them both bad men."

He looked down at her, his eyes wide and bright, despite the darkness. "Now I see a woman who want to be a pirate."

Normally such a slight would have put a fury in her, but she was feeling too good to muster anger over anything. "I never said that," she replied.

"But you are," Bastion said with a smile.

"You're mistaken."

Bastion tilted his head in humble concession. "Like I say . . . I don't know what a pirate look like."

A roar of laughter went up behind them. The pirates were singing and dancing bombastically around the fire.

Keith tapped Bastion on the shoulder, and the two of them left to join their mates. Kate sat up, rubbing her suddenly heavy eyes. Rum always made her groggy. She shambled back up the beach, moving past Hornigold's tent, which was much larger than the others. It looked inviting, and he undoubtedly had many furs to curl up in.

She found an empty hammock on the border of the jungle and climbed in. It was closer to the jungle than she would have liked, but the alternatives were sleeping in the sand or sleeping with Hornigold. She fell into the hammock and closed her eyes as it swayed right and left, gently rocking her towards sleep.

Something gripped her arm.

She woke with a gasp.

Hornigold was staring down at her, eyes gleaming furiously in the night. He yanked her out of the hammock. She landed awkwardly on her feet, twisting an ankle.

"What the bloody hell do you think you're—" she started.

"I'm going into that jungle to find one of the chests," he said, slurring every word. "You're coming with me."

She bent down to massage her ankle. "You're drunk."

"Everyone's drunk."

"I'm not going in there in the dark."

He seized her wrist and lifted her up forcefully. "You'll go where I say you'll go."

She tore free of his grip. "I am not yours to command."

"Listen to me," he hissed, breath hot and stinking of rum. "Harrow found no trace of anything in that jungle."

"He was in there all of two hours," Kate scoffed. "Hardly

time enough for a thorough search."

"I need to know something's in there," Hornigold insisted. "You've dragged me halfway across the Caribbean. I would have ratification."

"I *dragged* you?" she laughed. "I thought you controlled your own actions?"

His hand ascended swiftly, thumb and forefinger worrying away at his mustache. "A poor choice of words, influenced by heavy spirits."

Her husband had once told her, "Spirits give true voice to a man's soul." She briefly considered reciting that sentiment to Hornigold but thought better of it. "This can't wait till dawn?"

"It cannot," he said, pacing in the sand. "I will find no rest until I have confirmation of at least one chest."

"This is absurd."

"Do not leave," Hornigold instructed, pointing at her face. "I will fashion a torch."

She spread her arms and said, "Where would I go?"

She waited, leaning against one of the trees her hammock was tied to. She closed her eyes and nearly fell asleep upright, but she was jarred into consciousness when Hornigold came running up with a burning torch. He handed her a shovel and gestured to the nearest opening in the trees. "Let us waste no time."

She stared at him. "You know, most men simply pass out when drunk."

"Not I," he declared.

Kate sighed and followed after him. Hornigold drew his cutlass in one hand, held the torch aloft in the other, and plunged into the jungle. She hurried after him, moving on uncertain legs. She was instantly greeted by massive leaves slapping at her face. She shoved through them, focusing on the torchlight. The leaves scratched her arms and legs. She blinked, holding her hands in front of her face for fear of cutting an eye.

Hornigold was hacking through the leaves with his cutlass, but it wasn't doing much good. "Do you have any particular direction in mind?" Kate called ahead.

"If you care to offer a destination," he replied over his shoulder, "I'd happily alter course."

"I was hidden away in Griffith's cabin when his crew buried the valuables," she muttered. "I promised you the island and here you are. I never said I knew where each chest was."

Hornigold stopped and turned, slapping a leaf out of his face. He glared at her, knuckles white around the hilt of his cutlass. "I swear to God, Kate, if this was all some sort of ruse, I will leave you on this island."

Kate felt increasing pressure in her left temple, and she knew it would manifest into a headache soon. "Rum has dulled your senses, Benjamin. What purpose would a ruse serve me? Think hard. Take a moment, if you must."

His eyes darted back and forth as if he was working through many nefarious scenarios. "I see your point," he said at last.

"That's settled then," she said with a sigh. "I grow weary of your doubts. It is hardly my fault you leapt at the opportunity without deliberation, and yet accuse me of subterfuge with equal haste."

"You've made your point," he snapped, turning and continuing on his path.

She smiled, pleased with herself, and followed after. They pushed through the jungle for what felt like hours, and Kate's arms were soon traced with dozens of thin welts from the rough branches scraping past. She craned her neck and saw no stars, only wet branches and leaves glinting in the torchlight.

Finally, when Kate's patience had all but fled, they came to an opening. The trees and the brush dispersed into a sandy clearing, which ended abruptly in a wall of rock. Kate's eyes scaled the wall, which sloped steeply into the peak that towered above the island. The stars and moon shone clearly here, unbroken by tree cover.

Hornigold was staring at the peak, mouth hanging open. "Tell me Griffith didn't place any chests up there."

"I doubt it," Kate replied. "He wasn't gone nearly long enough. The chests would have been buried in haste."

"This is all speculation!" Hornigold exploded, hurling his torch to the ground. He advanced on her, lifting his cutlass high in the air, and for an instant she feared he would bring it down on her, but he flung it downward and stuck the blade in the sand instead. He aimed an accusatory finger, his mustache twitching. "You know nothing of value!"

Kate shook her head, exhausted physically and mentally. *This man is a joke. I should have waited for someone whose will isn't so easily broken.* Hornigold might have been a formidable pirate once, but Woodes Rogers had stripped him of what little resolve Edward Teach hadn't. Ambition had been enough to carry him this far, but it wasn't enough to sustain him.

"You are an impenetrable fog in the mind," he went on.

"Why, thank you," she quipped with a smile.

"You corrupt men with easy words."

"I am not a witch," she chuckled. "I have no magical powers over men."

"Are you certain? You turned my crew against me!"

"Last I looked, you're still captain. I merely reminded them who they are, as you would have done were you not so ashamed with yourself."

"I feel no shame!" he spat.

"You reek of it," she sneered. "The stench is enough to gag upon."

He gaped at her. "You're a ghastly woman. For the life of me I can't figure why Jonathan Griffith died for you."

She smiled obliviously. "I wasn't always so ghastly."

He shook his head. "One day something very bad is going to happen to you, Katherine Lindsay."

Her smile faltered a notch, but she held what remained. "One day something very bad is going to happen to every one of us, Benjamin Hornigold. Only fools think they can escape their end."

"Yes, well, it seems my end approaches much sooner than I had anticipated, thanks to you." He threw his hands to the sky. "You've killed another man's ambition."

"We've been here less than a day," Kate said with a woeful sigh. "Already you despair. If you regret your decision, that is *your* concern, not mine. You can't change what you've done, so you might as well make the most of it."

Hornigold waved a dismissive hand and faced the clearing, hands on his hips. His head fell. Kate stared at the back of his skull, hoping she might penetrate that black hair and see his thoughts unfold before her. His shoulders tensed suddenly, head lifting slightly. "A solution has sprung to mind," he said.

"Yes?" she replied hopefully.

He held out a hand. "Hand me the shovel, would you?"

She gave him the shovel. He gripped it with both hands and took a step further into the clearing . . . and then pirouetted on his heels, swinging the shovel in a great arc. She was too slow to register what was happening before the flat end glanced off of her forehead with a sickening metallic *thunk*, snapping her head back. Her knees buckled and the world tilted dizzyingly. She collapsed limply into the sand, cheek splitting on a sharp, fist-sized rock. She cried out, clutching her face.

Hornigold tossed the shovel aside and stepped over her, placing one leg on either side. His silhouette blotted out the stars. He straddled her and clutched her wrists, eyes gleaming. "I will not leave here empty-handed," he snarled. "If I cannot have Griffith's treasure, I will find solace betwixt your legs." He bent over her, licking her face, and when he lifted up, his mouth was wet with her blood. He released her left hand so he could fumble with the laces of his breeches.

She groggily struggled to recover her scattered senses as pain seared through her skull. *He only has one hand to work with, and his breeches are tightly laced. Think. Ignore the pain. Look around. Think.*

He stopped with his laces long enough to tear open her shirt, and she felt the warm Caribbean night air upon her right breast. Hornigold paused as he stared at her hungrily. He descended to lick her nipple.

Think. He is distracted.

Her right hand was firmly secured, so she looked to her left. She saw his cutlass sticking from the sand, but it was well out of reach. The torch had landed too far away, and the shovel even further.

Think. What can you use?

He was halfway through the laces of his breeches, hand working quickly. His tongue darted out to lick her blood from his lips. She wondered how badly the rock had mangled her cheek.

The rock!

"You fancy yourself a pirate?" Hornigold growled through clenched teeth. "You think yourself equal to a man? Then why do you crumble so easily beneath me? You haven't the strength, that's why. You're only a woman. You think yourself so smart, but in the end, all that matters is strength."

He struggled with the stubborn laces, cursing. Kate lifted her head and scooped up the rock with her left hand. She smashed it against Hornigold's nose, and blood squirted from his nostrils into her eyes. He loosed a warbled shriek that was almost feminine as he tumbled off her, slapping at his face.

Kate scrambled to her feet, blinking blood out of her eyes. She wiped her face with her sleeve, and the white cloth came away streaked in red. She couldn't be sure how much of it was her blood or Hornigold's. Her face was on fire, her forehead and cheek throbbing. When her sight merged from indistinct blurs to somewhat distinct blurs, she perused her options: A shovel, a torch, and a cutlass.

She went for the cutlass.

Hornigold howled like an animal. Every ounce of chivalrous tact spilled out of him in a murderous fury, along with the blood oozing from his nose, until there was nothing left but a disgraced fiend thrashing about in the sand. "My nose!" he screamed. "You cunt! You cunt! You fucking cunt!"

Kate returned to him, cutlass in hand. "Such language does not become you, Benjamin."

"Fuck you, cunt!"

She set the tip of the blade under his chin, lifting his head. "Look at me, you swine, or I'll put this straight through your jugular." He glared up at her through the ruin of his face, barely discernible as the handsome man he had been only moments ago. His crooked nose was already turning a shade of purple, dribbling blood all over his mustache.

Kate opened her other hand, showing him the rock she had bashed him with. "I found my strength," she said, smiling through the pain.

8

DILLAHUNT

"Your hair is uneven," Dillahunt scowled, fingering a dark lock of Calloway's hair that was distressingly longer than the rest.

The last candle had burned out in the captain's cabin, and their naked figures were swathed in nothing more than the monotone light of the waning moon, spilling through the murky aft windows. She was on top of him, her fingers interlocked over his chest with her chin resting upon her knuckles. The two of them were drenched in sweat. They had been at it three times over, yet Dillahunt found his manhood already rising against her belly.

"You're the one who cut it," Calloway replied with a weary smile. She shook her head briskly, and the lock vanished somewhere within the short tresses, but Dillahunt knew the wayward strands were still in there somewhere.

"I did a terrible job of it," he murmured bitterly. "A rapier is a poor shear. It finds better use impaling a man's belly."

"Something of yours threatens to impale *my* belly." She grinned naughtily, freckles bunching together. "And it's not a sword."

"The thing is inexhaustible," he sighed.

"So am I," she claimed, but her heavy eyelids told another story.

"I think you're finished," Dillahunt countered.

She slid closer, freeing a hand and slipping it downward. "I've got one more in me. How 'bout you?"

Her hand slid under him, fingers tickling his rear. He snatched her wrist before she could probe him. "My step is still ajar from the last time you did that."

"Just one finger this time," she grinned. "I promise to be gentle."

"Stop it," he said, tightening his grip until she flinched and pulled her hand away. "I require no encouragement."

"No fun." She seized his manhood instead. Her piercing blue eyes held his as she guided him inside her and began slowly swaying her hips. He was too tired to do more work, so he let her do it for him. She had lost much of her zeal, but the slow motion was a welcome massage for his aching loins. She nibbled his lower lip, moaning softly through her teeth. She continued writhing until he released, every muscle in his body tensing at once. She opened her mouth, freeing his lip, and sank her head beside his.

He stared at the low overhead. He preferred the dark, which made details indistinct. There were too many patterns in the wood, too many irregularities that played havoc with his mind. His mother told him he had a "condition." The word had been meant to comfort, but it had terrified him instead. In those days he would wake screaming from repetitious dreams that shouldn't have frightened him at all. Sometimes, he would dream he was painting a wall, desperately trying to match the previous color, but it was always a shade too bright or too dim. He would mix the paint with a lighter or darker color to find the proper shade, but it never worked. It was always off, sometimes elusively so, glimpsed only in a shift of the light. Other times he found himself trying to make structures out of blocks, but he never had enough blocks to finish. He would attempt to build a pyramid and only make it halfway to the top. Usually he would realize he was dreaming, but he was never able to jar himself into consciousness. This was the most frustrating part, and he realized that in order to wake, he would have to finish the menial task placed before him. When he was unable to finish, he swelled with panic and would finally wake thrashing in his sheets, doused in sweat.

The dreams grew fewer as he grew older, but his attention to trivial details had not dwindled, and even the dark offered less comfort than it once did. Lack of light did not change the fact that the patterns were still there, ingrained in the wood of the overhead, swirling this way and that, intermingling and dispersing, with no sense to be made out of any of it. He shuddered, struggling to push all thoughts from his mind or to focus on something else entirely. Sex was always a welcome distraction; otherwise, he never would have allowed Jacqueline Calloway to steal aboard his ship. He was not regretting the decision. She made his nights much easier. But sex only lasted so long, and the evil patterns were once again prodding at his thoughts.

Sounds, he reminded himself. Focusing on various sounds always helped.

He listened to the footsteps shuffling around up there. It was probably Jones Thompson, the navigator, scouting the horizon with his long silver spyglass. Or maybe it was Nathan Adams, pacing about the quarterdeck as he so often did. That young man seemed never to sleep.

"Do you fancy Adams?" Dillahunt blurted in Calloway's ear. The question had been on his mind all day, eating away at him much like the patterns of the overhead. She had casually informed him how easily Nathan had uncovered her ruse, inadvertently planting a seed of suspicion in Dillahunt. Or maybe she had meant to do just that. Women were funny that way. Either way, Calloway was already a little too familiar with Adams.

"You're ruining the mood," she whispered in his ear, eyes closed.

At least she has the sense not to feign surprise.

"He is young and handsome," he said. "Though, the missing arm is vexing. If it were my own, I would hack off the other to even both sides."

"I believe you would," she giggled, "but how would you cut off your arm with only one arm?"

Dillahunt paused. He hadn't thought of that. "Don't be daft. I would have someone else do it, of course. But that's beside the point. Your repeated attempts to change the subject have not gone unnoticed."

"Oh no," she yawned. "I'm in trouble."

"Do not make light of my concern," he grumbled.

She lifted her head and stared at him. Her lips parted in a wicked grin. "You are concerned?"

He blinked, frustrated. "I find myself in . . . " He struggled to find the words. "I find myself in a vexed bewilderment."

She frowned. "A vexed be-what?"

"A vexed bewilderment."

"There's a twist of the tongue."

"My emotions run high. A mouthful of words is required to relay them."

She rolled her tired eyes. "The boy is dashing, but I am yours, Captain Dillahunt. If I've been a bad girl for merely speaking to him, you must punish me accordingly."

"Punish you?"

She plopped her head alongside his, exhaling her words into his ear. "Mayhap a good spanking would set . . . me . . . straight . . . " Her voice trailed to a murmur, and then she was breathing heavily against his cheek.

Another perplexing pattern, Dillahunt thought as he stared at her naked form. Trying to get a handle on her was as elusive as trying to catch a trout in a flowing stream with nothing but bare hands for a net. *Young people are perplexing. They do not yet know who they are. They could be anybody. So many patterns running through their minds. So many possibilities laid out before them. They are everything and nothing.*

"I shouldn't have let you come," he thought aloud.

"Not this again," she murmured. "I was promised death and blood. Where is it?"

"You'll see too much of both before the end, I fear."

Nearly every night he asked her what she was doing here, and she always eluded the question. She would always reply with a query about the various ways a man could die. She certainly had an unhealthy preoccupation with gore.

Sometimes she would turn the question back on him, asking him why *he* first took to sea. He honestly could not remember. It had seemed the only option at the time. His father had been a captain before him.

Perhaps not even she knows why she's here, he realized. His obsession with detail often excluded the randomness of human nature. *Not everyone has a good cause for doing the things they do.*

The footsteps above grew heavier and more frenetic. *Far too much commotion for this late hour.* He guessed it was around midnight. He glanced at Calloway, and when he was sure she was fast asleep, he slipped out from under her. She rolled onto her side, mumbling something about sand and water. He threw on his black breeches and red shirt, leaving it unlaced at the neck, and started for the door.

The night air was warm, with only a slight breeze. Stars filled the clear sky, and the moon shone brightly even in its diminished state. Dillahunt had no trouble seeing where he was going, despite the lack of lanterns on deck.

That's odd, he realized. All the lanterns were extinguished.

"Captain," came a throaty voice from above.

Dillahunt turned round and looked up. Ogle, one of the gunners, was looking down on him from the quarterdeck. He was an imposingly tall bald man with a massive gut, but he was powerfully muscled. His scalp shined in the moonlight. Nic Lawsome had joked that Ogle plucked every single hair from his body in accordance with his head. "What is it, sailor?" Dillahunt called up.

Ogle pointed forward. "Just off the starboard bow, captain."

Dillahunt turned, but he couldn't see anything from this low vantage. He ascended to the quarterdeck. Nathan Adams, Jones Thompson, and Phillip Candler were up there too. Dillahunt looked across the ship to see what they were all staring at. The island was distant and black, but the height of its sharp peak made it hard to miss, like a pyramid in the sea. "Already?" Dillahunt asked.

"We made good time," Candler answered.

"Good thinking dousing the lights," Dillahunt said, setting a hand atop Candler's shoulder. Candler had been his friend for three years and had loyally served him as first mate for nearly the same length of time. Candler was only a few years younger, with thin blonde hair and a sharp blonde goatee that sloped to a point beneath his chin. He wore a long blue coat and white breeches.

"Wish I could take credit," Candler said as he shifted his gaze toward Nathan.

Dillahunt fixed Nathan with a glare. "Your idea?"

Nathan withered sheepishly, but Dillahunt thought the young man's modesty seemed a touch overstated. "I didn't mean to go over your head, captain."

"You've done well," Dillahunt replied, unable to deny it. He returned his gaze to Candler. "We will approach with caution. As soon as you catch sight of Hornigold's sloop, move around the island and slip from his view. I would catch the villain by surprise, if at all possible. They have no idea we're coming, so it's unlikely they are watching for us at this hour."

"And if they are?" said Thompson.

Ogle cackled. "Our guns will make lettuce of them."

Dillahunt nodded. "My only worry is Hornigold will turn tail and run. His sloop has the advantage of speed, but that is all. He would be a fool to face us in open combat, and he is no fool."

"Hornigold may be no fool," Nathan put in cautiously, "but he's grown sloppy. He abandoned his post on the promise of a *woman*. I'd wager he's scouring that island with his men, and only a small complement remains to man his ship. Even if they did spot us, Hornigold is cornered."

Dillahunt hated to admit it, but Adams was probably right. He was starting to like this young man, in spite of himself. "Given that he has no reason to expect our arrival, that's likely. Still, I will take no chances. We must take *Ranger* quickly, on the off chance Hornigold is aboard. Once *Ranger* is secured, we will we set upon the island and capture our prey."

"Secured?" said Ogle with a puzzled look. "Does that mean I get to use my guns?"

"Only if they use theirs first," Dillahunt replied.

Ogle's shoulders sagged. "Aye."

Dillahunt smiled reassuringly. "Don't worry, we will find something for you to shoot. These waters are still ripe with pirates."

Ogle's face brightened like a child entering a candy shop.

"Alert the crew," Dillahunt instructed Candler. "And tell them to keep their voices low as we approach."

Candler did as instructed and returned a half an hour later as men fell to their various positions. Gunners took to their stations and prepared the cannons. Ogle descended to the main deck to join them. Nathan remained on the quarterdeck, scrutinizing Dillahunt from time to time, his face unreadable. Soon, Jones Thompson glimpsed *Ranger* through his spyglass, moored far off the eastern beach.

"Give the island a wide berth," Dillahunt ordered. "Then move close and approach from the west. And watch the shoals. It would be embarrassing to report to Woodes Rogers that we ran aground trying to catch Hornigold unaware."

Dillahunt paced the quarterdeck in a circle for nearly an hour as *Crusader* slowly circumvented the island from the western side, making way toward the eastern beach. He made small talk with Nathan, asking him, "Did it hurt?" Nathan smirked at that, and Dillahunt wondered if he had fallen prey to some private jest. "Have I offended you, son?"

"No, captain."

"Then answer me. When my questions go unanswered, it makes me question my existence."

"A little," Nathan said. "I passed out before my arm was taken off."

"There's a kindness."

"I woke to find it missing," Nathan replied sharply. "That was not so kind."

It seemed hours before they caught sight of *Ranger* again. She remained haplessly bobbing in the water, far from shore, dark and silent. Thompson claimed no sign of movement. Dillahunt borrowed the spyglass to confirm. He saw nothing, though it was difficult to make out details in the night, with the moon now hiding behind the island peak. *Ranger's* canvas had been taken in, and she would not be able to flee quickly once set upon. "They must be sleeping."

"Or they've all gone to the island," Candler suggested.

"Would Hornigold leave his ship unattended?" Nathan asked. He seemed to already know the answer.

Dillahunt shook his head. "No captain worth his salt would be so irresponsible."

"Do you still think Hornigold worth his salt?" Nathan asked.

"We're about to find out."

Crusader moved silently toward its prey, and still there was no sign of crew on deck. *Crusader's* bow turned starboard, and she pulled port-to-port alongside *Ranger*. The gunners all moved to the port cannons, light on their feet so their heels did not rattle the deck and draw attention. Soon *Crusader* was running parallel to *Ranger*, a ship's distance apart. Still there was no movement on her deck. No shapes or shadows betrayed lurking crew. Nathan smiled confidently. "They've not seen us."

Candler shook his head. "Hornigold truly is a fool."

"He wasn't always," said Dillahunt uncertainly.

"Women have that effect," Nathan replied sourly.

There came a blinding flash. It was as though the sun had materialized upon *Ranger's* deck. A dozen villainous faces were illuminated. A deafening blast followed a second later, and the bulwark exploded in front of Dillahunt. A maddening pattern formed before his eyes, splinters of wood, big and small, thick and thin, spiraled toward him, riding the blast. In a split second his mind absurdly tried to estimate their number. *My god*, he thought, *there must be a thousand!*

The wooden needles perforated his body as the force of the

blast propelled him against the opposite railing. He fell to his knees and stared at his hands, which were doused in blood. Splinters were sticking from his arms and legs. He was afraid to look at his torso or touch his face. The pain was like nothing he had ever felt, riddling every inch of him. He had imagined a hundred deaths for himself, but none had been as creatively spectacular as this.

Dillahunt slumped against the railing, taking in his surroundings for what he suspected would be the last time.

Nathan was picking splinters out of his right leg with a mildly annoyed look on his face. The rest of his body had somehow eluded mutilation. The boy had been through far worse.

Thompson was crumpled against the railing on Dillahunt's left, gurgling thick black bubbles. A long shard of wood was jammed in his throat. His body lurched, mouth working open and closed, and then he fell silent.

Thunder sounded from beyond. Dillahunt heard both crews shouting insults across ships at one another.

Candler dropped to Dillahunt's side and stared forlornly at him, as a dog stares at his wounded master. He didn't appear to have a scratch on him, the lucky bastard. The look on Candler's face was so pitiful that Dillahunt found himself suddenly disgusted. "Stop that," he commanded. He tasted blood. When Candler continued to stare dumbly, Dillahunt shouted, "Stop looking at me like that! Your face is a twisted perversion!"

"You look affright," Candler said, his lip quivering.

"You must take command," Dillahunt urged. He had never seen Candler like this. Had the man never faced a tragedy? Dillahunt was having trouble recalling.

"You look affright," Candler kept saying.

"Yes, you said that."

Nathan stood up, wincing terribly, and hobbled over to them. He still had a few splinters in his leg, but he seemed to have forgotten them for the time being. Dillahunt noticed the right side of Nathan's face for the first time. Blood was steadily flowing from a thin splinter wedged in his scalp, just above his forehead. Nathan grasped it between two fingers and hissed as he yanked it out. "Did you hear the Captain?" Nathan shouted in Candler's ear. "They're firing on us, you fool! You must take command!"

Candler just looked at Nathan. "He looks affright."

"Adams," Dillahunt said without allowing his thoughts any further deliberation. It didn't matter who Candler had been, he was clearly not that man right now. Nathan Adams was. "You're captain."

"What's that?"

"I name you my replacement, with Candler as witness . . . such as he is."

"Captain," Nathan said, his lips twisting into a smile, "you're not going to die."

"My body insists otherwise," Dillahunt moaned. "I feel its individual functions shutting down, each at a time, without the courtesy of my pardon."

"That's just pain," Nathan said.

"N-n-no," Candler sputtered, gaping in horror. "I can see it in his eyes. He's dying. He looks affright."

"You see *blood* in his eyes," Nathan said with a derisive snort.

"It's death I see," Candler sputtered.

"Shuttup!" Nathan snapped. "You cower at the sight of blood, that's all. Find me someone who does not."

"Who?"

"The surgeon!" Nathan bellowed, spitting in Candler's face. "Bring the surgeon!"

"Aye, captain," Candler replied, and scrambled down the stairs to the main deck.

"I'm not your captain!" Nathan called after him.

"Yes you are," Dillahunt insisted. He clutched Nathan's shoulder.

A cannonball sailed over the quarterdeck, trailing into the sea. "Are the men returning fire?" Dillahunt asked.

"They require no instruction there," Nathan answered. "Hornigold's men are only firing three or four cannons. Most of his crew must be onshore, and Hornigold with them."

"A fine de . . . de . . . deduction," Dillahunt gasped, his chest suddenly heavy, as though someone had set a cannonball on him. Every breath sent a fresh jolt of pain through him. One of his lungs had probably been punctured, and he was going to drown in his own blood. "Order the men to sink the bloody . . . the bloody ship . . . that killed me."

"You're going to be fine, captain."

"Enough of that. Let me die knowing you will . . . sink that ship and Hornigold will ha . . . hang for murdering Thompson and me and . . . whomever bloody else he's killed. If it's not . . . too much trouble, have Hornigold's cock removed."

Nathan frowned. "You're in shock, captain."

"I'm not. I couldn't be more . . . lucid. I want Benjamin Hornigold's . . . cock removed. Shove the dainty thing in . . . Katherine Lindsay's mouth. That woman should be used to . . . a pirate's cock in her mouth. Deliver the pair of them . . . to Woodes Rogers."

"Aye, captain."

Pain gave way to a sweeping numbness that would have been a welcome relief if only he could breathe. He inhaled, but no air entered his lungs, and he knew they were filled to the brim with blood. He hacked something thick and gooey from his throat into his mouth and felt it dribbling down his lower lip. Nathan was doing his best not to look revolted. It was surreal to be on the receiving end of that look, which Dillahunt had given more times than he cared to remember. It was his turn now. He had never been so certain of anything in his life.

He was going to die.

He struggled to think of a profound final statement, but before he could do so, he was struck by a terrible realization. He seized Nathan's collar, drawing him close and rasping into his ear. "If I should shit myself upon dying . . . see that my breeches . . . are changed."

9

CALLOWAY

"Captain's dead!"

It was the first thing she heard when she emerged from the cabin, after hastily dressing herself. Candler wailed it loud enough for everyone to hear over the chaos, flinching as a cannonball whipped over his head. Several of the crew stopped what they were doing just long enough to stare at him in shock. Young Peter Lively, a gunner, took off his hat and clutched it to his breast. Nic Lawsome, who was crouched over the bulwark with a musket, looked up in shock. Gabe Jenkins, a handsome youth with a muscular build and curly black hair, mouthed a silent prayer.

Ogle merely sniffed. "Get back to it, men. Cap's not getting any deader, but *we* might."

Without thinking, Calloway plunged forward and seized Candler. "What did you say?" she hissed, forgetting to mask her voice. Luckily he was too dazed to notice.

"You heard me well enough," he said, looking at her but not seeing her. His eyes were lost in whatever horror he had just witnessed. His golden goatee was mottled with tiny dots of red.

"How? Where?!" She shook him.

"A cannonball took apart the quarterdeck. There's blood everywhere. I just watched the best man I'll ever know die."

She shoved him away and started for the quarterdeck. "You don't want to go up there!" he called, but she ignored him. She glanced only briefly at the enemy ship and saw dark figures rushing about its deck, hurrying to load cannons. The hull was riddled with smoking holes, and the mainmast was listing, threatening to topple. The ship was in terrible shape, but its crew seemed unaware, cheering and laughing. Were they all drunk?

One of the cannons flashed. The sound followed an instant later. Calloway ducked as the cannonball whooshed far above her, tearing through the main sail.

"Aim lower and you might hit something!" Ogle shouted across.

"The next will find your blubbery arse!" someone shouted from the opposite ship, inciting laughter among their ranks. "Won't be the first time he's had balls up his arse," shouted another.

Ogle laughed bitterly, his massive pecs vibrating. "Very funny. Comedians to the end."

Calloway regained her footing and continued up the stairs. When she reached the top, her breath caught in her throat. The port rail had a massive hole in it, with splinters of wood scattered all over the deck. Jones Thompson's dead eyes stared up at the sky, mouth hanging open with a shard of wood sticking out of his throat. Nathan Adams was crouched over a body, his head hanging low. She scrambled over and shoved him aside. He fell on his rear and stared at her through a face stained with blood.

She struggled to recognize Dillahunt beneath the crimson rivulets that covered his body in an intricate web. There must have been over two dozen splinters in him, with several lodged in his face.

"It looks worse than it is," she heard Nathan say.

"How could it be any worse?" she murmured. "He's dead."

Nathan scoffed as he struggled to his feet. "Candler is an idiot. Why Dillahunt saw fit to appoint that man first mate is beyond me. No matter, though. His wailing incites the crew's wrath."

"He's alive?!"

Nathan nodded. "For the moment, anyway."

Bellamy, the surgeon, ascended to join them. He crouched beside Calloway, setting down a weathered satchel and appraising Dillahunt with dispassionate eyes. He was a lanky man with silver hair tied back in a ponytail, a narrow face and bronze skin. He wore a light brown shirt and white pants, a red sash around his waist, and three golden bracelets on each wrist. He must have been the oldest man aboard the ship, probably mid-fifty.

"Is he breathing?" Calloway demanded. "I don't think he's breathing."

"He's breathing," Bellamy said.

"Are you sure?"

Bellamy looked at her. His irises were grey, nearly a match for his hair. "Last time we spoke, you had a man's voice."

Calloway shuddered as a chill of panic ran through her. She had forgotten to mask her voice since leaving the cabin, and she had also forgotten her hat. She had been so diligent about both until now. "Don't tell anyone, please."

"It's not my concern," Bellamy said with a shrug.

"No, it's not," said Nathan, his tone suddenly very firm. "This man's life is. I am captain now, and I command you to save him."

"Promoted yourself already, have you?" Bellamy said with a wry smirk.

"He promoted me," Nathan shot back, aiming a finger at Dillahunt.

Bellamy looked to Dillahunt. "Is that true, captain?" He turned back to Nathan. "He does not dispute it."

"I'm not lying," Nathan sighed, patience lost.

"Suppose your sudden promotion conveniently lacked a witness."

"Ask Candler if you don't believe me. I doubt he'll lie. He craves the job less than I do."

Bellamy went to work on Dillahunt, his bracelets clinking as he plucked out the smaller splinters with a pair of rusty pliers from his bag. "Makes no difference to me," he muttered. "I don't need to be reminded what my duty is, but if you speak the truth, you might look to your own."

Nathan took the not-so-subtle hint. He looked at Calloway. "He's right. I'll be on the main deck with the men."

She had no idea what she was supposed to say.

He lingered for a moment, as though he wanted to say something else. He was concerned for her, maybe. A man's courtesy for a woman in danger. "Keep your head down," was all he said, and then he hurried off.

"That's good advice," Bellamy said, tossing a clutch of red splinters behind him.

"Will he live?" she said, fearing the answer. She didn't like the careless way Bellamy was tearing wood out of Dillahunt's limbs. His pliers hadn't reached the face yet. She didn't think she'd be able to watch that.

"Surface wounds, most of them," Bellamy replied. "I'll

patch them up, but I can't say he won't die of infection, and he's lost a fair deal of blood. And there's always the chance another cannonball will land on our heads and send us all to Davy Jones. Barring all that, he'll live. That is, until he dies of something else."

That didn't make her feel any better. Bellamy was notorious for his lack of a soothing bedside manner.

"Why are you here?" he asked as he tugged at a stubborn splinter wedged securely in Dillahunt's wrist. "This is no place for a girl."

"I was bored," was the only thing she could think to say. As a cannonball whooshed overhead, she realized how ridiculous that sounded.

"Bored," Bellamy rumbled. "Bored, she says! Well I hope the sight of gore alleviates your boredom." The splinter slipped free, and blood streamed from the hole, collecting in a pool beneath Dillahunt. Calloway felt lightheaded. Not moments ago she had been snuggled next to this man, naked in his arms. Bellamy droned on obliviously. "Silly girl. This is a ship, not a whorehouse."

She flinched as if physically struck. "You do not know me."

"I know you steal into his cabin every night. I have eyes. Two of them, in fact. And I'm not the only one. Some of the men were starting to question the captain's proclivities. They'll be relieved to learn your true gender. They will be so relieved, in fact, that they'll celebrate by raping you. Not that a whore is concerned with rape."

Calloway clenched her fists and pretended that didn't frighten her as much as it did, but her hands trembled uncontrollably. "This whore chooses her own clients," she bracingly replied.

"Oh, a high priced whore," he said with a raised eyebrow. "They'll like that even better. Pirates fancy expensive things they can't normally afford."

"Pirates? This is not a pirate ship."

"No, but it is crewed by many former pirates. Surely you know that."

She knew that, but she hadn't really thought about it. She had seen pirates of every shape and size in Nassau, fair and ugly. She had also met many honest sailors, and it was often hard to tell the difference. They were all the same to her.

"When a captain dies," Bellamy continued, "pirates take what was his."

"If any of them so much as touches me, they had better pray this man dies of his injuries." But she said a silent prayer of her own: *Please don't let that happen, for my sake as well as his.*

Bellamy raised the pliers to Dillahunt's face, and Calloway turned away, setting her hands on the rail that overlooked the main deck. Nathan was down there, supervising the gunners, pointing out targets. The crew seemed to have accepted his promotion without quarrel. Only a few scowled at him when he gave them an order, but they did as they were instructed. Ogle accepted every order, but the rancid look on his face indicated he would have unhealthy words with Nathan later.

A cannonball bounced across the deck, obliterating a young deckhand's right leg. The boy collapsed onto his side and stared vacantly at what remained of his leg. As comprehension grew, he loosed a low, mournful wail that gradually elevated into high-pitched shrieks, breaking only to take short gasps. Nathan stepped away from him and kept to his duty. "Captain! Captain! Captain!" the boy cried in swift succession, reaching for Nathan.

"It won't grow back," Nathan coldly replied without looking at him. "Stay down until the battle is done."

Calloway heard Nathan say something about "chainshot." A minute later, Ogle's gunnery crew fired two cannonballs at once that spiraled through the air on a three-foot chain. The chain tore through three crewmen and wrapped around a fourth man's torso, spiraling him into the water beyond. "That's it!" Nathan bellowed, clenching his lone fist. "Do that again!"

He's enjoying this, Calloway thought. *He has no idea how much he's enjoying this.*

"Captain! Captain! Captain!" cried the maimed boy. He had crawled over to Nathan and was clutching his leg.

Nathan kicked the boy away. "Crawl to safety, man!"

Two deckhands seized the one-legged boy and dragged him to a less crowded spot.

Nathan turned to the gunners. "Now put her to the bottom of the sea!" They aimed the cannons downward, firing relentlessly. The enemy ship was listing on its portside, pieces of it tearing free and crumbling into the sea. Smoke wafted from dozens of holes pitted along the hull.

Three long planks suddenly extended forward, slapping down on *Crusader's* rails. Shadowed pirates leapt onto the planks and scrambled over. *Crusader's* crew drew their pistols, firing at them. A pirate's head snapped back, and he tumbled off his plank, lost in the dark abyss between the ships. Nathan took a step back, drawing his sword. "Push those planks off! They're boarding us!"

Ogle and a few others managed to lift one of the planks, but it was heavy with the weight of encroaching pirates, and they could not slide it far enough to one side to free its purchase. "It's no good!" Ogle shouted at Nathan.

"Then kill them all!" Nathan shouted back.

Calloway looked to Bellamy and found him staring back, jaw grimly set. "You'll need this," he said, and he handed her Dillahunt's pistol. "And when that fails, you'll need this." He handed her Dillahunt's rapier. "Gun first, then sword. It's easy.

Even a girl can do it."

"That's funny," she muttered without an ounce of delight.

"I'm the funniest surgeon you'll ever meet," Bellamy quipped flatly. He drew his pistol and sword as well, standing beside her, in front of Dillahunt's limp form. "You know how to use it? The gun, I mean."

"Yes," she said. One of her patrons had shown her how to shoot rocks.

"And the sword?"

She withered. "Grip the sharp part and stick the hilt in their belly?"

"You're funny, too," Bellamy drawled.

"Why do they board?" she asked. "Surely they are too few to take us."

"They're out of options. Our new captain has done his job too well. Now they'll fight like devils, for they have nothing left to lose."

"They could surrender."

Bellamy tittered in annoyance. "A white flag would afford them a long journey back to the gallows and little else. They opt to die like pirates, and I don't blame them. It's what I would do in their place."

"Why don't they just swim for shore?"

"That swim is longer than it looks. We'd be in our boats and on top of them before they ever got there."

Five grappling hooks shot from the enemy ship like splayed fingers, four of them latching onto the rigging. Pirates swung across, hollering war cries. Two of them were shot in midair and came crashing unceremoniously onto the deck. Both were instantly overwhelmed and impaled by cutlasses. Eight of the pirates made it successfully onto *Crusader's* deck. They fired pistols and swung their swords. A tall pirate barreled down on Ogle. Their blades clashed, and Calloway was shocked to see both men grinning. Then Gabe Jenkins stuck his sword in the tall pirate's back, downing him instantly. When Jenkins pulled the sword out, there wasn't nearly as much blood as Calloway had expected. Not at first, anyway.

Ogle shoved Jenkins down to the deck, screaming, "He was mine!"

Jenkins got back to his feet, tossing a lock of curly hair out of his pretty face with an angry flick of his head. "They're always yours, Ogle!"

Seven remained.

A pirate with a red bandana thrust himself at Nathan. The newly appointed captain dodged to his left and held out his sword, letting the man sweep himself across the blade. Red bandana fell dead.

Six now.

Two pirates fought back-to-back as *Crusader's* crew converged on them. Candler skirted the edge of the swarm, jabbing his cutlass through any gap he could find. On the fourth thrust, the point of his blade found a pirate's belly. Intestines snaked out of him, collecting in shiny curls at his feet. Calloway's mouth dropped open in awe.

"Like that, do you?" Bellamy said, watching her.

She forced herself to look away. "It's gross," she lied.

Candler continued to stab the man long after he was dead. "That's for my good friend, Captain Guy Dillahunt," he declared. "God rest his soul!"

Five.

As his partner sank behind him, the next pirate's back was left undefended, and three swords plunged into him at once. The tip of one sword exploded from his chest, splashing the deck with his blood. He gawked at the blade, face slowly relieving of tension, and then he tumbled forward.

Four.

A large man—so black that Calloway had trouble keeping track of him in the night—and a thin, distinguished looking pirate were cornered between two cannons. As the crew closed on them, they exchanged glances, nodded, and dropped their weapons. "I am Francois Laurent," the thin pirate declared in a thick French accent, "and I know when I am outmatched."

"Of course you're bloody outmatched," Candler sniggered. "Was it you who killed our dear captain?"

"It is entirely possible."

The large black man chuckled at his friend.

Calloway searched for the other two pirates.

A very young, very skinny pirate escaped the swarm, ducking his head low as he made a mad dash for the quarterdeck. His cutlass was dripping red. "Stop that one!" Nathan shouted.

"He killed the cook!" someone cried.

"He skewered Nic Lawsome!" someone else said.

Calloway braced herself, aiming the gun at the stairs. She set her finger against the cold metal of the trigger. Bellamy raised his gun next to hers. "Don't worry," he assured her. "One of us is bound to hit him."

"I look worried?" The barrel of her gun shuddered as she spoke.

The boy made it as far as the second step before he was shot in the back by Candler. He collapsed and slid down the stairs, big round eyes never closing. "That's two!" Candler shouted triumphantly.

"Bah!" Bellamy spat over the rail. "That one was ours!"

Calloway sighed and lowered her gun.

One left.

She looked over the main deck. The men were glancing about, swords ready. "Anyone spot him?" Nathan asked.

"Don't know where he got off to," Jenkins said.

"He was a big one," Peter Lively added.

"Maybe he jumped overboard," Candler suggested.

"Someone check the hold," Nathan ordered. He peered up at Calloway, and then his eyes went wide.

A massive hand shot over the rail, clutched Calloway's belt, and wrenched her violently toward the edge. A bearded hulk was crawling up from the main deck, desperation in his eyes. His considerable weight leveraged her waist against the rail. She struggled to aim her pistol, but the pirate easily snatched it out of her grasp and brought the steel pommel down on her skull. The world went fuzzy, and all sound fled her ears. Dillahunt's rapier fell from her other hand. She would have fallen back, but the pirate's hand was firm around her belt. Bloodshot eyes fixated on her, lips parting from yellow teeth in a macabre grin. He flipped the pistol around and aimed it squarely at her face.

Another hand appeared from behind her, gold bracelets glinting at the wrist. Bellamy grasped the ascending pirate by the throat, shoved the barrel of his pistol into the man's right eye, and squeezed the trigger. Calloway did not hear the crack of the shot. Sparks ignited in the priming pan. The pirate's eye disintegrated, and Bellamy's pistol sank into the red hollow. Brains erupted from the back of the pirate's skull, raining down on the crew. They shielded themselves from the gore, laughing as bits of bone and brain pattered their arms.

The dead man's fingers released Calloway's belt, and he dropped off the rail, and the back of his yawning skull smacked the main deck with a nauseating *squelch*, splattering gooey bits. Calloway collapsed against Bellamy. He made no attempt to hold her, and she slid down his legs, her ass landing on his feet. He kicked her off and circled around, glowering down at her. A mask of smoke rolled over his face, trailing from the barrel of his gun. Calloway couldn't hear anything, but she could easily read the question his lips formed.

"Still bored, girly?"

10

ANNABELLE

She gave the robe a slight nudge, allowing it to slip away from her left nipple. Jethro was thoroughly distracted, trailing off mid-sentence. The wooden handle of the pistol had grown hot in her grasp, concealed beneath the sheets with the barrel aimed at his oblivious face. Jethro crossed his legs and licked his lips.

"You were saying?" Edward Teach said from behind his desk. His hand rested on a weathered copy of The Iliad, which he claimed was his favorite book, though Annabelle had never seen him read it. The curtains behind him were parted, and he was framed in the darkness beyond the stern gallery window.

Jethro cleared his throat and returned his attention to Teach. "Apologies," he wheezed. "Your muse, she's most distracting, she is." The man seemed to have trouble finding the breath to speak, but that never stopped him. When first he had entered the cabin, the setting sun revealed an older man.

Now, the dim candlelight favored him, masking the bits of grey that speckled his short hair and mustache. He had taken off his black cap and set it on the desk, and he was strumming the tails of the red ribbon with thumb and forefinger.

"Then she serves her purpose," said Charles Vane, standing tall beside Jethro, hands on the back of the other man's chair. "While your thoughts linger on plunging your cock betwixt her ripe melons, you take no notice of the gun secreted beneath those sheets."

Annabelle sighed, lifting the robe back into place. Jethro looked disappointed to be robbed of his view. Vane smiled self-assuredly.

Teach's beard twitched. "A precaution, nothing more."

"Fuck your caution," Vane spat. "Had you any, you would not pursue a man so trivial as Benjamin Hornigold."

Despite his perpetually foul temperament, Annabelle could not deny that Vane was an extremely handsome man. He had curly, shoulder-length auburn hair, hawk-like green eyes, and a chiseled jaw covered in dark stubble. One eyebrow was always arced higher than the other, and his thin lips were ever in the various stages of a smirk. He wore a forest green coat that matched his eyes, with polished gold buttons, white stockings, and strapped shoes with gold buckles. His voice flowed with gentle ease, at odds with the belligerence that escaped his lips whenever they were moving.

"Hornigold aggrieved me," Teach evenly replied. "I must right that wrong. If I permit him free reign of my ocean after betraying me and siding with Woodes Rogers, I will be looked upon as a weakling unbefitting of the name Blackbeard."

"You might have killed him before he fled," Vane suggested, his green eyes glinting in the candlelight.

"I did not know the loft of his ambition," Teach said. "Or his cowardice."

"And now he's turned pirate once more, yet your wound still festers?"

"What a man does at the end of his life does not right his prior wrongs."

Vane laughed at that. "I know a priest who promises me otherwise. I keep him very close."

"Then Hornigold is truly damned," Teach said. "Either way, I have an image to maintain."

"I care naught for images or nicknames," Vane said, pacing behind Jethro. "Neither fills my holds with plunder."

"Oh, but you're wrong," Teach said. "They fall to their knees at the very sight of me, and gold spills out of their mouths quicker than words."

"Swipe their knees out from under them and they will fall just the same," Vane countered. "You waste too much time with theatrics. When Woodes Rogers finally apprehends you—and apprehend you he will, sooner or later—can you win him over with naught but fancy speech and a smoking beard? Will you tell him, 'nay, you cannot kill me, for I am the mighty Blackbeard'?"

Teach's cheeks folded into a smile above his beard. "Are you so frightened of Governor Rogers? You, who burned a ship in his harbor?"

"*My* harbor," Vane growled.

Teach shook his head. "No longer. We'll never take Nassau again, you know that."

"I have three ships now, Edward. I've placed Jack Rackham in command of *Ranger*. For the moment, anyway. Jack is a tad impatient."

Teach cackled. "The day I chance upon a pirate without a ship named *Ranger*, I'll shave my beard. Hornigold took that name as well."

Vane rolled his eyes and persisted. "And I trust you saw my

new sloop? Smaller than *Ranger*, but quite fast."

"Aye. Impressive." Teach didn't sound very impressed.

"Sacking Nassau would require but a small fleet with two great captains at the helm of two great flagships."

"Aye," Teach replied. He lifted a goblet of wine. His eyes narrowed as he peered into the glass. "I glimpse one such man before me. Let me know when you spot the other, for he be hidden from my sight."

Vane's smirk faltered only slightly. "It's good to see madness hasn't robbed you of your sense of humor, Teach. I will sob myself to sleep when I learn of your demise."

Jethro's eyes flashed apprehensively from one man to the next. "Gentlemen," he rasped, lifting diplomatic hands. "The issue at hand eludes us." The final three words were nearly a whisper as Jethro's strained vocals broke on them.

Vane flung his hands. "The fuck it does. Hornigold is no issue. If I should chance upon him, I would not waste the time it would take to feed him to the sharks. He presents no true obstacle. He is naught but Rogers' dog, and a tiny one at that. The kind that nips at your heels. He strained his chain and found it easily snapped, and now he skitters stupidly across the Caribbean, chasing after a bit of shine. We have far greater concerns."

Teach sat back in his chair, taking a long breath. "You bring me this man," he pointed at Jethro, "under false pretense, claiming to have knowledge of the bane of my existence."

Vane gave a lavish roll of his eyes. "I present two options, Teach, yet you remain stubbornly aware only of the lesser."

"No lie, sir," Jethro insisted. "I know where Benjamin Hornigold is, I do."

"My redundant friend speaks truth," Vane sighed. "I thought presenting him might afford me the opportunity to persuade you against foolery. Divided we are vulnerable, while our enemies converge as an army, gathering our own ranks against us. Together we would be an impenetrable spear, plunging through them to strike at their heart. The sight of our combined ships bearing down on Nassau would be a tale for the ages."

Teach was unmoved. "I have given the ages many tales without your aid, Vane."

Vane shook his head in dismay. "It seems I waste my time here. Oh well. At the very least, I will be compensated for bringing you Hornigold's whereabouts."

Teach fixed Vane with a dangerous glare.

"I *will* be compensated for the information," the handsome captain insisted, meeting Teach's gaze. "You crave Benjamin Hornigold more than sense, and I have all but dropped him in your lap. I expect payment. Should I vanish mysteriously within the next hour, my quartermaster will instruct the crew to unleash hell upon you. True, we're no match for the mighty *Queen Anne's Revenge*, but we'd leave a few scars you wouldn't soon forget."

"So distrusting," Teach sighed.

Vane raised a finger. "And still alive, I might add."

Teach set his palms flat on the desk. "You will be compensated. Speak to my cooper on your way out."

"The skinny shit, lame of leg?"

"Nay, that be Narrow Ned, the boatswain. The cooper is Hemett. Squat and ugly fellow with a red sash."

"That's helpful," Vane quipped with a smirk that was even more mischievous than usual. "Now I know to look for any man on this ship who isn't me."

Jethro sniggered.

Vane turned momentarily serious. "I trust your cooper knows the value of my information?"

Teach rolled his eyes. He plucked a quill from a jar of ink

and scribbled a number across a parchment. He handed the parchment to Vane. "I seem to have misplaced my seal, but if he gives you any trouble, have him speak to me."

Vane quickly scanned the parchment and tried not to look impressed. He casually flicked his head back, tossing a loose auburn curl out of his face. "Not quite the ass-fucking I had expected."

"That can be arranged, if such things be of interest," Teach drawled. "A few of my men have questionable proclivities."

Vane's lip curled in distaste. "Seems every ship has a few degenerates. I pretend not to notice."

Teach looked weary of conversation. "Don't let me keep you."

"No more smalltalk?" Vane made a sad face.

"Not everyone relishes the sound of your voice as much as you, Charles."

Vane inclined his head. "Very well, then. Give my regards to Queen Anne, when you see her. I hear her tits were as great as coconuts, and her juices twice as supple. No doubt she spends her afterlife impatiently awaiting your arrival, legs spread and thighs dripping." He adopted a regal, feminine voice. "'Oh, my dear Edward, how can I ever repay you for murdering all those innocent people in my good name? Come, rest that bushy beard of yours betwixt my thighs, but do extinguish those fuses first! I'll not have all that smoke filling my royal cunt! It's crowded enough in there as it is.'"

If Teach was amused, it didn't show behind his beard. "Goodbye, Charles."

Vane managed to frown and smirk at the same time. "I stand corrected. Madness *has* stolen your humor. And I had rehearsed that bit for days." He turned to Jethro. "And you, Jethro, have exhausted your usefulness on this little stint. Should you find yourself in a cell again, do not expect me to come to your aid."

Jethro nodded. "I'm grateful you did as much as you did."

"Oh, fuck off. You'll piss the favor away as you have every other." Vane favored Annabelle with a bow before leaving, not bothering to close the door behind him.

An awkward silence followed. Jethro broke it. "Going to miss his company, I will."

"Dishonorable wretch of a man," Teach sneered. "Does he still cheat his crew out of their fair portion?"

"They've come to expect no better. I hear he tortured the carpenter's boy just last week. Suspected him o' stealing a silver."

"Despite my affinity for torture," Teach said, "it be a thing best not turned on one's own crew. They'll have his head someday."

"I'm not so sure," Jethro sighed. "Fear him, they do. And even a stunted share o' Vane's fortune is greater than a fair share on most ships."

Teach finished his wine and dabbed at his beard with a handkerchief. "Enough about Vane. My thoughts fall to Hornigold, as so often they do of late. A malady soon to be remedied, thanks be to present company." Teach stood and poured Jethro a goblet of wine, handing it to him. "Tell me, how did you happen upon this information?"

Jethro sipped at his wine. His brow creased, and Annabelle suspected he didn't care for the vintage. He set the goblet down. "During my . . . holiday . . . in Nassau, I met a man destined for the gallows. Went by name o' Henry, he did. Served with Griffith on *Harbinger*."

Annabelle had only been half-listening to all this, but the name *Harbinger* jarred her attention. A chill coursed her spine as she recalled Edward Livingston's sadistic face.

"He was very talkative, he was, 'specially after his young

companion agreed to help Woodes Rogers track Benjamin Hornigold and Katherine Lindsay."

"Lindsay?" Teach thought for a moment as he sank into his chair. "The woman with the lofty reward on her head?"

"The very same," Jethro wheezed. "She and Hornigold went after some treasure Griffith supposedly stashed away on an unmapped island before his untimely death, God rest him. Henry's cellmate bought his life by agreeing to lead Guy Dillahunt to the island and capture Hornigold. Henry didn't take kindly to being left behind, and spilled everything to me before they carried him off to his death. I have the island's latitude put to memory, I do."

Teach was grinning. "Dillahunt. That man does not quit once set upon a task. Hornigold's chances slim by the minute."

"Aye," Jethro agreed. "It's possible Dillahunt has already apprehended Hornigold."

"Then we must apprehend Dillahunt."

Jethro nearly spit out his wine. "Apart from the man who just left, there's only one other you do not want to engage in combat with, and that's Guy Dillahunt."

Teach smiled. "Dillahunt's ship will sink as easily as any other. The trick be to weaken the beast from the inside before I ever fire a shot. Weasels work beneath Dillahunt's very feet. I employ as many weasels as Vane, if not more. You should know the value of weasels better than anyone, seeing how easily you escaped your cell."

"I see your point," Jethro conceded. "But the trouble with weasels is notifying them when it comes time to strike. Easy to free a man from a cell. Not so easy to notify a man at sea. You would have to get close to *Crusader*, and her guns would do far too much damage."

"A solution has yet to present itself," Teach admitted, "but that does not mean there isn't one. Who was your informant's cellmate?"

"A one-armed boy by name of Nathan Adams. Stubborn lad, that one."

Annabelle sat up in the bed, not bothering to secure her robe as it slipped away again. "What did you just say?"

Both men stared at her. "I said he's stubborn," Jethro replied, his eyes drifting downward.

"No, that's not . . . what did you say his name was?"

"Nathan Adams. You're familiar with the lad?"

"I was *very* familiar with him," she said without thinking. Then she glanced sheepishly at Teach. He gazed apathetically at her, and she immediately felt stupid for thinking he would care.

"Small world," Jethro said, eyes fixated on her breasts.

"Too small," she said, covering herself.

Something changed in Teach's gaze. Apathy surrendered to a curious sparkle. "How long did you know him?"

"We spent a month together."

The candlelight glinted in his pupils. "The boy fancied you?"

"He seemed to, for a time. I was his first woman. He said very sweet things and bought me equally sweet baubles. He demanded that I take no other man to bed while I was with him, and he paid handsomely to ensure his terms were met. Then he returned to sea, but not before . . . " She trailed off, not wanting to utter the name of the man who had raped and maimed her.

Teach leaned toward Jethro, and Jethro leaned forward with hyperbolic attentiveness. "Stunted romances often prove the most potent," Teach mused. "It's only when lust be afforded the time to gestate that love falters. A romance cut short, now that be a frustrating thing. The mind lingers on what it cannot have, God knows I know."

"Aye," Jethro said, nodding his head with a flaring grin, as though Teach had just imparted the meaning of the universe.

"But I haven't thought of him in some time," Annabelle protested. It was true. The memory of Nathan went hand-in-hand with that of Edward Livingston, as one had followed immediately after the other. She could not banish one memory without banishing the next.

"Nay, I suspect you haven't," Teach said. "The boy, on the other hand, may not share your ambivalence."

"It was many months past," she said with a dismissive snort. "He's had many whores by now, no doubt."

"There are few whores that look like you, my dear," Teach reminded her.

Jethro's eyes widened as a thought struck him. "Indeed not," he said. "Forgive me, but what was your name, girl? I know you told me already, but so many years o' sun beating upon my skull have not been kind to my memory."

"I hope your mind does not falter in recalling Hornigold's location," Teach bristled.

"I was only being modest on account of sparing the lady's feelings," Jethro replied, gesturing wildly at Annabelle and toppling his goblet. Wine rolled over the desk toward Teach, soiling maps and colliding with The Iliad. Teach frantically snatched up the book, gave it a fierce shake, and rubbed it against his coat. He glanced crossly at Jethro, frowning through his beard.

Jethro looked horrified, quickly dabbing wine off the desk with his sleeve. "I'm so sorry, captain."

"It's done," Teach said, setting the book on a dry side of the desk. "You were saying?"

Jethro sat back down and fretted with his sleeves, which were dripping wine. "Her name did not seem o' much import until now. I'm afraid I did not put it to memory."

"Annabelle," Annabelle said. "My name is Annabelle."

"My god," Jethro gasped. "The boy mentioned you, he did."

"Now you're lying," Annabelle said. She got out of the bed and held the pistol at her side.

Jethro observed the weapon respectfully. "It's no lie, missy. He said something about never seeing his Annabelle again. He went on at some length. Even said your name in his sleep, he did."

"*His* Annabelle?" She said, stunned.

"That's right. Destined for the gallows, he was, and at times quite downtrodden."

"Downtrodden?" She had never heard the word.

"It's a fancy way of saying he was sad," Jethro replied with a condescending smile.

Annabelle looked at Teach. He was sitting back, staring sourly at his red-stained book. His gleaming blue eyes slowly lifted until they met hers. She had seen the look many times, but never focused on her. She didn't like it.

"Annabelle," Teach said at last, "would you excuse us."

Annabelle hesitated. "Where should I go?" She knew very few of the crew and did not feel like mingling.

"See that Captain Vane is satisfied with his reward."

She stared at him. "Fully satisfied?"

He nodded slowly.

Jethro tittered. Teach glared at him. Jethro cleared his throat and made a somber face. "Apologies. A wayward musing entered the mind, unrelated to present conversation."

Annabelle set the pistol on the bed and straightened her robe. She left without looking back, gently closing the door behind her. She descended to the cut-down forecastle, trying not to think about whatever Teach was planning for her.

She found two of Vane's men, one tall and lanky and the

other squat and muscular, loitering before the broad ramp that had been extended between *Queen Anne's Revenge* and Vane's recently acquired sloop, *Valiant*. "What's your purpose, missy," said the squat man. He had a shiny bald head and deep-set, beady eyes that were nearly swallowed by the bulging folds of his face.

"I'm looking for Charles Vane, by order of Blackbeard."

The two men exchanged glances. "Vane's in his cabin," said the tall man. "Generally he don't fancy intrusions, but for you I wager he'll make an exception."

The two men moved out of the way, and Annabelle smiled sweetly at each of them as she stepped onto the ramp. She moved carefully across, lifting her robe slightly so she wouldn't trip and tumble into the black water below. She brushed past several gawking crewmembers, smiling at all of them along the way. "Captain's quarters, please?" she asked a heavyset young deckhand with rosy red cheeks and an innocent face. He stammered all over himself before pointing her in the right direction. "Thank you," she replied sweetly, and his cheeks flushed a deeper shade of red.

She did not bother to knock. She knew what type of man Vane was. He liked initiative in a woman. She swung the door wide, and her mouth fell open.

Vane was seated behind his desk at the opposite side of the cabin, one hand atop a painting of a nude woman, the other beneath the desk, stroking fervently. His coat was discarded on the bed, and his white shirt was hanging open, chest glistening with sweat. He looked up. If he was embarrassed, he failed to show it. He stood with his pants down to his knees. He seemed unashamed of his erect manhood. "I didn't expect you so soon," he said with a smile.

Annabelle turned her look of shock into one of pleasant surprise. She was good at that. She closed the door behind her.

"I hope you haven't finished," she said, slinking toward him. She slid her fingers down her cleavage, parting the robe from her breasts. Vane's lustful gaze fell between her legs as the robe slipped away. She watched as he grew harder. "I think you'll prefer me to a painting." She trailed a finger over the rough canvas of the nude woman as she rounded the desk to join Vane on the other side. He seized her waist, crushing her to him and kissing her. His tongue worked its way into her mouth, locking with hers. Her breasts mashed against his powerful chest. Her fingers found his cock, giving him a sharp squeeze. He gasped excitedly into her mouth. He slapped both hands against each cheek of her ass, hefting her onto the painting and splaying her across the desk. He parted her legs and shoved himself into her, setting his hands on her breasts and thrusting violently. Every thrust racked her entire body, like lightning surging through her.

She started to lift up, but he clutched her neck and forced her back down, glaring at her. "Don't you fucking move," he snarled.

"Then get down here," she said. She grabbed a handful of his auburn hair and jerked his face toward hers. He let out a little *yelp*, and then grinned in surprise. Both their mouths were open, but held an inch apart, breath hot on the other's face.

He pulled out halfway through climax, seizing himself and spilling the remainder of his seed into her naval with several firm strokes. He fell back into his chair, panting.

She remained flat on her back as his fluids streamed down either side of her stomach and saturated the painting beneath her. "Take me with you," she gasped, still out of breath. She rubbed at the soreness between her legs. "I'm wasted on him."

Vane looked mildly concerned. "He does not fuck you?"

She shook her head. "I am a puppet for his schemes and nothing more. He's plotting something nefarious right now, with me at the heart of it."

"And you will do whatever he commands?"

She propped herself up on her elbows. "I think he would kill me if I didn't."

He fixed her with a pointed gaze. "Is that why you came here? Because he told you to?"

An involuntary smile crept across her lips. "Well, some commands are easier than others."

He leaned forward. "What if he told you to kill me? Would you do it?"

She gnawed on her lower lip as she considered that. "I've never killed anyone before."

"Now there's a curious reply," Vane said, fascinated.

"How so?"

"If I asked twenty people if they would kill someone, ten would say they couldn't do it, though some might find it easier than they think if pressed into action. The other half would say of course they would, though some might find it more difficult than they imagined. But you . . . you simply say you've never done it. No denial or feigned resolve. In my considerable experience, that is the sign of a true killer." His lips pulled away from his teeth in an evil grin.

She sat up and slowly leaned toward him. "Take me with you."

"Would that I could," he sighed. "I have enough enemies as it is, and don't wish to make one of Edward Teach. You are right to fear him. Even from afar, he is dangerous. And if he would kill you for disobeying him, imagine what he would do to me for indulging your disobedience?"

"One day he'll be dead. You said it yourself."

Vane stood and lifted his pants, tucking his shirt back into place. "Aye, his time is running out, but even with a sliver of life he is not to be underestimated. Like all men, he will meet his end. Until that day, I shall dream of your bountiful tits every night, and curse the morning sun when it stirs me from slumber."

She looked away, making her disappointment plain.

"Do thank him for the reward," he said. "You *are* preferable to a palm and a painting."

"I'll relay your joy," she flatly replied, falling back down on the desk.

His eyes fell between her thighs. "I don't believe you've quite finished."

"It's difficult for me." She hadn't had an orgasm since she was raped. She wasn't sure it was even possible anymore.

"Lucky for you, I fancy a challenge," Vane replied. He sat back down and grabbed her by the legs, sliding her toward him and ducking his head between her thighs.

"Shouldn't I clean up first?" she protested, but already he was prodding her. The tip of his tongue found the right spot and lingered there, working diligently. She shuddered and clawed at the painting.

He lifted his head only for a moment. "No need. I relish the taste of myself."

11

HORNIGOLD

Hornigold's nose throbbed in agonizing waves. He stripped off his shirt, dipped it in the water, and pressed it to his face, but the blood would not stop seeping from his nostrils.

Over the bunched cloth he spied her. She was waist deep in a little black lake nestled in the rock beneath a long, narrow waterfall that drained from the summit. Her left cheek had a thin gash, but he doubted it was anywhere near as bad as his face must have looked. It was still too dark to see his reflection in the water, and he was glad for that.

The sky was gradually lightening, with deep purple hues intruding upon the eastern horizon. He wasn't sure how far they had walked. After their quarrel, neither felt like returning to camp. They had ventured out here to find treasure, and they weren't about to leave empty handed after dealing each other so much pain. At least they could agree on something.

He glared jealously at his sword, which was sticking through her belt. "This is mine now," she had informed him, after crushing his nose. She let him carry the shovel, but had wisely lingered behind him and maintained a safe distance as they walked. The torch had extinguished in the sand, so they had to let their eyes adapt to the darkness before they got very far.

She had taken off her black bandana and was washing her hair, not that any blood could be detected in those red tresses. Infuriatingly, the slice in her cheek somehow added confidence to her expression. It slanted from her cheekbone to one of the tiny creases flanking her mouth. *She actually has dimples,* he realized. Barely detectable, but there they were. She must have smiled a lot as a child.

She shuffled out of the water, breeches wet and tight around her hips, arms raised as she fastened her bandana over the top of her head. He could clearly see the small dark circles of her nipples poking against her wet white shirt as she stretched. A rush of blood surged through him. He turned away as yet another jolt of pain pulsated through his nose. His face was probably ruined forever, yet she was more fetching than ever. He hated her.

She will let her guard down, sooner or later, and then I'll take my sword back.

She stepped in front of him, setting a hand on her hip. "It's nearly dawn. Your nose looks terrible. We should get back so you can get it looked at."

"The doctor's dead, remember?" He was revolted by how nasally he sounded.

"I'm sure someone can patch you up."

"No," he insisted. "It's fine."

He lowered the shirt to reveal his face, and her lips peeled away from her teeth in disgust. She quickly looked away, adopting a vacant look and scratching the back of her neck.

"Is it really that bad?" he asked.

She shrugged, not looking at him. "We should press on." And then she added meekly, "Soon you'll have enough to afford a new nose."

He took a step forward, rage seething in his breast. The shovel was sticking out of the sand before him, where he had thrust it, and he had half a mind to grab it and lunge at her before she could draw her sword. He wouldn't make the same mistake again. This time he would beat her senseless before raping her. And after that, maybe he would drown her in the lake and leave her corpse to rot, with fishes nibbling her beauty away. "You're a dreadful person."

She set her hand on the hilt of the sword in her belt. "Only on the inside." She cocked her head keenly. "Would that I could say the same of you."

His teeth mashed together, and the pressure sent another torrent of pain into his nose. He did his best to ignore it, but water lined his eyes. "I can only imagine what horrors dwell inside you."

She bubbled laughter. "And only hours ago you were so desperate to get inside me. Or did I misread that? You were so very subtle, dashing me with a shovel, and all."

"Not nearly subtle enough, it seems," Hornigold grated. "I should have dashed harder. How is it you are not hunched in agony?"

"No need to question your strength, Benjamin," she said, rubbing the side of her head. "My skull still throbs from the blow, but the pain is slight compared to the memory of a pirate chewing through my ear."

"I should have finished what that man started and gone for the other."

She ruffled her hair and then straightened her shirt, fitting it back into her breeches where it had come loose. "There are many things you should have done, and far too many things you should *not* have done." She opened her hand to a narrow path leading away from the waterfall. "After you."

They followed the little path around the mountain, a steep crag on one side and dense jungle on the other. Hornigold crushed the shirt against his nose for a long time, and finally it seemed to stop bleeding. He sniffed too sharply and a stab of pain shot into his skull, as if someone had jammed an icicle up one of his nostrils. He leaned against the rocky wall, hissing through his teeth.

"You look like you're going to fall over," Lindsay said from behind.

The thought of his hands around her throat as her face turned purple, squeezing until her eyes bulged and all life escaped her, was all that kept him standing. His head was impossibly heavy, his back ached, and his legs were unsteady and numb. He would not collapse in front of her, not when she strutted about without a care, seemingly oblivious to pain.

"I can stand just fine, thank you," he said.

He lowered his head. A tiny droplet of blood splattered the sand. His nose hadn't stopped bleeding after all. He frowned. "We're close."

"Are you sure, or are you just following your nose?"

He threw a caustic look her way. Her head was down, hair in front of her face as she giggled softly. "Sorry. I couldn't help myself."

He pointed down at the sand before him. "There are footprints here."

Her head shot up. She rushed over to his side, hand firm on the hilt of her sword. *My sword,* Hornigold reminded himself.

A tree arched above, leaning against the cliff face to form a protective canopy that must have kept the footprints from being completely washed away. The hollows were soft around the edges, but the imprints of boot heels were unmistakable.

Hornigold exchanged a glance with Lindsay. His pain was momentarily forgotten. They continued in the same direction, finding hollowed prints here and there, wherever there was tree cover.

The scattered prints eventually led them to a beach that Hornigold assumed was on the opposite side of the island, for he could not see his ship anywhere on the horizon. The sky was brightening fast, a violet veil spreading from the east. The footprints vanished entirely in the sand, and Hornigold was once again acutely aware of the throbbing in his face. He sighed in frustration, but Lindsay seemed unworried. She searched about until she found another path into the jungle, then motioned for him to follow her in.

He delved in after her, whacking at massive leaves with the shovel. The leaves always swayed right back with a vengeance, smacking him in the face. If only he had his sword, he would shorten these stubborn leaves and maybe Lindsay's head along with them.

She was ahead of him now, focused on the ground, pushing leaves out of her path. "More prints," she said. "We're getting close."

"Yes, but close to what? One chest? There are many."

"One confirms the rest."

"Then you admit you are uncertain there are any chests at all!"

She turned, scowling at him. "I admit nothing. I already know what we'll find here, Benjamin. The evidence is trailed beneath your feet, yet still you doubt me. Your skepticism puzzles me, considering how easily you were coerced out of your duties."

"A man makes mistakes."

"You make more than most, but taking me at my word was not one of them."

"We'll see," he grumbled.

They continued on in silence. Hornigold's anger mounted with each leaf he shoved out of his face. The ground began to slope upward, presumably toward the summit. Hornigold's legs burned and his calves ached. He was starting to think they might end up right back where they started. He glimpsed the dim blue sky through the jungle canopy and one faint star that would be swallowed by the light of the sun in the next half hour. How long had they been out here? Six hours? His men were probably waking by now, wondering where he had gotten off to. Or maybe they no longer cared, and they were searching for the treasure on their own. Maybe they'd found a few chests already and were preparing to leave without him. More for them.

Just then the jungle opened onto a small clearing, little more than ten paces in diameter, where the parted canopy gave view of the sky and the summit towering above. The ground was caked with dried mud, strangely matted at the center. "Shovel marks," Lindsay nearly shouted, grinning at him.

Hornigold wasted no time. He plunged his shovel into the center of the clearing, where the mud formed a small mound. The dirt was thick and tightly packed. The first dozen or so thrusts were the hardest, and the muscles in his arms quickly started to ache. All the while, Lindsay just paced beside him, watching impatiently and biting a thumbnail. He glanced sideways and saw her eyes gleaming hungrily. She had found her prize, but she would have been nowhere without him. *Let her be happy. Let her think all is well. Let her drop her guard. And then strike.* He would have revenge for being humiliated. Lindsay would never leave this island.

Digging seemed easier the deeper he went. Maybe the ground was softening, or maybe he was just getting used to the repetitive motion. Then his shovel made a soft, squishy sound.

Hornigold glimpsed something pink and red and soft beneath the shovelhead. He tossed the shovel aside and dropped into the three foot pit he had dug, kneeling to inspect whatever he had uncovered. He poked at the object and recoiled as juicy flesh slid from bone. A nauseating aroma filled his nostrils. He saw a face in the dirt. A face that his shovel had cleaved nearly in half, from ear to ear. The eyes were gone, empty hollows packed with dirt. The jaw was gaping open, much of the right cheek had rotted away, and rows of teeth were visible through the holes. Stringy blonde hair tumbled from a dented scalp. The hole in the center of the dead man's forehead was unmistakable. An earthworm slithered out of the hole and dangled from it, glistening wet.

Hornigold leaned to one side and heaved violently, until the contents of his stomach erupted from his mouth. The vomit collected in a mottled brown pool beside the dead man's face. Hornigold scrambled out of the pit and leaned against one of the trees on the perimeter of the little clearing.

"Oh my god," Lindsay gasped. "That's Cunningham."

Hornigold wiped chunks of food from his lips and pressed his forehead against the tree. He focused on the texture of the trunk, hoping that would distract his mind from what he had just viewed. "You're sure?" he managed.

"I dunno who else it would be," she said.

Hornigold heard a *plop*. She had dropped into the pit, and her arms were moving. The shovel was beside the pit. Now was his chance, the best he was likely to get. Lindsay had said Cunningham died because he discovered who she was. He had died for *her*. It was only fitting that she share the same grave. Hornigold pushed himself away from the tree and shambled toward the pit, eyes locked on the shovel.

"Yes," she said. "It's Cunningham." She continued moving her arms, her brow creasing beneath the bandana. Hornigold bent down and wrapped his fingers around the shovel. She kept on moving her arms, focused on her task. He moved closer, until the tips of his boots were at the edge of the pit. She was bent over the corpse, her neck exposed as her hair fell away on either side. She grunted as she lifted the corpse out of the dirt, moving it aside as best she could.

The shovel fell from Hornigold's grasp, landing at his feet. "Is that what I think it is?"

Lindsay leered over her shoulder. "I'm not sure you're cut out for this sort of work, Benjamin. It's a good thing you haven't killed me yet, like you've been planning, because you'd probably walk away without digging any deeper." Before she could goad him further, he leapt down to join her. He hefted Cunningham's corpse out of the pit. The skin sank beneath his fingers, and he felt another wave of nausea rising to his throat, but he had nothing left to retch. He helped Lindsay scoop dirt off the lid of the black chest. The sky was bright blue by the time they had cleared enough dirt from the lid. Lindsay crawled out of the pit so Hornigold could open the lid. The unearthly golden glow from within nearly blinded him. He stared at it for a long time, but comprehension of the abundant treasure before him failed to settle in.

"And there are twelve more like this one," he heard Lindsay say.

Hornigold crawled out of the pit and stood beside her. "Let's get back," he said. "I'll need another man to help carry this."

They retraced their steps back to the beach and then walked the perimeter of the island. Hornigold's paranoia had flooded out of him, leaving room for a giddiness he had not felt since he was a boy. "Lindsay," he said, glancing back to make sure she was still following.

"Benjamin."

"I want to apologize."

"For trying to rape me?"

"Well, for that," he admitted sheepishly, "and for doubting you."

"Oh yes, the *doubt* was the most frightful part," she replied, oozing sarcasm. "The attempted rape was regrettable, but the nagging doubt is what kept me on edge. Far more troublesome than repeated attempts to creep upon my flank in hopes of dashing my brains in with a shovel. God only knows what you intended to do with my corpse."

Pain spiked through his nose as he gnashed his molars. "We've dealt each other a fair amount of injury. I'd say we're even, wouldn't you?"

"Is this still an apology?"

"Forget I said anything."

"Forgotten."

It was midday by the time they saw figures dotting the beach. There were far too many of them. Hornigold stopped in his tracks. He scanned the horizon until he saw a ship much larger than his, with a mermaid on the bow. His beloved *Ranger* was nowhere in sight.

"That's not your ship," Lindsay said.

"Of course that's not my bloody ship," he snapped. "And that's not my bloody crew." He turned, glaring at her. "How did they find me?"

Her eyes darted back and forth. "I have no idea," she said.

He jabbed an accusatory finger at her nose. "You're lying. You have *some* idea, I think."

Lindsay shrugged. She was quite good at looking mystified and helpless when she needed to. "I suggest we get off the beach."

"It's a bit late for that," came a surly voice from behind.

Hornigold and Lindsay spun in their tracks. Two very tall,

very mean looking men with orange bandanas were aiming pistols at their heads. They were shirtless, extremely tan, and barefoot. Their harsh features were uncannily similar, with protruding brows like cavemen, square jaws, and long black hair.

Hornigold's head fell, the inevitability of the situation overwhelming him with despair. He somehow managed to keep his knees from buckling. He had lost everything, but he would keep what remained of his dignity, all the way to the gallows.

He said, "Kate, meet Dick and Richard Maynard. You'll forgive me if I can't recall which is Dick and which is Richard. They're twins. And they work for Guy Dillahunt."

The Maynard on the left grinned. "That's right, missy, and Guy Dillahunt works for the governor."

The Maynard on the right grinned. "And the governor would like a word with the both of you."

12

NATHAN

Richard Maynard shoved Katherine Lindsay to her knees in the sand, tore off her bandana, and clutched a handful of her fiery red hair, jerking back her head so that her eyes met Nathan's. "Hello Nathan," she said, lips twitching into a pained smile. "I missed you."

Her hair was somehow more vibrant than he remembered, tumbling down around her face in wild, messy curls. Her face yielded less cares, in spite of the fresh slice that reddened her cheek. Her skin was darker than the last time he saw her, and anyone who didn't know her would think she had a bit of islander in her. The patches of dirt scattered about her face and arms did nothing to diminish her beauty. She had come so far from the skinny, pale, frightened girl tied to *Harbinger's* mast, teetering on the brink of death.

Nathan nodded to Richard. "Bind her hands." Maynard released Katherine's hair and produced a sash, turning her around and gathering her wrists. "From behind," Nathan urged. Richard nodded, securing her hands behind her back.

"What's my reward up to?" she asked casually. The question came off as a careless muse, forcing Nathan to swallow a surge of anger. She had left him to die rather than return to London, and now she pretended as though her fate was of no concern.

Nathan ground his teeth. "You look surprisingly healthy, Katherine. I thought I'd be returning a corpse to Woodes Rogers."

"It's just 'Kate' now. And you're as dashing as ever, I see. I'm sorry the arm hasn't grown back."

He winced. "Neither have your manners."

"I fear I left those somewhere in Griffith's cabin."

"You certainly didn't bring them to Nassau," he said, allowing a touch of resentment to filter through.

She smiled obliviously. "Still sore about that?"

"Not as sore as I expected to be," he replied, rubbing his throat.

Her smile grew. "You're funnier than I remember. Escaping death works wonders on the wit."

"And your company has scarcely improved."

Benjamin Hornigold glared at Nathan as he was dragged by Dick Maynard toward one of the tents *Ranger's* crew had erected along the beach, where he would be chained along with the rest that had survived the battle. His nose was black and caked with dried blood. "Where is Captain Dillahunt?" he shouted. "I demand to see Captain Dillahunt!"

Nathan ignored the man's annoying bleating.

"That's a good question," Kate said.

"The captain is incapacitated, for the moment. I've assumed his duties until he recovers."

Kate smiled knowingly. "How thoughtful of you."

Nathan had a mind to strike her, though he had never hit a

woman before. "Not everyone is moved by nefarious motives."

She almost looked wounded. "You think me nefarious?"

"You left me to die."

Her face flushed nearly as red as her hair. "When I meet a man who doesn't blame me for every stupid decision he ever made, that will be the day I perish of shock. I warned you, Nathan. God help me, I *pleaded* with you not to do it, and you did it anyway. You put yourself in a precarious situation and expected me to hand myself over and bail you out of it."

"It was the least you could do. I saved your life!"

"And not a day later, you plotted to sell me so you could find your way back to . . . to what? Some strumpet you thought you were in love with? I'm no object to be bartered in order to satiate your lust."

He thrust a foot forward, his boot scattering sand against her legs. "My life was at stake! Is returning to London so awful?"

"Yes!" she blurted, her voice breaking, water lining her eyes. She had not exhausted her tears after all. He almost felt sorry for her all over again, but reminded himself who he was dealing with. He would not abandon his resolve that easily. If she'd had her way, he'd be a rotting corpse dangling from the end of a noose right now, on display as a warning to anyone with aspirations of piracy.

"Perhaps I was misguided," he admitted with a bitter nod. "Maybe it was wrong of me to go against your will, but I was desperate. Was my *life* not more important than your selfish desires?"

"A man calls it selfish. A woman calls it freedom."

This absurdity was more than he could stand. "You call *this* freedom? Throwing in with pirates who would rape you at any moment?"

"No one has raped me, though it's kind of you to concern

yourself with my welfare. That's all you've ever been concerned with, isn't it? Kind acts with no thought of reward." She snorted loudly. "You're truly one man in a thousand, Nathan Adams."

He could no longer match her gaze. He pulled away and faced the ocean, great and blue and stretching on and on. Annabelle was out there somewhere, he knew it. The key to finding her was finally in his grasp. He had been so sure he hated Katherine Lindsay, and now he was finding it difficult to recall the vindication for that hatred. The sun beat heavily upon the crown of his head. His fingers started for an itch running along his left arm, and then he remembered that there was nothing to itch.

"Will you give me to Rogers?" she asked. Her voice was laced with anxiety. She cared more than she wanted to let on. *Of course she cares.*

"You are not the only prize on this island," he answered.

"Then you're not Rogers' man?" She sounded hopeful.

"I don't know what I am, Kather—Kate. I'm still trying to figure that out. When I do, you'll be the last to know."

Nathan motioned to Richard Maynard. "Take her to the tent with Dillahunt and stand watch outside. I don't want her touched, is that clear?"

Richard cackled. "What do you think we are, pirates?"

"I think you are men," Nathan said. "Should any ill fortune befall this woman, Woodes Rogers will know the name of the man who did it."

"Then we're going back to Nassau?" Richard said, puzzled. "What about the treasure?"

Nathan smiled. "Bellamy tells me Dillahunt needs a few days to recover before it's safe to travel. What we do in the meantime is no business of Rogers'."

Richard liked the sound of that, grinning broadly. "Aye,

captain." He lifted Kate to her feet and prodded her toward the largest of the tents, which Nathan guessed had belonged to Hornigold. Nathan watched until she descended under the tarp.

He strolled to the prisoner tent, ducking inside. Seven men were chained in a circle, plus Hornigold. Hornigold tried to stand when he saw Nathan, but his hands were chained behind his back, and he was jerked to a halt before his knees could straighten. A puff of air popped from his lips as he landed on his ass.

"Don't get up," Nathan said.

"Dillahunt sends a boy in his place," Hornigold grumbled.

"Consider yourself lucky," Nathan replied. "Dillahunt had very specific requests regarding you, which I don't have the fortitude or stomach to carry out." Nathan hoped he wouldn't be considered a mutineer for not removing Hornigold's cock.

"Guy Dillahunt would not chain me up like some mangy dog."

Hornigold's men cackled at that. "Captain always was too good for us dogs, wasn't he?"

"Aye, never could be bothered to eat with us or nothin'."

"That redheaded strumpet made a better captain, she did."

Nathan quieted them with a raised hand. "If you so desire your captain's company, take comfort knowing he will spend his final moments with the rest of you."

Their laughter died down as they seemed to remember their predicament. "Well that just soiled the mood," grumbled a fat prisoner named Farley.

"Where's Ryan?" Hornigold demanded, doing his best to ignore his perfidious crew. "Where's the boatswain?"

"If he's not here, he's dead," Nathan said. "There are two others we captured when we took your ship. You all will be joining them soon. They're in our brig, if you could call those cages such. A black man and a French man. Neither of them named Ryan. By my math, all but nine of your men are dead. Those that were smart enough not to shoot at us as from the beach sit beside you now. A few fled into the jungle. We'll keep an eye out for them, but if we don't find them, I'm not concerned. We have the man we were sent to find."

"My ship!" Hornigold remembered. "I did not see my ship. Where . . . where is it?"

"Oh, it's out there," Nathan assured him with a smile. "It's just beneath the water. Your crew fired upon us as we sailed in. Captain Dillahunt was wounded. He's lucky to be alive, in fact."

"We found a chest," Hornigold exclaimed, wasting no time. "A fortune beyond your wildest dreams!"

"Yes, I know," Nathan said with a dismissive wave.

Hornigold frowned, perplexed. "Lindsay told you? What a monstrous bitch! Is there nothing she won't do to save her—"

"Lindsay didn't need to say anything," Nathan interrupted, amused at Hornigold's fervor. "I crewed aboard *Harbinger.*"

Hornigold blinked. "Under Jonathan Griffith?"

"The very same."

Hornigold sighed in dismay as what little hope remained fled his eyes. "You crewed with Katherine Lindsay. Now I see why she isn't chained up in here with the rest of us. You're in league with the bitch."

"Hardly," Nathan chuckled. "She's to be returned to her family."

Hornigold's eyes filled with a murderous rage. "She's not to be executed?"

Nathan's chuckle became a laugh. "Of course not. She's a woman lost at sea."

"A criminal, far worse than any pirate! A demon!"

"A demon created by pirates," Nathan agreed. "She would

not have come this far without the aid of men like you."

Hornigold spat in the sand, his face contorting terribly. "She embraces her misfortune! You should have seen her instigate my crew into looting a vessel that came to our aid after a fierce storm!"

Nathan traded a glance with one of Hornigold's crew, a man who had surrendered willingly and politely introduced himself as Harrow. "We was pirates again," Harrow said with a shrug.

Nathan smirked at Hornigold. "You fled Nassau without leave of the governor. It looks as though your crew understood the implications of that crime, even if you did not."

"I would not have fled if not for that fire-haired cunt! Her words were topped with sugar, cloaking a venomous bite."

"I always thought her words more bitter than sweet."

"Then she presents you with an altered face."

Nathan shook his head. "Lindsay is many things, but a chameleon is not one of them. I think your memory sweetens her words. Maybe you weren't looking at her lips."

"A woman speaks with more than her mouth," Hornigold sneered. "Spoken or not, Lindsay makes promises she has no intention of keeping."

"You're pathetic." The words escaped Nathan's lips before he could withhold them. He was utterly revolted by this man.

The puffy black folds under Hornigold's eyes wrinkled painfully. "What?"

A captive with dark skin ardently shook his head, as though the foundations of everything he had built his life upon had just been torn asunder. "This is no way to talk to the captain," he murmured. Apparently Hornigold hadn't lost *everyone's* confidence.

"What did you just say to me?" Hornigold seethed. His nose deepened its shade of purple.

"I called you pathetic," Nathan answered.

The bruise seemed to be spreading from the center of Hornigold's face like a dark cloud. Nathan glimpsed the shadow of a once formidable man within those furious eyes. "On equal ground, boy, I would see your throat opened and your blood gush freely upon the sand."

"Life rarely affords opponents equal footing," Nathan replied. "A pirate should know that by now. I am only missing one arm, while the two of yours are secured behind your back. Yet even if they were not, you would claim Katherine Lindsay manipulates them. You truly believe she's the reason you sit in chains? That she is the lone catalyst to set your life off course? When you ascend the gallows, will you scream her name, claiming you had no control of your actions? Did she sprinkle magic dust under your nose? Did you wake one morning to find yourself spirited here, knee deep in the dirt with a shovel?"

Nathan turned away and started for the exit, hoping to keep Hornigold from getting a retort in. He was disgusted with the man, but also with himself for thinking Katherine Lindsay responsible for all his troubles.

"Don't pretend you're better than me, boy!" Hornigold called after him.

"I don't have to pretend," Nathan said.

"I know a pirate when I see one. I doubt you lost that arm as an honest sailor. I know the look of a man who craves what isn't his. I've captained a thousand boys like you. You're all so quick to part with innocence, but the lofty condemnation that accompanies youth is not so easily mislaid. You're all walking contradictions, the lot of you. Most of you are dead before you realize what you've become."

Nathan stopped at the flaps and tilted his head. "It's a pity I didn't meet you sooner, Hornigold. You've taught me much in a short time."

He pushed through the flaps and stepped into the warm sunlight. The sound of crashing waves greeted his ears. He inhaled deeply, smelling salt for the first time in a long time. He had forgotten how much he used to love that smell, before it became so common that he didn't even know it was there.

He found Calloway near the firepit, piling logs for the night's feast. "Captain," she greeted with an alluring smirk. Her large hat was not pulled as low as it used to be. Several of the crew had figured out her secret since last night, and the news had probably spread like wildfire. It was also likely that they knew she belonged to Dillahunt, and they wouldn't touch her as long as the captain lived.

"Boy," Nathan replied with a smirk of his own.

"You look like you want something."

"It's that obvious?"

"I know when a man wants something," she replied.

"And when does a man want something?"

She grinned. "When he opens his mouth."

"Well, your instincts serve you. I need a small favor. There's a woman in the big tent."

Her face was instantly racked with dread. "But, Guy is in there!"

"She's not that kind of woman," Nathan assured her. "Your man will go unmolested."

"Is it Katherine Lindsay? The one with the bounty on her head?"

"That's her. I want you to find Bellamy and have him see to her wounds. Stay by her side for a while and keep watch on her. You can pretend you're there to watch over Dillahunt. Don't try to hide your gender, as she'll figure it out quicker than I did. She'll be relieved to see another woman, I think."

Calloway regarded him skeptically. "Maybe."

"Don't worry, you'll like her."

"That doesn't evoke my confidence. Men are terrible judges of such things."

He rubbed his temples in exasperation. "Look, it can't hurt to try."

Calloway suddenly grinned. "Do you love this woman? Is this the one you were talking about? The girl who 'belongs to no one'?"

Nathan recoiled in horror. "What? No! You've got it all wrong!"

Calloway giggled.

"Stop laughing," he barked. "Do as I ask, or I'll pull your hat off in front of everyone."

She shrugged. "I think they've mostly figured it out by now."

"Just do it." Nathan turned to leave, then halted and raised a finger. "Oh, and her hands are bound. You might gain a bit of trust by freeing her and pretending you're doing so against my will."

"You're not afraid she'll try and escape?"

Nathan spread his hand and stump and made a big show of looking all around. "Where will she go? Is there another ship I don't know about on the other side of this island?"

"Why are you doing this?" she asked.

"She needs to be reminded of something. I think you are just the person to remind her."

Calloway lowered her head slightly, eyes shaded beneath her huge hat. "What am I supposed to remind her of?"

Nathan looked to the ship on the horizon, its once pristine sails now pitted with holes from last night's battle. A tingling sensation crept along his missing arm, taunting him with its absence once again. "Something too easily forgotten out here."

13

KATE

The girl's soft fingers brushed gently against Kate's wrists as they worked at the knotted sash that bound her hands behind her back. "This knot is stubborn," she muttered.

Richard Maynard smiled obscenely, gesturing downward. "I've got a stubborn knot for you to sort through." Sweat trickled down his leathery forehead, collecting on the thick ledge of his brow. His beady eyes gleamed from within deep-set hollows. He had not seen a woman in weeks, and now there were two in one tent.

"Captain Adams says you can wait outside," the girl coolly replied.

"I see *my* captain right there," Maynard said, shoving a fat index finger at Guy Dillahunt's unconscious form, heaped in blankets in a dark corner of the tent. His face was shrouded in bandages, save for the eyes and lower jaw. His arms and legs were wrapped as well. "He says nothing."

Kate felt the girl's fingers stop moving. "Shall I wake *your* captain and ask his thoughts on mutiny?"

Maynard slowly let the air out of his chest. "I'll be outside," he grumbled, ducking through the flaps. Bright rays of sun temporarily flooded the tent as the flaps opened and closed. Kate was relieved to see him go. The big oaf had done nothing but stare at her breasts since bringing her inside.

"And, there we have it," the girl said as the sash slipped free. Kate's wrists parted, freeing the strain in her shoulders.

"Thank you," Kate said, massaging her raw wrists.

"You're welcome." The girl possessed an amiable, soft voice. Her hair was cut like a boy's. She stood half a foot taller than Kate, and her shoulders were very broad, yet her face was delicate and youthful. When she first entered the tent, she had removed a large hat that Kate quickly deduced was meant to conceal her gender.

"The doctor will be here shortly to see to your face." The girl tentatively bit her lip as her gaze fell suggestively. "And any other wounds you might have."

"Just the face," Kate said with a light chuckle. She gestured at Dillahunt. "I trust it looks better than his."

The girl's young face fluttered with aggravation, but she swiftly veiled it with a smile. "You might need a stitch or two." She wandered over to Dillahunt and stared earnestly at him, biting a nail.

"You haven't told me your name."

"Jacqueline Calloway. Just 'Jaq,' where the men are concerned. They're so easily fooled, aren't they?"

"Only when they want to be," Kate said, scaling Calloway's long, slender legs. "I'd offer my name, but I think you already know it."

"What makes you think that?"

"You would've asked by now."

"Who says I'm here to talk to you?" the girl tersely replied, eyes steadfastly fixed on Dillahunt.

"Your new captain, I imagine."

Calloway confirmed Kate's suspicion with an apprehensive glance over her shoulder while chewing on a thumbnail.

"Nathan can't hold a grudge as well as he'd like," Kate went on.

The girl tilted her head, frowning. "I would think grudges easily preserved at sea, with nothing else to think on."

"He's inexperienced. Grudges come more naturally with *age*." Kate protracted the last word, studying the girl for a reaction.

The girl smiled sweetly, but her eyes gleamed abhorrently. "Some youths are more experienced than others."

"I expect he told you to free my bindings as well," Kate added. "Gain my trust, and all that."

"He didn't want you to know it was his idea."

"Nathan sends me a friend. How nice."

Calloway's jaw muscles tightened visibly. "Nathan might be captain for now, but he cannot command my friendship. I haven't decided I like you."

"Why the hesitation?" Kate wondered. "We're both women. There's no reason we shouldn't get along." *At least, that's how Nathan sees it,* she realized.

Calloway sighed. "I've known many women, most of them far less trustworthy than men. And now I see a woman among men, and I wonder what she has done to be held in such high regard."

"You're a strumpet, aren't you?" Kate hazarded.

"Of course I am," Calloway said, irritation doing little to diminish the sweetness of her voice.

Kate took a seat in one of the ornate chairs in front of Hornigold's desk, in the corner opposite Dillahunt. Hornigold had actually carted his furniture onto the beach. He'd even brought his wine cabinet. Kate set her hand on the desk, which had a freshly polished shine, despite a thin layer of sand it had already collected since yesterday. Had he meant to hold meetings in here? Discuss retirement plans with his men? The absurdity was more than Kate could subdue, and she snickered loudly.

Calloway turned round, annoyance painted plainly on her face. "Is something funny?"

"Not really."

The girl lifted a thin eyebrow, her mouth tweaking into a lopsided frown. "You're a queer woman, laughing at things that aren't funny."

"Spend a year with pirates," Kate replied, "and you'll find yourself laughing at all sorts of things that aren't funny."

The girl screwed up her mouth even further. "I honestly can't imagine what Nathan thought the two of us could have in common."

"Tits?"

Calloway allowed a chuckle, in spite of herself. "There is that, I suppose." Her eyes met with Kate's for a brief moment, before flickering back to Dillahunt. She kneeled beside him, lifting the bandages to peek at his face. "It's not as bad as it looks," she said.

"It looks pretty bad," Kate said, before she could think to stop herself.

"He'll be fine," Calloway snapped.

It was becoming obvious why the girl had stowed away on Dillahunt's ship. "So that's why you're out here," Kate said. "For him."

Calloway's freckles nearly vanished as her cheeks flushed. "Does there always have to be a reason?"

"No," Kate admitted, crossing her legs and throwing an arm

over the back of the chair. "But there usually is."

"What's yours?" Calloway asked. She took a seat in the blankets next to Dillahunt and hugged her legs.

"My husband died."

Calloway laughed. "No, that's not it."

Kate was too intrigued by this girl's gall to be annoyed. "I think I would know."

"Then why didn't you go back to London when you had the chance? You escaped your former captors only to throw in with more pirates? Seems a bit daft, doesn't it?"

Kate grinned. "So you *do* know who I am."

"Everyone knows," the girl replied indifferently. "Amazing what a bounty will do for your fame."

"A reward," Kate corrected.

The girl pursed her lips and shrugged. "Reward, bounty, it's all the same to the man collecting it."

A sudden gust parted the flaps of the tent, and the salty scent of the ocean swept in, along with blinding rays of sunlight. The tent billowed from the inside like a balloon. Kate felt her hair blow back, and she saw Calloway's expression change into something that was not disgust. "What happened to your ear?"

The breeze softened, the flaps fell, and the tent was dim once more. "A pirate made a meal of it."

"And what happened to that pirate?" the girl asked with trepidation.

"I killed him."

"Really," Calloway blurted excitedly. "How did you kill him? What did you do it with?"

"Does it matter?"

"Was it a pistol? A sword?"

"A sword," Kate said, massaging the leathery patch of skin where an ear used to be. She had visited with Hornigold's surgeon before the man was lost to the sea, and he told her how lucky she was the wound hadn't become infected.

"Where did you stick it? The sword?"

"I stuck it in his belly," Kate replied flatly. She had hoped to find some kind of common ground with the girl, but this was not what she'd had in mind. "I pinned him to the deck of a ship and watched him burn to death."

The girl shuddered, but she was smiling. "Did he deserve it?"

"He didn't seem to think so."

"Do you have nightmares about it?"

"I've answered enough of your questions," Kate said. "How about you answer mine, for a change?"

"What do you want to know?"

"Why are you here?"

Calloway laughed. "I don't know."

"Most would conjure a reason," Kate said, joining in her laughter.

Calloway stopped laughing at once, as though she didn't want her laugh mingling with Kate's.

"Not so long ago," Kate said, "although sometimes it seems like a century, I knew a pitiful surgeon. When I first met him, I immediately saw something in his eyes . . . something terribly sad . . . a dreadful calamity I didn't understand at first."

Calloway feigned a yawn. "Oh no. Is this going to be a long, sad story?"

"Sad, yes," Kate replied sweetly, "but not long."

The girl waved her hand, allowing her to continue.

"I knew very little about anything," Kate went on, "but I came to realize fairly quickly that this man wanted to die. He was not a pirate. He was not where he was supposed to be. They had stolen him and corrupted his purpose. He was forced to aid villains who brought harm upon innocents. It went against everything he was. He so desperately longed for release. I'd never met such a hopeless man. And then, after accepting the torture that his life had become, death came for him at last, welcoming him with open arms. But just then, right before the end, something changed."

"What?" Calloway said, unable to sustain her curiosity.

"He wanted to live."

After a moment of consideration, Calloway said, "That's very sad, but what's the point?"

Kate ran her finger along Hornigold's desk, trailing a smudge across the polished surface. Tiny grains of sand rolled beneath her finger, grinding thin, barely detectable scratches into the wood. "The point is no one really knows what they want until they're certain to lose it."

"Wants are fickle," Calloway said, adjusting a loose bandage on Dillahunt's forehead.

"You lost someone," Kate realized suddenly. There was a haunted, elusive wisdom behind the girl's blue eyes that often accompanied tragedy.

Calloway nodded. "My mother."

"I'm sorry. She was a strumpet too?"

"Yes," Calloway said. "Until one of her clients murdered her. There was no reason for it. My mother was very good at making men feel good about themselves, so I can't imagine she offended him. She knew all the right things to say. Any good strumpet does. Maybe he just wanted to see the color of her blood. Maybe he couldn't get off. I've seen men get angry when that happens. They pretend like it's your fault. Can't be anything wrong with them, so it must be something you did or didn't do. Anyway, he must have been very angry. The other girls heard the screams, but no one would go in there. They tried to stop me. I wish they'd tried harder." She had gone distant now, projecting some unimaginable horror upon the fabric of the tent. "I had no idea a person had so much blood in them."

"I'm sorry," Kate said.

"You said that already," Calloway snapped.

Kate stopped herself before she could apologize for apologizing. She looked down at her hands and started picking at her fingernails.

The girl kept going, sweet voice laced with disdain. "Ever since that day, when I see the color red, I see blood. I think I always will. Before then, I never realized how much red there is in the world. It's everywhere you look, really."

Kate looked up and found the girl surmising her with large eyes. Her pupils were dilated in the dim light, like a cat as it readies to pounce on a mouse. "I bet people tell you how beautiful your hair is all the time," Calloway said. "It *is* truly beautiful. So wild and perfect and so very, very red. How can hair be so messy and so perfect at the same time? That's what they say, isn't it?"

Kate shook her head. "No one's ever said that."

"I bet someone has," the girl said, nodding with a confident smirk. "If they haven't, they've at least thought it. You want to know what I think?"

"Not sure I do," Kate replied, staring at the sliver of light where the flaps of the tent parted. She suddenly wanted out of this stuffy, dark place.

Calloway's voice remained as sweet as honey. "When I look at your hair, all I see is blood."

14

NATHAN

On the dawn of the sixth day at Griffith's Isle, Nathan was stirred from a deep slumber.

He had been dreaming about Annabelle. They were naked on a little island with no trees. It was nothing more than an oval of sand amidst a shallow ocean, with the two of them in the center. The sand was warm and soft against his back, with no grain biting into his skin. The crystal water was no deeper than three feet for as far as the eye could see, and the sand shimmered beneath a fluctuating web of light. The sky made no sense. The sun remained directly above for the duration of the dream, never descending toward the horizon. Nathan was able to stare directly at it without squinting, and it was not hot upon his skin, but pleasantly warm. The sapphire sky darkened near the horizon, and stars twinkled along the circumference.

His left arm had grown back. Rarely was it missing from dreams. His subconscious had yet to catch up with reality. He knew it wasn't supposed to be there, but he was happy to fool himself for the time being.

He held Annabelle with both hands, and her skin was smooth against his, her kisses wet on his lips. Her dark hair blotted out the sun. He stared at her, but he could not fixate on any single feature for long, because her face was too deeply shadowed by her hair. There was an overall impression but no detail. The more he tried to focus, the less he could discern.

He wasn't sure what they were talking about. They giggled at each other's jokes and whispered sweetly in each other's ears. He promised never to leave her, and she promised the same in return, and the promises made as much sense as the hand he held against her back and the stars on a midday horizon.

She lifted her head and looked out to the sea. "A ship," she said.

"No," he replied. He wouldn't allow any ships infiltrating this dream. No pirates. No plots. No thoughts of treasure. No fear of death. They had their little island, and that's all they needed.

"Captain," she insisted, pounding on his chest. "It's a ship. A ship approaches."

"No it doesn't," he replied.

She balled her hand into a fist and brought it down hard on his chest, and the wind puffed from his mouth, and his eyes shot open.

Candler was hunched over him, fear etched in his face. "Captain, there's a ship on the horizon. It's big."

Nathan nudged Candler away with his stump as he sat up in his blankets. It was dim in the little tent, and beyond the parted flaps he saw the low purple light of early dawn. He threw on his shirt, which he had discarded at some point in the night, and retrieved his pistol and cutlass as Candler waited impatiently by the exit. He gestured for Candler to leave, and

Candler ducked outside, holding the flaps open for him. Nathan stepped out, greeted instantly by a nip in the early morning air. He scanned the purple horizon beyond *Crusader* until he saw a much bigger ship in the distance. And it was approaching fast. A chill ran through him, but he could not attribute it to the morning air. "That's a bloody frigate," he murmured.

"Ogle swears it's *Queen Anne's Revenge*," Candler replied at once.

Nathan started for the prisoner tent. Candler hurried after him. "Where are you going?"

"To ask the expert," Nathan said.

"Who's that?"

Nathan withered. "Benjamin Hornigold. The reason we're here, remember?"

"You think Blackbeard's come for him?"

"Amongst other things." Kate Lindsay had led them to the largest chest on the first day, and over the next week, the crew had discovered six more chests. All of the chests were concealed a little ways in the jungle, but Blackbeard would easily find them if he bothered to look.

Many of the men were gathered near the firepit, staring at the approaching ship. Peter Lively signaled Nathan to come over, but Nathan ignored him. He turned to Candler. "Give me the keys."

"The what?" Candler said, gawking at the ship.

"The keys to the prisoners' chains."

"Oh, of course." Candler slapped a ring with near a dozen keys into Nathan's hand. "It's the littlest one," he said.

"I won't need you," Nathan said, and Candler gladly took his leave. The first mate didn't like associating with prisoners. He had been extremely agitated when Nathan assigned him to look after them, but Nathan knew he could trust Candler not to stray too close.

Nathan reached the prisoner tent and pushed through the flaps. Most of them were asleep, sitting upright with their backs to each other, heads drooping. Hornigold was wide awake, staring expectantly. "I heard someone say *Queen Anne's Revenge*. Did I hear someone say *Queen Anne's Revenge*? I heard someone say *Queen Anne's Revenge*. He's come for me, Adams. He's come for me at last, as I always knew he would. He's come for me."

Hornigold had deteriorated considerably over the past week. He hadn't eaten much or taken much water. His cheeks were starting to sink in. His skin was a shade paler, lips cracked and bleeding, and he was constantly sweating. His hair was wet and stringy, resembling seaweed. Nathan was starting to feel sorry for the man. It was cruel to search for treasure at a leisurely pace while prolonging Hornigold's certain execution, but how could anyone pass up such an opportunity? Hornigold had made his choice.

"I was hoping you'd tell me," Nathan said as he bent down to unlock Hornigold's chains.

The one named Bastion was awake, eyes bright in the dark, though no other part of him was visible. "This is no good," he was saying, shaking his head.

"Thank you, Bastion," Nathan drawled.

"This is no good."

He freed Hornigold's wrists and helped him up. Nathan's knuckles raked over the notches of Hornigold's ribs. The disgraced captain was surprisingly easy to lift with just one arm. How had he lost so much weight so quickly? If they lingered much longer, Woodes Rogers would have to settle for dangling a skeleton from the noose.

Nathan helped Hornigold step out of the tent, steadying him from behind. Before the flaps closed, he heard Bastion say,

"This is no good," one more time.

"So tell me," Nathan said. "Is that *Queen Anne's Revenge*?"

Despite the dim light, Hornigold squinted as though it pained his eyes. Nathan watched his face decline from anxiety to a state of sheer terror. "You lingered here too long," he quaked. "Too long, Adams. You've bloody killed me. You've bloody killed me."

"So that's an affirmative," Bellamy quipped cheerfully as he approached, bracelets clinking. His silvery hair resembled polished metal in the low light.

Nathan handed Hornigold over to the surgeon. "See that he doesn't die before Blackbeard sets foot in the sand. That would be bad for all of us."

"You've killed me, Adams!" Hornigold shrieked.

Nathan glared at him. "Oh, now it's me who's killed you? I thought it was Katherine Lindsay."

"The whole bloody lot of you!"

Nathan chuckled bitterly. "Anyone but you, it would seem." He handed the keys to Bellamy. "Take him back inside and keep him as quiet as possible." Bellamy nodded, dragging the prisoner back through the flaps. Hornigold's enlarged, terror-ridden eyes flashed at Nathan before he was drawn into the darkness of the tent. "You've killed meeeeeeeeeee!"

Nathan snapped his fingers at Dick Maynard (Dick had slightly shorter hair than Richard). "Maynard, stand watch over this tent. Make sure Hornigold doesn't leave."

Dick grunted and lumbered to the tent.

Nathan joined the crew by the firepit. He stepped between Peter Lively and a middle-aged black man named Yarlow, who had very short, curly white hair and an equally white beard. Yarlow handed Nathan a spyglass. The silver shaft was dotted with blood. It had belonged to Jones Thompson, the navigator who was killed by the same cannonball that had earned Nathan his sudden promotion.

Yarlow gestured to the approaching frigate, which was just now coming to a halt parallel to *Crusader*. The token crew Nathan had left aboard were likely preparing the guns right about now. "Look at her colors," Yarlow said.

Nathan peered through the spyglass, scanning the horizon until he found the ship. He scaled the long mainmast, and at the top he saw a white flag fluttering in the wind.

"Mighty nice of Blackbeard to surrender before the fight," quipped Lively. "Not in his character, but let's not look a devil in the mouth, eh?"

"He's not here for a fight," Nathan said. "He's here for Hornigold."

"Then we'd best give him over," Yarlow urged. "That ship could sink *Crusader* just by looking at her."

"Not quite," Nathan said. "Ours would do a fair amount of damage before she sank, and Blackbeard knows that. Hell, *Crusader* might even get a crippling shot in before she went under. Not worth risking his precious *Revenge*. He hasn't made it this far by being stupid."

Nathan hoped the men he'd left on *Crusader* knew the meaning of a white flag. Some of them were quite daft. So far no one had fired. That was a good sign, at least.

"A white flag," Lively muttered sarcastically. "The mighty Blackbeard doesn't disappoint. I think I just shit meself."

"Only just?" said Gabe Jenkins. A lock of his curly black hair was matted to his forehead, which was glistening with sweat.

They waited an hour.

Nathan instructed the crew to act casually but remain on their guard at all times. He had Calloway light candles in the large tent and then asked her and Lindsay to remove themselves to another tent. He had been keeping both women sheltered and under close watch, along with Dillahunt, as those three were the most vulnerable members of the crew. He did not trust some of Dillahunt's men not to rape the women or murder Dillahunt in his sleep. There were too many former pirates here, and some of them had worked with Blackbeard.

The sun appeared as a boat from *Queen Anne's Revenge* slid upon the shore. A dark shadow stood tall at the bow, in a long coat and tricorn hat, arm resting casually upon a raised knee. He was flanked by five men. Four of them jumped off, and two of them helped their captain into the sand, taking care that his boots didn't get wet. He was at least six feet tall. He stepped in front of the quarter-sun that was ascending slowly from the water, and his towering silhouette seemed to swallow all light. He stood there, features indistinct in the gloom. The shadow emitted a guttural voice. "Where be Captain Dillahunt?"

Nathan stepped forward. "Captain Dillahunt is unwell. I act in his stead."

The shadow remained still. "Am I to guess your name?"

"Nathan Adams," Nathan said, doing his best to keep a firm, commanding tone.

There was a long pause. "That name be familiar to me."

Nathan frowned. "It shouldn't be."

"Nevertheless, it gives me pause." Blackbeard turned and snapped his fingers at the two men who had remained in the boat. "Return to the ship."

"You arrive under a white flag," Nathan said.

"Aye. Normally I would take what is rightfully mine, but respect for Captain Dillahunt stays my hand."

Nathan smiled thinly. "Respect, or fear of *Crusader's* many guns?"

"Don't fool yourself, boy," the shadow boomed. "*Crusader* would swiftly find herself at the bottom of the ocean if it served my purpose, and I would suffer a few holes in my beloved

Revenge to see the deed done."

"And what is your purpose, exactly?"

"A thing best discussed away from prying ears," the shadow said.

Nathan motioned toward the big tent. "Your men will have to wait here," he said.

"As will yours, boy."

"That's fair."

Nathan walked to the tent, hoping the tall man was following. He ducked through the flaps and into warm candlelight. Dillahunt was still comatose in his many blankets in a dark corner. Nathan turned.

The flaps parted, and Blackbeard stepped in. The top of his hat skimmed the roof of the tent. Even in the light, his face was shadowed by a bushy black beard. His piercing blue eyes, however, seemed to yield a light all their own. He glanced around. "A touch decadent for Captain Dillahunt."

Nathan took a seat behind the desk and gestured toward one of the two seats before it. Blackbeard walked over but refused to sit. He paced slowly, his hat gliding along the bowed canvas. He regarded Dillahunt for a moment. "If I didn't know better, I'd wager this man survived a battle with a shark."

"You might say that," Nathan replied.

Blackbeard's eyes found Nathan's. His right cheek was creased. Was he smirking under all that fur? "Did the shark survive?"

"I know why you're here," Nathan said, not in the mood for games. He knew he should be pissing himself with fear, but Blackbeard had nothing to hold over his head.

"And here I thought myself subtle."

"You want Benjamin Hornigold."

"Hornigold?" Blackbeard scratched his beard and looked up, as though searching for a clue. "That name be familiar to me as well, though far more troublesome. It's like I've put it away, for it harkens an unsettling history."

Nathan smirked. "I doubt you've forgotten the man that made you."

Blackbeard looked shocked. "You cannot make a man such as me; you can only watch in horror as I am born. Hornigold's name may find its way into a history book or two, but not without mine to context it. Give the man to me, and I will warrant him a chapter all his own. Unless Captain Dillahunt offers protest." Blackbeard turned, placed two fingers behind his ear, and favored Dillahunt with a moment's consideration. "It appears he does not." He turned back to Nathan. "Point me to Hornigold's whereabouts and I'll be on my merry way."

"Your merry way is littered with corpses," Nathan grated. "Don't think me evil enough to hand a man's life over to you with no better reason than making you happy."

Blackbeard feigned injury to his heart. "You wrong me, boy. I be nothing if not a fair man. You will of course be amply compensated. Emphasis on the 'ample.'"

Nathan spread his hands. "What could you possibly offer that I don't already have? A spare arm?"

Blackbeard shrugged. "Your life."

"Other than that."

"You do not wish to live?"

"Of course I do," Nathan said, confused.

"Of course you do not wish to live?"

Nathan hesitated. "Of course I wish to live. Doesn't everyone?"

"Do they not?"

Nathan sighed, irritated. "What are you playing at?"

"Strange," Blackbeard said, a crease in his brow. "Everyone claims a desire to live, but their words be so unclear when their life hangs in the balance."

"My words were perfectly clear," Nathan insisted. "It's your forked tongue that muddies them."

"Do not anger me, boy," Blackbeard suddenly glowered. "It's best to be clear with me, for my mind be easily scrambled, and my hand finds itself compelled by frustration." He laid his hand casually upon the hilt of his sword.

Nathan found a blade of his own tucked in the hollow of the desk. "If you came here to threaten me, you should have brought more than four men. I must say, I expected more from the mighty Blackbeard than childish word games."

Blackbeard was unfazed. "And I expected less from a child playing captain." He let his hand slide off the hilt. "I merely try your mettle, boy. Clearly there be more to you than meets the eye."

"Thank you."

Blackbeard slid out one of the chairs and slowly took a seat. Somehow, he still seemed very tall. His eyes held Nathan's. "You be quick to smile, but I see no glee behind it. Are you not a happy man, Nathan Adams?"

"What kind of question is that?"

"The inquisitive kind."

"Are *you* a happy man?" Nathan countered.

"I will be, very shortly. Fulfilled goals always leave a man contented, would you not agree?"

Nathan sat back in his chair, trying to appear more relaxed than he actually was. His fingers did not leave the hilt of the sword concealed beneath the desk. "Some would say happiness is in the pursuit."

"Then mayhap you will not want what I have to offer. Not yet, anyway. Shall I dangle her just out of reach, only to steal her from your grasp once more?"

Nathan stiffened in his seat. "Dangle who?"

"Her name is Annabelle. She tells me you are acquainted."

Nathan didn't even realize he had stood until he heard the chair topple distantly behind his legs. The sword fell in the hollow of the desk, clanging loudly. Blackbeard smirked at the sound. Nathan backed away, his calves touching the over-turned chair.

"I see she didn't lie," Blackbeard said.

"If you are lying," Nathan seethed, "you will not leave this tent."

Blackbeard choked out a laugh. "Ah, youth. I miss it so. Alas, my passion ignites only for revenge."

"Show her to me."

"My men row her to shore presently. I signaled them to do so when I first heard your name."

"A convenient bargaining chip," Nathan said skeptically. "How could you possibly know I would be captain?"

"I didn't know," Blackbeard admitted. "Your promotion be a stroke of fortune. I expected to bargain with you in secret, after talks with Dillahunt failed." He glanced at the wine cabinet. "My lips be parched."

Nathan moved over to the cabinet. He uncorked a bottle of wine with shaky hands and poured two goblets to the brim. He handed one to Blackbeard and then downed his own, wincing at each gulp. He had never much cared for wine, but he needed it right now. He quickly poured another. Blackbeard stared at him indifferently, sipping at his goblet. "Go easy, boy. Wine dulls the loins' ambition, and I suspect you'll need all you can muster."

"You are not what I expected," Nathan said, shuffling into the center of the tent.

"I am exactly what you expected," Blackbeard replied. "The present conundrum does not require the horrors foretold of me. They're all true. I would see your head mounted upon my bow, if it served my benefit."

"Lucky me," Nathan said, peering into his wine. He couldn't see his features within, only the outline of his head cast in blood.

"Do not mistake our bargain for amity."

"I've accorded to no bargain yet," Nathan reminded him. His voice was already slurring. He set his goblet down beside Dillahunt.

"You will," Blackbeard stated with no hint of ambiguity, lightly sipping at his wine.

"Who says I even have Hornigold?"

"You've hardly denied it. Shrewdness be earned with more than a lost arm, Nathan Adams. Wisdom be far more precious than an absent appendage. The trick is surviving youth, and more often than not that's a game of fortune."

"Fortune is relative," Nathan muttered. How many had died because Blackbeard had survived his youth? *And you're about to hand him another victim, if what he says is true.*

"Morals tug at you," Blackbeard said, sounding genuinely concerned. "Virtue be yet another appendage stolen with age. I sometimes forget that."

"You expect me to believe you were ever virtuous?"

Blackbeard shifted in his seat, staring at him. "There was a time, though mine was discarded long before yours. Virtue be no match for ambition."

The tent flaps parted, and Candler stuck his head in, tossing an uneasy glance at Blackbeard. "Begging pardon. Another boat approaches."

Nathan's heart beat against the inside of his chest, as though it yearned to burst free. For a moment he thought he was going to fall over. "If the boat carries a woman, bring her to me at once. If not, we'll be accommodating another prisoner, one that Woodes Rogers will be very pleased to see."

Candler nodded, and his head withdrew from the flaps like

a turtle retreating into its shell.

Nathan turned to find Blackbeard still looking at him. The huge pirate captain was smiling confidently. His beard was dripping red around his lips, where the short curly tendrils had dipped in the wine. "You'd better not be lying."

Blackbeard cackled. "Benjamin Hornigold threatened me once. His days were numbered from that moment."

Nathan scratched the stump of his left arm. "Our days are numbered from the moment we're born."

"Aye," Blackbeard conceded, "but if the water be teeming with sharks, will you take a swim?"

"No."

"Nay, indeed," Blackbeard said with a firm nod. "Our days be limited, but carelessness quickens mortality. A hard lesson learned, and too often the last."

"And you're the man to teach that lesson?"

"We cannot deny our appointed stations in life."

Nathan didn't know if the man was joking or serious, and he wasn't sure which was scarier.

Candler's head shot through the flaps without warning, and Nathan nearly jumped. "They have a woman, captain!"

"Send her in," Nathan ordered briskly.

Candler vanished. Nathan held his breath, watching the flaps wavering back and forth. A slender hand slipped through the gap, and then another. The flaps parted, and a copper-toned leg appeared, followed by the rest of her. She wore a silk white robe, belted at the waist. It plunged in a V at her neck, nearly to her navel, revealing the perfect curve of her cleavage. Her hair was as thick and black as he remembered. Her right cheek was badly scarred, but it did not diminish her beauty.

Nathan's heart had all but stilled in his chest. "Annabelle," he heard himself weakly murmur.

She nodded timidly. "Nathan," she said. Her great brown

eyes met Nathan's only briefly before fluttering away, as if the
tent's fabric held greater interest.

"It's good to see you," Nathan said, realizing instantly how
lame the words sounded.

"Mhmm," she replied.

Blackbeard stood. "You have your prize. Now take me to
Benjamin Hornigold."

Nathan started to turn, but he didn't want to take his eyes
off Annabelle for fear she wouldn't be there when he looked
back. Blackbeard grasped Nathan's shoulder, turning him with
surprising force. "That is, if your morals do not object." His
breath was hot on Nathan's face, steely blue eyes gazing into
his.

"They're mum on the issue," Nathan said.

"Good," said Blackbeard with a nod of finality.

"AAADDDDAAAAAAAAMMMMMS!!!"

The eerie howl seemed to billow the fabric of the tent and
shudder the ground, prickling the hairs on Nathan's neck and
arms. Nathan, Blackbeard, and Annabelle turned towards
Dillahunt, who was struggling to rise from his heavy blankets.
He stretched a trembling hand at Nathan, bloodshot eyes
bulging beneath the bandages wrapped around his face. "You
traitorous cunt . . . you strike bargain . . . with Satan! I will . . .
see your . . . cock removed!" With that, he collapsed back into
his bed and didn't stir again.

Blackbeard looked from Dillahunt to Nathan, raising his
eyebrows. "That puts a chill in the marrow. Do you want to
kill him, or should I?"

"No one's killing him," Nathan said.

"I suggest you act fast," Blackbeard said with a knowing
glance at Annabelle. "This bargain will be for naught if you are
parted from your cock."

Annabelle flushed with aggravation.

"I'll deal with Dillahunt," Nathan said.

Blackbeard started for the exit. "I suppose that be your problem." He brushed past Annabelle without sparing her a final consideration. She watched him go, jaw tight and arms folded. Nathan tried not to think on what their relationship had consisted of until now.

He stared at her. Her skin was so dark in contrast to the thin white robe that did so little to conceal her every curve. She was so perfect. He wanted to touch her and make sure she was really there, but he didn't know how. Part of him had always known he would see her again, but he had hoped for a much warmer reunion. Leaving her had been the hardest thing he had ever done, and now she looked at him with nothing more than vague familiarity. She hadn't even seemed to notice his stump. *She just needs time,* he reminded himself. *Who knows what she's been through?* He wondered if the trench in her cheek had been delivered by Livingston or Blackbeard.

"Annabelle," he said, lifting his lone hand to her face.

"Conclude your business," she stated flatly.

He lowered his hand, nodding. "We'll speak after."

"I look forward to it," she replied, but nothing in her tone suggested anticipation.

15

CALLOWAY

She watched through the flaps of a darkened tent as Nathan talked with most of the crew near the firepit. It was difficult to hear over the crashing surf, but she heard the names "Tortuga" and "Woodes Rogers" repeatedly. Most were nodding in agreement and exchanging enthusiastic grins.

"We're not going back to Nassau," came Kate's raspy voice from behind. She had been sitting quietly in the dark on a blanket for the past hour, with her legs crossed and hands in her lap.

"I figured that out all by myself," Calloway drawled. She looked down at the dagger she'd lifted from Bellamy's medical bag while he had been examining Dillahunt's wounds two days ago. She ran a thumb along the edge of the curved blade, which was shiny and new. Her thumb came away with a red slit that seeped tiny droplets. If Bellamy suspected she took it, he hadn't said a word.

She looked to the horizon. The sun was hanging just above the ocean, casting an iridescent column across the water, which was broken by the two ships moored offshore. She recognized the big ship by its shape alone as it had pulled in. She had first glimpsed that ship while walking the beach at Nassau one murky morning. It had appeared through a thick fog, dark and hulking. By the end of that day, her mother was dead.

And now that very same ship had come to claim another victim, though Calloway was not concerned with the fate of Benjamin Hornigold. Blackbeard had yet to emerge from the prisoner tent.

Calloway turned the dagger over and over. She smeared droplets of her blood over the hilt, darkening the wood. She tried not to think about the mysterious black-haired woman in the white robe that had been brought into the big tent. The woman was still in there, with Dillahunt. The dagger suddenly felt hot in her grasp.

"What are you planning to do with that?" Kate asked.

Calloway wasn't sure how Kate had even seen the blade. Calloway's back had been to her the entire time. "I'm going to stick it in his throat."

"Whose throat might that be?"

Calloway bit her lip. *I won't say his name.*

"Blackbeard?" Kate said.

She flinched. *I won't say his name. I won't say his name. Not until he's dead.*

"Is he the one that did it? The one that—"

"I don't want to talk now," Calloway barked.

She couldn't be distracted. Not now. She had to prepare herself. She knew he would emerge at any moment. He would be too occupied with his prize, Hornigold. She would catch him off guard in his moment of triumph. There would never be a better time. She wouldn't get another chance.

"Is that why you're here? To kill him?"

Calloway said nothing. She hadn't come to sea with any specific intention. She had been moved by a sudden and inexplicable desire to leave Nassau and sail with Dillahunt. She wished she knew herself as well as Kate Lindsay seemed to know herself. She had instantly resented Kate's confidence, the easy way she walked, and her careless disregard towards danger. It was as if nothing could touch her. Kate was a woman who had seen her vengeance fulfilled. Perhaps her easy demeanor was the result of that.

The only thing Calloway knew for a certainty was that fate was offering a chance for revenge, and that chance would slip away if she didn't seize it.

"It's strange," Kate mused. "Blackbeard has made so many enemies, yet no one has come close enough to kill him."

"Not yet," Calloway replied.

"No one but Jacqueline Calloway," Kate announced with a mocking flourish. "She's going to end the mighty Blackbeard."

"If I don't try, I'll hate myself."

Kate snickered. "And if you do try, you'll be dead, and there'll be no one left to hate herself."

Calloway looked back. A stripe of sunlight from the slit in the tent's flaps fell over one side of Kate's face. "You should know better than anyone, Lindsay."

"I do. I also know I'm very fortunate to be alive. I pray you're favored with the same fortune."

Calloway returned her gaze to the beach. "Save your stupid prayers. I won't rely on fortune."

"Fortune plays a bigger part in our lives than we'd like to admit."

"Then it *taunts* me," Calloway barked, squeezing the hilt of the dagger until her knuckles turned white. "Fortune brought that man before me."

"And Blackbeard's fortune will just as happily see you dead at his feet."

"What do you care, anyway?" Calloway snapped. "Is it because I'm a woman? I can't think of any other reason. You hardly know me."

Kate's voice was softer than usual. "And I probably never will, if you leave this tent."

"There seems to be another woman in Captain Dillahunt's tent. Befriend her, if you so desire womanly company." *You probably had plenty of friends in London, you silly bitch.*

Blackbeard emerged from the prisoner tent with a confident smile that his beard could not conceal. Two large men followed with Hornigold in tow, hands chained behind his back, face wrought in terror. Tattered clothes hung loose from his bony frame. He was the most hopeless creature Calloway had ever gazed upon.

I can avenge one life and save another. It just made sense.

A boat was approaching the shore, carrying only a few men. They hopped out as it slid into the sand, and they stood there waiting to accommodate the prisoner.

Calloway heard a light shuffling behind her. "Just hand me the knife." Kate's voice was alarmingly close. Calloway was shocked to see Kate standing over her, hand outstretched.

Calloway stood to face her. "I'll stick this in your belly if you get in my way."

Kate offered no reaction. She merely studied her in the same dispassionate way Bellamy inspected his patients' wounds. Calloway suddenly felt uncomfortable under the woman's gaze, but she would not allow her to see it.

"Good luck, Jacqueline," Kate said at last. "It was lovely to have met you."

"The feeling is not mutual," Calloway replied. She tucked the knife in her belt and burst from the tent. She locked on to

Blackbeard, who was nearly to the boat. He had fallen behind the two hulking men that were dragging Hornigold by the armpits, as if he thought Hornigold might try to escape from the rear.

Calloway looked left and saw Nathan still occupied with his crew. He wasn't even looking at the man he had condemned to death in exchange for some woman. Was that woman the lost love he had talked about with such reverence?

Calloway quickened her pace, hand falling to the hilt of the dagger. She knew Kate's eyes were on her back. *Would she truly be sad to see me killed?*

She shook her head. *It doesn't matter. Focus.*

She was catching up with her target. His back remained unguarded. He seemed to grow taller and taller as she drew near. Soon she was within ten paces of him.

Nine paces.

Eight paces.

She clutched the dagger.

Seven paces.

Six paces.

She freed the dagger from her belt.

Five paces.

My god, he's huge!

Four paces.

She drew back her arm for the killing strike.

Three paces.

Two paces.

A deafening *crack* sounded in Calloway's left ear, and the sand billowed upward between her and Blackbeard. She looked left, and Nathan Adams was moving toward her through a cloud of smoke that swirled from his raised pistol. "Jaq, no!" he screamed desperately, the veins bulging in his neck.

Blackbeard spun, whipping his sword from its sheath in a

smooth motion. The blade clashed with Calloway's dagger, sending it spiraling out of her grip. It landed harmlessly in the sand several feet away. She skidded on her heels and fell on her ass in the sand. He loomed over her, a towering black shadow that swallowed the sun. He raised his sword. There was no mirth in his eyes. He would strike her down just as easily as swatting a fly, and he would forget her only minutes later.

As he did my mother.

A flash of steel shot between Calloway and Blackbeard. Blades clashed, and Blackbeard's killing blow was brought to a premature halt. And then she saw anger sweltering in his evil eyes, which were now fixated on Nathan Adams instead of her. Nathan's cutlass trembled in his lone hand under the force of Blackbeard's heavy blade.

Blackbeard's guttural voice boomed like thunder across the beach. "You dare come between me and my prey, boy?"

"You'll claim no one else," Nathan said through gnashed teeth, his entire body straining under Blackbeard's weight against the blade. "You've got your prize."

"The boy tried to kill me!" Blackbeard protested.

"She is a member of my crew."

Blackbeard withdrew his blade, relieving Nathan's strain. "You mean to tell me a mere *girl* made attempt on my life, and you would deny me vengeance?"

Most of the crew had gathered around to watch, waiting with baited breath for Nathan's answer.

"I'm giving you Hornigold," Nathan said. "How many vengeances do you require?"

"I will drink my fill until I my lust be slaked."

Nathan sighed, sheathing his sword. "Then I fear the ocean will be drained."

Blackbeard pointed to his distant ship. "When her hull scrapes the bottom, I'll know my duty is done."

"Your ship will find the bottom," Calloway hissed. "One way or another."

Blackbeard frowned down at her. "I do not know what I've done to wrong you, girl, and neither will I linger to unravel the mystery. Do not think yourself special, for I have ruined many, and will ruin many more. Should we meet again, I will not recall your face."

He turned and joined his men, who were hefting Hornigold into the boat. Hornigold stared at her hopelessly, probably realizing that his last best chance had failed him. She looked away.

Nathan seized her hand and lifted her up. "What madness took you?" he demanded, shaking her. "That man is not to be trifled with, and you attempt to murder him? You nearly undid everything!"

"You undid everything yourself," she snarled in his face. "All for your whore! You can't go back to Nassau after trading Hornigold. None of us can!"

"You knew the risks when you stole aboard Dillahunt's ship."

"*Dillahunt's* ship!" she yelled. "Not yours!"

"The reward is worth the risk," Nathan stubbornly replied, looking to the ships on the horizon. "For all of us."

"Mostly for you," she said, struggling to free herself from his solid grip.

He dragged her toward the big tent. "You'll remain with Dillahunt, under close watch. I don't know what business you have with Edward Teach, and frankly I don't care. I thought Kate Lindsay would make trouble; I didn't expect any from *you.*"

"You're hurting my wrist."

"Good." They reached the tent, he shoved her through the flaps, and she fell to her knees inside. She heard him yell for both Maynards to stand watch outside. She remained on the ground, palms flat, staring at the back of her hands.

I'm sorry, Mother. I tried. You can't say I didn't try.

Her peripheral vision caught movement in the corner opposite Dillahunt. The woman from Blackbeard's ship was seated before the desk, a bare leg sticking through the slit in her white robe, crossed over the other. She regarded Calloway with a raised eyebrow. "Are you that Lindsay woman everyone is always talking about?"

"No," Calloway murmured softly. "I'm nobody."

16

HORNIGOLD

"I've concocted something special for you," Edward Teach said.

Hornigold had no idea where they were now, but Griffith's Isle had long since faded from view. The ship was surrounded by vibrant turquoise water. In the distance, off the starboard bow, there was a patch of little white sandy islands that barely broke surface level. The sun was in the middle of a cloudless sky.

He stood upon the cut-down forecastle. The entire crew had gathered round to watch, crowding the decks, perched on the rails, and dangling from the ratlines.

"Just get on with it," Hornigold pleaded. He was so tired. Since Dillahunt's men had apprehended him on the island, he hadn't been able to sleep for more than an hour without being stirred into consciousness by horrific dreams that explicitly detailed his own death. He'd hardly kept any food down, and the few times he did, he woke to find he had shit himself in his sleep, and not the solid kind.

"I won't be hurried," Teach said. "You've made me wait this long, Benjamin. It be fair that you indulge my theatrical side. I have an audience to placate."

"Fair?" Hornigold said, aghast. Speech sheared at his parched throat, but he supposed he could endure a little pain in his final moments, if it meant speaking his mind. "You would not exist if not for me."

Teach nearly bristled, but he calmed himself with a few deep breaths. "The only reason I won't deny that is because you so clearly regret it."

"With all my heart."

"From your woeful look, I'd wager you have very little heart left. I pray my concoction wakes you from lethargy." He took Hornigold by the shoulders and pointed him toward the main hatch, just as two hulking men lifted a long black crate from the dark. They set it upon the deck at the feet of Hornigold and Teach, taking care not to damage it. It didn't take long for Hornigold's weary mind to register what he was looking at.

"I went through many of these," Teach said, scratching his beard, "making sure it be just airtight enough, but not entirely airtight, if you get my meaning. There be a science behind it. Took months to get the first one right."

"The first one?" Hornigold said.

Teach grinned and squeezed Hornigold's shoulder, as though they were the best of friends. "You'll see for yourself soon enough."

It was a coffin, shiny and black, with four brass handles knotted with thick rope. On the lid, level with the intended victim's head, was a brass-lined porthole, inlaid with the clearest pane of glass Hornigold had ever seen.

"The porthole is new," Teach said, looking rather proud of

himself. "Cost a fortune to get it right. The glass was always too murky, or it cracked after ten feet."

Hornigold crumpled to his knees and retched. Only milky fluids emerged from his mouth. The entire crew boomed laughter. Teach chuckled softly. "Better here than in there," he said, gesturing at the coffin.

Hornigold looked up. Edward Teach's dark features were indistinguishable with the sun peaking just above his hat. "I beg you, Edward. Don't put me in that thing."

Teach pondered the request for barely a moment before firmly shaking his head. "If you'd let me catch you sooner, I might be persuaded to offer favor. Mayhap I'd set you on one of those little sandbars with a pistol and one shot. You'd like that, wouldn't you?"

"Very much," Hornigold gasped. Anything was better than that coffin. He just needed a little more time.

"However, you've eluded me so long that my mind be set upon task."

"Gold! I can offer you gold!"

Teach cocked his head. "Where be this phantom gold you speak of? Your pockets look scant."

"Adams has it!" Hornigold cried, the words slicing at the inside of his dry throat. "He probably aims to split it with Kate Fucking Lindsay."

"But I already know what Adams holds. The boy thinks me unmindful of his sudden wealth. One revenge at a time."

"How?" Hornigold demanded. "You're wasting time with me and your silly revenge while Adams slips away!" He needed to keep Teach talking. He had prepared himself for a quick, merciful death, but this was ridiculous.

"My grasp extends very far, Benjamin. You of all people should know that. Griffith's fortune will be laid at my feet in but a few days."

Hornigold seized Teach by the legs, shaking him. "You can't put me in that thing, Teach! You can't! Take off my head. Shoot me. Strand me on one of those islands without even a pistol, but don't put me in that coffin! For the love of God, man!"

"God," Teach said, eyes sweeping over his crew. They all laughed knowingly. They had heard every plea, and they knew every retort. There was no way to win this. No one ever had. "God does not want your love. He wants your fear, and when he's had his fill of that, he'll take your soul. I will deliver him both in one stroke."

Rage clouded like a thunderstorm in Hornigold's breast. He struggled to lift from his crouch, but his weak legs refused to cooperate. "You don't know what God wants," he sneered derisively.

Teach spread his arms wide. "I have eyes, Benjamin. I see a world of fear and death. If that world be designed by God, it be exactly as its maker wills it. If he be a kind maker, he would strike me down before you, would he not? Yet he has delivered you into my hands."

"I think your hands are moved by another," Hornigold said.

Teach directed a guttural laugh at his crew, and they laughed with him. "We've heard that one before, haven't we, men?"

"Aye!" they shouted in unison.

Teach turned to Hornigold. "The other you speak of . . . tell me his name."

"I will not."

"Say it."

Hornigold gazed up at the indistinct shadow that towered over him, the sun struggling for purchase beyond that black hat. "Lucifer," he said.

"Aye, Lucifer." Teach bent down to whisper in his ear.

"Mayhap he stands before you."

The last ounce of hope trickled down Hornigold's inner thigh. A stream of fleeting warmth collected in a little yellow puddle about his heel. His shoulders quaked as his head fell between them. He would have collapsed had Teach not placed a hand under the pit of his arm.

"I have a parting question for you, Benjamin Hornigold," Teach said. "I will not ask twice."

"Ask," Hornigold muttered.

"Do you not wish to live?"

Hornigold looked up suddenly. Some stupid part of him was still desperate for life. Why he would wish to endure more of this ridiculous world he couldn't say. Instinct trumped dignity. "Yes," he blurted at once. "God, yes!"

The crew laughed again.

Teach's face was so close that the bristles of his beard scratched against Hornigold's cheek. "Very well." He rose to his full height and gestured to his two hulking assistants. "Put him in the coffin."

Hornigold shrieked as they lifted him off of his feet. He thrashed his legs and pounded his fists, but the men who held him might as well have been statues. Two more men, who Hornigold recognized as Narrow Ned and Hemett, raised the coffin's lid, which tilted on thin silver hinges. The interior was plain and without cushions, painted in black. There was a goopy tar-like substance lining the seams. Silver shackles were chained into the base.

The hulks dropped Hornigold inside. He continued thrashing, sticking his limbs out of the coffin so they wouldn't be able to close the lid. One hulk held him by the shoulders while the other seized both of his feet, securing the shackles around his ankles. Narrow Ned placed two chained cannonballs at his feet, fastening them to the shackles. Ned disappeared and reappeared with two more cannonballs, adding to the others. "What in God's name are you doing?" Hornigold demanded.

Ned's lips peeled away from rows of rotten, yellow teeth. "It's a courtesy, Benji. Makes it so you go down rightways up."

Hemett seized his arms, forcing them into the coffin. Hornigold shrieked at him, and Hemett blinked as spittle pattered his face. Hemett released Hornigold's wrists at the last minute, and the lid snapped shut. The little porthole lined up perfectly with his face. His shrieking instantly fogged the glass. He managed to slip his right hand over his chest, raking his knuckles against the lid. He frantically beat at the glass.

Teach's face appeared in the hole. His voice was muffled through the glass, but his words were clear enough. "The last thing you want to do, mate, is break that glass."

Hornigold pounded at Teach's face, but the only thing he managed to break was his own skin, smearing the glass with blood.

"Goodbye, Benjamin," mumbled Teach. He offered a final smile, indistinct through the crimson sheen. "I will miss the chase."

And then he was gone.

Hornigold caught glimpses of the hulking men. They had something in their hands, but he couldn't see. And then rapid *thuds* racketed the lid, and the thin slits of light in the seams gradually started to vanish.

They're nailing me in. Oh God, this is actually happening. How can this be happening?

It can't be happening. It's not happening. I'm dreaming. That's it. I'm dreaming.

No you're not, Benjamin.

The coffin jerked suddenly upward. The main sail started to shift. Hornigold glimpsed men on either side, carrying him. Something *thumped* beneath him. He saw the sails rotating as the coffin turned clockwise. And then he heard and felt wood grinding over the railing beneath him. Suddenly his face mashed the glass and his knees hit the lid as he lifted into the air. And then the coffin came to a jarring halt, sending a numbing vibration down Hornigold's spine as he was crushed against the backboard. He wiped blood from the glass with his sleeve, and he saw that the coffin was suspended by four lines of rope, and he saw the hull of *Queen Anne's Revenge*. Four of Teach's men were slowly lowering him over the side of the ship.

This is a dream. It's too ridiculous to be anything else. Wake up, wake up, wake up.

Teach was above, dark and blurry, but his eyes gleamed, wide and curious. He was leaning forward like a kid struggling to see a dolphin.

You're going to drown, Benjamin.

NO I'M NOT! I'M DREAMING! IT CAN'T END LIKE THIS!

The rest of the crew were lined up along the starboard side of the ship, smiling and laughing and elbowing each other. He knew half of them. He had captained many of them, before Edward Teach. Some had been trusted friends. He had shared food and drinks with them, played games with them, laughed with them.

Betrayed them.

The coffin came to a gentle halt and immediately started to bob up and down, tilting this way and that. Water streamed over the porthole. *Queen Anne's Revenge* and her jovial crew slowly slid out of his view.

And then there was nothing but blue sky through a small porthole.

It wasn't long before the coffin began to tip downward, feet first.

Oh God, save me. Don't let this happen. Don't let me die like this.

He heard the cannonballs roll and clink together as they bunched at his feet. Two of the smallest toes on his right foot were crushed.

Something cold touched his heels, and he tried to recoil, but succeeded only in rattling his shackles. He looked down and gasped hoarsely at what he saw. Water was streaming in from either side of the lid, near his shins, collecting in a pool at the base. The pool spread until it covered his feet and the cannonballs, and the coffin tilted until it was nearly vertical. His knees buckled against the interior. Soon the coffin was so deep that waves lapped at the porthole. The water inside rose to Hornigold's knees, and outside the water lifted above the porthole. The coffin was completely submerged. Hornigold planted his face against the glass and watched in horror as the surface slowly lifted above him. The sun shimmered beyond the glassy canopy. He saw colorful fish swimming in schools, their scales glistening softly in the diminished light. He saw a shark that was either very small or very large and far away.

The water filled the coffin to his waist and then tickled his stomach. The blue world outside gradually darkened. His chest heaved rapidly, unable to supply his lungs with enough oxygen.

Maybe I'll pass out first. Please, God, let me pass out first.

It's not real. It's a dream.

It's real. If you're lucky, you'll pass out first.

It's a dream, it's a dream, it's a dream.

His teeth were chattering uncontrollably, even though the water wasn't all that chilly. His body shook, arms knocking the slim confines. The coffin started to groan all around him. He pressed his face to the glass, looking downward. The bottom was surprisingly close. Teach had chosen a spot that wasn't too deep, so Hornigold would not be deprived of light. *He wants me to see my grave.*

Long strands of gnarled seaweed stretched up like fingers from the sand. He saw strange black columns within the seaweed. He counted twelve. Seven were standing vertically, and the other five had toppled over. As he descended, details came into focus.

He was looking at coffins, much like his.

It was a graveyard.

One of the coffins had broken open, and a skeleton was suspended above it, chained at the ankles and gently swaying in the seaweed. Bits of cloth and white flesh clung to the skeleton, and little fish nipped at what remained on the skull, which grinned at Hornigold.

It wasn't long before the coffin hit the bottom, settling in the graveyard amidst its companions. Hornigold pressed his face to the porthole. The surface was no more than sixty feet up, and the orb of the sun taunted him, casting oscillating rays upon his final resting place. He saw the black keel of *Queen Anne's Revenge* in the distance, slowly moving off.

Dark shapes darted between the seaweed and coffins. He saw a long thing with tentacles trailing behind a bulbous head. He saw a shark that was half the size of a man, weaving deftly through the graveyard, cold black eyes scanning for its next meal. A huge crab skittered atop of one of the coffins, claws raised as if in reverence to some great crab god above. Something struck the right side of Hornigold's coffin, and a shadow blotted out the porthole, and he thought he glimpsed white teeth before it passed.

The water lifted to his chest.

He beat his fists against the lid in frustration, and he kept on beating until blood oozed from his knuckles. When the porthole cracked, he stopped pounding. A web spread rapidly before his eyes.

Oh God, this is it.

His scream was a terrible thing, tearing at the inside of his throat as it warbled out of him. It went on and on, until only a tiny, shrill sound emerged, as if a very small man was trapped somewhere in his stomach. A triangle of glass popped out of the porthole, striking him painfully in the cheek. Hornigold inhaled to summon a final pathetic wail, but saltwater gushed into his mouth and filled his lungs. He gasped for a breath that refused to come, his eyes bulged from their sockets, and he knew at last that he was not dreaming. He beat his hands against the slim walls, and his legs writhed, but he wasn't going anywhere. Agonizing torrents pulsed from his lungs, and his muffled gagging filled his ears as he convulsed violently. He beat his forehead against the glass until it shattered completely. His blood swirled about him in tendrils, drifting through the porthole.

The monsters gathered outside, waiting patiently.

17

ANNABELLE

Once she found Ogle, who was exactly as Teach had described, she told him to summon Peter Lively, Gabe Jenkins, and Red Devil. All four had two things in common: They were highly respected among the crew, and they owed various debts to Blackbeard. For their covert meeting, Ogle suggested a cave he had discovered while searching for treasure. As Annabelle wandered alone through the jungle, with twilight darkening the sky, she hoped Teach had been right about the loyalty of these men. If he was wrong, she didn't want to think about what they would do to her. The only thing worse than one Edward Livingston would be four Edward Livingstons.

"They won't pluck a hair from your pretty head," Teach had assured her, but her confidence was waning with every step she took further into the jungle. She thought she'd have enough light, but she quickly regretted not bringing a torch. Croaking frogs, buzzing insects, and chirping birds merged to form an incessant chorus. A beetle the size of a walnut zipped toward her, colliding with her forehead before altering its course. She set a hand on a tree, and a long lizard slithered over her fingers, needlelike claws gripping her skin.

If she disappeared out here, no one would care to question her absence except Nathan Adams. Slipping out of his tent had been easy. Nathan was too occupied with supervising his crew as they ferried the chests from the shore to *Crusader*. She had counted nine chests in total. There were supposed to be four more, but after Blackbeard's visit, the pirates seemed eager to leave.

She had been here less than a day. So far she and Nathan hadn't consummated their reunion. After their first meeting, he returned with a plain brown shirt and black breeches for her to wear, instead of the skimpy robe Teach had presented her in. She tried to undress in front of him, but he made a hasty exit before the robe fell. She found the clothes uncomfortable. She had been so used to wearing next to nothing for most of her adult life, but without the protection of Blackbeard, it was probably best not to tempt this crew.

After that, Nathan checked in occasionally throughout the day, briefly making eye contact before departing prematurely. He clearly didn't know how to act around her. Confusion and joy seemed to be fighting a war within him, and she wasn't sure which was winning, nor did she care to find out. There was a time when that sort of thing would have endeared her, but now she just found it needlessly tiring. Nathan had obviously been through hell—and emerged with one less arm—but he was still every bit the indecisive boy she had spent a month with in Nassau.

If he hadn't left her there, things would be much different. She had been so naïve then. She knew she couldn't go back to that life even if she wanted to.

It was sad how foolish he looked when she first entered the tent, with his mouth hanging open and a little smile struggling at the edges. Was he really that stupid? The coincidence of her sudden appearance was so unfathomable, she hardly believed it herself. Perhaps that's why he couldn't look at her. He didn't trust her.

She smirked. *No.* A man who distrusts a woman does not shamefully pull his eyes from her. Nathan clearly felt guilty for leaving her behind. He had chosen piracy over her, and that choice had cost him more than he bargained for.

I'll show you a real pirate, Nathan.

Eventually, Annabelle came to a small clearing in the jungle, with two trees crisscrossing at the center, and she turned left just as Ogle had instructed. His directions were made easier by his leftover footprints, which remained in the muddy patches. She almost took a wrong turn once or twice, and then another footprint would clue her to the correct path.

After several twists and turns and no shortage of maddening uncertainty, the jungle opened onto the base of the mountain at the center of the island. At the foot was a black cave, with a yawning entrance wide enough to fit the bow of a sloop through. Cold air swept out of the darkness, riddling her arms with goose bumps. She heard a constant rush of water from somewhere deep within.

"Took your time," sounded a gruff voice from the black.

She nearly shuddered. "Who's there?"

"Who do you think?"

The man slowly stepped out of the darkness, and then she caught the familiar shine of his bald head. His gut jiggled as he walked, but the muscles of his arms and legs were as hard as the rocky walls of the cave. He smiled obscenely. "The others ain't here yet. What should we do while we wait?"

"You're too big for me," Annabelle smirked.

"You're used to little men like Adams?"

"I'm used to *men*, not giants," she countered.

"Once you've had a giant inside you, you won't want a man."

She lowered her head and pinched the bridge of her nose between thumb and forefinger, closing her eyes. "My employer would kill you if he knew we were having this conversation."

Ogle kept his smile, but one of his eyelids flickered. "I trust he knows a jest when he hears one."

"He knows a jest," she replied with a sweet smile, "but he might not find it very funny."

That shut him up.

They waited in silence outside the cave. The sky was littered with stars by the time Lively, Jenkins, and Red Devil arrived. Red Devil was carrying a torch, and the flickering orange glow made his skin appear blood-red in the night.

"Shall we, gents?" said Ogle, intoning the air of a British gentleman as he gestured toward the cave.

"After you," said Jenkins, adopting a similarly haughty tone.

"You first," Ogle replied.

"No, I insist, ladies first."

Annabelle slipped between them and descended into the cave. She heard them giggling like little boys behind her. She shook her head wearily. *These are the men he tells me to rely on? I'll be lucky to leave this cave with my life, let alone my clothes.*

The cave gradually blossomed with orange light as the four men fell in behind her. Red Devil remained in back, his torch casting their shadows upon the uneven walls. She wondered how deep this cave went. The rush of water filled her ears, echoing loudly. She would have to raise her voice to be heard. She cleared her throat and turned to face them. "You know who I serve."

"Served him well, I'd wager," laughed Lively. He nudged

Jenkins in the ribs, who winced and glowered in return.

Annabelle had to force herself not to stare at Jenkins, as he was an extremely attractive young man. She liked the way his thick long hair curled so naturally about his chiseled face. She cleared her throat. "I'm here to remind the four of you of your obligation."

Lively's laugh trailed down the cave, lost to the sound of water. He crossed his arms. "Aye, I know who you serve, and apparently he knows me. But he don't know me well enough to summon me like a dog. I crewed with him but a month. We're all of us free men, last I looked. I don't recall signing no contract when I stepped aboard *Queen Anne's Revenge*. How about you gents?" Lively looked around for support, but Ogle and Jenkins suddenly looked anxious, heads angled away from their loudmouthed friend.

Red Devil merely smirked at the back of Lively's head. When he spoke, his voice seemed to rumble across the walls like thunder rolling over the sea. "You'd do well to mind your tongue, boy."

"You'd do well to let your brain talk instead of your cunt," Lively shot back. "I'm not scared of you, red man, and I'm certainly not scared of some faraway pirate with delusions of grandiosity. What, he wears black and lights his beard on fire, so I'm supposed to piss meself at every mention of his name?"

Red Devil shook his head slowly and merely said, "Hmm."

Jenkins moved to the wall and started picking at a small jut of rock, trying not to look as nervous as he clearly was. "What carved this cave, you think? Water?"

"Water carves everything," Red Devil said.

Jenkins frowned. "It's strange we put so much of it in our bellies, then. I'm sticking with rum from now on."

Annabelle couldn't tell if Jenkins was being serious or not. He was difficult to read.

Lively scoffed. "If all the oceans were filled with rum in place of water, the whole bloody world would burn through."

Annabelle rolled her eyes. "I'm sure you can continue this discussion later. I need to know which of you I can count on. More importantly, I need to know which of you *Blackbeard* can count on, because he will surely dispose of those he can't, when the time comes."

Ogle spoke first. "What is it you'd be counting on us to do?"

"Remove obstacles."

Ogle placed his hands flat on his great round belly. "When you say 'obstacles,' would you be meaning 'people'?"

"People who would cause a problem, yes. But they mustn't be removed one at a time. They mustn't suspect anything is amiss until it's too late. They must all be removed at the same instant."

"Jesus," Lively exclaimed. "She'd have us murder our mates in cold blood."

"Starting with you," Annabelle said, aiming a finger at him. She nearly hesitated, but the words were out of her mouth before she gave them leave. She needed to know these men would do as she instructed, and Lively was the weak link of the group.

Lively's face went sour. "What did you just say?"

The torch fell, embers cascading down the rocky floor. Red Devil seized Lively by the scruff of his shirt and secured him easily. Lively squirmed in the huge man's grip, but it was no use. Red Devil's knife was at the boy's throat in a flash.

"Not you, Red," Annabelle said with a raised hand. She knew Red Devil was a killer from the moment she had laid eyes on him. She didn't need to test his willingness.

She looked to Jenkins. "*You* do it."

The light of the dying torch did little to soften the white

sheet that passed over Jenkins' pretty face. His Adam's apple bobbed in his thick neck as he swallowed. "Do what, miss?"

"Take out your pistol and put a shot through your friend's skull."

Lively loosed a sound that was somewhere between a laugh and a snivel. "This is a joke. Yes, it's a joke. I get it now. Very funny. You made your point. Let me go and I'll mind me tongue. It gets away from me sometimes."

"Yes," Annabelle said. "That's what concerns me."

"It need concern you no more," Lively assured her.

She moved closer, looking into his eyes. "I believe you," she said. "But I need to know that your friends will do what I command."

"They will," Lively bleated. "I know they will."

"I'm not convinced," she said. "Right now I think your friends are considering shooting me instead."

Ogle confirmed her suspicion with a keen nod. "I can't say I fancy a bitch telling me who I can or can't kill."

A surge of adrenaline filled Annabelle's chest. She was acutely aware that she was enjoying the imminent danger of the situation. She advanced on Ogle, knowing it might be the last move she ever made. "And you'd get away with it." She cocked her head, allowing herself a sly smile. "At least, you'd *think* you got away with it. And then, one day, when you least expected it, maybe a month from now or maybe even a year, *he* would come for you, just as he came for Benjamin Hornigold. He specifically named you four men. Do you honestly think he'll let you get away with murdering me? I think a part of him wants you to do it."

Ogle's eyelids fluttered uncertainly.

She called over her shoulder, "Jenkins! Why haven't you shot this man yet?"

Stone-faced, Jenkins drew a pistol from his blue sash.

Ogle looked at the ground.

Red Devil was grinning, rows of white teeth splitting his crimson face.

Lively started to sob desperately. "No, Gabe."

Jenkins leveled the pistol at Lively's temple. Lively tried to twist out of the barrel's line of sight, but Red Devil clutched a handful of his hair and held him in place.

"Gabe," Lively sniveled, snot dribbling out of his nose. "Gabe, no. Remember that time we—"

The shot brightened the cave and cracked in Annabelle's ears. For an instant she saw Lively's face frozen in the flash, a small red dot in his temple, mouth drooping open, and one eye closed. Annabelle squeezed her eyes shut, and when she opened them, a cloud of smoke roiled toward her. She clenched her teeth and struggled not to cough, but a muffled choke belched from her throat. She waved the smoke away. The three men were staring down at Lively's limp body. The shot was clean, with no exit wound. Just a hole in his temple, with a thin line of blood streaming into his hair.

Ogle seemed to have no trouble breaking awkward silences. "'Remember that time' you what?" he asked. When Jenkins didn't respond, Ogle palmed him on the back of his head. Jenkins shook violently, staring at him. "'Remember that time' you what?" Ogle demanded. "He didn't get to finish."

"I dunno," Jenkins barked defensively. "Could've been anything. What's it matter?"

Ogle looked flustered. "Shoulda let him finish. Now I'll be wondering at it all night!"

Red Devil retrieved the torch and held it aloft. "There's a stream down there," he said. "We'll put the body in the water."

"Someone will miss him," Jenkins muttered, knuckles white as he tightly gripped the smoking gun.

"Not enough to wait for him," Annabelle said.

"She's got a point," Ogle said. "The men are aching for Tortuga. All that coin won't spend itself."

"They wouldn't be so eager if they knew it's all going to Blackbeard," Jenkins sulked.

"Teach is a fair man," Ogle replied. "So long as he's not crossed. I don't want to be looking over my shoulder the rest of my life. We've more than enough coin to split. We'll deliver him his share and be on our way."

"That's the plan," said Annabelle.

"What of Adams?" Jenkins said. "He's been a good captain. Surprised us all, to be honest."

Red Devil scowled at Jenkins in disgust.

Annabelle smiled sadly. "Adams made his choice when he didn't tell Teach about the treasure. He'll die with the rest."

"And who gets to kill him?" Red Devil asked hopefully.

"I do," Annabelle replied easily.

Ogle looked skeptical. "Have you ever killed a man? With your own two hands?"

"No," she said with a shrug. "But Adams is as good a place to start as any. Teach knows our course. Failure will mean the death of everyone on that ship." She pointed at Lively's corpse. "If a few must die to save the rest, that is far less a cruelty than the alternative." She looked at Jenkins. "Yes?"

Jenkins nodded somberly and slipped his gun back in his sash. "Suppose so."

She turned to Ogle. "Sway those that you can, but do not bother with those that remain fiercely loyal to Dillahunt or Adams."

"No one's loyal to Dillahunt," Jenkins said. "Their eyes all lit up when they saw the first of that treasure. Just today Adams told us he plans on keeping Dillahunt under lock and key until such time as he can set him loose and be quit of him."

Annabelle smirked. *Just today, eh?* Her presence had nudged

Nathan back to piracy. Otherwise, he probably would have carried out Dillahunt's mission and sailed back to Nassau with Hornigold as his prisoner. *Silly boy.*

"Fine," she said. "But now they're loyal to Adams, who earned them their fortune. You must dispose of those who cannot be swayed. You have five days, and then we take the ship for ourselves. Spend those days wisely, gathering allies, and then strike. Teach wants no resistance."

"Why not?" Jenkins asked. "*Queen Anne* could take us."

"Use your head, boy," Ogle growled. "*Crusader* would go down, sure enough, but she'd also take Teach's share of the treasure with her. Why risk that?"

"There's a smart man," Annabelle said.

"What of the redhead and the girl?" Ogle wondered with a sadistic gleam in his eye.

Annabelle shoved a finger in his face. "No raping," she sneered. She would not have any of the women assaulted while she was in charge. Not after what Livingston had done to her. No one deserved that.

"You don't tell me who I can or can't rape, woman."

"No raping, or you'll answer to Blackbeard."

Red Devil laughed. "Because he cares?"

"The women are valuable," said Annabelle.

"Lindsay is," Ogle agreed, "but no one will miss the black-haired girl. She tried to kill Blackbeard."

"All the more reason to leave her intact. Teach will decide how he wants to handle her."

Ogle giggled like a little boy. "I've been wanting to handle her since I found out she was a she."

Annabelle advanced on him. "Touch her and Blackbeard will hear of it."

The big man backed off, nodding submissively. "Fine, fine."

She looked around, realizing she had nothing left to say.

Jenkins was still staring at Lively. She had half a mind to ease his troubles. *Maybe later.*

"I'll leave you boys to clean this up. Don't speak to me again unless I speak to you first." With that, she started back for the beach, leaving them there to dispose of Peter Lively. She could only imagine what they were saying about her. She didn't care, so long as they did as she asked.

The journey back seemed quicker than the journey there. She heard a rise of boisterous laughter before she came upon the beach. When she exited the woods, the crew were dancing and singing around a huge bonfire, and the smell of roast pig and sizzling chicken teased her nostrils. Her mouth watered, but she didn't know who she could trust yet, nor did she feel like making friends with someone who might be dead in five days. All of them were clearly very drunk. Katherine Lindsay was sitting close to the fire, chatting with a group of them, who looked enthralled with whatever she was saying. Surely they were more enthralled with her casually laced shirt, which did little to conceal her cleavage. Her red hair blazed in the glow of the flames. She didn't appear to be lamenting the absence of Benjamin Hornigold. Lindsay was clearly a survivor, and Annabelle suspected she would fall to the winning side when the time came.

And if she is truly responsible for sinking Harbinger, I must remember to thank her. She wondered what horrors Lindsay had suffered at the hands of Livingston. The man had uprooted Annabelle's life in a matter of minutes. Lindsay had been at his mercy for a year. If she could survive a man like Livingston, she could survive anything.

Annabelle skirted the edges of the camp, remaining in the shadows until she reached the big tent. She ducked inside and found the tent dark, with the exception of a single candle atop the desk where Nathan was hunched over a map, with a mostly neglected plate of chicken next to his lone hand. Dillahunt had been removed to a smaller tent, presumably under guard with the girl who had attempted to murder Blackbeard. Nathan glanced up at her, a distinct flutter of irritation passing over his face.

"I was worried," he said.

"I've been cooped up in a ship far too long," she replied. "I needed a walk."

"Long walk."

She took a seat across from him, setting her elbows on the desk and resting her chin on her knuckles. He looked up, found her staring at him, and looked away quickly. His eyes slowly trailed back to meet hers. A little smile played at the edges of his lips. She returned it.

He is so easy.

She looked at the chicken, hoping he would take the hint. He slid the plate across to her. "Go ahead."

"You're not hungry?"

"Not especially."

She picked up a plump chicken leg and sank her teeth into it. Her eyes closed, and she smiled happily as she swallowed the first piece of juicy meat. She quickly stripped the leg to the bone, tossed it back onto the plate, and licked her fingers. Nathan stared at her, eyes widening. She cocked her head, sliding a finger from her mouth. "What're you staring at?"

"A woman I feared I'd never see again."

"Yet now that you have me, you avoid me."

"I'm trying to get us out of here," he said, jutting his chin at the map indicatively. "There'll be time enough for us later. When we're safe."

"When do we leave?"

"At first light."

She let her smile grow suggestively. "Then there's time

enough for us now."

He fixated on the map. "I should really—"

"Who knows what time we really have?" She stood and slowly rounded the desk. His eyes lifted, following her hips. She sat on the desk and nudged his leg with her own. He put his hand on her thigh. She placed her hand atop his, moving it up into a gap where her shirt had come untucked. The shirt lifted as she continued to slide his hand up her midriff. His calloused palm was like gravel running over her smooth skin. He stood, lips drawing near, his breath heavy on her face. He looked horrified and excited all at once, as he had during their first encounter. His fingers grazed the underside of her right breast and hesitated there, tickling her flesh. She jerked his hand upward to cup her, and he squeezed eagerly. He lifted her shirt over her head, freeing her large breasts and mashing his face against them. She held his head there, spreading her fingers through his sandy blonde hair. She slid her other hand into his breeches and curled her fingers around his hardening manhood. She felt his tongue circling an areola, his teeth lightly pinching the nipple. His hand fell to the small of her back, pulling her to him as she stroked him fiercely.

He kissed her neck, and she let her head fall back, wincing pleasurably as he nibbled at her skin. He was going to leave raw marks on her throat, but she supposed that was only fair.

18

KATE

She was on the last boat that ferried back to *Crusader*.

She had been nervous that Nathan would leave her on the island and sail away without a single look back. Her anxiety increased when he ferried the prisoners over before her, but she was determined not to let him know. At the last minute, he snapped his fingers at Candler and said, "Bring Lindsay." She would have thanked him, but she suspected he had deliberately withheld his intent in order to worry her. If so, it had worked.

The trip over seemed long, with the hot midday sun beating down. The boat was crammed with the last of the crew, all of them sweating heavily. The stench of body odor was difficult to ignore. The sun was unbearably hot, and there was no breeze to soften it. Kate leaned over and trailed her fingers in the water, but that provided little relief.

She made three attempts at conversing with Candler, but each time he replied only in frenetic grunts, angling his head toward the sea and stroking his golden goatee. She gave up on Candler and turned to a muscular young man with thick black locks. He was wearing a blue sash. His handsome brow was pinched at the middle, and his eyes were distant, as though something was worrying him. "What's your name?" she asked.

"Gabe Jenkins," he muttered sullenly. "You're Kate, yes?"

Her belly fluttered. *The gorgeous boy knows my name.* She scowled at her sudden girlishness. *Of course he knows your name, you silly woman. Everyone knows the name of a woman with a reward on her head. Don't be daft.*

He was staring at her curiously. "Are you alright? Your face is doing funny things."

"No it's not," she scoffed defensively. "*Your* face is funny."

"What?"

"I don't know," she said, looking away and withering with embarrassment. After her experience aboard *Harbinger*, she wasn't sure she could ever be attracted to men again. Now that she found herself undeniably attracted to someone, she had no idea how to act. Part of her wanted to die for being so silly, while another part was giddy just to realize she could still feel that way.

He frowned. "Are you sure you're alright?"

"I'm fine." She cleared her throat, banishing the silliness, and casually asked, "Do you know where we're going?"

"To the ship," he said, pointing at *Crusader*.

She rolled her eyes. "And where would said ship be taking us?"

Jenkins winked. "Probably I'm not supposed to tell you. Not with our dear captain and his bonny lass right over there." Nathan had taken a seat at the front of the longboat, as far removed from Kate as possible, with his beautiful strumpet at his side.

Kate leaned close and whispered in Gabe's ear, "You mean

his whore?"

He smirked. "Maybe I did, but I'm not sure which one of them is more deserving of the word."

Kate laughed. *Smart boy.*

Jenkins continued to glare. There was something dangerous in those pretty eyes, barely concealed beneath the surface. Was it jealousy? Did he fancy Annabelle? Kate couldn't be sure. Either way, this was probably not someone she wanted to get involved with. *Even if he is one of the prettiest boys I've ever seen.*

She looked away, refusing to let herself look at Jenkins any longer.

Her gaze settled on Nathan and his beautiful strumpet. It was obvious why he was so infatuated with this woman. She had just the right amount of curves, amazing black hair, and a supple face, apart from the scar. Her wicked eyes and the evocative arch of her back suggested she knew more about sex than she did about anything else. She whispered something in Nathan's ear that made him laugh, and then she glanced at Kate, and Kate knew the jest had been about her.

Make all the jokes you want. I was just having a laugh about you with Mr. Jenkins here.

It was midafternoon when Kate climbed aboard *Crusader* for the first time, helped up by Jenkins. He favored her with half a smile and took his leave. He seemed very distracted, and she doubted he would even remember he had met her.

The deck was a mess from the battle with Hornigold's ship. There were splotches of blood here and there, and splinters everywhere. The port bulwark was pitted with large holes.

Kate stared at Griffith's Isle as *Crusader* pulled away. She was confident that she would never set foot on those cursed sands again. Nothing good had ever happened there. It was a graveyard.

When she turned away from the island and started walking

along the deck, she nearly ran into Nathan. He stared in surprise. "Kate," he greeted . . . and immediately started in another direction.

"Nathan," she called.

He halted and slowly pivoted. "Yes?"

There were a hundred things she wanted to ask. She wanted to ask him what he was thinking, trading a man's life for a strumpet who in all likelihood was far more interested in the hold's plunder than she was in Nathan. She wanted to ask him why he was risking his neck yet again for piracy, after Rogers had set him free. She wanted to ask him why she of all people was free to roam the deck, instead of being secured with the others. She wanted to ask him why he had locked up poor Calloway for trying to put an end to a notorious murderer. Above all, she wanted to ask how someone so smart could be so stupid.

Instead, she shook her head and said, "It's nothing. Never-mind."

He grunted and abruptly walked off toward his cabin, where Annabelle was likely waiting for him. Kate glanced around at the crew. Some of them were scowling at Nathan behind his back. *He's already losing them,* she realized.

Late that night, as *Crusader* sailed through a calm sea with no land in sight, Kate descended to the hold. She made her way through the many crates, to the two crude square cages in the back. Hornigold's men, who now totaled nine, were secure in the larger cage. She knew all their faces. Harrow, Bastion, Dumaka, Laurent, Clemens, Elegy, Fat Farley, Billie, and his older brother Avery.

Dillahunt and Calloway were huddled in the smaller cage, which was tucked further away in a dark corner. Dillahunt's state hadn't changed, wrapped in bandages and blankets. Calloway looked up, eyes red with fury. "Why are you out there while I'm in here?" she demanded.

"You'll find no argument," Kate said, raising her hands. "I've been wondering the same. It's not fair."

Calloway opened her mouth, preparing for a retort, before she realized Kate had agreed with her. "No, it's not," she replied stubbornly.

Kate smiled. "While I'm out here, can I get you anything?"

"A pistol, maybe?"

"Anything other than a pistol?"

"Food?" she said hopefully. She held up a half-eaten clump of dried bread. "This is all they gave us. I didn't eat the other half, by the way. It came like that." She indicated a pile of white cloth between her and Dillahunt. "Nathan was nice enough to provide new bandages, but forgot to send real food. Occupied with his whore, I suppose. He's forgotten everything else. We'll probably rot in here. I thought him a friend."

"He's just a little out of his mind," Kate assured her. "I'll get you some real food."

"It's for Dillahunt," Calloway barked defensively.

Kate doubted Dillahunt was doing much eating these days, but she didn't want to press the issue. It was obvious that the girl didn't want to be indebted to her. That was fine. Kate would allow her to maintain her stubborn pride, so long as she ate. "I'll be back later."

"Please hurry," Calloway said.

Kate walked past Hornigold's former men on her way out, and they started talking all at once. "We didn't get no food neither," groaned Jeremy Clemens.

"Aye, where's our love, love?" said Andrew Harrow. "We shared our rum with you, remember?"

Kate scoffed. "I *took* your rum, remember?"

"Well there you go," Harrow said, shoving a pleading hand through the bars. "You owe us."

Francois Laurent flashed a suggestive grin. "I'd be eternally indebted."

"Can't live off scraps," Dumaka muttered.

Fat Farley just stared at her with sad eyes.

"My belly is screaming," said Gabriel Elegy, rubbing his stomach.

Kate put a finger to her mouth, quieting them. "I'll find food for all of you, but you have to keep quiet about it."

"Oh, bless you, missy," said Harrow.

Avery Dowling grunted. "I'll believe it when I see it."

"I'll make a believer out of you yet," she promised him.

"To what end, eh?" he asked, crossing his arms. "What's in it for you?"

She shrugged. "I sailed with you boys. We are bonded."

Avery snorted. "Not in the way I'd like."

She slapped the bars. "You're lucky you're not the only man in that cage, Avery Dowling, else I wouldn't be standing here taking orders like a serving wench in some seedy tavern."

Avery made a sour face and turned away. "No one's nice without a reason. Mark my words, men."

"She's a woman," Harrow said, as if the answer was obvious. "Women have good hearts. They like to make things right when things is wrong."

"Aye," agreed Clemens, although his face turned red as he stifled a laugh.

Kate managed not to bluster. She hastily took her leave. As she ascended the stairs to the main deck, she allowed herself a smile. She had just secured a handful of allies.

She had a feeling she would need them.

19

DILLAHUNT

Whenever he woke, the world was in chaos. His environment kept changing.

First he found himself in an oversized tent that stretched away from the little corner he was huddled in. He was covered in blankets and drenched in sweat, yet shivering violently. Filthy, bloodstained bandages were wrapped tight around his face, chest, arms, and legs. His throat felt like a desert, with tiny cactuses prickling his gullet whenever he swallowed. It pained his facial muscles just to part his lips.

Nathan Adams had been there too, conversing amicably with . . . *no, it couldn't have been him.*

Yet it couldn't have been anyone else.

Edward Teach.

Blackbeard.

And Adams was striking a deal with the man, handing him Benjamin Hornigold in exchange for some strumpet. Dillahunt cursed his stupidity in promoting the boy to captain. What madness had seized him? He should have promoted Candler. The man was a fool and a coward, but at least he'd remained loyal over the years. Then again, that loyalty only went so far. Candler must have been serving Adams now, or else he would have been in a cell with Dillahunt.

Is there no one I can trust?

Adams clearly had his own agenda, though it was directly at odds with a prolonged life. Bargains with Blackbeard rarely ended favorably. Dillahunt recalled shouting something at the two of them. Blackbeard had looked on him as a boy looks on an ant before squashing it underfoot. And then Dillahunt was lost to darkness, followed swiftly by those strange dreams just like the ones he had as a boy, where he was assaulted with unsolvable patterns. On and on the dreams went, and he wandered lucidly through them but was unable to stir himself into consciousness.

The next time he woke, he found himself in a much smaller tent, with Jacqueline Calloway sitting beside him, hugging her knees while she rocked back and forth. When she noticed he was awake, she leaned in close with a sad smile. Her boyish black hair had grown half an inch since last he saw her. Her skin was darker, freckles more prominent. Yet her smile yielded no comfort, and her blue eyes were distant and somehow less bright than he remembered. She picked at his face, and he glimpsed the edges of a white bandage, mottled with red. "You're healing," she said, but she looked distressed.

Darkness swept in along the perimeter of his vision. He tried to focus on her pretty young face, but his eyes slowly rolled upward in their sockets without asking his permission. The dreams and their infuriating puzzles returned. A mess of thin white sticks was scattered before him. As he struggled to arrange them in bundles, he realized they were bones. Leg bones, arm bones, here and there a rib, a femur, little fingers and toes, and finally a skull. He arranged them properly, constructing a full skeleton on the ground. When he had finished, his nostrils picked up a foul scent. A fly trailed before him, taunting him with an annoying *buzz*. His eyes tracked the fly as it buzzed around his head, sailed downward and landed on a glistening mound of hot, steaming flesh. Dillahunt sprang forward uncontrollably, moved by an inexplicable urge, and plunged his hands into the flesh without thinking. He had trouble scooping it up, as the squishy red chunks slid through his fingers. He bowled his hands, filling as much as possible, and began piling the flesh atop the skeleton. The pieces fit together like a jigsaw puzzle. He kept going until the skeleton was completely covered, save for the skull. He gathered the final bits of flesh. Pieces of a face, two ears, the full cap of a scalp with brown hair permeated with light blonde strands, and two eyeballs that dangled on red nerve stems. He quickly assembled the face and stuffed the eyes into the two dark hollows.

He recoiled as he looked on what might have been a mirror image. "Thank you," the other Dillahunt said. "I feel much better now."

He awoke in a dark hold, with strips of light streaming through slits in the planking above. He was surrounded by bars. Calloway remained at his side. Her forehead was beaded with sweat. Her skin had lost some of the color it had gained during the journey to Griffith's Isle. She looked at him, but this time offered no smile, sad or otherwise. "Oh, you're awake," was all she said.

He raised his hand to his face and felt the bandages. He wondered how bad he looked, but he wasn't sure he really wanted to know. Calloway would probably lie if he asked. Some of the bandages had been removed from his arms and legs. His right leg was almost completely freed, with thin lacerations that had healed nicely, but his left was shrouded, except for the knee. His arms were sporadically wrapped, and his chest was completely covered. *I'm only half a mummy, now.*

He tilted his head to the right, where he saw several black chests with gold accents occupying a far corner of the hold. Griffith's fabled treasure, no doubt. That fortune had lured Hornigold to his death. *How many more lives will it claim before this journey is done?*

He heard male voices and swiveled his head left, peering between two large crates. Through the gap, a group of nine men were exchanging bitter words. They were in a cage of their own. He recognized a few of them from Benjamin Hornigold's ship, *Ranger*. Francois Laurent, a Frenchman he had met in a tavern in Nassau, was staring back at him, nudging a huge black man beside him. "Looks like Dillahunt's waking up," he said. This provoked the curiosity of the other men, who crowded together to see through the gap.

"Him won't like what Captain Nathan did with Captain Benjamin," said a man with dark skin. "Him won't like that one bit."

"And what's he going to do about it in his condition?" spat Avery Dowling, who had served under Dillahunt a few years ago, with his younger brother Billie, who was presently sitting quietly beside him. "And in a cell, no less. We've just got to keep kissing Adams' ass until he lets us out of here."

"Adams don't trust us," said a thin lad Dillahunt did not recognize.

"Why should he?" replied a very fat man. "We attacked first."

"We was under Hornigold's orders, we were," the thin lad said with a shrug. "Adams ain't exactly on the side of the law no more hisself. He'll have to let us out someday."

"Or he might just leave us here to rot," the fat man sighed. "He barely feeds us. I'd starve if not for Kate sneaking us a good meal now and again."

"You're always starving, Farley," quipped the thin lad. "And why does Lindsay get to roam free, anyways?"

"Don't know, but I'm glad she does," Farley replied as he rubbed his stomach.

"Adams is probably afraid to lock her up," Laurent laughed.

"Bah!" Avery sneered. "She's just a woman."

"She's always been nice to me," said Farley.

"She wasn't nice to Bart," scoffed the thin lad.

"Bart fell off the ship," the dark-skinned islander replied.

"You keep telling yourself that, Bastion," chuckled the thin lad. "I'd wager he had a bit of help over the rail."

"He probably deserved it," said Laurent.

Billie Dowling picked at the blistered skin on one of his arms. "No one deserves to die in the ocean, all alone."

Avery cackled scathingly in his little brother's face. "Billie here captains his own ship, did you know that? It's called *The Obvious*."

"Didn't know Billie's tongue still worked," Laurent said, shocked. He set a hand on Billie's shoulder. "We thought you'd gone mute, boy."

"I'm tired, is all."

Avery waved a dismissive hand. "We're all tired, boy."

After that, all of them fell silent and stared distantly as they pondered their dire situation.

Dillahunt looked at Calloway, who was rocking slowly back and forth. He lifted his head slightly, straining the muscles in his neck. "How long?" he managed. He felt his lips split when he talked. He ran his tongue over the flaked, dry surface.

She gazed woefully at him. "It's three days since we left the island. Nathan is taking us to Tortuga."

"Skullduggerous little shit."

"He gave you new bandages," she replied in a halfhearted defense.

"Bah! I shall see his cock removed and stuffed up his ass." He frowned. "Why are *you* in here?"

She blinked, looking away. "I tried to kill Blackbeard."

"Oh," he said, nodding. "Right, then."

She didn't seem to want to discuss it, so he didn't inquire. Her face was somehow less complicated than he remembered. Her smile was slow and steady, as though calculated, or maybe just difficult to muster. As much as patterns vexed him, the notion of a simpler Calloway made him profoundly sad, though he couldn't explain why.

He struggled to sit up, wincing as pain spiked through his stomach muscles. His arms ached from lack of use, riddled with scabbed lacerations wherever the bandages had been removed. The wounds beneath the bandages that remained must have been truly dreadful. Calloway helped him lean against a crate that had been placed inside the little cell. "Drink this," she said, handing him a half-drained bottle of rum. He took a hefty swig, letting it trickle down the sides of his mouth and saturate the bandages on his chest.

"Nice of our captors to supply us," he said, handing the bottle back to her.

"It was Lindsay," Calloway said with a flicker of irritation. "She visits when everyone else is sleeping. Brings extra food and drink. All good deeds, that one."

"Until you get in her way," he grunted. "Lindsay's keen enough to know how quickly the tide can change."

Calloway's freckles bunched in a perplexed scowl. "She's always trying to talk to me. It's like she wants to be friends. I try to be mean. I say horrible things, and she puts on a stupid sad face, but she keeps coming back, always asking if I'm okay or if I need anything. It's maddening!"

Dillahunt shrugged as though it was obvious. "She's lacking for female company."

Calloway's head sank between her shoulders. "I'm a poor substitute for that."

Dillahunt set a hand on her leg, lightly stroking with his thumb. "You're far more skilled at being a woman than you think. As a boy, you're an utter disgrace."

She giggled in spite of herself.

"Good God!" Dillahunt jerked his hand from her leg and stared at his nails, which were long and jagged, like shards of broken glass. "I might have slit my own throat in my sleep! Did no one bother to trim them?"

She snorted. "Hygiene is not a priority on this ship."

"Bloody savages!" Dillahunt exclaimed. "The next time Lindsay is about, have her fetch me some clippers, elsewise I might saw through these bars with my fingers. Jesus! I dare not look at my toes!"

"I think Nathan will let us go in Tortuga," Calloway said hopefully.

"Stop calling him 'Nathan,'" he huffed, folding his arms. "When we get to Tortuga, I shall find the nearest blacksmith and fetch a sword to run across that boy's throat."

Her face twisted acrimoniously. "He occupies your cabin, diddling that strumpet he traded Hornigold for."

"Hornigold is surely dead by now," he said. "Rogers will have my head for this, mounted above his desk as a warning to all others who would fail him so miserably."

"But you were mutinied against. He must understand that."

Dillahunt chuckled through his teeth. "There was no mutiny. I handed my ship to Adams on a platter. If Candler hadn't been pissing all over himself, I might have roused from slumber in proper quarters, rather than a cage."

"Candler's an idiot," Calloway reminded him. "And were he truly your friend, he would be in this cage with us, refusing to aid Adams. Instead he struts about freely. He checks in on you occasionally, and I think he's disappointed when he sees you have not perished."

Without thinking, he started to scratch a scab on his right arm, finger probing between two bandages, and Calloway snatched his wrist. "Don't," she snapped. "You'll make it worse." For a fleeting moment, her concern for his wellbeing revitalized her face, crowding it with several emotions at once. She withdrew just as swiftly, and the complexity was gone.

"Have you stayed by my side the entire time?" he asked.

She tilted her eyes his way without moving her head. "I tried to get away, but these damned bars made it difficult."

Dillahunt smiled. It was good to know Calloway was still in there somewhere, ready to emerge at any moment. Resolve was no match for youth.

"I have to take my ship back," he said.

"You're not giving up?"

"Why should I?"

She angrily flicked one of the bars with her middle finger, and it made a ringing sound. "Because we're in a cage! Most would stop there."

"Most would," he grinned, ignoring a plethora of pain as the raw skin of his cheeks stretched taut. "An opportunity will present itself. Half this crew is not to be trusted, and the other half just wants to live. Adams doesn't realize the danger he's in."

"I wouldn't underestimate him," Calloway said.

"Oh, clearly I don't," Dillahunt said, glancing irritably at the bars. "But the odds are against him. We need only wait."

A few hours later, Phillip Candler timidly descended the stairs at the far end of the hold. It seemed to take him an hour to make his way through the crates and barrels. He approached Dillahunt's cage with the look of a mouse hoping to befriend a cat. "I thought you might never w-w-wake," he stammered.

"Disappointed?" said Dillahunt.

"Relieved," Candler insisted, though his obvious trepidation suggested otherwise.

"You don't look it," Dillahunt replied. "Set yourself at ease, Phillip. You've committed no treason."

"The hell he hasn't," Calloway spat. "He serves pirates now, or hadn't you noticed?"

Candler seized the bars in desperation. "Pirates who surely would have killed me had I not shifted allegiance!"

Hornigold's nine men burst into fits of laughter.

Candler's face darkened against the bars.

"They may kill you still," Dillahunt reminded him.

"And what would you have me do?"

"Set me free," Dillahunt replied.

Candler pushed himself away from the bars. "So you can do what, precisely? Confront Adams and die for your trouble? I think not!"

"Adams is no killer," Calloway objected.

"He killed plenty of Hornigold's men!"

"Aye," called Andrew Harrow from afar.

"In self-defense," Calloway said.

"Those were pirates," Dillahunt reminded Candler. He jabbed a thumb against his own chest. "I am no pirate."

"Shame, that," shouted Harrow. "You'd make a fine one."

"Quiet, Andrew!" urged Fat Farley.

"Or what?" Harrow balked. "He'll slip out of his cage and box me ears? I gave him a compliment!"

Farley shrugged. "We might be on his side when we're sprung."

"You, fat sir, are on no one's side!" Dillahunt shouted over.

"You are all traitorous dogs, and I'll see you all at the end of a noose."

Calloway's fingers dug into Dillahunt's arm. "We might need them," she hissed.

Avery Dowling chuckled. "We'll see what a few more days makes of the good captain's resolve. I wager he'll look to us as mates soon enough."

Candler was backing away from the cell. "I must return topside. I only meant to check on you."

"Certainly not to *aid* me," Dillahunt growled. "Do not check on me again, unless you bring a key."

Candler nodded sadly and hurried off.

Later that night, after Katherine Lindsay had snuck in more food, Dillahunt was drifting in and out of a light slumber when he heard whispers, low and conspiratorial from a far corner of the hold. He glanced through the seam of the crates that separated his cell from Hornigold's men and saw them all fast asleep, except for Avery who was wide awake. The carpenter was sitting against the bars with one arm casually strung across a bent knee. He briefly locked eyes with Dillahunt, drawing his index finger to his mouth and shaking his head. He tilted the finger in the direction of the two shadows.

They were hunched near a dark cluster of double-stacked barrels, grunting as they pulled one of the barrels from the top and set it down. There were two of them, both very large.

"It's Ogle and Red Devil," Calloway whispered, opening her eyes but not getting up.

"Treacherous swine," he hissed.

She reached over to grasp his hand. "Keep your voice down. Those two worry me. Whatever they're doing, they don't want anyone to know about it."

"I'm not afraid of them," he scoffed.

The two men turned an empty barrel on its side and rolled

it toward the stairs. As they stepped into the soft amber light flowing down from a lantern on the deck above, Dillahunt glimpsed the two men's faces. They looked rather nervous.

Under her breath, Calloway said, "Every night they come down here and remove a few empty barrels."

Dillahunt frowned. "Why?"

She shrugged. "Hornigold's men have been trying to figure that out. No one knows."

Red Devil suddenly started for Dillahunt and Calloway, moving at an alarming speed. Dillahunt sank into his blankets. Red Devil looked at the cell. But he didn't stop. He continued on to the black treasure chests, which were striped with lantern light from above. He opened one, and the light fell on brightly colored silks. Red Devil plucked a few silks from the chest and slammed the lid closed. He returned to Ogle, stuffing the silks into the barrel. "Let's take them up," Ogle said. Red Devil nodded, and they worked together to heave the barrel up the stairs.

"That can't mean anything good," Dillahunt said.

20

NATHAN

Nathan cocked the hammer and tightened the screw that ran through the jaws, securing a fresh chunk of flint between the clamps. It had been raining all day while he attended to his duties on deck, and the powder was soaked through. He sprinkled fresh powder into the priming pan and covered it beneath the L-shaped frizzen. He spent another few minutes polishing the pistol and then set the weapon on the little round table beside the bed, as had been his ritual for the past five days.

He looked over at Annabelle. Her breasts slowly lifted and fell. Her body was slick with sweat from their lovemaking. She had been even more energetic than usual, as if she had feared she might never make love again. She wouldn't even let him get on top. When it was over, she rolled off of him, sighing happily, and was soon asleep.

As exhausted as he was, he had no wish to join her. When

he slept, he saw Hornigold's face, desperately pleading with him or furiously accusing him, while the monster Blackbeard dragged Hornigold kicking and screaming across the sand toward a roiling black sea. Blackbeard was always impossibly tall in the dreams, dwarfing Hornigold, who was barely larger than a young boy, hopeless in his captor's grasp, lost beneath the shadow of a giant.

Nathan slid quietly out of the bed, taking care not to wake Annabelle. *If she's actually sleeping.* He looked at the gun on the table. *There it is, my love. If that's what you came here to do, there will never be a better time.*

He slipped on his pants and threw on a clean white shirt, leaving it unlaced at the neck. It took too long to lace a shirt one-handed. He stepped on deck, closing the door without looking at Annabelle again. The main deck was dim, with only two lanterns flickering softly, as per Nathan's instructions. He didn't want *Crusader* to appear as a beacon of light for miles around. Most of the pirates up top were sleeping, save for Ogle, Gabe Jenkins, Red Devil, and a few others he didn't recognize, all huddled near the capstan, engaged in a game of dice. Ogle and Jenkins smiled all too generously at him as he passed, while Red Devil merely nodded, with a strange twinkle in his eye that suggested he knew something Nathan didn't.

"Evenin', captain," Jenkins called. "Nice night, isn't it?"

Nathan nodded curtly at him. He wasn't sure what to make of Jenkins, who always seemed uncomfortable around him, rarely making eye contact.

Nathan wandered to the bow, where light didn't reach. A shadow was lingering there, too slender for a man, with wild hair tossing in the breeze. She was hunched over the port bulwark, gazing into the darkness below.

"Kate," he called, not wanting to startle her, for fear she'd plunge something sharp into his belly.

"I wondered when you'd start speaking to me," she replied.

"I've run out of reasons not to," he admitted.

"Maybe if you hadn't locked up poor Calloway, you could have sent her again. She fancies me, I think. Especially my hair."

"Really?" he said, pleased. "I was hoping you'd get along."

"It was a joke, Nathan. She hates me."

"Oh."

"But I might be wearing her down. She reminds me of you, a bit."

He was suddenly intrigued. "How so?"

She grinned. "Not so good at holding a grudge."

"I wouldn't say that. She did try to murder Teach. I think she's got more in common with *you*."

Kate smirked. "If she was anything like me, Teach would be dead."

"I can't trust her," he said, stepping beside her to join in the view, not that there was much to see. The sky was black with clouds, allowing the sea no reflection. It seemed as though *Crusader* was sailing through an endless abyss. "She nearly ruined everything, and she's infatuated with Dillahunt."

"Why does everyone think Blackbeard an unkillable wraith? You should have aided her."

Nathan stared at her. "Killed Teach?"

"Why not? You had your precious Annabelle. You could have easily overpowered the men he brought with him."

"And *Queen Anne's Revenge* would have sunk *Crusader* in retaliation."

"*Crusader* could hold her own against Teach's ship."

"The odds are slippery," Nathan argued. "Not everyone is favored with your brand of luck."

Kate's lips curved wickedly behind wavering strands of hair. "I am lucky, aren't I? Is that why you let me roam free?"

He chuckled lightly. "You'd be far more dangerous in a cage."

"You know me." She turned around and propped her rear on the rail, looking down on him. She wobbled slightly, and Nathan started to reach for her leg, to steady her in place, but stopped himself.

"Besides," he added, "the crew likes you."

"The happier the crew, the less inclined they are to murder you."

"That's one way to look at it."

"That's the only way to look at it, Nathan," she reminded him. "These are very dangerous men, and you're as careless as ever."

He smiled up at her. "I'm not the one dangling over the bow of a ship. Do you know what happens to a person swept under the keel of a ship?"

She smiled. "If I were in any danger of stumbling off a ship, I would have done so a long time ago."

"Why are you out here?" he wondered.

Strands of hair blew in her face, but she seemed oblivious. "Where else would I be?"

"London."

She scoffed. "If I ever chance upon you in London, I'll ask why you're not in the Caribbean."

Nathan moved to cross his arms but remembered he only had one arm to cross. "London sounds nice, actually."

"Change always sounds nice. Until it's no longer change."

"Maybe you'll tire of the sea," he suggested.

"Maybe I will," she said with a careless toss of her hand.

"And when you do?"

"I'll go somewhere else."

He shook his head and smiled. "It's all so easy for you, isn't it?"

"For now," she said. Her gaze trailed off toward the darkness beyond the ship. "But that will change. Might be a year. Might be a month. Might be a minute. Nothing lasts."

Nathan nearly shuddered as he recalled the shriek Kate had unleashed when Jonathan Griffith plunged his sword into her husband's breast. He shook the grisly memory from his head and cleared his throat. It had been little more than a year, but Kate was already so much more than that naïve, pale girl in a spotless saffron dress. "What will you do when we get to Tortuga?"

She shrugged. "I dunno. Disappear with my share of the plunder, probably." She lifted a finger before he could think to object. "And you *will* be giving me my fair share. I earned it just as much as you, if not more. You know that better than anyone, Nathan."

"Yes," he admitted. "I know."

"Of course, this is all assuming Blackbeard doesn't arrive to claim it all for himself."

Nathan shook his head. "Blackbeard has no idea we have it."

Kate loosed a terrible, raspy laugh. "The woman in your cabin knows."

"And you think she serves Blackbeard still?" Nathan's laughter overpowered hers. "How do they communicate, exactly? Carrier pigeons?" He spun around, scanning the sky. "She must dispatch them at night, because I haven't spied any wings flapping in the day."

"It's all too bloody convenient," Kate grated.

"You think I don't know that?"

"You don't seem concerned."

"And you are?" It was hard for him to take her seriously, given that she'd left him to die so she could gallivant around the Caribbean.

She shook her head. "You're a fool to allow this farce to continue."

His laugh was bitter. "It seems I'm a fool either way."

"That's the smartest thing you've said yet."

"You know for a fact it's a farce?" he asked with a flourish of feigned curiosity, for he knew she had no evidence. "If you've heard something I haven't, now would be a good time."

She looked away in frustration. "Of course I haven't heard anything. It's obvious to anyone with two working eyes."

He massaged the rough end of his shortened arm. "I won't know anything for sure until she takes action."

"You mean until she kills you. When you're a ghost, drop in for a visit so I can say I told you so. I enjoy being right."

"Maybe I would deserve it," he said as he stared into the black. "I was wrong to trade that man's life."

"Hornigold was an idiot," Kate spat. "He should never have left Nassau."

Nathan stared at her, appalled. "You mean he should never have listened to *you*."

"That was his choice," she replied with a relaxed shrug. "He knew the risks. Just as you knew the risks when you traded Hornigold for your precious Annabelle." She cocked her head as though struck by a sudden thought. "Such a sweet name. How could anyone with so sweet a name be capable of evil?"

Nathan slapped his palm on the rail. "You give me too little credit."

"You deserve none!" She slid closer and leaned downward, trying to get his attention. "Do I have to spell it out for you? That woman is here to murder you."

"She's taking her time!" He tried to avoid her unrelenting gaze, but he felt her eyes burrowing holes in his skull.

"You really don't know anything, do you?"

His hand shot upwards and seized her throat, shoving her

backwards and suspending her over the water. Her legs slipped around his waist, tightening. She smiled, even as her face turned red. "All it would take is a little shove," she rasped.

He pushed forward a little, letting her hang precariously for a gratifying moment. The comely masthead waited just below her, oblivious to her plight. If Nathan released her throat, the mermaid's pretty face would be the last thing she'd see before being dragged under the keel.

Kate didn't relinquish her smile. "What are you waiting for?"

"That's not what I want," he said at last, jerking her toward him. Her ass slipped from the rail, and she crumpled against him. She placed both hands on his chest, struggling to push off, but he slipped his fingers around the back of her neck and brought her forward. Her lips peeled away from clenched teeth, and her eyes burned furiously. The muscles in her arms strained against his pull, until her elbows buckled. Their lips came together. He shoved his tongue into her mouth. Her teeth parted, and he feared she was letting him in just so she could bite down, but then her tongue curled around his. For an instant, her body softened in his grip, leaning into him, and Nathan realized how desperately he wanted her.

But it was only an instant. Her tongue abruptly stopped moving, and she shoved him away with greater force than he thought her capable.

She glared at him, wiping her lips with the back of her hand.

"I'm sorry," he said, though he wasn't sure he meant it.

A warm breeze washed over the deck, ruffling the sails. Kate's reproachful look faded. "I just can't do that, Nathan. Not to you."

"Not to me?" He couldn't hide his sudden aggravation.

Her face twisted painfully, and her eyes lined with tears, and he was reminded that there was still a very young woman in there. "I've done enough," she said.

His mind drifted to the dark cell in Nassau, where he was certain he would face his death because she had abandoned him. Her hair, which looked so full and beautiful before him now, had been a dreadful, fiery vision that plagued his thoughts. Now he wanted nothing more than to lose himself in her. A question emerged methodically from his lips. "If you had to make the decision you made in Nassau again . . . would you?"

"Yes."

He nodded slowly.

She added a remorseful smile. "But I would feel terrible about it."

The walk back to his cabin was not nearly long enough. The ship felt very small, and he yearned to be back on an expansive beach, where he could stroll for hours without encountering another soul. He didn't want to go to sleep and dream of Hornigold again. Falling into bed with the very woman he had traded Hornigold for would only make it worse. She served as a constant reminder of his dark deed.

He flinched angrily at his nagging thoughts, flinging his hand through the air. One of the sleeping pirates stirred, turning over and adjusting his blanket. *The bastard was already dead,* Nathan reminded himself, as he had done over and over in the past five days. He was tired of thinking about it.

He shouldered through the door to the captain's cabin, forbidding himself further opportunity to dwell on decisions he couldn't change. Annabelle hadn't budged and neither had the pistol beside the bed. Nathan sat down at the desk on the opposite side of the cabin, setting his hand atop a map of the Caribbean. He circled his index finger around the island of Tortuga, smiling. What better place to vanish? It would take him three lifetimes to spend his share of the treasure.

He heard Annabelle shuffling out of bed behind him. "Where'd you go?" she murmured groggily.

Nathan tilted his head but didn't look back. "Needed some fresh air. Go back to sleep. It's late."

"Come back to bed," she groaned.

"Soon."

"Fine." He heard her fall back into bed, and then nothing. He looked at Tortuga again, far south and slightly west of *Crusader's* current position, with the islands of Maguana and Leneago between the ship and its destination. He blinked, and the map grew blurry beneath him. He rubbed his eyes and yawned, and he realized how tired he was as exhaustion swept over him.

He stood and turned . . . and Annabelle was standing three feet from him, with his gun in her hand, aimed at his face. He hadn't even heard her move. She'd slipped on her white robe. Her arm was steady, and the gun's barrel didn't budge.

"It's what you want, isn't it?" she said. "You made it so easy for me. Every night you spend an hour polishing and loading this goddamned thing, and you put it on that table, and then you walk away, always with your back to me. What are you doing? Testing me? Do you think that makes me feel good about myself? Do you think that makes me feel *wanted?*"

He sighed. "I was wrong to trade that man's life for yours."

The deep scar across her right cheek seemed redder than usual, drawing attention to itself. Perhaps it was amplified by the candlelight, which normally made her mahogany skin that much more beautiful. "Am I not enough?"

He leaned casually against the desk. "I thought you were."

She cocked her head. His lack of fear seemed to intrigue her. "Better to die than spend the rest of your life with your prize?"

He chuckled. "My prize wants to murder me."

The gun's barrel wavered a notch. "I wasn't always certain."

"That's comforting."

"But you just had to test me, didn't you? You'll always want what you can't have, just like every other man. You need a goal. Without it, you feel useless."

He shook his head. "I want the woman I fell in love with."

"That woman never loved you, and you've always known that. I gave more fancy to your purse."

He sighed in genuine relief. "Thank you. Thank you for finally admitting it."

"I never claimed anything else." A crease formed between her eyebrows. "I cannot live with a man who resents me."

"I don't," he insisted. "I only resent myself. Maybe I just need time."

"Time is the one thing you don't have," she assured him confidently. "Well, that and Kate Lindsay."

"What?"

She cackled. "Oh, don't pretend you don't fancy her. I've seen the way you look at her. You didn't come all the way out here to find *me*. You came out here to find *her*."

"For the governor," he insisted.

"I wish you could see how silly you look, trying to deny it," she sneered, flinging the gun slightly.

Nathan was baffled. "You don't love me, but you're playing the part of jealous lover?"

"I'm only casting light on your falsity," she sneered, "which you seem blissfully ignorant of. After I've put a hole in that silly face, I'm going to have a chat with your pretty little bitch. See, I have this suspicion she couldn't care less what happens to you. When I show her your corpse, I'll know the truth. A woman knows a woman. Of course, if she falls to her knees and weeps, I'll have to kill her too. But I don't think that's going to happen, do you?"

Nathan sighed. This had gone on long enough, and he was too disgusted to let it continue. "Part of me considered leaving the shot in that pistol."

She frowned. "What?"

He pointed at the barrel. "It will make a very loud noise, my ears will ring, and the crew will rush to my cabin and find me unkilled, and you with a smoking gun. They'll have at you, and I don't think I'll be able to stop them even if I want to."

She kept on frowning at the pistol. She wasn't getting it. He allowed himself a little smile at her expense. "I wish you could see how silly you look, trying to figure it out. It's quite simple, really. I loaded the powder, but not the shot."

The barrel declined, and her eyes trailed with it. A variety of emotions darkened her face, like storm clouds merging on the horizon. Her eyes darted this way and that, desperate for a solution to this startling turn of events, hoping for the answer to materialize somewhere in the cabin. For an absurd instant, he nearly felt sorry for her.

And then all uncertainty left her face, and a grin formed in its place. Her shoulders trembled as giggles bubbled out of her. Dread seeped into Nathan's gut as he realized what a fantastic actress she had always been.

"You think I'm so stupid that I wouldn't check? I loaded it while you were on deck." She returned the gun to its former height, level with his forehead. "So tell me, Nathan, did I pass your little test, or fail?"

As he opened his mouth to answer, he heard something snap.

21

KATE

The crack of thunder gave her a violent start. It was alarmingly close and there had been no lightning to foreshadow it. Kate pushed off the rail, scanning the horizon aft of the ship, in the direction she thought the report had sounded from.

A flurry of moving shadows on the main deck seized her attention. She took a few cautious steps forward. A man rushed up to the lantern nearest the bow, and she glimpsed the comely face of Gabe Jenkins before he doused the light. An instant later, the second lantern was extinguished, and the entire deck was pitched in darkness.

She heard a shuffling of feet, maybe ten or twelve men rushing about. She heard a man gasp, then a strange groan that trailed into silence. Someone protested, "Wait, no! Please!" and then said no more. Another man said, "Ogle? Is that you?" followed by a gurgling noise, and then fell silent. A would-be scream was smothered in its infancy. Shadows were moving from spot to spot, crouching and rising.

When she saw the sharp outline of a cutlass, she ducked low, clutching the hilt of her own. How many had they killed already? She retreated to the bulwark, setting her back against it, and prayed no one knew she was there.

There was a muffled shriek from somewhere below. A flurry of movement trembled the deck. Someone shouted, "I yield! I yieeeeld!" and then howled gruesomely.

Jaq is down there, she reminded herself. Not that she could do anything for the girl now. They were too far removed.

She let her eyes adapt to the darkness, watching for more shadows, but she saw no further movement. *They must have all gone down to the hold.* She slid along the starboard bulwark, hunched low, moving toward the captain's quarters. She had to get to Nathan. He was the only one she could trust right now.

If he's still alive.

Her toes caught on something soft, and she went tumbling over it, landing hard on her palms. She dragged her legs off of whatever she had tripped over. She reached out to the dark mound, and her fingers sank into something wet and squishy. She fought an instinct to recoil, sliding her fingers up the surface, which was mushy in places and hard in others, until she felt hair. It was a human face, completely bashed in. She jerked her hand away, gasping hoarsely in terror.

Something shuffled behind her. She spun, whipping her cutlass from its sheath in a single fluid motion. Her arm seemed to hit a brick wall, halting in midair. A shadow loomed over her, clutching her wrist. He shoved her away and she crumpled to the deck before him. "I'm not your enemy, lass," said a familiar voice.

"Bellamy?"

The surgeon leaned close, offering his hand. She took it, and he helped her back to her feet.

"They're killing everyone," she nearly shouted.

"Quiet," he said. "That was Yarlow you just stuck your hand in. Candler's dead too."

Kate was in the process of wiping the goo off her hands on the rail, but she stopped as the words registered. She clutched her stomach, struggling not to vomit as the metallic taste of bile saturated her mouth. She had met Yarlow her first day aboard *Crusader*, and she liked him instantly. He had seemed to enjoy her company in return, recounting his horrific capture by slavers in Africa to his recruitment by Guy Dillahunt, who had intercepted the slave ship that was transporting him.

Candler, on the other hand, she had met only briefly. The man had seemed intimidated by female company, and she was never able to speak more than two words to him before he hurried off in another direction.

"Why would anybody kill them?" she rasped, gripping her belly. "They were harmless!"

"I don't know, but I'm not waiting around to ask."

She almost laughed. "Where are we going to go?"

He hesitated. She couldn't see his features, but she knew he was thinking. "I don't know. We'll take one of the boats if we have to."

"We have to get to the cabin first."

"I know," Bellamy muttered grimly. "I heard it too."

"I thought it was thunder."

"It wasn't."

The surgeon moved ahead and she followed closely behind, hand on his shoulder. They continued along the starboard side until they were nearly to the captain's cabin, when the door slammed open and light spilled out. Annabelle emerged, a gun in her hand. Bellamy pulled Kate down low, back to the rail. Annabelle looked around cautiously. "Ogle?" she called.

Ogle ascended from the main hatch. He stepped into the

orange column of light streaming out of the captain's cabin. He was covered in blood and smiling like a child. Red droplets fell from his blade, pattering the deck. "The deed is done," he proclaimed.

Annabelle smiled with confidence. "Teach will be pleased." She shifted suddenly, aiming a finger at Kate and Bellamy. "Grab those two."

Bellamy stood before Kate, drawing his cutlass. His silver hair shimmered in the light of the cabin. Ogle approached eagerly, licking his red lips. "Put away the blade, old man. You'll only cut yourself."

"I've cut many men," Bellamy replied casually. "Both with scalpel and sword. Never cut myself."

Ogle advanced until their blades crossed, and the metal screeched as the edges scraped. "And I've killed twelve men tonight. What makes you think you'll be the man to end my spree?"

The surgeon grinned. "I've never doubted your skill against snoring opponents, but I have the advantage of being awake."

A third blade appeared, resting on Bellamy's neck. Kate looked sideways, and there was one of the Maynards, grinning broadly. She had no idea whether it was Dick or Richard. "We'll put you to rest soon enough," the Maynard assured Bellamy.

Bellamy's eyes swept from Ogle to Maynard, back and forth. After a moment he released his blade, letting it clang on the deck.

Annabelle stepped forward. "That's better. Now, who is your captain, old man?"

Bellamy frowned. "What kind of question is that?"

"Don't be rude to the lady," Ogle grated. "She asked who you serve."

"I don't answer daft questions."

Kate shrank behind Bellamy's legs.

Annabelle tilted sideways to get a look at her, and then she looked at Bellamy again. "You'll find this daft question far more difficult to answer with a sword in your belly. Who is your captain?"

Bellamy spat at her feet. "Enjoy your lofty position while you can, girly. It won't last long."

The strumpet sighed impatiently. "I'll ask once more. Who is your captain?"

The Maynard leaned close and whispered in Bellamy's ear, "This is the part where you say, 'Blackbeard.'"

Bellamy wrenched his face in disgust. "This is the part where I tell you to fuck a pufferfish. I'm a surgeon. I serve the wounded."

Ogle looked around. "Then you serve no one. They're all dead." He plunged his cutlass into the surgeon's gut. Bellamy doubled over Ogle's shoulder, his face turning purple, eyes bulging from their sockets. Ogle jerked the blade sharply upward, shearing through the old man. Kate glimpsed the sharpened tip moving up his back in a red line. When the sword moved no further, Ogle pulled it out, and Bellamy fell dead.

With her shield gone, Kate was completely exposed before Annabelle, Ogle, and the Maynard. They gathered around her, with Annabelle in the center, hands on her hips. "I'll have a word with you now, unless you'd care to join your dead friend in . . . well . . . being dead."

"He was more of an acquaintance," Kate said as she got to her feet as casually as possible and stepped over Bellamy's corpse.

"Until a few moments ago, I'm sure," Annabelle quipped with a shrewd smile. She offered her hand. "You're skilled at making friends when you require them."

Kate moved past her, toward the cabin. Annabelle followed, with Ogle and the Maynard flanking her. Kate struggled to keep her breath shallow as she stepped through the door. She knew Annabelle would be studying her for a reaction.

There are no surprises in here. You know what you'll find.

He was splayed on his back across the desk, legs hooked over the front. The shot had penetrated his brow, just above his left eye. Blood streamed out of his ear, collecting upon a dark red mass that had oozed from the back of his skull. A final expression of stunned comprehension was frozen on his face.

Nathan, you bloody idiot. Were you truly surprised?

Ogle's cutlass shrieked against the inside of its sheath as he put it away, nearly causing Kate to jump out of her skin. She managed to keep her feet firmly planted. She glanced sidelong at the big man, wondering if she could snatch the weapon from his belt and elude his sweaty, bloody hands quickly enough to sink it into Annabelle's neck. A few hacks to sever that pretty head from those perfect shoulders.

The strumpet's voice was gently modulated. "He gave me little choice, I'm afraid."

Kate sensed Annabelle's eyes on her back. She knew better than to turn away from Nathan too quickly. She crossed her arms and gradually swiveled to face the terrible woman. "So it's true what they say."

The strumpet cocked her head inquisitively. "What's that?"

"Blackbeard holds grudges."

Annabelle's eyelids fluttered in bewilderment. "I have to confess, I expected a different reaction."

Kate put on a honeyed smile. "Expected, or hoped for?"

"I worried that I might need to kill you. I worried that the sight of Nathan's corpse might drive you to do something rash. Forgive the theatrics, but I had to know." Annabelle gestured at Nathan. "You should have another look, before we give his body to the sea." She frowned. "Sailors always say that. 'Give his body to the sea.' Like it's some gentle thing of comfort. Does that make them feel better about dying at sea? I think it's horrific. Imagine what happens to a body down there, nibbled apart by fish. I can't think of anything worse."

"I don't think the dead care," Kate mused carelessly. "Only the living dwell on such things."

You fucking whore, she wanted to scream.

"You're so smart," Annabelle said, but Kate detected a hint of sarcasm. "Really, you should have one last look. He was your friend, wasn't he?"

"I saw him," Kate promised. Her cheeks felt as though they might burn away. She prayed she wasn't turning red. "It's a good clean shot. Do you make a habit of killing?"

"What do you think?" The strumpet spread her hands. "I just claimed a ship in naught but a few moments."

"With your *own* hands, I mean."

Annabelle tightened the belt of her robe. "He was my first."

"And you're eager for more?"

Annabelle's hands slid away from the belt. "I'll do what I have to do. Whether I enjoy it or not is beside the point."

Kate hazarded a step forward, and out of the corner of her eye she saw Ogle clutch the hilt of his cutlass. "I'm worth nothing dead."

"You're worth nothing to me either way," the terrible strumpet argued. "I can't exactly claim your bounty, can I?"

"Oh, I'm certain Blackbeard has his ways. He just took a ship without lifting a finger. One of his spies could turn me in and relay the reward to him. But you already know this, or you would have killed me by now."

Annabelle's eyes narrowed. "You're a keen woman. Come now, are you not the least bit sad?"

"Nathan was a fool," Kate replied with a lazy wave of her

hand in the general direction of Nathan's corpse. "I tried to kill him myself once, did he tell you that? Probably not. Five days isn't a generous amount of time to get reacquainted. I'm sure most of the catch-up was spent in the bed, yes?" Kate managed a playful smile, somehow.

I'll fucking kill you, you fucking whore.

Annabelle reached out to touch Kate's arm. It took everything she had to not flinch away abhorrently. "He was interested in little else," the strumpet giggled. "You know how it is."

Kate joined in her laughter, but Kate's laugh was distinctly bitter. "Oh yes, let's bond over the men we've killed, shall we? Did Nathan murder your husband and take you against your will as well?"

Be careful now. But it was so very hard.

Annabelle took a step forward, raising her hand, and for an instant Kate was certain she was going to strike. Annabelle's fingers delved into her hair, pushing it back from her missing ear. "That must have been painful. What happened?"

"Jonathan Griffith's quartermaster was hungry."

Annabelle recoiled. "Edward Livingston?"

"You knew him?" It was strange to hear that name spoken aloud again. Kate could not resist a shudder. She wasn't sure the beautiful creature before her was any better than the hateful beast that had taken her ear.

Annabelle's eyes darkened. "I wish I didn't." She put her back to Kate, looking at Nathan's corpse. It was a while before she spoke again. "I wonder where I'd be if not for that man."

Kate was very curious to find out what Livingston had done to this woman. "Set you on a dark path, did he?"

Don't blame him for what you are, you fucking whore.

"That's a matter of perspective."

Kate couldn't help herself, blurting, "And you've smartly

murdered anyone who doesn't share your perspective."

Annabelle turned and placed a hand flat across her chest. "I love how funny you are."

"I wasn't trying to be funny."

"Probably not," the strumpet replied with a saccharine smile. "You have a natural sort of wit." She tapped her chin with her index finger in contemplation, eyes descending. "I'm curious. Would you be so amusing without your clothes?"

"I don't follow."

The strumpet grinned, perfect white teeth contrasting her dark mahogany skin. "Let me help you." She snapped her fingers at Ogle. "Unburden her."

Ogle stared at Annabelle questioningly. "What, now?"

Annabelle sighed. "Take off her clothes."

Ogle's eyes brightened as comprehension struck him, and he stepped forth without hesitation, huge hands grasping at Kate's clothing. She made no attempt to pull away as the big man easily shredded her shirt and tossed it away. She crossed her arms over her breasts.

Annabelle continued to tap her chin indecisively. "Despite the little bits of skin you like to tease the men around you with, I think you prefer wearing clothes."

Kate smiled obliviously. "If you're hoping for equal ground, I have a lot of catching up to do." This did not hurt her. This was nothing compared to the dead young man on the desk. The worst had already happened.

Annabelle looked at Ogle. "Why have you stopped? Don't you want to know what she looks like down there?"

Ogle nodded hungrily and proceeded to slide Kate's pants down her legs. He stared at her crotch the entire time, never blinking.

"Oh, you match!" Annabelle exclaimed with a wicked smile, biting her fingernail. "How exciting! You never know with redheads."

After Ogle had drawn her breeches down to her ankles, his clammy hands slipped around one of her thighs, grasping tightly. He smashed his face against her skin. Kate remained still as his tongue darted out of his mouth and slid up her thigh, tugging at her skin like the underside of a slug. He gradually made his way toward the nook between her legs. She let her mind wander. She thought about the gently rolling waves of the ocean on a clear day. She tried to imagine how lovely the warm Caribbean water would feel against her bare skin, with the hot sun beating down on her shoulders.

"That's enough, Ogle," Annabelle barked in a surprisingly stern voice that lacked its prior ease. When he kept licking, she snapped, "That's enough!"

Ogle pulled away, though it seemed as difficult as prying a magnet from a metal beam. He let out a pained groan as he returned to Annabelle's side, hanging his shiny bald head low, like a dog scolded by his master for following his instincts.

Annabelle shook her head apologetically at Kate. "I question this one's inclinations. Too eager to prove his lust."

"You what?" Ogle said, scratching his head.

"Nothing." She reached into the cleft of her robe and produced a rolled parchment. "Find a man best suited for a trick at the helm. Appoint a navigator and sail to this location."

Ogle took the scroll, unrolled it, and scowled. It wasn't what he expected. "What is this?"

"Our destination."

He studied her skeptically. "And this is where we meet Blackbeard? It's in the middle of nowhere."

"Good a place as any," Annabelle replied haughtily.

Ogle lingered. "And what do we do with the prisoners?"

"What prisoners?"

"The survivors from Hornigold's ship, locked up in the

hold. All those men fled with Hornigold when Rogers offered pardon. They can't be trusted."

She shrugged. "Leave them to their cage. I think there's been enough killing for one day. Keep them fed. They may be of use. And don't let any harm come to Captain Dillahunt. He could be a valuable hostage."

Ogle inclined his head, favored Kate's loins with a longing glance, and took his leave. The Maynard (she still didn't know whether this one was Dick or Richard) lingered. His eyes were shaded beneath his protruding brow, but she knew they were trained on her. She wondered how long she would have to stand here in the nude. She imagined she looked rather silly. Her thigh was cold where Ogle left smears of sweat and saliva.

Annabelle's finger returned to her chin, tapping slowly as she decided what she wanted to do next. She turned to the Maynard. "Which Maynard are you? Dick or Richard? Forgive me, I get you confused."

"Richard," he rumbled absently.

"Lovely. Richard, escort Mrs. Lindsay to the brig. Put her with Dillahunt and the girl, where she won't be violated."

"How thoughtful," drawled Kate. She bent down to lift her breeches.

"No," Annabelle interjected. "You'll go as you are."

Kate didn't miss a beat. "Fine," she said, and she stepped out of her breeches and kicked them aside.

"Richard," Annabelle went on, "make sure everyone gets a nice view of her as you lead her down, will you?"

"Aye," Richard said, stepping forward. His hand closed around Kate's, and he jerked her into motion. Kate allowed herself a final glance at Nathan's lifeless form before she was yanked outside.

Most of the mutineers had gathered on the main deck. The lanterns had been lit again, and there were several bodies littered about, though not as many as Kate had expected. Apparently Blackbeard's influence was stronger than she imagined. They all turned their heads and gawked at her as Richard dragged her toward the hold.

"I fancy our new captain's methods already," said the other Maynard.

Gabe Jenkins was there, too. To his credit, he looked downright ashamed. He briefly met Kate's gaze and then turned away.

She heard the rest of them jabbering excitedly as Richard took her down the hatch into the large hold. They snaked through the maze of cargo, and several more dead bodies were sprawled about. Three of them had died in their bunks, throats slashed. Four had put up a fight but were clearly outnumbered, with cutlass wounds in front and back. One of the dead was still standing, slumped on a cutlass that had been thrust through his midsection, pinning him against a crate. He had died gaping at the cutlass, with a sliced hand resting atop the blade.

Maynard dragged her past the prisoners from Hornigold's ship. Eight of them lowered their heads respectfully. Avery Dowling wasn't so kind, staring at her with a sinister smirk. Avery had refused to acknowledge her as any more valuable than the juicy meat she had been sneaking them every night, even as he greedily consumed it.

Richard brought her to Dillahunt and Calloway, who both raised their eyebrows and then looked at each other in shock. He unlocked the door and shoved her in, slamming it behind her. "Enjoy your new quarters, missy," he sneered and trotted off.

Kate smiled sheepishly at her two cellmates and crouched, hugging her knees. Calloway stared dubiously for a while, as if she suspected this was some sort of ruse. When she apparently concluded it was not, she snatched one of Dillahunt's blankets and moved to Kate's side. She set the blanket over Kate's shoulders, concealing her, and then returned to her spot next to Dillahunt. "Thank you," Kate said.

Calloway looked away. "These people are monsters."

"Disgraceful," Dillahunt agreed. He sported fewer bandages than before. The upper half of his face was mostly covered, with his hair spilling out of the top, but his broad jaw was uncovered. The bandages resembled a bandit's mask. There were a few slices on his cheeks, but they weren't terribly deep. His bare chest and right arm were still heavily bound. He had thrown on a pair of black breeches and his characteristic black coat. She had to admit, he looked sort of dashing this way.

He opened his mouth a few times, hesitating repeatedly, before he finally asked, "Did they . . . do anything to you?"

"Other than strip me naked? No. Annabelle's taken the ship."

Dillahunt's jaw fell open. "A *woman* has taken my ship?"

Calloway shook her head. "They just started killing people down here."

"How many dead up top?" Dillahunt asked.

Kate shook her head. "Maybe ten."

"That makes about twenty total," he concluded. "Did they get Candler?"

She nodded. "And Bellamy."

Calloway gasped.

Dillahunt let the news sink in for a moment. "And Adams?"

Kate lowered her eyes.

"How?" Calloway asked.

"Does it matter?" Kate said. "He's gone."

"He deserved no better," Dillahunt replied with a smug air of vindication.

Kate flinched angrily. "If you hadn't promoted him he'd

still be alive. What were you thinking?"

He snorted. "If the boy hadn't traded Hornigold he'd still be alive. When you spend your life making mistakes, one day you make the mistake that kills you."

A sharp headache was swiftly materializing between Kate's eyes, muddying her vision. Her stomach growled noisily, and she realized it had been too long since her last meal. She would probably have to wait a lot longer until the next one, if it came at all.

"Where are they taking us?" Calloway asked.

Kate hesitated. "To Blackbeard."

Calloway's blue eyes went distant and icy. Her head sank between her broad shoulders, and she suddenly looked very young and very lost. "We're all going to die."

"One day," Kate replied. "But not yet."

"How can you be so cavalier?" Calloway demanded. "He was your friend, whether you knew it or not."

"I knew it," Kate said, taken aback by Calloway's sudden fervor.

"He wanted to hate you," she went on, "but he couldn't. I don't know what did or didn't happen between you two, but I think he loved you, in a way. He's been dead five minutes and you've forgotten him already. What kind of woman are you?"

"I haven't fucking forgotten Nathan!" Kate exploded, forgetting to hold onto her blanket. She tugged it angrily back in place. "How could I forget? That dreadful cunt of a whore just rubbed my nose in his corpse! And I had to smile and pretend I didn't care, because if I cared, she was going to stick a sword in my belly." Kate didn't realize she was crying until she tasted the tears on her lips. She furiously wiped a hand over her face. "And as you can see from my lack of wardrobe, that still wasn't good enough for her."

Calloway withered against the bars, instantly repentant.

Dillahunt's eyes swiveled in the slits of his bandages, from one woman to the next.

Kate composed herself, refusing to allow more tears to flow. "Nathan's gone, and weeping won't magic him back to life. We're alive, and I mean to keep it that way."

22

CALLOWAY

She watched as Red Devil and Ogle rolled another barrel toward the stairs, as they had been doing every night since leaving Griffith's Isle. She no longer cared if they saw her watching.

It had been two days since the murder of Nathan Adams, and with Kate locked up alongside Calloway and Dillahunt, there was no one to bring additional food. They got one meal every day, consisting of hardtack and rancid water. Whenever she forgot how hungry she was, her stomach growled loudly enough to remind her. She was tired of leaning against the bars, but there was nothing else to lean against. Her rear ached from sitting on the hard planking. Even when she folded a blanket and sat on it, it wasn't thick enough to provide much padding. She squirmed constantly and never got a good night's sleep, so she was always exhausted.

Whenever sleep finally came, usually in the early hours of

the morning, just before the ship became a flurry of activity, she would dream of her mother. The dreams always took place in Nassau. They would be walking the beach or perusing the market, conversing normally, and Calloway would not realize until she woke that her mother was long dead.

Upon waking, her eyes were always drawn to Kate's brilliant red hair, matted about her head like a fiery cushion as she slept. Calloway marveled at how soundly the woman slept after all that had happened. She had wanted to despise Kate, though she couldn't explain why. Kate wouldn't have it. She dodged every insult Calloway had hurled at her, no matter how subtle or brash, and remained infuriatingly sympathetic. And when one of those insults finally injured her, after Nathan's death, Calloway was ashamed of herself. But she was also relieved to discover that Kate was a person after all. Kate had feelings. Kate could be damaged. Kate was not untouchable. Somehow, that made her impossible to hate.

Dillahunt's slumber was even more frenetically uncertain than before his injury. He would often wake rambling about puzzles and patterns and splinters. Sometimes he would feel his face, as if to make sure it was still there. When he realized he was in one piece, he would fall back to sleep.

He was asleep again now, breathing heavily. His scarred face was mashed against his arm, which he had folded under his head in place of a cushion. She was hopelessly in love with him. There was no point denying it. She loved the way he looked at her, as though he wanted to protect her from all the evils of the world and was genuinely sad that he could not. He seemed perplexed by his own feelings toward her, and that made her love him all the more.

If she ever escaped this cage, she would never return to whoring. She had moved out of the whorehouse because she wanted to seek out her own clients. She didn't like the men choosing her. She preferred choosing them. And now that she'd found a man she truly loved, she knew she could never go back to that life. Unfortunately, freedom was looking less and less likely every day. One way or the other, it seemed she would spend the rest of her days at Guy Dillahunt's side.

"Dammit!" Ogle hissed while rolling a barrel across the hold.

"What?" Red Devil said, looking around.

"Splinter," Ogle answered, sucking on his finger.

Red Devil sighed. "Shame Bellamy's dead. You might bleed to death without him."

"Bugger off," Ogle spat.

"What's she looking at?

Calloway swung her gaze to Red Devil and was shocked to see him staring directly at her. She looked away immediately. His heavy feet thumped toward her. He pressed himself against the bars. "What are you looking at, little boy, or girl, or whatever you are?"

"I couldn't sleep for all your racket," she shot back without looking at him.

He clutched his crotch. "I've got something that would put you right out."

Dillahunt stirred, but Red Devil kept his voice too low to wake him. Whatever he and Ogle were up to down here, they didn't want anyone above to know about it.

Calloway stood and glared at him, but maintained a healthy distance from the bars. "I don't want your red cock."

Red Devil seized the bars and shook them, his eyes and teeth showing fiercely within that dark crimson face. "Boy or girl, I'm going to fuck your ass bloody."

She looked into those white pools for as long as possible, until she could look no longer. She turned away. His hot breath blasted the back of her neck. "I won't forget this, little boy," he snarled. "I can't wait to hear the pitiful little squeaks you make when my red cock splits you in twain."

He returned to Ogle, chuckling to himself. The two men rolled a barrel to the opposite end of the hold and carried it up the stairs.

Calloway fell into her blankets and lowered her head in shame, wishing she was as strong as she thought she was when she snuck aboard Dillahunt's ship back in Nassau.

"They like to remind us of how weak we are," said a raspy female voice. Calloway refused to look. She didn't want to face Kate right now. "The truth is they fear us, because they need us. So they keep telling us how much stronger they are."

"They *are* stronger," Calloway replied bitterly. "They're bigger. They have muscles."

In her peripheral vision, she saw Kate's hair shimmer as she shook her head. "Strength is always within reach, Jacqueline."

"Really?" Calloway said, looking around the cage. "Where is it? I don't see it."

"That's because you haven't looked."

"And what am I supposed to see?" she demanded. "I see bars. I see a bucket of shit." She pointed to the rusty, stinking pail that all three of them had been relieving themselves in.

"Exactly," said Kate. "A man with a face full of shit will quickly forget his lust. And while he's busy wiping it out of his eyes, you bring that bucket down on his head until his skull caves in."

Calloway stared at Kate dubiously. Kate shifted uneasily in her blanket, clutching it to her breasts. No one had brought her clothes, so the filthy blanket was all she had to conceal her nakedness. "I don't understand you, Kate."

Kate shrugged. "I can't make myself more plain. When a man tries to rape you, use whatever is within your grasp to prevent it."

Calloway shook her head. "No, I understand that. I don't understand *you*. What are you doing out here? You could be home, safe in London right now. There's no good reason for you to be here."

Kate smiled at her. "Haven't you asked yourself that same question?"

Calloway looked at Dillahunt, oblivious in his slumber. "I followed a man."

"That's not why you're here."

"Stop pretending you know me," Calloway barked.

"Then stop confirming that I do," Kate replied easily. "You're out here for a reason, and it's not for this man. Maybe you've got a lust for death. Maybe you wanted to face your mother's killer."

"I never expected to face him," Calloway growled.

"Maybe you wanted a change."

Calloway chewed on her lower lip. "If you want the truth, I don't really remember why I wanted to come. Maybe I never knew."

"You saw a chance for something new and you took it."

Calloway's face twisted as she fought a sudden upsurge of emotion before it could manifest tears. "I was safe in Nassau. I had everything I could have wanted."

"Clearly you didn't," Kate replied with a little laugh. "Wants are never satiated. In fulfilling one desire, we neglect another."

Calloway glanced bitterly at the bars. "I know I didn't want this."

"No." Kate smiled. "But you *want* to get out. And when you do, you'll swiftly forget your hardship here. Your mind will be too occupied with fulfilling its next desire."

23

ANNABELLE

No vegetation lined the charcoal-hued islands protruding from the ocean like the serrated teeth of some monstrous prehistoric shark. The eight volcanic islands were gathered in a lopsided ring, which was five miles wide. They were pure rock. The northernmost island was the largest, with the other seven tapering off in a circle, growing smaller with each.

Crusader sailed between the two smallest islands at the southern end, into the huge circular gulf, and continued toward the big northern island. Its giant volcanic mountain was split down the center by a canyon, which was open to the sea. The canyon looked like a slender crack from here, but Annabelle knew this was just a trick of the distance, given the canyon's great width in relation to the relatively small ship she could see moored just outside it. As they neared, the canyon grew massive. The other ship's features came into view.

Ogle joined Annabelle at the helm, scratching his bald head

anxiously. "Uh, Miss Annabelle? The men are starting to worry."

She folded her arms, refusing to meet his gaze. "You might call me 'captain,' just once."

"I would, but my tongue refuses."

"Your tongue doesn't seem to be of much use," she shot back.

"*Captain,*" he mustered, though it seemed to severely pain him. "The men recognize that ship from her colors. And it's not *Queen Anne's Revenge.*"

"You know bloody well whose ship that is, Ogle. I expect everyone else does, too."

"Aye," he said. "That be Charles Vane's flag."

She glared at him, letting her hands fall to her hips. "And he is a friend to Blackbeard, yes?"

"That's a rickety alliance at best," he replied.

"Too late to alter course," she said. "To do so would draw him down upon us."

He stepped closer, until his nose was nearly touching hers. His foul breath blasted her cheeks when he spoke. "If you lie, missy, I will be the first to savor a piece of your thighs. I won't care if you're dead."

She waved him away, making a face. "Your breath stifles my thoughts."

He fell back to his former position, but his eyes were hard with suspicion.

Just a little further, Annabelle told herself.

They sailed forward, with *Crusader's* recently appointed navigator, Red Devil, staring mistrustfully at Annabelle. She merely nodded at him with a little smile. She was relieved this journey was nearing its end. She had endured Ogle and Red Devil's contempt and doubt for far too long. Their fear of Blackbeard kept them at arm's length, but she knew that couldn't last forever. They were pirates, and impatience would win out eventually.

Crusader sailed toward the tall canyon that severed the mountain. The crevice was ominously dark in the late afternoon light.

Vane's sloop, *Valiant*, curved to intercept. A tall blonde man in a bright red coat hailed them, and Annabelle instructed Jenkins to shout back, "Mistress Annabelle here, commanding *Crusader*. We have prisoners, Captain Dillahunt among them." Jenkins delivered the message with an uncharacteristically firm voice, the wind blowing back his curly black hair.

The man in the red coat disappeared for a moment, then returned and signaled for them to continue ahead. *Crusader* sailed past *Valiant*, into the shadow of the mountain. The entire deck went dark as the ship descended into the canyon channel, and for a nauseating moment Annabelle felt as though the towering charcoal walls on either side were moving to swallow her. She craned her neck to see the thin line of sky through the slit above. The canyon curved slightly, until she could no longer see the entrance behind them.

As Annabelle's eyes adapted to the dark, details came into focus. There were two docks on either side of the channel. A fancy brigantine was moored at the large dock on the eastern side, and a small, neglected schooner at the much smaller dock on the western side. The brigantine's deck was a flurry of activity as the men unloaded supplies.

Far more impressive was the wall above the eastern dock, hollowed like a beehive with dozens of orange-hued half-caves. Each hollow was decorated like an apartment, with lanterns, paintings, shelves, and haphazardly scattered furniture. Men were moving about within them. Rope ladders and wooden stairways lined the canyon wall, giving it a very industrialized appearance. Precarious walkways slanted from each hollow to the next. Annabelle watched a pirate stroll casually across a walkway while the thin planking bowed under his feet. A few ramps had fallen into disrepair, and the unreachable hollows they had once led to were now dark and empty. Some of the smaller caves seemed to cut deep into the mountain, like mineshafts, fading into darkness. She wondered how deep they went.

Annabelle looked up. High above *Crusader* three little bridges extended from one side of the canyon to the other, providing access to a few caves on the western side (though most of the population seemed to dwell on the eastern side). A man halted halfway across one of the bridges to stare at the approaching ship directly below.

The dark, still water was blanketed with a fine layer of mist. The air was dense and humid, and sweat trickled down her temples. In the distance she could see where the canyon slanted to a close. Apparently it didn't run all the way through the mountainous island, which meant there was only one entrance, easy to defend.

"Heard about this place," Jenkins said. "They call it 'Pirate Town.' Thought it was a myth."

"That's why it's still here," Ogle said with nervous awe. His hairless skin was already covered in perspiration, and his shirt was nearly soaked through. "No one thinks it's real, not even the governor. I'm sure Vane wants to keep it that way. We'll be lucky if we leave here alive."

Annabelle smirked. "Everyone who keeps their mouths shut will be fine."

"And how do you know so much, missy?" Ogle demanded. "How did you even know to find this place?"

"That's a good question," muttered Red Devil, flashing her with a dangerous glare.

She raised one shoulder in a cavalier half-shrug. "Men are

forgetful of their possessions when happy. I stole a map from Vane's cabin."

Red and Ogle exchanged a woeful glance. "This woman is going to be the death of us," Ogle growled.

"Should we kill her now?" Red Devil wondered aloud.

That stirred her heart into a panicked frenzy. "I don't think Vane would appreciate that," she objected promptly.

"She knows what she's doing," Jenkins insisted. But then he swallowed. "Right?"

Annabelle shrugged. "We'll find out."

"Too late to do anything about it," Ogle said, pointing at a ledge jutting from the eastern wall, where a thirty-two pound cannon was trained on them, with two men manning it. Ogle pointed at the opposite wall, at yet another ledge supporting another large cannon. As Annabelle scanned both walls, she spotted several smaller nine and six pounders nested on ledges, along with some mounted swivel guns.

"This place is a fortress," said Red Devil.

"Could hole up in here forever," Ogle said.

They docked behind the brigantine. Two dozen very serious pirates crowded the dock to greet *Crusader*, brandishing guns of every shape and size. Ogle and a few others extended a ramp to them. Annabelle went first, figuring they would be much less likely to shoot at a woman. A single stray shot could trigger a battle. As she descended the narrow ramp, the pirate crowd dispersed at the middle, and Charles Vane stepped through. He was wearing that same forest green coat he had worn last time she saw him, which so nicely complimented his eyes. His auburn hair was slightly trimmer than she remembered, but his red stubble was a little thicker.

The only thing missing was his perpetual smirk, which he had presently swapped for a perplexed scowl. Annabelle and Vane reached the foot of the ramp at the same time and stood two paces from one another. His eyes trailed her body. The smirk returned for a fleeting moment. "There's a good reason for this, I'm sure. Because if there isn't, I will politely ask you to depart."

She teased him with a smile. "And if I don't obey?"

One of his eyelids flinched, revealing tiny crow's feet at the corner. "I will politely fuck you to death with my cutlass."

Annabelle took an involuntary step back. "That's no way to treat a woman bearing gifts."

Vane's strong jaw worked furiously. "I had wondered what happened to my map. I tortured a man I suspected of thieving it from my cabin. He maintained his innocence, even as the last of his guts were drawn into a bucket."

Annabelle swallowed. "I'm sorry for your man."

"I never liked him," Vane replied. "Tell me you are here at Teach's behest."

She shook her head. "Teach has no idea I'm here."

He drew his cutlass and set it to her neck. "An old sailor once told me that the brain works for a full minute after the head is parted from the body. The eyes still see. I never really believed that, but right now I pray it's true."

Annabelle forced a little smile, but her heart was thudding violently in her chest. "After everything we've been through?"

Vane scowled. "I've been through many women."

"Not like me."

His scowl softened. "I'll admit, you were memorable. But that changes nothing."

"Don't you want to see my gift?" The words came out a tad shakier than she intended.

"I've seen it." He leaned on the sword, and she felt a thin sting. "Return to your ship and go. That is the best I can offer you. Had anyone else walked down that plank, they would never have left. Consider it an act of . . . nostalgia."

She lingered until the edge of the sword bit too deeply. She turned and started back up the ramp. Her legs wobbled, threatening to give out from under her. A trickle of blood ran down her neck, collecting on her white shirt. The crew was gathered at the rail, their expressions conveying a mixture of emotions, relief chief among them. They wanted out of here.

How would she control them after this? Someone else would surely take command the minute they had safely sailed from Pirate Town. Probably Ogle, since he was the loudest. He'd sail straight for Teach and inform him of her treacherous intentions, and if she was lucky, Teach would dispatch her swiftly, instead of favoring her with one of his more creative torments. He had an arsenal of deaths to choose from, many of which he had relayed to her in great detail. Vane might as well have killed her on the dock. It would have been a kinder end.

She made it five dreadful steps before Vane called, "Wait!" Annabelle halted, relief pouring over her like cold water on a blistering hot day. She listened to his footsteps thumping up the ramp behind her, and she didn't dare turn. "Show me," he said when he reached her. "And I don't mean your cunny."

"Follow me," she said, continuing up the ramp.

She led him down the stairway to the hold and through the maze of crates and barrels. Vane glanced at the prisoners in both cages, pausing for a moment to appraise Dillahunt, who looked like he'd emerged from the business end of a meat grinder. "Captain Dillahunt," Vane said. "Did someone mistake your face for a chamber pot?"

Dillahunt glared through the slits of his bandages. "I found myself in disagreement with a cannonball."

Vane leaned in for a closer look, lips curling. "I'm afraid the cannonball won."

Annabelle continued to the treasure chests, beckoning Vane to follow. Vane pointed at Dillahunt and said, "We'll pick this up later, Guy. Don't go anywhere."

He caught up to Annabelle. She opened one of the chests and took a step back, allowing Vane time to digest what he saw within. He pretended not to be impressed, even as his smirk steadily returned.

"Still wish to violate me with your sword?" she asked.

"Not with this one," he said, sheathing his cutlass at last. "However, Teach may wish to fuck us both with something unpleasant, namely the bow of his ship. He'll skewer us like pigs on a spit, and we'll make pretty mastheads, with your lips to my ass."

"What Teach doesn't know won't kill us," she assured him.

Vane wiped sweat from his brow. "Edward Teach has ways of knowing things he has no way of knowing. You used his men to take this ship, yes?"

She didn't want to answer that. She wanted him to believe it had all been her doing, that it hadn't been as simple as following Teach's instructions and enlisting the proper men. But that's exactly what she had done. She lifted her chin and looked Vane in his pretty green eyes. "Yes. Two men named Ogle and Red Devil."

"That must have been frightening for you," he said. The crease in his brow lengthened sympathetically. "Being forced to command traitorous brutes who might have split you from the ass up at any moment."

"I took the job gladly," she said, maintaining a confident tone.

He winked knowingly. "With every intention of betraying your master."

She flinched.

He raised a diplomatic hand. "It's nothing to be ashamed of. Bravo, I say. But I can't exactly trust you, can I?"

She hazarded a step closer. "I would think less of you if you did."

"Thank Christ for that," he muttered sarcastically. "A whore's regard is so very important to me."

"Don't pretend you didn't miss me." She trailed a finger between her breasts. "You promised you would."

"You may have ventured across my thoughts once or twice, without warning, and I may have pleasured myself to the memory of your ample tits." He looked away, blinking rapidly. "But I digress."

"A welcome digression," she teased.

He ignored the flirtation. "Captain Dillahunt seems well accommodated, with no less than two women." Vane frowned. "Is the redhead naked under that blanket?"

"Yes," Annabelle sighed.

Lindsay shifted her bare legs so Vane couldn't see between them and met the pirate captain's leer with an unrelenting stare of her own.

"Who is she?" he asked.

"That's Katherine Lindsay."

He looked at Annabelle in shock. "Truly? Your hold is filled to the brim, it seems."

Annabelle bit her lip as a proud smile fought for purchase.

Vane pointed at the other cage. "And who are they?"

"Hornigold's men," she answered, "captured by Dillahunt before Dillahunt was mutinied against."

"By you?"

"No, by Nathan Adams."

He scratched his head. "And this Nathan Adams was then mutinied upon by you?"

"Yes."

"This ship's a bloody tragedy!"

"Anyway, I figured I couldn't trust Hornigold's men, so I left them in there."

Vane nodded. "They will find my brig a bit more cozy, at least until I decide what to do with them. I do need more workers. Would seem a waste to kill them all, much as I enjoy torture."

"Just keep them separate from Dillahunt," she cautioned.

"You think I'm an idiot?" he snapped, face reddening. "I won't have a potentially valuable hostage murdered in his sleep. Who knows what this man's life is worth to Woodes Rogers?" He squinted. "Who is the long-legged girl?"

The girl lowered her head innocuously.

Annabelle shrugged. "Dillahunt's woman, I think."

"Dillahunt, you dog!" Vane called at him. "She's young enough to be your daughter."

Dillahunt glared back. "I heard you fucked a baby."

Vane's laughter filled the hold. "I've fucked many things, if you believe the gossip. I'm told I once fucked a squid. The logistics are maddening."

"You may yet get the chance," Dillahunt sneered. "If you listen to anything this treacherous cunt tells you, you'll swiftly find yourself at the bottom of the ocean. Do you really think you can trust a crew that has twice mutinied?"

Vane turned to Annabelle. "You know, he has a point there."

She had an easy answer to that. "Kill Ogle and Red Devil. The rest will fall in line." She couldn't bring herself to mention Jenkins, despite his undying loyalty to Teach. She had been meaning to ask Jenkins what debt he owed Teach, but she hadn't found the right moment.

Vane stroked his chin. "So, those are the shepherds?"

"The rest are sheep," she said. "You might want to do away with Richard and Dick Maynard as well."

He rolled his eyes. "Perhaps a list would set me straight?"

"I'll introduce you."

"No need, I've got it," he sighed, tapping his temple. "I hope they enjoyed their final glimpse of sunlight."

Annabelle giggled. "I'm afraid they were too fretful to enjoy it."

As he looked at her, Vane's eyes glimmered with something that might have been respect. "Rightfully so."

They returned to the dock, while the crew of *Crusader* watched anxiously from the main deck. Annabelle assured them everything was going to be fine. Ogle looked particularly twitchy, which filled her with satisfaction. She winked at him before descending the ramp. *Goodbye, Ogle.*

Vane called for his quartermaster. Jack Rackham was a tall man with an athletic build. He had a handsome, sleek face and long blonde hair that was pulled into a ponytail. He was in his late thirties and dressed all in calico, which had earned him his nickname. A large gold earring drooped from one of his ears, and he wore a big black tricorn hat with a bright red feather.

"Remove the prisoners from the hold to our brig," Vane instructed Calico Jack. "Keep Captain Dillahunt and his woman separate from the others. The rest of the crew are free to wander, but keep them from our treasure room. Also, find *special* quarters for four of them going by names of Ogle, Red Devil, Dick Maynard and Richard Maynard. Got that?"

Calico Jack nodded conspiratorially. "Aye, captain."

Before the quartermaster could spring into action, Vane grabbed him by the arm. "Oh, and bring the redhead to my quarters, along with a chest full of women's garments. I'm sure we've stolen plenty of those. And have Harry's boy draw her a bath."

Annabelle's chest swelled with a murderous fury. She stomped toward Vane without thinking. "Captain!"

Vane smirked at her. "Yes?"

Annabelle halted, grinding her fingernails into her hips.

"Nothing."

"Alright," he replied with a raised eyebrow. He moved past Calico Jack. "I'll be in my quarters."

She hurried after. "Shall I join you?"

"No," he grunted without looking back. "I'll send for you when I'm ready. We have an extensive kitchen. I suggest you pay it a visit while you wait."

As Vane abruptly rushed off, Annabelle felt the voracious eyes of Pirate Town's seedy occupants creeping over her body, while the mounting doubt of *Crusader's* crew weighed heavily upon her back. She clutched her fluttering stomach, resisting the urge to vomit on the dock in front of everyone.

I should have killed that bitch when I had the chance.

24

CALLOWAY

Calloway and Dillahunt were the last to be escorted out of the hold. Hornigold's men were taken first, secured together with chains lined through their shackles. A tall blonde man in calico took Kate next. Kate glanced uncertainly at Calloway on her way out. Calloway offered a meager smile, secretly hoping this was not the last time she would see her. Though Calloway would never admit it to her face, Lindsay was a fascinating woman. Over the last few days, Kate had recounted the past year of her life. The tale made incarceration far less tedious.

Two big shirtless men appeared. One had thinning locks of stringy blonde hair, and the other had a shaved head. The bald one took Calloway by the arm and led her out of the cell while the blonde man snatched Dillahunt to his feet and shackled his wrists. Calloway's numb legs nearly buckled a few times as she was ushered toward the stairs. The journey up the steps was surprisingly difficult. She hadn't walked more than two paces in weeks. The bald man nudged her every time she slowed, and she shot angry looks at him, but that did nothing to slow him. He gave her arm a sharp squeeze and said, "Move!"

When she emerged on the main deck, Calloway's breath caught in her throat. As she gawked at the honeycomb of flickering hollows in the canyon wall, she felt tiny, like a fly trapped in a giant beehive. She had never seen anything like it.

Dillahunt looked like he was going to be sick. "Those walkways are tragically misaligned," he gasped, eyes wide behind the slits of his white mask.

"Where are we?" Calloway wondered aloud, staring at the darkening slice of sky between the canyon walls far above.

"Move!" the bald man barked again, pounding her back so hard with his fist that her breath burst from her mouth like a popping balloon.

"Go easy with her, man!" Dillahunt demanded. "Have you never handled a woman before?"

The bald man swiveled his head and snarled like an animal, with a string of white spittle dangling from his lower lip.

Dillahunt withdrew in horror. "My god. Somewhere a dog is prancing about with a man's brain, carrying on civilized conversation."

The man with stringy hair laughed. "That's why we call him 'Mongrel.' He don't talk so good."

"Neither do you," Dillahunt quipped, "but it doesn't seem to stop you."

"You're lucky Captain Vane wants you kept alive, funny man. Still, wouldn't be my fault if you slipped and took a little dive into the water, would it?"

"I disagree," Dillahunt said, fervently shaking his head. "You'd do better to drop one of those chests into the water. I'm worth twice as much."

"Is that so?" the stringy-haired man balked. He nodded at

Calloway. "And what's *she* worth?"

Dillahunt paused to consider. "Priceless."

For the first time in weeks, Calloway grinned. The muscles in her cheeks were nearly as unwieldy as her legs, twitching uncertainly.

Most of *Crusader's* crew were on the dock now, conversing with their new mates, although Calloway thought the overall mood was a bit tense. The smiles and laughter on both sides seemed false.

Dillahunt and Calloway were taken past the dock, skirting a thin wooden walkway suspended just above the impenetrable black water. They plunged into one of the smaller caves, which led to a dim tunnel. Every twenty paces or so, the rocky walls were lit with gothic iron sconces bearing large candles. Thick beads of orange wax dripped between wickedly sharp prongs. The shadows of each prong danced across the tunnel walls in the wavering flame.

The snakelike passage was narrow, and they were forced to duck in several spots. Calloway couldn't be sure if the passage was manmade or carved out by water.

"What do you think they've done with Kate?" she asked Dillahunt.

"I haven't a clue," he said. "You miss her already?"

"I only hope she's alright."

"That woman can take care of herself."

The stringy-haired man giggled. "Captain Vane will take good care of her."

They encountered three forks in the passage, splitting off into separate tunnels. They took a left on the first fork, a right on the second, and another right on the third. Calloway silently mouthed, "Left, right, right" repeatedly, committing the path to memory.

The tunnel sloped steeply upward, and it wasn't long before

Calloway's unused legs started to ache. Her bare feet had difficulty finding purchase on the worn ground, which was far smoother than the rocky walls. Apparently this passage was heavily traversed. She inevitably began to slow down, until she was nudged forward by Mongrel. "Move!"

"Is that all you know how to say?" she asked in annoyance.

"Move!" he answered.

"Right," she grated warily.

A hundred agonizing paces later, the tunnel leveled off and opened upon a long cavern. Stalactites drooped from the arched ceiling. Four torches decorated the wall on her left, flaring brightly. The right side was sectioned off by thick rusty bars that reached from floor to ceiling, penetrating the rock. Hornigold's nine survivors were locked behind the bars. They were appraising their larger cell with satisfied nods. They even had bench and a long table, topped with dice and cards.

"Care to join us, Captain Dillahunt?" said Andrew Harrow cheerfully.

"We've got plenty of space," said Francois Laurent.

"This is much better," said Bastion.

Dillahunt smirked. "I'd rather not, gentlemen. I'm afraid I cannot endure a knife in my belly."

"Aww, come now, captain," Harrow protested. "We would never!"

The stringy-haired man rattled Dillahunt's chain. "Don't worry, captain. Vane don't want you nowhere near the riffraff, seeing as your balls are made of solid gold."

Laurent looked at Harrow. "I hadn't heard that."

Calloway and Dillahunt were led past Hornigold's men. At the end of the long cavern there was a smaller, dimly lit hollow, enclosed by bars. "Our cell isn't much of an improvement from the last," Calloway drawled.

"Don't worry, lassie," the stringy-haired man said. "You'll

be staying with me."

Before the words could register, Dillahunt twisted free of the stringy-haired man's grasp and spun behind him in a single motion, reaching over his head and pulling the chains tight around his neck. The man's stunned face quickly turned a sickening shade of purple as Dillahunt drew him back.

Mongrel tossed Calloway aside and drew his cutlass. He wasted no time and charged at Dillahunt. Calloway hit the ground hard, but she managed to stick out a leg and catch Mongrel's toes. His momentum carried him through the air, until he crashed against the ground face-first, sword clanging noisily.

The stringy-haired man reached for Mongrel, fingers working like a dying spider's legs. Dillahunt jerked the chain harder into his captive's neck, dragging him away. The stringy-haired man's tongue jutted from his mouth, and his eyes puzzled with bloody veins. "Anyone know this man's name?" Dillahunt yelled to Hornigold's men.

Fat Farley shrugged. "We just call him Rotter."

"That'll do," Dillahunt replied with a firm nod. "Listen to me, Rotter. I'll strike a bargain with you, right here. It's quite simple. The girl stays with me, and you don't strangle. Nod if you can understand me."

Rotter gurgled something unintelligible.

"What was that?" Dillahunt demanded. "I said nod if you understand."

Rotter nodded frantically.

Mongrel was just getting to his feet. Blood oozed from his nose, collecting in a little puddle beneath him. He retrieved his cutlass and raised it threateningly.

"Stay back, Mongrel," Dillahunt urged, "or your friend's neck will—"

A grotesque *snap* echoed throughout the cavern. Rotter's

head slacked over the chain, tongue hanging from his yawning mouth like a bloated slug. A long and pitiful fart sounded as the contents of his bowels darkened his pants.

Dillahunt frowned. "Shit."

Hornigold's men tittered with joy as they crowded against the bars of their cell. "That's going to stink something awful in a minute," Harrow said.

Mongrel growled furiously as he stood, aiming the tip of his sword at Dillahunt's face. "Move!" he commanded, jerking the sword toward the cell in the back.

Dillahunt loosened the chain and let Rotter's head slip free. The corpse crumpled at his feet. "This did not go as I had intended," he groaned.

Mongrel seized Dillahunt's shoulder and dragged him to the cell, opening the little barred door and hurtling him inside. Dillahunt crashed against the opposite wall and slid down it. Mongrel slammed the door shut, produced a ring with five keys on it, and locked it. Dillahunt quickly sprang to his feet, thrusting himself against the bars. "Vane ordered you to put the girl with me!"

Mongrel raked his sword across the bars, and he would have sliced off Dillahunt's fingers had Dillahunt not jerked them away just in time. "Vane will hear of this!" Dillahunt protested.

The bald man pocketed the keys, turned, and started for Calloway. She scurried into a far corner, panic flooding her gut.

"Do not harm a hair on her head!" Dillahunt bellowed.

"I don't think it's her head he's interested in," Avery Dowling replied.

Mongrel grinned sadistically. He clutched the hair at the very top of Calloway's head and lifted her onto her feet. She shrieked as pain seared across her scalp. He released her hair and wrapped his arm around her waist, dragging her toward the tunnel they had entered from.

Dillahunt's shouts echoed behind her. "Jacqueline! Bring her back here, Mongrel! I'll bloody kill you! I'll kill all of you!"

As Mongrel dragged her down the tunnel, Dillahunt's protests faded. She beat at her captor's arms and kicked his legs, but she was useless in his iron grasp. They reached a fork in the tunnel, and Mongrel turned a sharp corner, and she was no longer certain where she was. She dragged her hands along the walls, bloodying her fingers and palms.

"Strength is always within reach," Kate had said. Calloway looked around desperately, but she saw nothing she could use against Mongrel.

He made another turn at a fork. Calloway clutched a sharp rock protruding from a wall. Mongrel tugged at her until her fingers slid loose. "Move!" he commanded, thrusting her forward, into the light of the next wall sconce.

A sconce!

She stared at the four sharp prongs that held the burning candle. When Mongrel dragged her close enough, she seized the sconce, lifted it from its hook, and swung it wildly. Fire curved around her in a wide semi-circle. Mongrel dodged too late, and the sconce smashed into his skull, dousing his bald head in hot wax. One of the prongs shredded his scalp to the bone, and wax instantly seeped into the wound. He loosed an inhuman wail, slapping frantically at his face as blood and wax washed down in steaming rivulets. "Move!" he shrieked. "Move! MOVE!! MOOOOOOOOOOOOVE!!!"

Calloway reared back, angled the torch downward, and plunged the four prongs deep into Mongrel's bare belly. The candle exploded across his torso, blood spurted from his gut, and fire gripped his skin. He sank to his knees, clutching the handle of the sconce, struggling to pull it out. His mutilated face twisted in anguish. He collapsed onto his back with the sconce protruding from his belly. He convulsed violently for a full minute. The wax hardened in the trenches it had seared into his flesh. The fire burned out, dimming the passage.

Calloway crumpled against the opposite wall, unable to pull her eyes from the dead man. *I did that,* she realized distantly. *I killed him.*

She was allowed no time to dwell on what she had done. Distant voices echoed down the tunnel. They were growing louder, and footsteps soon followed. The walls gradually brightened as the men approached. One of them must have been carrying a torch, but the curve of the passage kept them from view. Calloway got to her feet and ran in the opposite direction. She came to a fork and skidded to a halt, trying to figure out which direction Mongrel had dragged her from. She went left, and soon she came to another fork. The voices were further now, but she still heard them. She went right this time and continued on for a long time, until she was certain that she had taken a wrong turn.

When the sconces ended and she was suddenly immersed in darkness, she decided to turn back, feeling along the rough walls. How had it gone dark so quickly? After a long walk in the dark, without any sign of the sconce she had passed, she started to panic. Had she really turned around, or had she turned full circle and continued in the same wrong direction? Did these passages run on forever? She ran her fingers over the wall on her right as she stepped cautiously onward, worrying that she might plummet into a bottomless pit at any moment. Her eyelids were peeled, yet she saw nothing.

The close echo of her own frantic short breaths filled her ears. For all she knew, she was a mile deep in the mountain and would never find her way back.

25

KATE

Harry's boy, who apparently had no name of his own, stole glances at Kate's rear as she stepped timidly into the steaming hot water. Her eyelids fluttered involuntarily when she sank into the copper bathtub. "Is that warm enough, miss?" the boy asked nervously. He couldn't have been more than twelve, with shaggy brown hair, a narrow face, and twig-like arms and legs.

"It's perfect," she said.

The boy snatched up the two large buckets he had used to ferry water into the tub and scurried off, afraid to be in the same room with a naked woman for very long. "Give me a shout if you need anything," he called over his shoulder. "I'm in the next cave over." He disappeared into a dark passage in the back of the cavern.

Kate closed her eyes and rested her head against the back of the tub, smiling as the hot water stole away all her troubles.

Vane's lofty cavern overlooked the canyon below. Calico

Jack had led Kate up a frightfully narrow stairway that zig-zagged up the eastern wall, then into a little tunnel that arched up and around to one of the three bridges stretching across to the western wall, right into Vane's cavern. As she stepped onto the thin bridge, with the ships and the channel far below, she discovered she had a paralyzing fear of heights. Calico Jack had to guide her across. His every mannerism toward her had been chivalrous, and he would flash a smile any time their eyes met. "I know a woman just like you," he said in his strong, fetching voice.

"I doubt that," she had replied. "There aren't many women like me."

"Then I have been most fortunate," he said, giving her hand a squeeze. Her stomach fluttered, though she couldn't be sure if it was caused by Calico Jack's smile or the wavering bridge. "Are you alright?" he asked, studying her. He looked so very concerned.

"I've never been this high," she said.

"Few have," he replied.

The expansive cavern was luxurious. The large canopy bed in the center of the room was carved of solid mahogany, stained with a deep burgundy finish. Gold leaf accents spiraled along the bedposts. Maroon silks draped from the canopy, elegantly braided. The mattress was covered with spotless ivory sheets, topped with shimmering gold cushions. The figure of an octopus was carved into the headboard, tentacles spreading outward from the bulbous center. Each tentacle curled at the end, grasping white pearls inlaid into the wood. A little round table stood to the left of the bed, flanked by two gold-cushioned chairs. Beyond that was a giant armoire, set against a rocky wall, nearly touching one of the many stalactites. On the opposite side of the bed was a dressing table, with a mercury mirror hanging on the wall behind it in a gold leaf frame. The floor was uneven, so all the furniture was slightly angled. Candles were scattered all over, wax melting upon natural ledges in the rocky walls. The flames flickered in the soft breeze that occasionally drifted in through the wide entrance.

Outside, a dark blue starry canvas twinkled above the black wall of the canyon's eastern side. A bout of laughter rose from the dock somewhere below.

The hot water soothed Kate's aching limbs. She had been sitting in a cell far too long, never able to find a comfortable position on the hard deck. This was heaven.

If nothing else, the long stretch in the cell had given her ample opportunity to wear down Calloway's defenses. Kate hoped the girl was safe. She had inquired with Calico Jack as he escorted her to Vane's quarters, and he assured her Calloway would stay with Captain Dillahunt. Kate wanted to check on her, but she couldn't exactly run around a pirate fortress in nothing but her skin. She felt guilty enjoying a hot bath while Calloway was being transferred from one cell to another, but she wasn't about to pass up an opportunity to clean up, especially when there was nothing else she could do. Maybe she could convince Vane to release the girl. Then again, maybe Calloway was safer in a cell.

Kate closed her eyes, and the blotted remnants of the many candles shimmered like blurred stars against the back of her eyelids. She drifted in warm darkness, wondering distantly if this was what the womb felt like. A woman emerged from the black, strolling towards her, smiling with an outstretched arm. Kate couldn't see the woman's features from so far a distance, but based on the long red hair and the bright yellow dress, she knew it was her mother. That was her mother's favorite dress, and she wore it so often that eventually it faded, but now it was as bright and spotless as the first time she had worn it. She had been dead ten years, but Kate had never forgotten her face. As she neared, she saw that her mother had aged ten years, as if she'd been alive all this time. Faint lines curved from the corners of her eyes and mouth, and her dimples were not as smooth as they used to be. Still, she was as beautiful as ever. Kate fell into her arms, squeezing her tightly, so she wouldn't be able to escape. "I missed you, mother."

Her mother didn't speak. She simply smiled warmly. The smile was a combination of amity and pride, though Kate couldn't imagine why her mother would be proud of her. "I have so much to tell you," she said uncertainly, burying her face in her mother's bosom and trembling in her grasp. The tears fell freely then, darkening her mother's dress. She wept and wept, until she couldn't possibly have any tears left to shed. She squeezed her eyelids shut, until the tears stung her eyes and forced them open again. The yellow dress was soaked through, completely translucent, but the skin beneath had an ethereal greenish tint. Kate looked at her mother's face, but the elegant face that looked back was not her mother's. Her hair had gone black and straight. Her eyes were gone, replaced by illuminated blue orbs. The yellow dress dissolved into water, splashing at her feet, revealing a lithe, green figure.

"I remember you," Kate muttered, pulling away in terror. "You came to me on Hornigold's ship."

The petite mouth split into a wide grin, revealing rows of pointed teeth. The wraith burst into a fit of giggles, aiming a long finger at Kate. "I'll have you yet," it said.

Kate jerked into consciousness, splashing water over the side of the bathtub. For a moment, she had no idea where she was or why she was there, and she sat there gripping the rim of the tub until her memory slowly returned. The water had lost some of its heat. She didn't think she'd been asleep that long. She contemplated getting out before the water went lukewarm, but she couldn't bring herself to leave just yet.

Vane entered through the tunnel in the back of the room. Two very large men followed after him, carrying a big brown chest between them. Kate sank further into the water to avoid their leering eyes. They set the chest before the bed and then started back the way they came, with Vane snapping his fingers at them.

The captain took off his coat and threw it over the chair in front of his dressing table. He produced a ring of keys and jingled them at Kate. "My two jailors are dead, and Dillahunt's woman is missing. What do you know about her?"

Kate lifted up slightly, frowning. "We barely talked," she lied. "I know Dillahunt fancies her." *And he would be very upset if anything happened to her.*

"Dillahunt refuses to talk. I might have to torture him."

"I doubt that will do you any good," Kate replied.

"You're probably right." Vane set the keys on his desk, and Kate pretended not to notice them. "Well, these problems have a way of working themselves out. If the girl doesn't turn up soon, she'll starve."

Kate tried not to think about Calloway fumbling in the dark, scared and alone. But then she thought of the tall, lithe girl in the dream, with the pointed teeth and black hair. It had looked a little like Calloway, she realized. *More than a little.* But that didn't make any sense, because she'd dreamed of that scary creature *before* meeting Calloway. She shook her head and cleared her mind before such thoughts could drive her mad.

Vane took a step toward her. "I'm sorry about the tub. I've been attempting to procure something nicer to match the rest of the room."

Kate snickered dismissively. "I've been relieving myself in a bucket in front of two people for the past week. The tub is just fine."

His expression went rancid. "I'll do my best to forget that

statement."

"Turn around," she said. He did, and she stepped out of the tub, quickly wrapping her old blanket around her. She was shocked at how much dirt she'd left in the water.

Vane unlatched and opened the chest. It was packed full of colorful garments. He rummaged through them for a long time before he produced a thin black chemise. Kate shook her head. "I prefer breeches."

He curled his lip in revulsion. "Your mouth is moving, but nonsense is flowing out."

"Breeches, or I'll stick with the blanket," she insisted, clutching the blanket to her breasts. "I've grown fond of it."

"Fine. At least put on a bodice. Your tits could use the boost."

"I might try one," she said, curious how her breasts would look.

She slipped into a pair of dark brown breeches that might have hung loose a year ago, when she was thin as a rail. She laced a long-sleeved, cream-colored shirt only so far, leaving her shoulders bare. He helped her into a sleeveless black bodice intricately embroidered with two dozen roses that were the same shade of red as her hair, with thorny brown stems that intertwined. She couldn't help but smile when she looked down. The bodice boosted the top of her breasts above a low neckline. She adjusted the sleeves of her shirt as Vane laced up the front of the bodice. He turned her around and adjusted the backside.

"You're good at this," she said.

"I'm better at getting you out of it."

"Maybe another time."

He pulled her to him, reaching around and cupping one of her breasts. "Maybe *now*." His other hand slid around her waist and down her stomach.

She grasped his hands, holding them still. "But you just went to all that trouble to get it on."

"I enjoy unwrapping my presents."

"I am not a present." She slipped out of his embrace and swiveled to face him, stepping behind the tub. "And you already have a woman."

"You mean the whore?"

Kate put a finger to her lip. "I was certain she had a name."

He circled the tub to get at her. "Has she? It seems to have slipped my mind."

"No it hasn't," Kate said, positioning herself behind the tub. "She's brought you a fortune." She brushed a fleck of dust from her bodice, murmuring, "Possibly misfortune."

When she looked up, Vane had stopped moving and was studying her skeptically. "Do you know something I don't?" he asked.

She recalled Nathan's expression of shock, frozen forever on his young face. "I know she murdered my friend, Nathan Adams, and betrayed her master, Blackbeard." She glanced at the ceiling. "Or did she? I'm indefinite about that last bit. Oh well, I suppose we'll find out soon enough."

Vane grinned shrewdly, wagging a finger. "You are trying to raise my suspicions."

Her head sank into an innocent shrug. "Merely voicing my own." But she knew she had him.

"You're a devious woman," he said, moving around the tub. "And I'm hard."

She backed away. "And I'm sorry."

"I want you."

"Out of the question," she replied, evading him. She crossed the room to the dressing table and appraised herself in the mirror. "But thank you for the clothes. I rather like the bodice. The thorns are a particularly nice touch." She poked one of her breasts with her index finger. "And these *do* look fantastic."

Through the mirror she saw Captain Vane adjust himself in frustration. "I'm not accustomed to being denied," he fumed. "I could take you right now, if I wanted to. I doubt Griffith gave you a choice in the matter. How long was it before he took you? The first night or the second?"

"The taking was mutual."

"I find that difficult to believe."

She shrugged. "I don't care what you believe."

"Did you pretend to enjoy it? Or worse yet, did you actually enjoy it?"

"I enjoyed it," she answered. "When he was inside me, I thought about all the ways I might do away with him." She drew her hair away from her missing ear, running a finger over the rough, red skin. It looked hideous. She was thankful it was so easily concealed. "And one day, when he dropped his guard, I finally did it."

"And did that make it all better?" he asked.

She nodded at him through the mirror. "Yes."

Vane glanced downward. "Oh dear. I seem to have gone soft."

Kate tried to adjust her hair in the mirror even though she knew it was futile. The red tresses were wild and scraggly beyond repair. Her skin had gone a bit lighter, after being deprived of sun for a week. The wound on her cheek had healed to a thin indent, detectable only in angled light, offering a faint reminder of her short time with Benjamin Hornigold. She didn't miss him.

Vane walked to the edge of the cave and locked his hands behind his back as he looked down on his kingdom. Kate pulled herself from the mirror and crossed the room. She approached the edge cautiously and leaning forward until she could almost see the eastern dock below. Most of the caves had gone dark, but a few were still lit, and she could see men within. Vane had built quite a community, hollowed in the rock. One man was framed at the edge of his cave, staring into the canyon while sipping from a silver goblet. Another was pacing in circles, lost in thought. A third was relaxing in a chair, with his legs crossed. She saw another man shimmying up a ladder toward his cave, wobbling as though he was very drunk. She wondered how often pirates plunged to their deaths here.

"You see that brigantine?" Vane said, pointing at the eastern dock. "The one your ship docked behind?"

"Yes," she replied nervously, unable to bring herself any closer to the edge.

"That's *Ranger*."

Kate rolled her eyes. "What an original name."

He ignored the jest. "I'm allowing Jack Rackham to captain her. I've half a mind to take her back. *Valiant* is fast, but she's no *Ranger*."

"It's a very pretty ship," Kate said. She slowly backed away from the edge, for fear of passing out from nausea and toppling over.

Vane guffawed in pleasant surprise. "It's good to see you're afraid of *something*."

"I fear a great many things," she assured him.

He scratched the back of his head, suddenly perturbed. "I do wish you'd ask me something about, well . . . me."

She resisted a laugh. "What should I ask?"

"Oh, I dunno," he said, looking around. "There must be something you want to ask me. Anything. First question that springs to mind. You must have a hundred."

She bit her lip. "I can't think of anything."

He sighed, pinching the bridge of his nose. "Maybe you're curious how I came to pirating?"

"Not really."

His jaw hardened.

Kate saw movement in the cave at the opposite end of the bridge that extended into Vane's loft. A stout man with a red bandana and a bushy red beard emerged and started over the bridge. He wore a red shirt and brown pants, shredded at the ankles. His feet were massive, with gnarled toes. He was sweating terribly, and his muscular chest heaved as though he'd been running. "Captain Vane, sir," he called.

"What is it?" Vane said with a touch of irritation.

"I know it's late, sir," the stout man gasped, unable to catch his breath.

The captain feigned confusion, looking at the stars. "Is it? When did that happen?"

"It's one of *Crusader's* men, sir," the other man went on. "One of them you wanted placed in *special* quarters, if you catch my meaning, sir. Goes by name of Ogle."

"Yes," Vane grated impatiently. "Get fucking on with it."

The stout man glanced uneasily at Kate. "Well, it's just that we was torturing him . . . "

"Naturally," Vane replied, rolling his eyes.

" . . . and he said something I wager you'll want to hear."

Vane embellished a sigh. "Spit it out, Bigfoot."

Bigfoot swallowed. "I think you should hear it for yourself, captain, sir."

"Fine," Vane sighed, ushering him away with several flicks of his wrist. "Off with you. I'll be there presently."

Bigfoot nodded and started back across the bridge.

Vane retrieved his coat, but he left the ring of keys on the dressing table. Kate pretended not to notice them. "You're welcome to wait until I return," he told her.

"In your bed?" she replied with an exaggerated swoon.

He grinned. "It is quite comfortable."

She teased him with a smirk. "Save it for Annabelle. I'll not divvy a man with another woman, let alone the woman who murdered my friend." She inclined her head, adding casually, "Not while that woman's alive, anyway."

26

ANNABELLE

The kitchen was a long, cavernous room, which was accessible from the eastern dock by a thirty foot tunnel that burrowed into the mountain. Four sconces ran along either wall. Two long benches stretched across, and there was a massive oven in the back, carved into the rock. A heavyset chef was plucking feathers from a limp chicken, while his black assistant prepared a stew in a large iron pot. Chickens strutted along the ground, pecking at crumbs. The wobbly floor was matted with hay. The air was teeming with the competing stenches of hay and chickens and raw meat, and Annabelle nearly gagged when she first entered.

She had been wandering Pirate Town for hours, well aware that she should be impressed by everything she saw, but all she could think about was what Vane had been doing with Kate Lindsay all this time. She hadn't seen Lindsay since Vane had invited her to his quarters. *That bitch gets to see his quarters before I do?* Annabelle wanted the woman dead, reward be damned. *I should have tossed her to the sea alongside Nathan. He would have liked that.* She knew Nathan had fancied Lindsay more than he'd ever been willing to admit. *Who wouldn't?*

Killing Nathan had been easy. Truthfully, it was easier than she thought it would be. Her body had shuddered as the pistol kicked in her arms with more force than she expected. One minute he was alive, the next his brains were leaving his skull. His last moment was clearly one of comprehension. He finally understood who she was, and that he had underestimated her. After his body vanished into the deep, she'd hardly given him another thought.

But she hadn't been able to murder a woman, let alone a woman with whom she shared indignities at the hands of Edward Livingston. A woman who had survived Livingston deserved to survive anything. Annabelle realized now that she had used the reward as an excuse to spare Lindsay's life. She had humiliated her instead, to remind her who was in control, but even that had been a thinly veiled excuse not to kill her. *Crusader* carried enough treasure to last a hundred lifetimes, and procuring Lindsay's reward would be problematic at best. There had been no real reason to keep her alive, other than respect.

I should have been stronger, she told herself. *I should have been ruthless, like Teach. That's why he's still alive.*

She would correct that mistake. Lindsay was just a woman, and she was made of the same flesh and blood as any other. She wasn't invincible. She could die as easily as anyone else, and Annabelle knew just the man for the job.

Gabe Jenkins was seated at the far end of the room, near the oven, hunched over a steaming bowl of stew. His shirt was tight across his muscular back. Thick curls dangled over his brow, darkening his eyes. His jaw worked slowly as he chewed.

He didn't look at her as she approached, but a slight tilt of his head told her he knew she was there. She took a seat beside him on the bench and scooted close, nudging him with her hip. "I was looking for you," she said.

He glanced apprehensively at her. "What do you want?"

"You're mad," she said, making a sad face.

He stirred the mysterious contents of his stew with a large wooden spoon but didn't take another bite. "You figured that out, did you?"

Annabelle resisted a smile. *He's fetching when he's angry.* This wouldn't be difficult. If he was angry, it meant he cared. "You feel betrayed," she said. It wasn't a question.

He tried to shrug casually, but his bulky shoulders were too stiff. "What do you care?"

"I'm here asking, aren't I?" she said.

He shook his head, snickering loudly, and swept his curls back into place with a furious hand. "You're here because you want something. Don't pretend. Only time you pay attention to anyone is when you want something. Everyone knows that now. Shame Adams figured it out too late."

She flinched. "That's not a very nice thing to say, Gabe Jenkins."

"The truth isn't always a nice thing to hear, is it?" he shot back. "Anyway, it doesn't matter what I think. Only thing that matters is what Teach will think when he finds out what's happened here, and I have a feeling that'll be sooner than you expect."

An icy chill of doubt riddled her arms with gooseflesh. She clutched his wrist. "Do you know something I don't? Answer me."

"No," he replied, staring at her hand as if it was a very large spider. "But I know how Teach works. No one escapes him for long. You should know that better than anyone, having spent so much time with him. It baffles me that you'd try something like this and honestly think you can get away with it."

"I *did* get away with it," she reminded him.

"Everyone thinks that," he chuckled sardonically, "until *Queen Anne's Revenge* is bearing down on their stern. Captain Hornigold probably thought that too, but he didn't count on being traded for a woman."

"Teach can't get in here," she assured him. "This place is a fortress."

"He'll find a way," Jenkins replied. "Why do you think Vane's been so careful not to get on Teach's bad side? He's afraid of him. He may not say it, but he is. Everyone is, as well they should be."

Her palm slapped the table in frustration. "Vane was quick enough to accept the plunder I brought him."

His laugh was bitter. "I heard a song once. I can't remember the lyrics, save for one. 'A bit of shine sets every pirate out of his mind.'"

She leaned closer. She knew he liked it when she was close, even though he pretended he didn't care. "Well, it's not like you're going to tell Teach, right?"

An amused look passed over his face, followed swiftly by grim certainty. "I don't have to. He'll find out with or without my aid. He knows things. I don't know how, but he does."

"What do you owe him, anyway?" she asked. "It must be something important, if you'd kill a friend over it."

He slapped the spoon into the stew, splattering the table. "But I didn't kill a friend under Blackbeard's orders, did I? I only *thought* I did."

"I am sorry about that," she said, trying to sound as genuine as possible, though she couldn't even recall the name of the man Jenkins had killed in that cave. "I needed to know who I could trust."

"You don't look sorry," he returned. "I'm a bloody idiot."

There was a long, uncomfortable silence. Her stomach broke it, unleashing an embarrassingly loud growl. Jenkins slid the bowl her way. "Sounds like you need this more than I do. I'll be dead soon anyway."

She laughed. "Why do you think that?"

"Because you're going to have me killed, just like Ogle and Red Devil. No one can find them. You told Vane to do away with them, didn't you?"

She nodded slowly. "Yet you're still here. What does that tell you?"

He frowned, unable to come up with an answer.

She dipped the large spoon into the steaming muck and brought it cautiously to her mouth. The stew was permeated with strips of chicken, chunks of potato, and maybe bread, but she couldn't be sure. It wasn't particularly tasty, but it was better than nothing.

"So if you're not going to kill me," he said finally, "what is it you want? You must have kept me alive for a reason."

She narrowed her eyes and licked the spoon clean. "Two reasons, actually. The first is, well, I fancy you."

He rolled his eyes. "And the second?"

Pretend you don't want what's between my legs, Gabe. Pretend for as long as you can stand it. "The second," she continued, "is I want something."

He threw up his hands. "Here it comes. Who do you want me to kill this time?"

She glanced at the cook and his assistant. Neither seemed particularly interested in their conversation, but she lowered her voice to a whisper nonetheless. "I want you to kill Kate Lindsay."

He thought about that for a minute, eyes shifting. When he came to a conclusion, he chuckled that same sardonic chuckle.

"I just remembered something. You're not my boss anymore, lady. Teach is. Seeing as you don't really have his best interests at heart, I can't help you."

"Don't you want to know what you'll get in return?" She slid a hand over his leg, fingers tantalizing his crotch.

He shifted uneasily. "I know what I'll get. A knife across my throat. If I'm lucky, you'll sit on my face first."

She jerked her hand away and folded her arms. "You're in a foul mood tonight. Maybe I *should* have you killed."

"Go ahead," he said, smirking. "Or do it yourself, if you've still got the stomach for it. I'm not killing anybody else for you, certainly not for a quick fuck. There are plenty more whores where you came from."

She raked her nails across the table, but she swallowed her rage and kept her voice at a low hiss, so the cook wouldn't take notice. "Are you scared, is that it? Do your hands shake?"

His glare was icy. "They used to. Not anymore, though. You have no idea what I've done, or what I'm capable of. Keep pushing me and you might see for yourself."

"Good!" she exclaimed cheerily, reaching for his wrist. "That means you're stronger now."

Jenkins pulled his hand away and stood, stepping over the bench. "You're right about that," he said. "You want her dead? You'll have to do it yourself. Shouldn't be a problem for you."

"I suppose I'll have to," she concluded haughtily. This had not gone at all as she had hoped.

He aimed a finger at her face. "You think killing makes you stronger? It doesn't. It only makes you weaker." He turned and hastily made for the exit.

"Gabe," she called, but he didn't look back before vanishing into the tunnel.

Annabelle lowered her gaze. The uncertain contents swirled in the murky brown stew. She saw a scar reflected within.

There might have been a face behind it, but it was impossible to see. She pushed the bowl aside.

27

VANE

Five of Ogle's teeth were scattered about his knees. His bald scalp was striped with red lacerations that seeped red fingers down his pallid face. A sliver of skin dangled from his left arm, exposing pink muscle and a hint of bone. Despite his woeful condition, he was grinning broadly. "You're all going to die," he mumbled through a broken jaw.

The dark cave was thick with the stench of death, wafting from a pit in the back, where they had dumped recent bodies. Water dripped from gnarled stalactites, pattering the various torture devices that Vane had collected over the years. He was up to nearly two dozen now. There wasn't always a good reason to torture a man, but he didn't want to see his collection to go to waste.

Bigfoot stood behind Ogle. Calico Jack was leaning casually against an iron maiden, arms folded. Tanner, a lanky man with shifty eyes and long blonde hair, studied a table full of knives and tools, pondering his next option while stroking his pointed chin.

Vane placed his hands on a double torture chair, which consisted of two bulky wooden chairs placed back to back, with dozens of rusty iron spikes protruding from the backrests, and two collars tethered on a short chain. It was designed for two victims, who would inevitably pull each other against the spikes. Vane adored the simplicity of it. He smiled down at Ogle. "I had intended this chair for you and your red friend. You would have made a lovely pair. Sadly, my quartermaster has informed me that he's gone missing."

"You'll never find him," Ogle said. "Red Devil knew that cunt wanted us dead."

Calico Jack and Bigfoot laughed heartily, and Tanner stared at them inquisitively. The torturer was never known to join in laughter. "We'll chance upon him one day," Calico Jack said, "and unless his bones are as red as his skin, we won't concern ourselves with who they belonged to."

There were too many places a man could disappear in these caves. But that didn't matter. Red Devil would have to come out of hiding eventually. There was no food to be found anywhere on this barren, mountainous isle, save for what Vane's men ferried in from a lush island many leagues away. Red Devil wouldn't last long on his own.

"What about the brothers?" Vane asked Calico Jack.

"The Maynards put up a fight," Calico Jack said, shifting his eyes elsewhere. "Found the two of them in a corridor, talking in whispers. One of them came at me. I put my sword out and he ran right into it. The other went mad when he saw his brother dead, saying he was going to kill us all. There was no approaching him, so we shot him."

Vane suspected Calico Jack wasn't being completely honest about what had gone wrong. The quartermaster too often gave men a chance to do the right thing. That made him sloppy. Still, Jack Rackham was one of the few men Vane considered a friend, which afforded him far more leeway than anyone else.

"*Crusader's* crew brings fortune both shining and ill," Vane grated. "Maybe I should kill them all and be done with it." *I've already lost two jailors.*

"Too late for that," Ogle said.

Vane snickered. "Where'd you find this one?"

"In the kitchen," the Calico Jack answered, "putting grub away like he didn't have a care in the world."

Vane kneeled close to Ogle, peering into his eyes. The big man reeked of sweat and dirt and salt. "Did you know you were enjoying your last meal?"

Ogle shrugged. "I take every meal like it's my last."

Tanner plucked a massive serrated knife from the table and inspected it closely. It looked like he might kiss it. "Oh my, what a pretty girl you are."

Calico Jack shuddered. "It's not a girl, it's a knife."

Tanner stared at Calico Jack as a religious zealot stares at a blasphemer. "They're all Tanner's girls," Tanner insisted. "They're his sharp little girls."

"You've been down here too long, friend," Calico Jack said.

"There's no better place for him," said Vane.

"No better place for him," Tanner agreed with a fervent nod. He had always been a despicable creature. His eyes lit up whenever Vane brought him a new torture device.

Bigfoot thrust a foot into Ogle's back so hard that he nearly fell into Vane. "Tell him the thing you told me," Bigfoot urged. "The thing about you-know-who."

Ogle sat upright, filling his great chest with air. "He's on his way."

Vane smirked. "Who?"

Ogle grinned, blood oozing from the gaps in his teeth.

"Blackbeard."

Vane maintained his smirk, but his jaw was tightening. "And how would that be possible? My scouts spotted no other ship trailing yours."

"He wasn't following close enough to be seen," Ogle laughed.

Vane returned the laugh. "How could he follow what he couldn't see?"

"We never trusted that strumpet," Ogle said. "She was handing out orders from the start, before we even left the island. Well, that didn't settle too well with me and Devil. We knew we couldn't trust her to lead us to Teach. So we dumped barrels over the stern every so often, when she wasn't about. She spent so much time in her cabin, it wasn't hard. We fixed the barrels with pretty garments, so they could be seen for miles. We did that from the start. From Griffith's Isle all the way till she changed course on us, and then all the way here. A pretty trail leading straight to you, Charles Vane." He cackled, blood and spit dribbling down his chin. "You should have turned us away when you had the chance. By my wager, Teach is already here."

Vane stood and looked down on Ogle's shredded bald scalp. Ogle slowly raised his head, glaring up from beneath a bloody brow. His shoulders shook as he chuckled. "He will give you no quarter. He will not wait on your account. He will burn every cave and every man within. You know this."

"Pirate Town is not easily penetrated," Vane reminded him.

"He'll penetrate your little hideout one way or another," Ogle said. "He'll find a way. And if he doesn't, he'll wait outside until you starve."

Vane's molars scraped as his lower jaw worked back and forth like a saw. A sharp pain spiked through his right cheek, tugging at his eyelids. One of the molars had gone rotten over a month ago. He knew he would have to remove it eventually. That would be a hard day, if he lived long enough to see it.

He patted the double-torture chair. "Strap him in."

Bigfoot nodded enthusiastically. "Right. And who else?"

"You."

Bigfoot eyed Vane suspiciously for a few seconds before he broke into jittery giggles. "That's funny, captain. You got me, there. I almost pissed meself."

Vane looked at Calico Jack and Tanner. "Put him in the chair. And get a bucket, in case he pisses himself."

Bigfoot sprang forward and clutched Vane's arms. "Captain, sir, whatever I done, I'll set it right."

Calico Jack and Tanner seized Bigfoot, wrenching him off of Vane. Vane brushed off his sleeves. They shoved Bigfoot in the chair, and he shrieked as his back mashed against the nails. He stiffened as they strapped him in.

Vane leaned in close. "It's more what you *didn't* do, you little shit. You dragged me all the way down here instead of relaying the news in my fucking quarters. Every minute you wasted brought Edward Teach that much closer."

"Captain, sir, please, no!"

Tanner tittered with excitement.

Vane snapped his fingers at Calico Jack. "Where did you last see the whore?"

Calico Jack sighed. "I told you how many times, Charles? Don't snap your fingers at me. I'm not one of your dogs."

"This is hardly the time to fuck with me, Jack," Vane growled. "Where did you last see the whore?"

After a long, sullen glare, Calico Jack answered, "Probably in the kitchen by now. She asked me where it was earlier."

"Thank you," Vane replied with exaggerated obligation. "When you're done here, ready the guns and secure all exits. Teach will not take Pirate Town without a fight."

Calico Jack nodded. "I say we barricade the entrance with *Valiant*. *Revenge* will have to get past her and every man on her before Teach sees the inside of this canyon."

Vane hesitated. "I rather liked that ship."

Calico Jack shrugged. "Plenty of ships in the sea, eh?"

"Aye," Vane nodded. "When *Revenge* breaks through, she'll have our mounted cannons to deal with."

"Them little cannons won't save you," Ogle said, sputtering blood and laughter. "You think *Revenge* is coming alone? You're all going to die."

Vane turned on Ogle, clutching the man's bloody cheeks so tightly that his lips bunched together. "That might be true, but you'll know nothing of it. This cave is very deep and very difficult to find, as I'm sure you noted on your way down. Teach's men will never find you here, not even when you scream at the top of your fucking lungs. And scream you will."

Ogle continued to laugh. "I'll take comfort knowing that cunt will die."

"That's the only comfort you shall receive," Vane said, shoving Ogle's face away. He looked Calico Jack. "Put him in the other chair."

Vane grabbed a torch and started back up the long passage to surface level, with Bigfoot frantically calling after him. "I done nothing! I done nothing! CAPTAIN!!"

Bigfoot's wails soon faded, and Vane was alone with his thoughts. Ogle was right. Teach would offer no quarter, let alone allow Vane a chance to explain himself. Not that there was anything to explain. No lie would be sufficient. It was obvious what had happened.

Plunder stiffens my cock and clouds my brain, Vane realized. He had always known treasure would be the death of him. The epiphany had occurred to him several times over the past two years, usually as he was engaged in battle on the deck of an enemy ship, parrying blades, with musket and cannon fire zipping past his head. Since he had aided Henry Jennings in raiding Spanish ships that were in the process of salvaging the wreckage of a treasure fleet off the coast of Florida, the promise of fortune at the end of a battle had urged him heedlessly forward.

He pounded a fist against the wall, splitting a knuckle on a sharp rock. The pain was bracing, coursing up his arm. "Fuck!" The curse reverberated down the tunnel. When he finally reached the first of the sconces that lined the upper passageways, he cast his torch aside and cradled the wounded hand in his other, massaging the shattered knuckle with his thumb. He hunched as he walked, passing many sconces, moving through light and darkness.

He wound through several passages, taking left and right turns without deliberation. When he had first discovered this isle, which had been mined by the Spanish half a century before his arrival, he dared not venture too deeply into the tunnels. Now, he knew them like the back of his hand. The entire volcanic rock was a honeycomb of intertwining tunnels, both natural and manmade. Vane had insisted that his men commit the necessary passages to memory. He didn't want outsiders learning anything about his hideout. When he caught one of his men sketching a crude diagram of the tunnels, which Vane had specifically ordered against, he had the man tortured to death. The diagram proved inaccurate, but Vane still had to set an example.

It was nearly an hour's walk from the torture chamber to the kitchen. To Vane, the thick aroma of poultry was nearly as nauseating as the stench of dead men. Annabelle was no longer there. The cook's assistant, a wiry black man named Roach, who was busy polishing the pots, informed Vane, "She go to your quarter, captain. She say she make you real happy."

"Oh, she will," Vane hissed.

A damp breeze swept across the face of the eastern wall as Vane scaled the stairs that snaked along the side. His heart thumped violently against his ribcage. Halfway up, he looked back toward the entrance of the great rift in the island. A fog was drifting in. *Are you lurking somewhere out there, Teach? Waiting for me to run?*

Annabelle was sprawled in his bed, naked and smiling with the sheets cast aside. He was fully aroused by the time he crossed the bridge into his loft. She traced a finger down her perfect stomach, inserting it into the cleft between her legs. "I got tired of waiting."

He slipped out of his coat, tore off his shirt, and lowered his breeches. He leapt on top of her, spreading her legs and thrusting himself within. "Are they dead?" she gasped beneath him. "Ogle and the others?"

"Dead or dying," he answered, thrusting dutifully.

"Good," she said, reaching for his face. He seized her wrist and held it beside her head. She whispered, "I have another name for you."

"Oh?"

"Gabe Jenkins."

His molars gnashed. "I don't know who that is."

"I'll show you."

He slapped a palm over her mouth. "No more talking." A nasty look flashed across her face. He wondered if she would be his last, before Teach's men found him hiding away in some dark cave. There was always Katherine Lindsay, of course.

As he imagined Lindsay's vibrant red hair splayed about the pillow, he released unexpectedly. He lowered his head and groaned. Annabelle shoved his hand away from her face and stared at him expectantly. "That was fast. My turn?"

"Your turn," he replied. He scooped his arms under her and

lifted her out of the bed. She squealed in delight. "But first, my pretty strumpet, I want to show you the view."

Her smile wilted as he carried her toward the edge, and her eyes began to dart frantically back and forth. "What are you doing?" she demanded, placing a hand on his chest.

"I'm sending you off, my dear. You seem an adaptable sort. Mayhap you'll sprout wings on the way down."

"No, wait!" she cried, raking her nails over his chest as she curled her fingers into a fist. He winced as she tugged at his curly auburn hairs. She kicked her legs, glancing frantically at the approaching edge.

"You've fucked me," he answered. "I must return the favor."

"I can set it right, whatever I've done."

He laughed. "That's the second time I've heard that today. Nothing can set Edward Teach right."

The edge was near. He walked slowly, allowing her time to process what was about to happen. Her frantic expressions shifted rapidly through denial, fear, despair, and renewed determination. "There's no way he could know!" she bleated, eyes wide and resolute.

Vane chuckled softly. "And yet he does."

She writhed in his arms like a cat, small sinewy muscles emerging beneath her dark skin. Her body was elegant even in struggle, her face beautiful even in distress. It would be a shame to destroy something so lovely. Then again, it would be less shameful than allowing her to grow old, withering into a hideous hag. She would never be more beautiful than she was now. *Better to shatter a crystal cup than let age chip away at it, one piece at a time.* The scar wedged in her cheek was only the first of many chips. *A sign of things to come.*

"You don't want to do this," she pleaded.

"I really do," he replied.

"You'll need me when Teach arrives. He'll want to see me

punished. He'll want to do it himself. He'll be furious if you've killed me!"

"Then I'm doing you a favor," Vane said. "You might buy yourself a little extra time, but Teach will kill you slowly, and then he'll kill me anyway. He's no fool." He smiled down at her. "I rather like you, so I'll do you the honor of killing you promptly."

"This is insane!" she said, eyes swirling desperately in their sockets, arms and legs flailing. "With me alive at least you'll have a chance!"

"You mean you'll have a chance to escape before Teach gets here."

"Where would I go?"

He shrugged. "You're resourceful. I'd rather not find out."

"It will look even more suspicious if I'm dead and you've taken the treasure for yourself!"

"You might be right," he said as they came to the edge. His biceps ached as he held her over the precipice. The mist had crept between the docks, surrounding the ships in a milky blanket. "Mayhap it's in my best interests to keep you alive."

She locked eyes with him. He tilted her legs downward and set her just before the edge. Relief softened her muscles, tense knots withdrawing into smooth mahogany. She crumpled against him, sobbing softly into his chest. "Thank you. Thank you. Thank you, thank you, thank you."

He cocked his head, as though a thought had just struck him. "Then again, you've brought me a redhead to replace you. That was either very thoughtful or very foolish."

"Katherine Lindsay is worth nothing dead!" she reminded him, cheeks blooming with rage. "Would I have been wiser to murder her?"

"Yes," he stated bluntly.

"She'll slice off your manhood before she lets you betwixt

her thighs. Remember what happened to Captain Griffith? She's poisonous. You should lock her up with the rest of the treasure, until such time as you can trade her."

He smiled. This one was cunning when she needed to be. Unfortunately, it was the kind of cunning that arose from desperation rather than deliberation. Vane grasped one of her breasts, which was somehow soft and firm. "I must admit, there's more to you than a fantastic pair of tits."

She smiled gratefully up at him.

"If I were a wiser man, I'd take what I have and sail away with you right now, to some tropical isle where we would fuck like rabbits for the remainder of our lives. Or at least until you grew ugly, or my cock went niggardly, though I suspect the former before the latter."

She stood on her toes and drew her lips toward his. "Then be the wiser man," she urged.

He sighed, swirling the tip of his finger around an areola. "Sadly, I've never been very good at resisting base inclinations." He pinched her nipple and twisted hard, as if he was tightening a loose screw. She cried out, face racked with sudden pain. He gave her chest a light shove. It was just enough to tip her balance. She flung her hands at him, but she had already tipped too far, and she toppled over the edge, unleashing a terrible shriek that echoed off the opposite canyon wall. He leaned over the edge, watching her naked body spiral downward, toward the schooner at the western dock. Three men working on the deck scattered in separate directions. Annabelle impacted the planking like a meteor, splintered bits jutting up around her. The sound of the impact reached Vane's ears a moment later, silencing her warbled scream. Bloody stakes protruded from her torso, legs, and arms. Her wide, terrified eyes were fixated on Vane from within a garbled ruin of pink and red flesh. Her broken body slowly bent inward at the middle, sinking into the hole she had punched in the deck. She slipped through the gap, into the dark hold below, and vanished from sight.

The three men surrounded the hole, peering within. They looked up at Vane, then each other, and then back up at Vane. "The fuck are you looking at?" Vane bellowed down at them. "Clean up that mess!"

28

CALLOWAY

She pushed herself onward, moving faster and faster despite the ache of her bruised and bleeding legs, and the light at the end of the passage grew brighter and brighter. She emerged into the gloom of pre-dawn, with the endless ocean spread out before her. A wonderful breeze swept over her, cool against the sweat that layered her entire body. She crumpled to her knees, not caring as they gnashed into gravel. She had already scraped them many times in the pitch black of the tunnel, which she thought she would never leave. The sun wasn't up yet, but it might as well have been. Her eyes had grown so used to the darkness that the early gloom caused her to squint.

She suspected she had emerged on the far eastern side of the mountain. It was ugly and grey, with no plants or white sand. The mountainside sloped into a slim rocky beach. Stars twinkled in a moonless sky, fading eastward into an increasing violet ambience.

She skittered down the rocky hillside toward the beach, feet sliding on rolling gravel. Waist-high waves broke over the pebbled shore below. She wanted to dive into the water. Of course, it wouldn't quench her thirst, but maybe she could find a pool of fresh water somewhere afterward. She didn't care. Her body sweltered from nonstop movement. She hadn't taken the time to rest in the tunnel. She had been afraid to stop, fearing that her burning muscles would cease to muster, and she would be forever lost in darkness. Her lungs seared with every breath, and she wheezed hoarsely.

She was halfway down when she spotted a dark blotch out of the corner of her eye. It was a huge three-masted ship, moored to the north. At the top of its mainmast a black flag with a horned skeleton fretted in the wind. One skeletal hand raised a chalice in toast, while the other threatened to skewer a red heart with a spear.

A chill shuddered through her. She tried to skid to a halt, but her legs slid out from under her and she landed hard on her ass. She slid a bit further, teeth chattering as she bounced along. She grabbed hold of a boulder that was twice her size and huddled behind it, pressing her face against the cold damp rock.

In the relative silence between the crashing waves she heard voices. They had to be coming from somewhere along the beach.

"Didn't get a look at his face before I put it through his skull," one of them said.

"I got a look," said the other. "He's prettier now."

Both howled laughter.

Calloway slowly crept down the hillside to another boulder. She peered over it to the beach below. A hundred paces north, she saw two men standing before a small wooden shack with a smoldering campfire just outside it. A body was slumped beside the fire, blood gushing out of his gaping skull. He had stringy grey hair and was wearing black rags.

"'You're not supposed to be here,' he says," laughed a lanky man that leaned awkwardly on a bum leg.

"Aye, that's a new one," agreed a compact man with a fat belly bound by a red sash. "I'd wager he'd been out here a while. He wasn't very sprightly."

"Vane got what he paid for," said the other.

Calloway saw a small boat bobbing in the water, tethered to a stake. These two must have come from the ship offshore. Was there nowhere safe on this cursed isle?

The squat one stretched his neck and looked Calloway's way. She ducked low, heart thudding rapidly. "Must be a way in somewhere around here," she heard him say.

"Maybe. Or maybe Vane shipped him over and left him out here."

"Rotten job. Almost feel bad for bashing his face in."

"Almost," said the other, and they both laughed.

They were silent for a few minutes. Calloway waited, hands flat against the boulder, listening to the waves crashing over the pebbled shore. When one of them spoke again, his voice was alarmingly close, and she jolted in shock. "Has to be a way in. Why else would Vane put a lookout all the way over here? He was meant to warn Vane if he saw anyone, and he probably would have if he hadn't been asleep."

"He shoulda stationed two out here," said the other, also very close. It sounded like they were just on the other side of the boulder. "That's what I woulda done. One to watch while the other sleeps."

"That's just commonly sensible. You heard what Teach said. Vane's getting sloppy."

"Oy, what's that?"

"Eh? What's what?"

"Looks like a hole in the mountain."

"Hello! Told you!"

She heard their feet shuffling in the gravel, on either side. *They're coming around!* Calloway flattened herself against the rock, closed her eyes, and prayed that they would walk right past her.

"What have we here?" A hand snatched her by the collar and tossed her onto her back. The squat one set his foot on her chest and leered down at her. "It's a boy. Second lookout?"

"That's not a boy, you oaf," said the lanky one.

The squat man scowled. "Hair's cut like one."

"Oh, then it must be a boy then," drawled the other.

"Teats are too small. Maybe I should check between its legs." The squat man bent down and reached for Calloway's crotch. She seized his foot and shoved hard. He fell backwards and collapsed against the rock, growling furiously. "You'll pay for that, you . . . whatever you are!"

The lanky one drew a dagger and circled behind, shuffling on a bad limp. "How is it you came to be out here?"

"I killed one of Vane's men," she answered quickly. If these were Teach's men, she had best ally herself fast. "Didn't think he'd appreciate that, so I ran."

The lanky man lifted an incredulous eyebrow. "How old are you?"

"Fifteen," she chirped quickly, hoping youth would encourage their sympathy.

The squat man shrugged. "I've killed younger."

She licked her lips, thinking fast. "You want to get through that passage, you'll need me. I just came through. It was very long and confusing."

The squat man glared at her. "If you stumbled through it so easy in the dark, I wager we won't have no trouble finding our way with torches."

"I was lucky," she said.

"I wouldn't call this lucky," the lanky one chuckled.

"Let's see if you really are a girl," the squat man said. He drew his knife and advanced.

"Now hold on a minute," the other interjected, stepping between them. "Let's not be hasty, Hemett."

"Yes," Calloway agreed, setting her hands on the lanky man's shoulders and taking refuge behind him. "Let's not be hasty, Hemett."

"And why shouldn't I be, hmm?" Hemett said, puffing his chest. "It's been months since I had a woman. I'm throbbing, Ned. Strapped Bodice was my favorite whorehouse, you know that! And Rogers took it away from me when he took Nassau! Now I have to go all the way to Tortuga or Mariposa for my pleasure. I can count on two fingers how often we been to either in the past year."

Calloway shrank behind her human shield, skinny though he was. She had probably met these two during her time at The Strapped Bodice, but there were too many men to remember. She was thankful they didn't recognize her. Her shortened hair apparently worked wonders in altering her appearance.

"You didn't even know this was a woman till I told you it was," Ned replied.

"He makes a good point, Hemett," Calloway said, peeking over Ned's shoulder.

Ned flashed an irritated glance back at her. "Stay out of this. It's none of your concern."

She frowned. "But I'm the subject of the conversation."

"That's besides the point," Ned insisted. He looked at Hemett. "We should bring her before Teach."

"Oh, you don't need to do that, Ned," Calloway protested, pushing off of him.

"I told you to stay out of it."

"I'm finding it hard with my life in the balance."

Ned turned on her. "Teach will want details. He's powerful furious with Captain Vane. You've been in his hideout. You know things."

She shook her head. "I don't remember much."

Ned wagged a finger. "One minute you're promising to lead us through caves, the next you don't remember nothing. I don't think you've worked out your story, missy. But don't worry. Edward Teach is good at sorting through fibs."

Before she could offer further protest, the two men seized her by each arm and ushered her to the boat. Ned lifted her off her feet and deposited her in the boat. Hemett pushed them off and crawled in, rolling onto his back. He spent half a minute trying to right himself, his compact body and stumpy arms refusing to negotiate as he wobbled to and fro like an upended turtle. Calloway sat at the front of the boat, which was barely large enough for the three of them, as they rowed toward the distant ship.

Most of the stars in the east had faded by the time they reached the huge vessel. The three masts ran dizzyingly high. The bow towered above the little boat, its long bowsprit ending in a spritsail topmast with a round base. A huge bald man with a red beard was perched on the base, legs dangling over. He glared down at Calloway as the little boat sailed under.

Teach's parting words on their prior meeting were fresh in her mind: "Should we meet again, I will not recall your face." She prayed that was true, but her botched attempt on his life had not been so long ago.

They pulled up to the starboard side. Men were crowded at the rail, watching silently, silhouetted against the faint sky. A knotted rope was tossed down. Ned urged Calloway to go first. She latched onto the rope and closed her eyes as they lifted her up. Two hulking men helped her over the rail to the cutdown forecastle. One of them accidentally grasped her breast along the way and then looked at her in shock. His lips curved into a leer.

The crew gathered in a dense perimeter. Their eyes crept along her body, and they whispered to one another.

A shadow pulled at her peripheral vision. Edward Teach was waiting at the quarterdeck rail, staring down impassively. From her low angle, his long black coat seemed to merge with the deck, as though he was an extension of his ship. His beard twitched slightly, but she didn't think he recognized her. "What's this?" he called down.

"Escaped Vane, she did," said Hemett as he climbed over the rail.

Teach cocked his head. "She?"

"That's right," said Ned, following after Hemett.

Teach descended the stairs as Ned and Hemett rushed to join him at the bottom. "We found a hole, captain," Hemett said excitedly.

Teach looked from Hemett to Calloway and back again. "I don't want to know."

"No, in the mountain," Ned said, looking like he was on the verge of explosive laughter.

"Aye, in the mountain, captain," Hemett nodded fervently. "The girl came through it, all the way from Vane's hideout."

Teach's eyes widened. "Quartermaster!"

The quartermaster emerged from the crowd.

"This be the stroke of fortune I needed," Teach told him. "Take one-hundred and fifty men into the passage and beyond. Kill everyone you find, save for Charles Vane or that whore what crossed me, should you find either of them. I want them alive. *Adventure* is already on her way to block the gap. We'll join her shortly, while you raid the bowels of Pirate Town. We'll take *Valiant* swiftly. And after we've slaughtered them all, we'll take back what that bitch owed us, and any other plunder Vane claimed. Aye?"

The crew unleashed a deafening howl.

He's brought another ship, Calloway realized. No one was going to escape Pirate Town alive. She thought of Dillahunt in his cell. They would kill him too, and there was nothing she could do about it. And she didn't even want to think about what would happen to Kate.

As the quartermaster went about gathering men, Teach's eyes fixed on Calloway. She realized he was frowning beneath that bushy beard. She clenched her fists at her sides and tried not to tremble as he drew within a foot of her.

This is the last face my mother saw. Her mother was dead, and the man Calloway loved was next, both at the hands of this man. Teach was going to take everything from her.

His steely blue eyes narrowed shrewdly. "It seems my eyes be puzzled by familiarity. Have we met?"

"Would you remember if we had?" she sneered without thinking.

It slowly dawned on him. "The lass on the beach with a mind to end the mighty Blackbeard!"

"Your memory is better than you think," she said.

"Fate be very kind to me or very cruel to you."

"So you'll kill me now?"

He nodded gravely. "You will not leave this ship alive."

Her head fell. In a way, it was a relief. If she was going to die, she could say everything she wanted to say. She raised her head, renewed. If these would be her final moments, she wouldn't waste them. "Fitting that the dog who murdered my mother should do the same for me. And make no mistake, Edward Teach, you are naught but a dog who has deluded himself into thinking he's a man."

If he was offended, he hid it well. Instead, a curious look

crossed his face. "Who was your mother, girl?"

"Her name was Elise," she said. "She was beautiful, and you took her from me."

"A strumpet at The Strapped Bodice, yes?"

"Yes," she answered.

"I remember her," he said, arching his head and looking to the heavens.

"As well you should."

His rigid gaze fell on her again. "I have murdered many men," he said. "Most of their faces be lost, adrift in a sea of hundreds, but surely I would remember killing a woman."

She scoffed, folding her arms. It distantly occurred to her how ridiculous she must look, sassing the mighty Blackbeard. "You expect me to believe you've never killed a woman?"

"Women have perished because of me," he admitted, "but never have these hands done the deed."

Her smirk faded instantly. "You're a liar. You just told me you're going to kill me. Did you forget already?"

He held up a finger, correcting her. "I said you won't leave this ship alive. I did not say I would kill you. I'll leave that to my men."

She jabbed a finger in his chest. "You killed my mother! I saw her body."

He glanced at her finger, as if struck by a fly. "What would a lie gain me? A man lies in order to shroud his guilt. I feel no guilt, not for murder and certainly not for a life I did not take."

"You were her last visitor!" Calloway insisted, balling her hand into a fist and beating it against his chest.

His hand nearly dwarfed hers as he closed his fingers over her fist. His voice deepened to a low, guttural growl. "I have yet to murder a woman, but I promise you, the day I do, I will not open her wrists for her. That be too slow a death."

Calloway wrenched free of his grip and took a step back,

shaking her head at him in disbelief. "Lies, lies, and more lies!" she cried.

He offered a sad smile. "When I arrived for my pleasure, I came upon a corpse. It seems she did not wish to suffer my company. Not even for an hour."

Calloway blinked until her vision glazed over. She clenched her teeth and looked the other way. *Don't cry, not now.* That would only confirm what she had always known but had fought for so long to avoid, suppressing all her mother's sad smiles and long silences. *He's still responsible,* she tried to tell herself, but she knew that wasn't true either. It would have happened no matter what. There was no stopping it.

Her knees crashed to the deck. The pain was distant, as though the lower parts of her body had stretched far away. Her head fell, and she sobbed uncontrollably in her hands. A shadow stepped before her. "Tell me your name, girl," Teach said.

"What does it matter?" she sobbed.

"It matters."

She pulled her hands from her face and stared at the tears in her palms. "Jacqueline Calloway," she muttered.

"I have a parting question for you, Jacqueline Calloway."

"Ask what you will."

"I will not ask twice."

"Ask your question!" she yelled at the deck, refusing to look at him.

He kneeled before her and placed a finger under her chin, lifting her head. His steely blue eyes penetrated her blurred vision, like twin beacons in a black fog. "Do you not wish to live?"

29

KATE

She was jolted into consciousness by a tremor that rattled the long table. An empty plate and bowl jittered along the surface, sliding a few inches. The walls rumbled, and thin trails of dirt fell from the jagged ceiling, collecting in hourglass piles on the tables and floor. Just as the rumbling started to die down, a tremendous *boom* resounded through the cavern, followed by another protracted tremor.

Kate stood, unsure what she should do. The kitchen was empty at this hour. She had gorged herself on bland meat and mysterious stew and then fell asleep with her head on the table, arms pillowed beneath her. The food was tasteless, which had allowed her to stuff herself before she realized she was full, making up for the scant rations she had been given during her incarceration on *Crusader*.

She knew she had slept a long time. It was easy to sleep with a full stomach. She was thankful she didn't dream of the glowing-eyed drowned woman again. Or maybe she had and just didn't remember.

She wasn't sure what time it was now. Her body told her it was early morning, but she had no way of knowing in here. A bracing chill sifted in through the exit, giving her a shiver.

The room rumbled again, and she considered running for the exit. The passage out was a short walk, but she didn't want to get caught in a collapsing tunnel. Then again, she didn't want to spend the rest of her life in a smelly kitchen, with food rotting around her. She started for the exit.

She was halfway across when Charles Vane stepped into the room, blocking the exit. His comely face was racked with distress, and his forest green coat was covered in dirt, but he had managed not to lose his arrogant smirk. He was sweating so heavily that his auburn curls were nearly black. His shirt was open, and there was a long red slash running down the center of his chest, between his pecs. He held a cutlass in one hand and a smoking pistol in another. He stood there catching his breath.

"You look awful," was all Kate could think to say.

He spat blood and grinned. "Nonsense! Your loins are steeping at the disheveled sight of me." He paused to regain his breath. "Don't pretend otherwise."

She rolled her eyes. "What's happened?"

"Blackbeard's men have infiltrated my fortress." The edges of his jaw stiffened sharply. "I should have killed that cunt when she first arrived."

"It's never too late," Kate offered buoyantly.

He waved his pistol dismissively. "Oh, she's quite dead, mind you. I just wish I'd done it sooner."

"She's dead?!"

Vane nodded nonchalantly. "I lobbed her off a cliff. A quick death, but she had time enough to realize she was going to die.

That's important. I ordered my men to string her up to the canyon wall. Last minute decision, that. Rather inspired, I think. The whore's corpse will be the first thing Teach sees when he sails in."

Kate bit her lip, but she was unable to prevent a bout of girlish laughter from gushing out of her. Annabelle's death wouldn't bring Nathan back, but at least some sort of justice had been served. Her only regret was that she hadn't been able to do it herself.

Vane scowled at her. "What are you so fucking giddy about? Did you not hear me? Blackbeard's men have come to kill us all. Those blasts you've been hearing are my men rolling barrels of gunpowder down the passages and blowing them up. My idea. Unfortunately, it's not enough to keep them out. There are too many."

She gestured at his chest wound. "What happened there?"

He glanced downward. "What, this? I had a run in with Red Devil not a half an hour ago. Believe me, he looks far worse."

"Did you kill him?"

"Depends on whether or not a man can survive a sword in the brain."

Another blast sounded somewhere behind Vane, causing him to flinch, but he tried to preserve his cool demeanor. "We have to leave. My scouts tell me there's only one ship near the entrance to the channel. It appears to be *Adventure*. My sloop, *Valiant*, will engage very shortly, and when she does, I will seize the opportunity to escape in *Ranger*. But we have to leave now. *Queen Anne's Revenge* is never far behind *Adventure*."

Kate cleared her throat. "So you'll sacrifice everyone on your sloop just so you can get away?"

He almost shrugged, but stopped himself. "Ah, yes, women and their gentle hearts. Does that sort of thing concern you?"

"Not really, but it does interest me. By the way, if you're in such a hurry to leave, why are you here?"

He stabbed a bench with the tip of his sword and leveraged his weight against the hilt. "I came for you, obviously."

She grimaced. "No doubt you'll keep me in your cabin?"

"Of course," he said, grinning suggestively. "You'll be safe there."

"I can't go with you."

"That's strange," he said, scratching his head with the barrel of his gun. "You seem to be under the impression you have a choice in the matter."

"I'm not going. I don't want to argue about it."

He tossed his gun on the table, let go of his sword, and moved toward her. "You'd rather linger here to be raped and murdered than leave with me?"

"No, I'd rather leave with my crew."

"You have a crew?"

She nodded. "They're locked up in your brig, last I heard."

He stopped within two paces of her, studying her narrowly. Another distant eruption shook the walls, and a stream of dirt fell between them, collecting at their feet. "Why?"

"I left a friend behind once," she answered. "I won't do that again."

Vane shook his head. "You're a stubborn bitch, Lindsay. I could put a fist in your gut, toss you over my shoulder, and carry you out of here, if I really wanted to. That would spare you whatever misguided moral obligation you think you must fulfill."

She cocked her head defiantly. "So why don't you?"

His answer came quickly and easily. "You'd probably slit my throat in my sleep, or something worse. Griffith was a fool to turn his back on you."

That made her smile. "Thank you." Nevertheless, she was

overpowered by a nagging urge to correct him. "I didn't shoot him in the back, by the way. I shot him in the—"

Another blast sounded before she could finish. This one was much closer. Vane craned his neck to the ceiling as it shook.

Calico Jack stumbled out of the dark tunnel, setting a hand against one of the long tables and catching his breath. Blood streamed down his forehead from a wound somewhere in his scalp. His right sleeve was sheared, and a long red stripe ran down his arm. "We have to go now, Charles, before they take the dock."

Vane glanced over his shoulder, and then quickly returned his eyes to Kate, as though he was afraid she would vanish if he looked away for too long. "Wait for me at the dock, Jack."

"We can't afford to waste—"

"I'm right fucking behind you," Vane grated.

Calico Jack nodded. He composed himself and left the way he'd come.

Vane didn't budge. After a moment, Kate said, "Good luck, Charles." She hoped he was done trying to convince her.

He sighed lavishly. "That's not something I rely on. I'm sure you understand."

"Everyone needs a little luck."

He snorted. "Speaking of luck, I suppose you'll be needing the keys to the cells before I go, if you want to save your friends." He smacked the side of his head with his palm. "Oh, what am I thinking? You already have the keys, don't you?"

She withered sheepishly. The keys were tucked securely in the front of her bodice, between her breasts. *Probably the first place he'll look.*

Vane nodded confidently. "Did you sincerely think me fool enough not to notice their absence?"

She reached out to touch his arm in a friendly gesture and withdrew just as quickly. "I thought you a busy man with a lot on your mind."

He seemed to appreciate the clarification. "I put them out in the open on purpose, to see if you'd take them."

"Of course you did," she said, humoring him. "You're quite cunning."

His smirk grew. "I will have a kiss, before we part ways."

"Hmm? I didn't hear you?" she said, backing away.

He advanced. "I almost forgot you're missing an ear." He raised his voice to a condescendingly loud decibel. "I SAID I'LL HAVE A KISS!"

"Captain Vane," she gaped, placing a hand to her chest in shock, "I had no idea you were a romantic."

"I'm not," he sneered in disgust. "I may be dead within the hour, if my plan goes to shit. I will have a kiss from a stubborn bitch first. Seeing as you're the only stubborn bitch still alive, you'll have to do."

She scanned the room, but there was nowhere to go. He was between her and the exit. If she tried to run, he would easily corner her. There was a plate and a bowl on the table beside her, but she doubted either of those would serve as much of a weapon. There were some big pots over by the oven. Assuming she could make it all the way over there, and had strength enough to lift one, she might be able crush it over his head.

Or maybe you could just let him kiss you. At least he wasn't hideous to look at. And there was no time for it to go any further. *It's just a kiss. It won't kill you.*

"What if I say no?" she murmured weakly.

"It's not a fucking request," he snapped. His hand struck with the speed of a viper, seizing her by the belt. He drew her close and shoved his tongue in her mouth. His lips tasted of blood. She grappled against his solid embrace, but not nearly as much as she might have.

30

DILLAHUNT

After a restless night of tossing and turning on the uneven rocky floor of the little cell, Dillahunt finally started to doze off. His mind swirled with a plethora of gruesome fates for Jacqueline Calloway, and he could think of nothing else no matter how hard he tried. He had waited all night for them to bring her back, but that hadn't happened. He could only assume Mongrel had disposed of her after having his way with her. Dillahunt cursed himself. He should never have let her board his ship. He knew it then, but he had not stopped it, because he was excited at the prospect of a woman sharing his bed every night.

His wounds itched terribly beneath the bandages. He tried to ignore it, but neglect only made the itching increase until it burned, and he had no choice but to scratch.

Two men had appeared earlier in the night to dispose of Rotter's soiled corpse. Hornigold's men in the big cell cheered when the body was dragged away, happy to be relieved of the stench. Later, they tried to make conversation with Dillahunt, but he ignored them. Most of them fell asleep eventually, with the exception of Avery Dowling, who sat on the long bench with his back against the wall, staring at nothing in particular. Dillahunt had never seen the man sleep.

It must have been early in the morning when Dillahunt's eyes finally started to close. As he faded, he was oblivious to the tingling of his wounds, and he momentarily forgot Calloway's fate.

And then he was stirred by the distinctive crack of gunfire, somewhere far down the passage. He jerked awake, rattling his shackles. He glanced over at Hornigold's men. Half of them were sitting up, looking around.

A distant *boom* sounded from somewhere in the tunnels, and the ground trembled in a rolling wave, displacing tiny pebbles. The rest of Hornigold's men popped up.

"Bloody hell was that?" muttered Andrew Harrow.

Bastion was rubbing his right ear, with one eye squeezed shut. "Too loud," was all he said.

"Sounded like gunpowder," Avery said, his face remaining apathetic.

"That weren't no gun," Jeremy Clemens replied.

"I didn't say it was," Avery grated.

A second *boom* shuddered through the dungeon, this one louder than the last.

Dillahunt got to his feet and grabbed the bars of his cell. "That was closer."

Everyone fell silent and listened intently. Smaller blasts sounded every minute or so, with cracks of gunfire sprinkled between. Dillahunt's mind tried to sort out a pattern, but the shots were maddeningly sporadic.

Five minutes later, a slender figure emerged from the dark

passage, stepping into the torchlight. She wore a black bodice embroidered with roses. Her hair shimmered like blood.

"Lindsay," Dillahunt muttered in disbelief.

"I have a first name," she quipped. She stopped before his cell, produced a ring of keys from her bodice, and set about finding the right key.

"Where'd you get those?" he asked.

"Vane," she said.

"I probably don't want to know how you managed that."

She tried four keys before the latch clicked and the cell was open. He stepped forward and thrust out his shackled hands. She found the right key after two attempts, and Dillahunt was free of his binds.

"What about us?" Harrow said.

Kate started for their cell. Dillahunt grabbed her shoulder. "What are you doing?" he demanded.

She stared at him as if it should have been obvious. "We need a crew."

"A crew?"

"Don't you want to get out of here? There's a fight going on in the caves, in case you hadn't heard. Vane's men are dying."

"Teach," Dillahunt realized. "He followed us."

Kate nodded. "If we don't take *Crusader* now, someone else will. But we need a crew, unless you think the two of us can sail her on our own."

"That's right," said Francois Laurent, standing. "You'll need a crew."

"Those are Hornigold's men!" Dillahunt protested.

"Hornigold's dead," Kate reminded him, moving to the big cell. She fingered through the keys, trying each one in the lock. "These are your men, now, Captain Dillahunt. And you'll pardon all of them for their aid when we return to Nassau. Isn't that right?"

Dillahunt bunched his fists. The bandages felt like they were constricting around his eyes and temples. "Fine," he growled through clenched teeth. "When they slaughter us in our sleep, it's on your head."

"Whose crew was it that turned to murderous mutiny?" Kate said, glancing upward for the answer. She looked at him pointedly. "Oh, wait, I just remembered: It was yours."

"That's very funny," he replied stolidly.

Kate unlocked the cell, and Hornigold's men spilled out, one after the other. Harrow, Bastion, Dumaka, Laurent, Clemens, Elegy, Fat Farley, Billie, and finally Avery. Of the nine, Avery was the only one who didn't thank Kate. "You're welcome," she told him anyway. He grunted.

"Let's waste no more time," Dillahunt said. They started down the long, winding passage. Kate took point, insisting she remembered the way. Dillahunt was secretly glad for that, because he had no idea which forks they had taken on the way into the dungeon. These tunnels all looked the same to him. Everything looked familiar and unfamiliar. It gave him a headache.

"Have you seen Calloway?" he finally asked Kate. He was terrified she would have an answer, but he had to know.

Kate glanced over her shoulder as they passed a sconce, and the light of the flame lined her grim expression. "I don't think she's alive, Guy."

He nodded. They didn't speak of Calloway again.

The journey through the tunnel seemed longer than before, and Dillahunt started to get nervous. He glanced at Kate, but she betrayed no signs of uncertainty, so he didn't question her. The loud blasts had ceased, with only an occasional crack of gunfire.

Harrow and Laurent started to bicker about whether or not they were ever going to find an exit. Dillahunt hushed them.

They came to a fork in the tunnel, heard a bloodcurdling shriek from one passage, and quickly took the opposite. Light appeared at the end of the tunnel. Dillahunt stopped, and he felt Hornigold's men crowding at his flank.

"Right then," said Harrow. "Why did we stop?"

"I pause to assess the situation," Dillahunt murmured.

Clemens looked puzzled. "What's his ass got to do with the situation?"

Dillahunt progressed cautiously, the light growing larger and brighter. When they came to the end, Dillahunt brushed past Kate to move in front. She smirked at him. He emerged into the post-dawn light, stepping onto a slim walkway. A dead pirate with a slit throat was slumped over the walkway, the lower half of his body resting in the water. Dillahunt nudged the corpse with the tip of his boot and watched it slide into the black. He motioned for the others to follow, and they made their way to the eastern dock. Bodies were scattered everywhere. Thin trails of smoke wafted from several discarded pistols. Dillahunt picked up a sword. Everyone else followed suit, including Kate. *Like she knows how to use that,* Dillahunt inwardly scoffed.

Crusader remained at the dock, waiting to be claimed. The schooner across the way had been burned, and only its charred mast and upward tilted bow jutted from the water.

Beyond the schooner, hanging ten feet above the western dock, was the naked, mutilated body of a woman with long black hair. Her arms were stretched over her head, wrists bound together by a rusty chain that was nailed to the cliff face eight feet above. Her limbs were awkwardly tilted, and a jagged white bone jutted from her right shin. Her left foot was tilted inward, the ankle twisting around like a spiral of rope. Pieces of wood stuck out of her belly. Her contorted face was caked in blood, cheeks split open, jaw angled sideways. She stared blankly down at the dock through glassy, red eyes. A thick pool of blood had formed below her, but she had long since stopped leaking.

A shudder ran through Dillahunt. The woman's body was so pulverized beyond recognition that for a terrible moment he thought it might have been Calloway, until Kate's impassive, raspy voice relieved his horror. "Annabelle," she said.

He sighed in relief, but that didn't make the sight any less gruesome. He pulled his eyes from the corpse. "Charles Vane is a monster."

Kate was chewing on her lip, and Dillahunt realized she was wrestling against a smile.

"Shame," Clemens chimed in. "Waste of a fine pair of teats." Everyone stared at him, and he shrugged innocently. "You're all thinkin' it."

Dillahunt returned his gaze to the eastern dock. Vane's brigantine was nowhere to be seen. "Where's *Ranger?*"

Kate shrugged and looked away. "Looks like Vane escaped."

"The dog is surely dead by now," Dillahunt snorted.

Kate smirked wistfully. "Something tells me he's not."

A few men moved about *Crusader's* deck. Their swords were bloody, their expressions sadistic. Teach's men were always easy to spot. "Only three," Dillahunt whispered to the others.

"That we can see," Avery replied.

"More in the hold, maybe," said Dumaka.

Dillahunt grunted. "Then kill these three fast, and set upon anyone that comes out of that hold."

"Aye, captain," Harrow replied with a vigorous gleam in his eye. "Haven't killed anything in quite some time."

Dillahunt led the charge up the ramp to the main deck. The first of the three came at him and then skidded to a halt when he saw the other men teeming behind Dillahunt. He tried to run, but Dillahunt raked his sword across his back, splitting him open. The man slumped, groaning. Harrow moved around Dillahunt and thrust his blade into the downed man's back, growling viciously.

Laurent, Elegy, and Clemens charged for the next man, who barely had the time to raise his sword before three blades simultaneously entered his abdomen. They pulled their swords out of him, and he crumpled.

The third man ran for the stairs to the hold, screaming, "Get up here! We're under attack!" A *crack* sounded, and something whizzed past Dillahunt's ear. The man's head jerked sideways, a crimson mist scattering from his skull, and his momentum carried him several feet across the deck. Dillahunt turned. Kate Lindsay stood behind him, smoking gun in hand, which she must have lifted off of one of the dead men.

Hornigold's men gathered around the entrance to the hold, waiting. A huge black man with a red bandana emerged, aiming a gun. He got off a shot before he was skewered by four swords. Laurent's blade went through one of his eye sockets and came out the back of his head. He collapsed onto the stairs below.

Billie Dowling fell onto his back, blood pouring out of a hole in his cheek. Avery Dowling howled, dropping to his little brother's side. Billie twitched in his arms. Avery covered Billie's cheek, but blood spurted between his fingers. Billie's eyes rolled back in his head, body convulsing violently. Half a minute later, he was dead.

Avery sobbed over his brother while the others traded sad glances. Bastion placed a hand on Avery's shoulder, and Avery shrugged it away, eyes red with tears and fury. "Don't touch me!" he spat. Bastion nodded and pulled away.

Dillahunt looked up at the masts. The wind was blowing toward the exit of the canyon. That was a stroke of luck. "Time to leave," he said. "Unfurl the mains."

"Aye," Harrow replied. He snapped his fingers at Elegy, Bastion, and Clemens, and the three of them went to work unfurling the sails.

Dillahunt looked at the large man. "Farley, is it?"

Farley nodded. "Yes, captain."

"I'm appointing you quartermaster."

"Me, sir?"

"Yes, you. When they're done with the sails, have them ready the guns."

Farley's rosy cheeks went pale. "Are we going into battle, captain?"

"Best to be prepared. We don't know what waits for us out there. Snap to it."

"Aye, sir."

"We need a helmsman," Dillahunt called.

"I can do that," Dumaka volunteered, stepping forward.

Dillahunt had never seen a black man steer a ship. He wasn't even sure such a thing was possible. "Beggars can't be choosers," he muttered.

"What's that?" Dumaka challenged, glaring fiercely. "I don't think I heard you."

"Nothing. Get to work. You have my utmost confidence." Dillahunt smiled reassuringly. *He'll probably run my ship into a canyon wall.*

"Guy," Kate said, tugging on his sleeve. She pointed. He set his hands on the starboard rail and looked down. Nearly forty men emerged from the caves, like ants fleeing an anthill, flooding the dock below in a panic. "Those are Vane's men," she said.

Teach's men followed, thrusting their swords and firing weapons. Dillahunt had no idea how many more were on the way. He turned. "Avery, help me with the ramp!"

"Fuck you," Avery said, still hunched over his brother.

Dillahunt looked at Kate. She smirked. "I think I can lift a bloody ramp," she said. The two of them ran to the ramp and crouched before it, but Vane's men were already storming up it with desperate looks on their faces. Two men stumbled and fell into the water below. Dillahunt and Kate grasped the bottom of the ramp, but it barely lifted under the tremendous weight of the approaching men. Kate squeezed Dillahunt's wrist. "I might have a better idea."

"Yes?"

"We take them on."

"No!" Dillahunt protested. "No more bloody pirates! I'll not have it!"

"You'd prefer to die? We don't know what's out there. If Blackbeard is waiting, we'll need all the men we can get. Vane abandoned them."

The man in front slipped and fell flat on his face on the ramp, and the others struggled to crawl over him. "Let us on!" one of them cried. "You've got the room! Don't leave!"

"We need them," Kate insisted.

"They'll take this ship for themselves."

"Not if you pardon them."

"Pardons for everyone, is that it?" Dillahunt said, shaking his head in disgust. "These men have no loyalty to anyone!"

"That's the beauty about pirates," Kate replied. Without allowing him another word of protest, she stood, bellowing to the men below, "KINGLY PARDONS FOR ALL WHO JOIN AND FIGHT FOR CAPTAIN GUY DILLAHUNT!"

Kate stepped aside, and Dillahunt followed suit, and Vane's men came filing up the ramp, sweeping onto the main deck. At least thirty of them made it onboard, while the rest remained below to fight the onslaught of Blackbeard's men, pouring from the caves. Vane's men gathered round Dillahunt and awaited orders, swords at the ready.

Dillahunt glanced at Kate. She muttered, "I think it worked," under her breath.

"You're an impudent woman," he muttered right back.

She beamed. "Thank you, captain."

Dillahunt shook his head. The bitch had forced his hand. He faced his new recruits. "Cast off that ramp!"

"Aye, captain," they cried in unison, and two of them lifted the ramp and tossed it into the water.

"Weapons are in the hold," Dillahunt told them. "Assuming you haven't removed them per Vane's instruction."

"No, Captain Dillahunt, sir," said a tall man in black with long blonde hair. "We only took the treasure."

"The treasure," Kate moaned, slapping her forehead.

"Do you think Rogers would have let us keep it?" Dillahunt asked. "The question is rhetorical."

She stared at him, suddenly nervous. He knew what she was thinking. "Don't worry," he reassured her. "If we survive this, I will not turn you in. I owe you."

"Yes," she said. "You do."

The sails rolled down, billowing instantly. *Crusader* pulled away from the dock as Vane's remaining men were overwhelmed by Blackbeard's forces. *Crusader* made a wide turn, from eastern wall to the west, bow scraping the opposite dock and hull grinding over the blackened ruin of the schooner as she curved back around. Soon she was facing the exit, with the wind urging her forward. From the eastern dock, muskets and pistols trained on *Crusader*. Shots rang out, pattering her hull and piercing her sails. One of Dillahunt's new recruits was struck in the throat and sank to his knees.

Dillahunt ordered the remaining sails doused. The canyon walls moved faster and faster, and soon *Crusader* was speeding for the exit. Dillahunt gazed up between the slit in the canyon to the brightening sapphire sky. They were almost free.

Calloway isn't.

But he couldn't afford to distract himself with whatever ghastly fate had befallen her. Not right now. There would be plenty of time to mourn her later. In fact, there would be nothing *but* time when they had escaped to open sea.

They rounded the canyon bend until they saw the exit, but it was blocked by two ships just outside, running parallel and trading cannon fire. Both were sloops. The sloop on the right was listing terribly. It was flying Vane's flag. The sloop on the left stood tall, bombarding its prey, and Blackbeard's colors flapped in the wind.

"*Adventure*," Dillahunt muttered gravely. He called to Avery Dowling, who was still cradling his brother. "Mr. Dowling, if you're quite through, it's time to make your brother proud!"

Avery looked up, his face red and smeared with dirt and tears. He looked absolutely pitiful. Slowly, an angry scowl formed. "And how do you expect me to do that?"

"I would sever *Adventure's* mast and prevent her from giving chase after we've sailed past her. In my hold, I've concocted a very special chainshot for an occasion such as this. It consists of two cannonballs bound by an eight foot chain. You will need to fire it from two cannons at the very same moment, with the chain stretched between them, understand?"

Avery nodded slowly. "I think so."

"It will require precise timing. Find a gunner to help you prepare and fire it."

Avery lowered his head, giving his brother's corpse a final mournful regard. He slowly stood, wiped his face, and hurried off.

Kate moved close to Dillahunt, so no one else would hear, and said, "Have you ever tried this before?"

He smiled. "Never. But I'm certain that if it works, it will work very well."

"And if it doesn't?"

"They will take this ship, rape you to death, and probably gag me with my own cock before hanging me from their bowsprit." For the first time he glimpsed fear in those pretty eyes. "I suggest you keep a pistol for yourself."

She jutted her chin defiantly. "I can take care of myself."

"That is precisely what I'm suggesting," Dillahunt said, "should the need arise."

Crusader plunged toward *Adventure*, waiting at the exit of the canyon channel. Vane's sloop was sinking fast. *Adventure* wasn't even firing on her anymore. She was done. *Dammit,* thought Dillahunt. *If only she had held out a little longer.*

He looked up at his dark helmsman. "Hold her straight and true!"

Dumaka frowned. "Captain, if we—"

"Betwixt the two ships," Dillahunt interjected.

"Aye, captain," Dumaka said, shaking his head in disbelief.

Harrow threw up his hands. "Well, we're dead. Who cares? I certainly don't! Never much liked living, anyways!"

Clemens nodded knowingly. "Downright frustrating at times, it is."

"Aye!" agreed Harrow. "Here's hoping we go out painfully, with guts spilling out our bellies!"

Clemens shook his head. "That's a bit much."

Avery Dowling and Francois Laurent emerged from the main hatch carrying the modified chainshot, each holding a cannonball. The two cannonballs were connected by a long chain that skittered along the deck. They loaded the cannonballs into two port cannons, with the chain stretching across the barrels.

Dillahunt approached. "You must fire at the same time," he reminded them. "If you do not, one cannon will act as an anchor, and the fired cannonball will swing back around and wrap you in the chain. That would not be a pretty sight. As you can see, I've given this tremendous consideration. My mind is not easily silenced once set to task."

Avery and Laurent exchanged a nervous look. "Fire at the same time," Laurent said.

Avery nodded. "Fire at the same time."

The canyon walls spread further apart as they neared the exit. *Adventure* remained where she was, bow pointed into the canyon, with her crew gathering at the port rail. Vane's sloop continued to sink, stern slanting down into the water. It was too close to the western canyon wall for *Crusader* to go around it, using it as a shield. *Crusader* would have to go between the two ships, making her a clear target for *Adventure's* cannons.

"Prepare yourselves!" Dillahunt bellowed, and his crew fell to the port side, aiming their guns.

Dillahunt casually strolled away from Avery and Laurent, who stood ready to fire their cannons. If the timing was off, he didn't want to be anywhere near them.

Adventure was close now. She was a smaller ship, but she was much faster and could easily catch up once they zipped past. With a larger crew, Dillahunt would be confident of taking her in a fight, but he only had around forty men, and *Adventure* looked to have near a hundred.

Gunshots cracked.

A chase gun sounded from *Adventure*, and a cannonball glanced off of *Crusader's* port bow. *Dillahunt's* men returned fire as *Crusader* sped closer. *Adventure* began to tilt toward *Crusader*. Her captain must have realized *Crusader* was not going to stop, and they would have to give chase.

You won't get the chance.

Crusader plunged through the gap between *Adventure* and

the sinking sloop. A hail of cannonballs and gunfire rained down from *Adventure*, tearing through *Crusader's* hull and sails. A cannonball struck Gabriel Elegy in the stomach, flinging him across the deck. When he came to rest, his upper and lower half were barely held together by a few strings of flesh and muscle.

When the two ships were parallel, running port to port, Dillahunt bellowed, "FIRE!" at Avery and Laurent. The two men wasted no time, firing the twin cannons in perfect sync. The modified chainshot was a beautiful success, sailing toward *Adventure* without spinning. The chain was pulled taut between the two cannonballs, and it sliced off the heads of two men not quick enough to duck as it arced over *Adventure's* port rail. The chainshot didn't stop until it hit the mainmast, both cannonballs wrapping around it. The mast snapped like a twig, careening downward as men scattered to get out of its path. Blood splattered the white cloth as the sails cascaded over the deck with a tremendous crack of wood and bone.

Crusader sailed past with only superficial damage, leaving *Adventure* crippled, her crew scattering about the deck in chaos.

They were free of the canyon and sailing into an expanse of ocean surrounded by a huge ring of mountainous islands. "Where are we?" Dillahunt gasped.

"Worry about that later," Kate replied.

Dillahunt set a hand on Dumaka's shoulder. "Good sailing, dark sir. I didn't know you had it in you." Dumaka nodded curtly. Dillahunt pointed ahead. "Make for the gap between those two islands."

"Captain!" Harrow shouted from the deck below, pointing.

Dillahunt followed his gesture, and off the starboard bow he saw the black shadow of *Queen Anne's Revenge* approaching fast.

Dillahunt wanted to hammer his fists on the rail and scream at the top of his lungs, but he had to remain strong for his new crew, dastardly though they were. He needed them to function properly. He ascended to the quarterdeck, joining Dumaka. The quarterdeck was still a mess, with a huge chunk torn out of the port railing, and he winced as the memory of splinters flashed through his mind. He retrieved a long silver spyglass that was resting beside the helm. He aimed the spyglass at *Queen Anne's Revenge* and peered through, closing one eye.

"She's coming about, captain," Dumaka said.

"Yes, I can see that quite clearly through this miraculous device," Dillahunt drawled.

Revenge's deck was not nearly as crowded as he expected. There couldn't have been more than one-hundred and twenty. Given how many of Teach's men had flooded the dock, it was possible he had split his forces.

Dillahunt looked back at *Adventure*, which was far behind now, at the mouth of the canyon entrance. She was no longer a problem, but Dillahunt was starting to think he'd wasted his modified chainshot on the wrong target.

"What course, captain?" said Dumaka.

Despite the wind, waves, and jabbering of crew, Dillahunt clearly heard his teeth grinding in his mouth. He approached the rail overlooking the main deck. His new recruits stared up at him, awaiting orders. He imagined he must have looked both dashing and terrible, bound in shredded, dirty bandages, with his long black coat flowing in the wind. "They're coming too fast," he announced. "Our sails are a mess. They'll sink us before we can even think of escaping."

Harrow stepped forward. "So what do we do?"

Dillahunt smiled. "We stand our ground!"

"Better to surrender!" someone called.

Dillahunt laughed at the sky. "Blackbeard came here to kill

you all! His men offered no quarter in those caves, and they will offer none now! We fight, and we may die. We don't fight, and we will surely die!" When no one replied, he added, "And they'll likely slice off our cocks and shove them up our own asses before the end!"

The crew exchanged uncertain glances. "What did he say?"

"Well, I like my cock right where it is!" Dillahunt bellowed. "So, we fight! We take *Queen Anne's Revenge!*"

He waited for the thunderous cheer that generally followed his speeches, but nothing happened. He went on as though they were enthused, raising his sword high. "Make ready the guns! Prepare to broadside!"

The crew went to work, grumbling to one another. It wasn't the reaction Dillahunt had hoped for, but he supposed it was the best he could ask of men who had shifted their allegiance not half an hour ago. They were loading the cannons and preparing their weapons, at least.

He turned to Dumaka. "If the rumors are true, Teach has fitted his ship with cannonades. Fierce at short range, but not very accurate. A slimmer target will be harder to hit, and she'll spend too much time reloading. That's when we'll attack."

"You mean to board her, captain?"

Dillahunt smiled. "Aye."

A short time later, Kate Lindsay joined Dillahunt on the quarterdeck. The red roses of her bodice were vibrant in broad daylight. She pushed her wild hair out of her face, fighting the constant wind. "You truly mean to attack *that?*" she said, aiming a finger at Teach's ship.

Dillahunt looked at her. "You shouldn't be here, Kate. This is no place for a woman."

She rolled her eyes. "So I've been told. But if I wasn't, you'd still be rotting in a cell."

"Is this truly where you want to be?"

She tossed her head in annoyance as a strand of hair teased her cheeks. "Everyone keeps asking me that."

"It's a simple question."

She sighed, placing her hands on her hips. "After all this is over, I'll answer it."

He looked over his new sword. It was a rather crude cutlass. He missed his rapier, which had been lost sometime after his injury. "After all this is over," he said, "we'll probably be dead."

Kate shrugged. "Spares me the bother of coming up with an answer."

31

CALLOWAY

She had no idea why she was still alive.

She had run through the events in her mind several times over. "Do you not wish to live?" Teach had asked, and she had met his query with a firm, "No," because in that moment, she had truly wished to die. Her mother had ended her own life, why shouldn't she? Dillahunt would soon be dead as well, and she would have no one left. There was no point to any of it. In the end, everyone died. *I might as well get it over with,* she had thought. Maybe Nathan Adams was the lucky one, killed in the prime of his life with no time to ponder his imminent demise.

Her answer had given Teach pause. He twirled a lock of his dense beard with an index finger, the sheen of his steely eyes narrowing into slivers. "So be it," he had said at last, and he walked away without another word.

"Why didn't he kill me?" she had asked Narrow Ned. He

replied with a mystified shrug, while the rest of the crew murmured in hushed, baffled tones.

After that, Teach yelled, "Weigh anchor! We make for the gap!" He ascended to the quarterdeck and disappeared into his cabin. The sails fell into place, and *Queen Anne's Revenge* started around the island.

As the ship rounded the bend, Calloway saw the familiar shape of *Crusader* burst from the canyon gap, with Teach's sloop, *Adventure*, crippled in her wake. Teach emerged from his cabin and stood at the edge of the quarterdeck, but he was no longer Edward Teach. He was Blackbeard now, with smoke trailing over his face from the fuses he had fixed to his beard. A sling ran from his shoulders down over his chest and stomach, with three brace of small pistols hanging in holsters. He raised a massive cutlass to the sky and bellowed, "Bring her alongside! No quarter for Charles Vane or any man serves him!"

"But that's not Charles Vane!" Calloway shouted up at him, but her cry was lost in the uproar that followed the order. She climbed the steps and approached him, bold and steady, and he fixed her with a malevolent glare. She stopped within two feet, refusing to cower as any other woman would. *Maybe even Kate,* she thought with a flutter of satisfaction. "That's not Charles Vane!" she repeated.

His jaw worked beneath his beard. "My eyes glimpse a ship escaping Vane's hideout, yet you tell me it's not Vane."

"That's *Crusader*," she insisted. "Guy Dillahunt's ship!"

"And you be sworn to this man, yes?" He raised the blade of his massive cutlass to her neck. She felt the cold, jagged edge biting into her skin.

"There's no need to attack him," she pressed, struggling not to shy from his blade. "He's not the man you're after."

"There be plenty need," Blackbeard replied. "He attacked my sloop, as you can see."

"No doubt your sloop would have attacked first."

"Aye, that be true," he admitted. "Yet I cannot ignore a nagging concern. *Crusader* be a plump whore of a ship, plagued by a shifty crew slight of loyalty and feeble of will. Why should I believe Dillahunt has magically regained his captaincy, when your eyes tell me you scarcely believe it yourself?"

"So hail them and find out!" she screeched.

Blackbeard lowered the blade and frowned at her. "I must confess, you mystify me, Jacqueline Calloway. My puzzlement prolongs your life. You'd be wise not to spoil your mystery with common trivialities."

He looked across the ship to *Crusader* in the distance, which was slowly coming about to intercept. "Nay," Blackbeard said, shaking his head. "I will put that ship to the deep once and for all."

"What if Griffith's plunder is still in the hold?" Calloway said, thinking fast.

Blackbeard loosed a guttural laugh. "If you'd met me as a younger man, those words might have stayed my hand. Alas, treasure no longer holds sway over me."

"Then what is your purpose here?"

All humor fled his face. Smoky tendrils rolled up the curls of his beard, swirling about his eyes. He straightened his back and towered over her. Calloway was eye-level with most men, but he was taller still. "I have been wronged," was his answer. He didn't bother to elaborate.

She gripped the railing as *Queen Anne's Revenge* hurtled toward *Crusader*. The other ship, which had seemed so large when she was on it, looked miniscule from Blackbeard's frigate. The men below crowded the starboard side, loading cannons and readying guns. Many of them held granados.

Her nails ground into the wood of the rail. If Dillahunt wasn't on that ship, he was probably dead. If he was on that ship, he would be dead soon enough.

Blackbeard stood several feet from her, shouting orders. Her eyes descended to the many pistols holstered along his upper torso. She took a careful step forward. *I could end him right now.* Maybe he hadn't killed her mother, but he was still a murderer, and he was about to murder many more.

As if he had read her thoughts, Blackbeard tilted his head and stared at her. He angled his steely gaze down at her feet. And then he grinned. "You are not the first with notions of creeping upon my flank, and neither will you be the last."

Chase guns fired from *Revenge's* bow. *Crusader* returned fire as she neared. Pistol and musket fire was exchanged between ships. A musket ball struck the rail between Calloway and Blackbeard. She jerked away, but Blackbeard remained steady.

While Blackbeard's crew hollered war cries, *Crusader's* men gathered at the starboard rail, pale-faced and relatively silent. There couldn't have been more than forty of them. And then she saw him, standing proud atop the quarterdeck, with his long black coat flowing behind him, bare chest and the top half of his head bound in tattered bandages. He held a sword high and bellowed, "No quarter for Edward Teach!" That roused a few of *Crusader's* men into scant cheers.

Blackbeard laughed at that. "I see Dillahunt hasn't lost his sense of humor!" He called down to his men, "Ready the cannonades! They'll be sunk before they can fire a shot!" The crew hunched before the stubby, fat cannons, ready to fire.

Crusader was maybe one-hundred meters off of *Revenge's* starboard bow, and she was slowly pulling to her port side, away from *Revenge.* "What's he doing?" said Blackbeard, looking baffled. "He means to run at the last second?"

Just then, Dillahunt shouted, "Drop anchor!"

The anchor impacted the water in a colossal splash. The chain suddenly stretched taut. With a tremendous groan of buckling wood, *Crusader* tilted sharply to her starboard side, bowsprit arcing around toward *Revenge*. Calloway grinned as the brigantine shot toward the frigate like a spear, arcing on its anchor.

"Duck!" someone called out. Sounded like Narrow Ned, but Calloway couldn't see him anywhere.

"Belay that!" Blackbeard yelled. "FIRE!"

The cannons fired all at once, and a thunderous volley cascaded toward *Crusader* . . . but she was steadily pointed at *Revenge* and made for too thin a target. Most of the cannons sailed harmlessly past. Only four hit *Crusader's* bow, and two of those glanced off, leaving little more than dents. One hit the masthead, shattering her scaly thigh. The last punched into the hull, disappearing into a black cavity.

On the cutdown forecastle, *Crusader's* bowsprit crashed through *Revenge's* starboard bulwark, impaling a man in the abdomen. The bowsprit burst from his back and lifted him skyward, raining blood upon the deck. The brigantine reared up, bow devastating the starboard bulwark, tossing aside four cannons like they were leaves in the wind. The mermaid splintered at her torso and toppled forward. Her upper half smashed one of Blackbeard's men before he could escape. Calloway shuddered with delight as his blood splattered from beneath the masthead. *Murdered by a mermaid's tits,* she mused.

Over a dozen granados hailed down from *Crusader's* upturned bow, thumping the deck. Blackbeard's men tried to scatter, but a dozen of them were instantly killed in the ensuing explosions, and many were wounded. A few of Blackbeard's men tried to return fire, chucking their own granados, but they bounced off of *Crusader's* bow and came right back, killing two more.

The smaller ship remained perched on the bigger ship's rail, slanting up to form a makeshift ramp. Dillahunt's crew ran up the front, tossing grappling hooks at *Revenge's* ratlines and swinging over. Dillahunt's strategy had worked, and his men were gaining enthusiasm, cheering as they boarded *Queen Anne's Revenge*. They likely had no illusions about winning this fight, but they would at the very least meet a glorious end.

Nearly twenty of them dropped to the cutdown forecastle, immediately engaging in battle. They impaled several of those who had been wounded and/or knocked off their feet by the granado blasts. They exchanged pistol fire with the two dozen or so of Blackbeard's men who were still standing in that section.

On the quarterdeck, three men with muskets dropped to the rail on Calloway's right, firing down on Dillahunt's men. Her teeth clacked together with each earsplitting report. The smell of gunpowder filled the air, along with an impenetrable smoke that wafted into the sails. The three musketmen started to reload. They were intensely focused on their task, indifferent to the surrounding chaos.

One of Dillahunt's men scurried up the stairs with a cutlass held high. Calloway recognized him as Francois Laurent. The musketmen had already finished reloading. Three shots struck him in the chest at once, and Laurent went tumbling back down the way he'd come.

Crusader started to slide back toward the sea, grinding against *Revenge's* bulwark. But then she came to a jarring halt, her keel catching on something, and *Revenge* lurched sideways. Pirates from both sides hurtled toward the starboard side, wailing desperately. Many of them couldn't stop and rolled right over the edge and into the water below.

Hemett slid toward the underside of *Crusader's* bow, scrambling frantically on all fours. There was already too much blood on the deck, and he couldn't find purchase before his squat body slid into the wedge. His feet were caught first, and he was slowly crushed between the two ships as *Crusader* bobbed up and down in the water, grinding back and forth against *Revenge's* deck. Halfway down, Hemett's shrieks were silenced when a thick ball of blood exploded from his mouth. Calloway watched in awe, unable to pull away. The last she saw of Hemett was his twitching right arm, before it too was milled beneath *Crusader's* keel.

"It's Dillahunt!" exclaimed one of the musketmen.

Calloway scanned the lower deck until she found Dillahunt, near *Crusader's* upturned bow.

"I've got him," said the one nearest Calloway.

"Nay!" called Blackbeard. "No man kills Captain Dillahunt but I." He lifted the sling that held his six guns over his head and dropped it to the deck. He seized Calloway by the neck, drawing her face near his, and said, "And I've got just the bait."

His huge fingers tightened around her throat, and he pressed her back against the rail. "Dillahunt!" he called down. "Face me, or see the color of your woman's blood!"

Calloway looked over her shoulder and caught a glimpse of Dillahunt's shocked expression. He was frozen in place, deaf to the sounds of men fighting and dying all around him. He obviously hadn't expected to see her alive again, let alone on the deck of Blackbeard's ship.

Calloway grasped at Blackbeard's chest, raking her nails over his leather coat. He had been wise to cast his guns from her reach. She choked as the smoke from his beard wafted over her face. She could barely see him through the haze, save for his evil blue eyes. She raised her right hand, fingers plunging into the scruff of his beard, until they touched something hot. Instead of jerking away, she grasped hold of it, and fire scorched her palm. She clutched tightly, despite the pain jolting up her arm, cramping her muscles. She wrenched the fuse loose, and he cried out as the hemp cord tore away from the curls of his beard.

"You should have killed me," she said, and then she thrust the burning end of the hemp into his right eye. His eye sizzled, and she pressed the cord deeper into the socket, until she heard a *pop*, and milky fluids drizzled down his cheek. The stench was nauseating. His lips peeled from his teeth, and he thrust her back with tremendous force. The rail fell away from her. She saw her legs flailing above her and realized she was going to hit headfirst. She curled forward. Her back hit with a sickening *crack* and splayed her arms and legs flat across the blood-smeared deck.

Before her eyes closed, she saw the huge mainsails flapping madly in the wind, dispersing the clouds of black smoke that roiled from the deck.

32

KATE

Crusader's bow was beginning to tear free of *Revenge's* bulwark when Kate saw Calloway plummet from the quarterdeck. Blackbeard crushed his hands to his face, howling like some kind of animal. Calloway landed somewhere below, but Kate's view was cut off by *Crusader's* upturned bow.

She surged forward without thinking, racing up *Crusader's* forecastle and leaping from the bow. A rope was still dangling from its grapple, and she latched on in midair, swinging over *Revenge's* deck. She quickly realized she had made a mistake. She swung in a wide arc, feet dangling over several dueling pirates, and she crashed into the foremast. Pain shot through her right shoulder and hip where she took the brunt of the damage. She bounced off and started to swing back around, her palms burning as she slid down the rope. If she didn't let go soon, she would smash into *Crusader's* bowsprit. She opened her fingers and came crashing down on one of Blackbeard's men, near the capstan, laying him flat in a puddle of someone else's blood. He was painfully skinny, and no matter how much he squirmed, he couldn't get out from under her. She scooped up a discarded cutlass and plunged it into his shoulder blades. Blood fountained out of his back and splattered her face. She blinked rapidly until she could see again.

She looked around for Calloway.

There were bodies everywhere. Feet hammered the deck like skittish drums following a frenetic tune. Swords clashed and pistols fired. Pirates dueled on the quarterdeck, pirouetting and swiping. For an absurd instant Kate was reminded of dancers twirling about a dance floor, much like the parties she and her husband had occasionally attended in London.

She stuck her sword in the deck and leaned on it in order to stand. A bald pirate lunged at her, screaming. He hesitated for a split second when he saw she was a woman, and she thrust her blade into his belly and pulled it free just as quickly. He dropped to his knees, clutching himself as blood streamed between his fingers. He gave her a final look of disbelief, unable to fathom that he had been killed by a woman, and fell on his face.

She spotted Calloway's lifeless body near the bottom of the stairs that led up to the quarterdeck. Dillahunt was already making his way up, slashing through two pirates that tried to block his path. Blackbeard lowered his hand, revealing a black, smoking hole where his right eye had been. He raised his cutlass and charged at Dillahunt, steam pouring out of his beard and missing eye. Dillahunt saw him coming and charged as well, the loose strands of his many bandages tapering behind him. The deck seemed to tremble when their blades met.

Kate dropped to Calloway's side. She lightly slapped the girl's cheeks. "Jaq?"

Calloway's eyelids slowly parted. "Is it over? Did we win?"

Kate looked around. "Not quite."

"Your face is red," she said, reaching up to touch Kate's cheek.

At least she can move her arms.

"We can't stay here," Kate said.

Calloway groggily shook her head, one eye closing while the other was barely a slit. "Let's just go to sleep right here. I'm tired. The wood is nice and wet."

"That's not water," Kate reminded her.

"Oh, what is it?"

"Get up!" Kate seized her by the wrists and peeled her off the deck with all her strength. Calloway came up . . . and then dipped into Kate, nearly knocking her over. Kate wrapped her arms around the girl's waist, balancing her.

"Tired," she said.

"You hit your head," Kate replied.

"It doesn't hurt," Calloway assured her. Her brow lifted when she saw Kate's bodice. "Are those roses? How dainty."

Crusader's bow finally slipped off the starboard rail, crashing into the water. Freed of the weight, *Revenge* pitched toward its port, and pirates living and dead were catapulted. On the quarterdeck, Blackbeard and Dillahunt stumbled out of view with their blades locked in a crisscross.

Kate and Calloway fell together, sliding along the deck until they hit the bulwark. Kate got up and struggled to get the girl back on her feet. "We can't stay here, Jaq!" she shouted in her face. The girl opened her eyes a little more.

Half of Dillahunt's men had taken the fighting up to the quarterdeck, but several were still fighting on the cutdown forecastle. If Kate and Calloway stayed here much longer, they would be ripped to shreds.

Kate finally got Calloway back on her feet. Two fighting

pirates nearly collided with them, and Kate veered out of the way. She looked to *Crusader*, but it had pulled too far from *Revenge* now and was tilting parallel, with the remaining crew firing muskets and swivel guns.

Kate spotted an open hatchway set in the deck before the capstan. She made for it at once, dragging Calloway along. The girl was taller, but Kate weighed a bit more, with stronger arms and legs. Still, it was no easy task. She zigzagged through two pairs of dueling pirates, brandishing her cutlass with her free hand. One of them was Andrew Harrow, who barreled into his combatant in order to make room for the women. "Go on!" he barked over his shoulder, knowing where they were headed.

Fear gradually enlarged Calloway's eyes as she regained her senses and realized where she was. Kate bent down long enough to pick up a dead pirate's pistol, shoving it down the front of her pants. A granado rolled across the deck as the ship swayed. "Grab that!" she told Calloway. Calloway fell to her knees and picked up the granado before it could roll past. Kate lifted her back up and continued for the hatch.

Just as they reached their destination, a hulk of a pirate popped out of the hatch, raising his sword. Kate thrust her blade through his neck. The tip stuck in the base of the capstan behind him. His eyes rolled up in their sockets and his mouth dropped open, chin resting on the flat of the blade. She wrenched the sword free, and he collapsed back into the hatch, rolling down the stairs. "Go!" Kate said, urging Calloway inside.

She looked over her shoulder and saw a dozen more of Blackbeard's men emerging from the dark hollow beneath the quarterdeck. Only five of Dillahunt's men remained on the cutdown forecastle, and they were about to be overwhelmed. The rest were dead or raiding the higher levels. Kate gave Harrow a final look. He hacked away at his opponent's blade until the man's knees buckled, and he kept on hacking until his blade split the man's skull. Blackbeard's men surrounded him, cutting him off from Kate's view.

She ducked into the hatch and followed after Calloway, who was stumbling over the corpse of the hulk, which had collected at the foot of the upper stairway. They hurried through the slim door into the crew's quarters, lined with hammocks and bunks. The hull slanted to a point at the far end, forming the bow. Fortunately, no one was inside, save for a corpse with a red bandana. He was still gripping a pistol. Kate ushered Calloway forward, shoving her into a dark hollow between two bunks. She pried the pistol from the dead man's fingers and handed it to Calloway. "Stay here," she said.

The girl set the gun and granado in her lap and rubbed the back of her head, squeezing her eyes shut. "That smarts. What happened?"

"You fell," Kate reminded her. "I'll be back. And if you have to shoot anyone, make sure he isn't one of Dillahunt's."

"Where are you going?"

Kate snatched the granado from Calloway's lap. "To find a powder keg."

She sheathed her cutlass in her belt and drew her pistol. She left the crew's quarters with pistol in one hand and granado in the other. She took the stair down into the dark cargo hold. She made her way around the stacked water casks in the middle of the hold, stepping over ballast stones. The starboard side was brighter, with beams of light shining through where *Crusader's* bow had pulverized the hull.

She approached a slim passage to what she guessed was the powder room. A figure emerged from the dark, stopping her in her tracks. Underneath a black cap adorned with a red ribbon he had short grey hair and a deep scar running down his forehead. He wore a white shirt and maroon breeches. And he was aiming a gun.

"Who might you be, girly?" His voice was barely above a whisper, difficult to hear over the screaming and thumping of feet and cracks of gunfire above.

"I might be Kate Lindsay," she answered, aiming her pistol.

He scowled at the name. "I don't believe you."

"I don't care," she replied.

"Well," he said, straightening his back, "whoever you be, my name's Jethro, and I'll wager from the granado in your hand that you're here to get at the powder magazine, yes?"

"You wager correctly," she said.

Jethro nodded indicatively, and Kate glanced over her shoulder. Another hulk of a man had crept up behind her, cutlass in hand. He looked a lot like the hulk she had killed on the stairs. Maybe they were brothers.

Jethro smiled, keeping his gun level. "Odds aren't in your favor."

"I'm used to that," Kate said with a smile.

"Best to just lower that gun, missy," Jethro urged.

Her eyes trailed downward. "Those are very pretty breeches, Jethro. What color is that?"

He frowned, glancing down. "Why, thank you. I believe that's called—"

Kate pulled the trigger. The hold flashed white, capturing Jethro's hapless expression for an instant. The shot penetrated his upper lip. Kate sidestepped as he toppled forward, dropping her gun and snatching his out of his hand as he fell, all in a single motion. She spun around and aimed as the second hulk charged with his sword held high. His face ran right into the barrel as she pulled the trigger, and his brains scattered into the darkness. He landed atop Jethro, sword clanging harmlessly on the ballast stones.

Kate stepped into the slim passage. Three kegs were stacked

horizontally against a bulkhead. She gripped the plug of one of the kegs, wrenching it loose. Black powder spilled out in a steady stream. She smiled. "Beautiful."

She moved back into the cargo hold, cocked the hammer of Jethro's pistol and set the fuse of her granado against the frizzen. She pulled the trigger. The flint struck the frizzen and the spark ignited the fuse. She tossed the sizzling granado into the powder room, dropped the gun, and ran.

She nearly stumbled over the ballast stones but grabbed hold of a water cask to steady herself. She ran back up the stairs and into the crew's quarters.

Before she got to Calloway, a tremendous *boom* sounded, and something slapped her from behind and lifted her off her feet, hurtling her forward. She didn't stop until she hit the crease where each side of the ship's hull met the bow. Her forehead split on a beam, pain lancing into her skull. She crumpled, clutching her face. Her hands came away slick with blood.

33

DILLAHUNT

Dillahunt's back was pressed flat against the port rail when the starboard side of the cutdown forecastle erupted in a blinding yellow fireball, showering *Crusader* in flaming splinters.

Blackbeard halted mid attack, sword suspended in the air, and swiveled his huge head.

The men Dillahunt had brought over to *Revenge* were all but spent. As far as he could tell, seven remained. Five were fighting on the quarterdeck. The other two were somewhere below, last he looked, although the explosion had probably claimed them.

"What in God's name?" Blackbeard muttered.

"Not God," Dillahunt replied, swinging his blade. "Last I looked, he doesn't deal in fire."

Blackbeard parried without even looking at Dillahunt. "My ship," he said, dazed. "What's happening to my ship?"

Dillahunt almost felt sorry for the man. He knew better than anyone that a captain's bond with his ship was nothing to make light of, and *Queen Anne's Revenge* was one of the most impressive ships he had ever seen.

"You knew this couldn't last forever," Dillahunt told him.

Blackbeard looked at him. From the creases in his cheeks, he might have been smiling sadly beneath that impenetrable beard. "Aye," he said. "The end always comes too soon."

The ship began to list toward its starboard side. The fire quickly reached the mainmast, slithering up to the sails. The heavy winds urged the fire across the sails in successive beats. Before long, blackened hemp was flaking away like dried leaves that had been dead too long. Dillahunt would have marveled at the sight, if he hadn't been fighting for his life. An explosion of that magnitude could only have originated from the powder magazine, which meant the keel had likely ruptured, and water was already filling in.

Blackbeard hacked at Dillahunt's blade and gradually inched toward the six pistols he had discarded during his attempt to make a hostage of Calloway. Before he reached them, the harness of pistols slid down the slanted deck, right through two rail posts, and landed on the quarterdeck.

Dillahunt grinned. "Now you'll just have to kill me fairly."

Blackbeard returned the grin. "I seek merely to curtail the inevitable. That's all I've ever done. The only certainty in life be death."

"Even for you, Teach."

"I've never claimed otherwise."

The men on the quarterdeck made a mad dash for the stairs. Five were on fire, shrieking and thrashing. Several of *Revenge's* crew ran right past Dillahunt and Blackbeard, darting up the ladder to the poop deck. Dillahunt's men joined them, their quarrel momentarily discarded.

"Cowards!" Blackbeard spat at them. "Do not flee the cleansing fires nipping at your back, for you'll be immersed eternally soon enough!"

Dillahunt thrust at an opening, but Blackbeard parried. "And where are you bound, Teach?"

His remaining eye rolled back to Dillahunt. "That be for God to determine. I have only ever served by his design."

Dillahunt laughed. "You have no idea how insane that sounds, do you?"

"Mayhap," Blackbeard admitted. His voice lacked the fury Dillahunt would have expected, but his resolve was unhindered. "One thing be a certainty: If my beloved ship be destined for the depths, you shall follow."

The muscles in Dillahunt's arms ached as Blackbeard's giant cutlass beat down upon his repeatedly. With his back to the rail, he could retreat no further unless he leapt into the sea, and he wasn't about to run away like a coward. He would see the monster dead before he left this ship, or he would never leave at all.

As he blocked every blow, waiting for an opening, his mind inevitably wandered to Calloway. Last he saw, Lindsay was dragging her toward the capstan. When he looked again, they were both gone. If they were in the hold when the powder ignited, they were both surely dead.

Blackbeard lowered his blade and jabbed at Dillahunt's waist. The tip pierced his belly, and he jerked sideways before it could enter further. Pain pinched the muscles in his stomach. He brought his blade down on top of Blackbeard's, pinning it to the rail.

"Your thoughts meander," Blackbeard said, pulling his blade free. "You make this too easy for me. Your mind be easily fogged. I glimpse that much in your eyes. You are assailed by questions, too many at once, aye?"

Dillahunt winced, a red spot blooming in his bandages from the fresh wound in his abdomen. "What would you know of it?"

"All too much," Blackbeard sighed. "We be of like minds, I think. We do not settle on simple answers to thorny queries, and thus we find hidden truths others do not see. That be equal halves boon and burden. If I were to pose a troublesome riddle, your thoughts would not readily relinquish it, no matter how badly you wished it gone. Should you leave here alive, with me dead, that riddle would gnaw at your mind long after the fish have gnawed at mine."

"Speak plain English," Dillahunt spat.

"Oh, I think you understand me."

Dillahunt slid around a cannon, making for the ladder to the poop deck. Blackbeard advanced fast. "Seek refuge with cowards and I'll split you down the spine."

Dillahunt glanced up at the poop deck, where men were scrambling for purchase as the rear of the ship lifted out of the water.

"We can't stay here," Dillahunt said. His feet were starting to slide. The deck slanted as the starboard bow inclined toward the water. The fire had made its way up the stairs, touching the quarterdeck. Beyond that, the ship was engulfed. A sail fell away from the mainmast, disintegrating in the wind. If they lingered much longer, both men would be pitched into the fire.

"You've somewhere better to be?" Blackbeard taunted, spreading his arms. The wind swept over him, whipping at his coat and nurturing the fuses in his beard. Smoke swirled before his face.

Dillahunt swiped at Blackbeard's blade. "I would spend my last moments in fairer company."

Blackbeard cackled a laugh. "And what company be that? Your dainty lover is likely dead by now. If it's any consolation,

I didn't intend to harm her. She forced my hand." He jabbed a thumb at the black hollow where his right eye had been. "Quick thinking, it were. Impressed though I be, I'd gladly return the kindness. Eye for an eye."

"Ha!" said Dillahunt. "You would've murdered her either way."

"Nay," Blackbeard protested with surprising vigilance. "The girl be much more interesting alive."

Dillahunt delivered a jarring blow, leaning into his cutlass, and Blackbeard stumbled back a few feet. "For once we're in agreement."

Blackbeard's teeth emerged, tightly clenched, as his lips split in a macabre grin. "You simple fool. Have you not yet realized who shares your bed?"

Dillahunt halted his blade mid-swing. He frowned. "What?"

Blackbeard opened his mouth to give answer . . . but so too opened the deck. The planking split apart beneath his legs like rows of gnarled teeth along a yawning mouth. Fire burst from the fissure in a bubbling cloud, enveloping him. Blackbeard's final expression was strangely impassive as he looked down to consider his fate. He didn't scream. His lone eye reflected the blaze as he plunged below, and his beard took flame along the way. And then he was gone, supplanted by fire. His tricorn hat landed on one side of the disjointed deck, smoldering.

Dillahunt peered into the blaze until his eyes could no longer endure the heat and light and most of all the swirling, endless patterns. He cast aside his sword, crawled over the port rail, and dove toward the water below. And all the while, Blackbeard's final riddle gnawed at his thoughts.

34

KATE

A dense cloud that reeked of sawdust and gunpowder rolled into the crew's quarters. The deck jolted violently beneath Kate's hands and knees. The roar of fire was reciprocated by a thunderous current of water splashing into the hold.

Kate shook her head, fighting off fatigue. The gash in her forehead had swiftly manifested a throbbing headache. Thick drops of blood pattered the deck, dripping from the matted strands of her hair. Her head felt light and vacant, but her muscles were tight and cramping all over. She was all but spent, but this wasn't over yet.

She crawled over to Calloway, who had remained safely tucked in the space between the two bunks. "What happened?" the girl asked, hugging her knees and trembling.

"I found the powder magazine," Kate replied.

They both started coughing from the smoke. "We have to

get out of here before we suffocate," Kate choked.

"Your forehead," Calloway gasped.

Kate blinked as blood spilled over her eyes. "Is it bad?"

Calloway's mouth was hanging open in fascination. "I think I see your skull," she answered. She raised a hand. "Can I touch it?"

Kate snatched Calloway's wrist. She suppressed the nausea rising in her stomach. "I've had worse."

She looked around, blinking dust and blood out of her eyes. She took the red bandana from the corpse and fastened it tight around her head. She crushed a palm against her forehead, and already she felt the cloth soaking with blood. She hoped the pressure would be enough to stop the bleeding.

She tried to stand and nearly toppled. She grasped one of the bunks and looked down. "We're sinking."

"Oh no," Calloway said. "What did you do, Kate?"

"Maybe I saved us. Maybe I killed us. We'll find out." She offered a hand. "Get up. We're leaving."

Calloway took her hand, and Kate lifted her up. They stumbled toward the exit, slanting forward to compensate for the upward slope in the deck. The smoke made it difficult to see more than two feet. They reached the stairs, and the hatch they had entered through was blocked by flaming debris. Cinders rained down the steps, and smoke was swirling down.

"So much for leaving," Calloway said.

Kate looked down the stairs to the hold. Water splashed violently below. The ship creaked, wood buckling as it was slowly being pulled under. "We're still leaving," Kate said. "Just not the way we came."

She yanked Calloway's hand, pulling her down the stairs. "Wait," Calloway said. "Wait, wait!" she cried.

Kate stopped just before the water. The air was painfully thin, as though it was being sucked from her lungs before she could inhale. The entire overhead was churning flame, and splintered planks bowed inward at the center, threatening to collapse into the hold. The casks that were still above the water were on fire. The hold was filled to waist level, with the ocean pouring in from a black void in the back, where the powder room had been.

"The explosion gouged a hole right there," Kate rasped, pointing. "Given how fast the water's flooding in, it should be wide enough to swim through."

"Oh, no, no, no," Calloway said, voice rising to a panicked pitch. She gasped for breath. "I'm not going to drown."

Kate whirled, slapping Calloway hard across the face. "That's exactly what you'll do if you stay here, cowering and pissing yourself!"

"I can't swim through that!" Calloway insisted. Her face was twisted in fear, and Kate was reminded how much younger this girl was.

"You don't have a choice!" She yanked on Calloway's wrist, lugging her into the water. Kate trudged against the current, its icy fingers biting at her legs. Smoke swirled against the water, curling away before it could touch the surface.

Calloway was yelping frenzied protests, but Kate ignored her. She maintained a firm grip, dragging the girl through the water. A burning cask rolled off of the others, nudged by the slant of the ship, and splashed into the water behind them, prompting Calloway to increase her pace.

The deck wouldn't hold out much longer. Wood popped and cracked as the fire chewed away at it. Flaming chunks rained from above, sizzling when they hit the water. One of them struck Calloway's shoulder, hissing against her skin. She cried out, clutching the raw mark it left behind.

The ship dipped sharply toward its starboard side, and three more casks rolled into the water. The impact propelled the girl into Kate, and both of them collapsed in the water. They emerged, blinking and coughing hoarsely. Smoke filled Kate's lungs with every breath. Calloway's face was bright red, her throat bulging as she hacked up water.

The ship had tipped to a ninety degree angle, and the sea was churning up out of the breach in the hull. Kate took hold of Calloway, ushering her toward the hole. "No!" Calloway protested, struggling against her pull. "I can't do this!"

Kate touched Calloway's cheeks, drawing her near. "It's just a little swim, Jaq. Just a little swim and then all this will be over."

Calloway's eyes glazed with tears and her chin quivered. "I'm scared, Kate."

"I know," Kate said. "I'm scared too."

"No you're not. You're not scared of anything."

"Who told you that?" Kate wondered. She attempted a laugh, but it came out as a throaty cough.

The deck above bent further inward, a crack forming down the middle. Flaming debris tumbled through the seam and into the hold, slapping the water. Steam rose from every impact. The ship shuddered.

"I need more time!" Calloway insisted.

"You don't have it!" Kate said, and shoved her headfirst into the bubbling water. She grabbed Calloway's upturned feet and heaved her downward with all her might. The girl disappeared into the black.

God, I hope she knows how to swim. She had forgotten to ask.

She looked up just as the deck collapsed. A massive wall of fire descended toward her, breaking apart as it fell. She inhaled deeply, filling her lungs with smoky air, and dove into the breach.

The current did its best to push her back up. She grasped at the darkness until her fingers grazed a jut of wood. She grabbed hold and pulled herself downward, swinging her arms and kicking her legs. She found another piece of wood and used it as leverage. She glimpsed the jagged circumference of the breach, black against the faint blue glow of the deep, and knew she was almost out. She thrust herself forward, through the opening . . . and was suddenly jarred to a halt. She thrashed in the water but gained no headway. Something had taken hold of her back. She peered over her shoulder. The lace of her bodice was caught on another jut of wood. She beat her elbows against the hull and kicked violently in the water, but the bodice refused to come free.

She fumbled to unlace the front, but the lace was so tight. Seconds seemed like minutes. Salt water singed the gash in her forehead, sending throbs into her skull. She shook her head spastically, hoping that the frantic motion would somehow gain her lungs more air.

She was halfway through the laces when her fingers hit a knotted tangle that refused to budge. She threw back her head and loosed a warbled, bubbly shriek.

The tension left her muscles, and she let her arms and legs drift. There was no point fighting it anymore. She was out of air. She scanned her surroundings, but the water was too dark to see anything.

As fitting a place as any, she thought. She braced herself. The first breath would be the worst. She had heard from Bastion that drowning wasn't so bad, once you got past the *drowning* part. She inquired how he could know such a thing, and he claimed to have drowned once. She had laughed heartily at that.

It didn't seem terribly funny now.

Her lungs started to convulse. Her chest heaved. She squeezed her eyes shut.

And then the ship's hull shuddered, and her bodice shook

loose of its snag. Her eyes shot open. She spun around and considered swimming back up into the breach to regain the breath she had lost in her frustration, but the fire above was distinct even through the murky water. The deck had touched down. The only way out was under the keel of the ship and all the way to the surface.

So she bent her legs and pushed herself off. She swam faster and harder than she would have guessed humanly possible. She made her way up along the curve of the keel, until she saw the ripples of the surface and the shimmering blot of the sun. She saw the underside of *Crusader*, and next to it was Calloway's slim form, legs kicking. The girl had made it.

Everything seemed to slow to a crawl. Kate felt as though she was swimming through a pool of clear mud. Her lungs convulsed viciously. She shook her head frantically, fighting the inevitable. Her vision narrowed.

Just a little further. Just a little further. Oh, God. It's right there. I can see it. Just a little further. I can see it. Oh, God. Just a little further. Just one more push, Katherine. You can do it. Just one more—

She was five feet from the surface when she involuntarily inhaled. Water poured into her lungs. Her chest clenched, muscles ceasing. She grasped at her ribs, tearing at her bodice. She thrashed and thrashed, sucking for air that wouldn't come. Needles of pain shot into her skull through her temples. Her hands lifted from her chest to clutch her throat, fingernails grinding into her skin. She heard herself gagging.

The surface was slowly falling away now, and she realized she had stopped kicking. Before the ocean went dark, she gave her legs a final thrust.

EPILOGUE

When Kate's red hair appeared next to Calloway in the water, she knew something had gone dreadfully wrong.

Jeremy Clemens dove in and swam to Kate's limp body, wrapping an arm around her before she could sink. The men above tossed Clemens a knotted rope, and he hefted Kate over his shoulder. The two of them were lifted up to *Crusader*.

Calloway followed shortly after. Her arms ached as she grasped the rope and was lifted up the side of the ship. After she was helped over the rail and onto the deck, she gasped. Dillahunt was alive. He was slumped on a barrel, soaking wet and clutching a bleeding stomach, but he was alive.

Her excitement, however, was tempered when she saw Kate splayed gracelessly on the main deck, head drooping to one side. Her face was pale and her mouth was hanging open. Four red trails ran down her neck where she had clawed at her throat. Clemens was hunched over her, prodding at her ribs, as if that would do any good. Avery Dowling was pacing with his arms crossed, trying not to look as concerned as he clearly was. Occasionally his eyes would flash Kate's way. Farley's face was bright red and all twisted up like he was trying not to cry.

Bastion appeared at Calloway's side, staring down at Kate. "She drink too much water?" he asked.

"She *drowned*, you idiot!" Calloway snapped uncontrollably.

Bastion burst forward. "Get out of the way!" he shouted, shoving Clemens aside. He kneeled beside Kate, leaned over her . . . and kissed her.

"Oh, for the love of God!" Dillahunt exclaimed, standing.

Bastion pulled away and stared at Kate's face. He looked dismayed. He leaned down again and delivered another kiss, cheeks puffing out like a blowfish. Nothing happened. He kissed her again.

The crew started to murmur uncomfortably to one another.

Calloway couldn't believe what she was seeing. Kate was dead, and this sick islander was groping her corpse. "Someone stop him!" she cried.

"I've had quite enough of this perversity," Dillahunt said, bunching his fists and stomping toward Bastion.

Bastion held up a hand and shouted, "Wait! I forgot something." He plugged Kate's nose between thumb and forefinger and kissed her again. Kate's cheeks ballooned. Her chest lifted. Her lips popped, and water burst from her mouth, splattering Bastion's face before he could pull away. She rolled over and hacked water for a long time, veins bulging from her temples and neck. Her face was purple by the time she was done. Blood seeped from her bandana, trailing between her eyebrows and down her nose.

Dillahunt had stopped in his tracks, gawking stupidly.

"Sorry to disobey, captain," Bastion said, lowering his head.

"It's quite alright," Dillahunt murmured.

Calloway dropped to Kate's side, squeezing her arm. Kate attempted a smile, but it was quickly lost to another fit of coughs.

"How did you know to do that?" Calloway asked Bastion.

"I drink too much water once. A man did this to me. Him learn it in the East. Him say you breathe into a person, it make them breathe." Bastion shrugged modestly. "It don't always work."

"It worked this time," Kate said in a throaty, pained voice.

Farley scratched the back of his neck. "Someone should make a note of that."

Clemens aimed a finger at Bastion. "You stay away from me from now on. And keep that dead woman away from me, too. Black magic, that was. I knows it when I sees it." He ran for the decks below.

Kate continued to cough while Calloway held her hand. Kate squinted gratefully up at Bastion. "Thank you," she said. "I'd kiss you, if we hadn't already."

When she was sure Kate wasn't going to die all over again, Calloway told her, "I'll be right back." She stood and moved to Dillahunt's side. She expected he'd be thrilled to see her, but he merely glanced at her. When he didn't say anything, she said, "Kate needs stitching. She's got a nasty cut under that bandana. I could swear I saw a bit of her skull!"

Dillahunt nodded. "Right. Any man here a surgeon?"

A timid little blonde man stepped forward. "I mend sails and fabrics well enough."

"There's a medical kit in my cabin," said Dillahunt. "See to Mrs. Lindsay's wound. And do take care. She's the only reason any man on this ship still draws breath. And after you've finished with her, my stomach could use some mending as well."

Calloway glanced over the remainder of the crew. There

were about half as many as before the assault on Blackbeard's ship. Of the twenty men that had gone over, only Dillahunt had returned.

Dillahunt appraised them with a proud half-smile. "You shall all receive free pardons, as promised."

Some of them cheered halfheartedly, but most were too tired to muster the enthusiasm. Some were still staring at Kate in disbelief.

"Helmsman!" Dillahunt called up to Dumaka. "Take us out of these infernal islands."

"Aye, captain."

Dillahunt faced *Queen Anne's Revenge*.

Calloway forced herself to look as well. The front half of the ship was completely submerged now, with the stern sticking out of the water, engulfed in flame. Several of Blackbeard's men splashed in the water, begging for help they would never receive. A few of them were swimming over, even as *Crusader* started to pull away. "Don't leave us!" they were screaming. "We'll drown!"

Dillahunt chuckled sardonically at that. Calloway watched him closely, wondering what he was thinking. "I'm happy to see you," she said.

"As am I," he distantly replied.

"You don't look it," she blustered, jabbing his arm.

He attempted to reassure her with an idle smile. It didn't work.

Later that night, after *Crusader* had sailed far from the circular island chain, Dillahunt finally joined Calloway in the captain's cabin. She had been waiting a while, her back propped against the headboard of the bed. She had lit a few candles, stripped off her clothes, and collapsed onto the soft mattress. She ached all over, especially the back of her skull, where it had smacked the deck. She bandaged the hand she had singed when she tore the fuse from Teach's beard. When they returned to Nassau, she would be sure to find some aloe for the burn.

Dillahunt smiled briefly as he entered. He removed his belt and sat at the edge of the bed, struggling out of his boots. He collapsed beside her, and she snuggled close to him, placing an arm across his freshly bandaged torso. His face, however, was still wrapped in the old dirty bandages. She plucked at them, and he jerked his head away.

"I want to see you," she said. He sighed and allowed her to continue. She didn't stop until his head was completely unwrapped. The wounds that riddled his rugged face had scabbed over. He didn't look so bad. In fact, she thought it made him look even more handsome.

His gaze was steadfastly focused upward. She touched his chin, nudging it toward her, but his eyes did not follow. She sighed, rolling away from him onto her back. "Are you done with me, then?"

"Don't be daft," he said, rather lazily. "I'm just tired."

"You seem vexed." She entwined his leg in hers and nudged his crotch with her knee. "What can I do to fix it?"

After a while, he propped himself on an elbow and looked at her. She wanted to kiss him just for acknowledging her presence, but she resisted. "It was all for nothing," he said. "Hornigold is dead. Griffith's fortune might have made up for that, but it too is lost. Probably in the hands of Charles Vane, if he isn't dead in a cave somewhere. And before I had the chance to take Edward Teach's head, he fell from my grasp."

"Teach is dead, then?" Calloway said hopefully.

He looked at her, nodding slowly. "Claimed by his own ship. There is no way any man could have survived that fire. Does that make you sad?"

She screwed up her face in disgust. "Why would that make

me sad? You know how I loathed the man."

He stared at her. "Yes. We never talked about that. You made an attempt on his life. Odd that he didn't kill you when he had the opportunity to return the gesture."

Calloway shriveled under his judicious gaze, feeling culpable without knowing why. "I'd rather not think about it," she said.

"No, of course not," he replied, looking away. He almost sounded disappointed.

She didn't want to talk about Teach, because that would inevitably lead her to dwell on her mother's suicide. She was tired of the past. "How is Kate?" she asked in a suddenly chipper tone, hoping for a change of subject.

"Resting." He leaned back and placed his hands behind his head. "As we should be."

"Don't look so glum," she said, pressing against him. "You still have me. We still have our lives."

He smirked. "And nothing else."

She chewed on her lower lip. She had been giving something a lot of thought over the past few hours, but she wasn't sure how to present the idea. "You know, this ship carries yet another treasure."

Dillahunt sat up in a huff, pressing his back against the headboard. He winced as his stomach curled inward. "I know what you're getting at," he grated. "I'll not sell Lindsay back to her family. I gave her my word. We struck a bargain. True, it was not a bargain among men, and women are fickle with their words, but it was a bargain nonetheless. I needn't remind you that she saved all our lives, many times over."

"Yes," she agreed. "And we can return the favor."

He regarded her skeptically.

She crawled on top of him, straddling him. "How much longer can she last out here, living like this? Today was nearly the end of her."

"Today nearly ended us all," he reminded her.

"Your desk is stained with Nathan's blood. I don't think it will come out even with the most vigorous scrub. How long before a red blemish is all that remains of Kate?"

"That has nothing to do with this," Dillahunt stubbornly replied. "Adams was a fool. He played with fire and he got what he deserved. I'll not hear his name again. It repulses me to think he fucked that whore in this bed."

"Nathan wasn't an idiot," she objected. "He was weak for a woman, that's all."

"Bah," he said, waving a hand.

Calloway sighed. "Kate needs to go back, Guy. Whether she realizes it or not. She thinks she can gallivant around the Caribbean forever, from adventure to adventure."

He glared at her. "I suppose the considerable sum her family is offering has nothing to do with it? You said you'd never return to whoring. Kate's reward would ensure that decision, wouldn't it?"

She folded her arms and fortified her tone. "It's the best outcome for everyone. We split the money and Kate goes home safe."

The scars on his face contracted as he wrestled with his thoughts. "She will hate you for it. She will see it as a betrayal, and she will spend the rest of her life cursing your name. Are you prepared for that?"

She blinked, doubt swelling in her chest. She swallowed it before it could reveal itself. "Yes."

He nodded. "Very well. When we arrive at Nassau, we will turn Kate over to the governor and pray he doesn't string her up for treason."

"He won't hang a woman," Calloway scoffed. "Such a thing would cause uproar, and besides she's worth too much. Her husband belonged to a powerful family."

"We must do it quickly," he said, "before she has a chance to disappear with another pirate. There will be no dallying in port, is that understood?"

"It is."

"And you must not alert her to your intent. You must act normal. She is a shrewd woman, and I needn't remind you that she is dangerous when cornered. Yes, her actions saved us all, but in doing so she saved her own life. Do not forget that."

Calloway considered arguing that point. Kate had recklessly leapt onto *Queen Anne's Revenge* and rescued her without any regard for herself. She would have died, if not for Bastion's magic kiss.

Instead of arguing, Calloway sighed and said, "I know."

"Then it's settled," he concluded. "We need discuss it no further."

She forced a smile, even though she wasn't feeling happy. She needed a diversion, so she started to grind her hips against his. He failed to rise beneath her. Finally, he grabbed her arms and gently forced her off. "Not tonight," he said wearily. "This day has twisted my stomach in knots. I am spent. Maybe tomorrow." He turned over and went to sleep. It was hours before Calloway was able to join him.

Dillahunt hardly spoke to her over the next few days. She knew something was troubling him, and it wasn't just the decision to turn Kate in. His eyes rarely met hers. She assumed he would return to normal after they made it to Nassau and procured the reward. That would set everything right. She reminded herself that Dillahunt had been through a lot in the past weeks. *He just needs time.*

Six days after the battle with *Queen Anne's Revenge*, on a particularly vibrant midafternoon, the lush island of New Providence appeared on the horizon. Calloway found Kate on the forecastle deck, eyes closed with her face angled at the sun.

Kate had been resting during most of the journey, recovering her strength. Her forehead was bandaged. She had dark circles under her eyes and a big ugly bruise on her chin. Four pink lines ran down her neck. Despite all that, she was as striking as ever. She was wearing a loose white shirt and tight black breeches. Her wild red tangles flowed behind her.

As Calloway approached, she glanced over the port bow. They were already nearing the long harbor. She glimpsed the familiar structures of Nassau in the distance, surrounded by greenery. Any other time, it would have been a beautiful sight, but it was the last thing she wanted to see right now.

She placed her hands on the rail next to Kate. She was acutely aware that this was the last time they would speak as friends, while Kate was blissfully ignorant as to what was about to transpire.

Calloway tried to think of something to say.

Fortunately, Kate spoke up first. "Can't seem to escape this place," she said, nodding at Nassau. Her broken voice was even raspier than usual.

Calloway forced a smile. She caught herself doing that a lot, lately. "I don't want to go back."

Kate returned the smile. Her chapped lips were etched with red fissures. "I *do* miss Sassy Sally's turtle soup."

"Mmm, yes," Calloway agreed. "We should go there first thing." She blurted the words without thinking. Guilt instantly pinched her brow.

"Everything alright?" Kate asked without looking at her.

Calloway couldn't bring herself to lie. *No, everything is not alright.* "Why did you save me?" she asked suddenly. "You had no reason to board that ship. Why did you come for me?"

"I don't know," Kate admitted. "I didn't really pause to consider it. If I had, I might not have done it."

"I don't think I could have done the same." Calloway heard

shame in her own voice.

Kate smiled at her, and for a moment Calloway was reminded of her mother's sweet face, doting on her. "Until such a moment comes," Kate said, "no one can say for a certainty what they would do."

Calloway could tell Kate was still in a great deal of pain, even though she was deft at masking it. She was slightly hunched and breathing shallowly, as though her lungs still tortured her. Her eyes were tight around the edges, and her jaw too firmly set. "Are you alright?" Calloway asked, touching her shoulder.

"I will be," Kate assured her.

Calloway looked to Nassau, even closer now. *This ship moves so quickly when you don't want it to.* Beyond the ships in the harbor, she saw the skinny figures of several boys darting along the white sands of the beach, oblivious to the dangers that awaited them. As she watched them, she said, "Don't you ever worry about what's coming next?"

"I used to," Kate replied. She looked up to the sky. Despite the anguish in her eyes, there was a subtle curve to her lips. "The truth is it doesn't really matter. This is the only thing that matters, right here and right now. The sun on your cheeks, the smell of salt on your skin, and the wind sweeping through your hair."

ACKNOWLEDGEMENTS

Infinite gratitude to my editors, Mark Baumgartner, Claire Edwards, and Jon Padgett for not being afraid to tell me where I screwed up, and ultimately making this a better novel for the readers.

Thanks to all the fans who contacted me via email with kind words for the first book, and their interest in seeing Katherine Lindsay's adventures continue. I wasn't sure whether or not to write a sequel, but you all convinced me.

And a big thank you to Randall Chan, the first person to read a jumbled draft of the first book so many years ago. He gave me some wonderful advice that he probably doesn't even remember (I did).

COMPLETE THE TRILOGY!

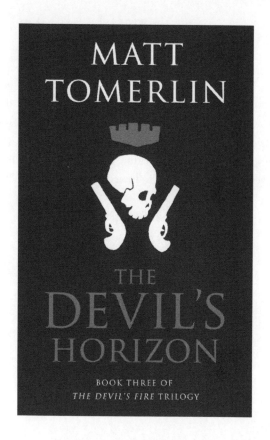

Available at Amazon
and other stores

facebook.com/thedevilsfire
TheDevilsFire.com

ABOUT THE AUTHOR

Matt Tomerlin awoke one morning with an inexplicable urge to dispel the romantic notion of pirates. He began work on a screenplay titled, "The Devil's Fire." After extensive research on piracy, the screenplay became a novel. He published the novel several years later, and followed it with two sequels.

Tomerlin currently resides in Southern California.

Printed in Great Britain
by Amazon.co.uk, Ltd.,
Marston Gate.